16

9-10
$3.00
Fic

ALSO BY KEVIN GUILFOILE

Cast of Shadows

THE THOUSAND

THE
THOUSAND

Kevin Guilfoile

Alfred A. Knopf · New York · 2010

THIS IS A BORZOI BOOK
PUBLISHED BY ALFRED A. KNOPF

Copyright © 2010 by Kevin Guilfoile
All rights reserved. Published in the United States by Alfred A. Knopf,
a division of Random House, Inc., New York, and in Canada
by Random House of Canada Limited, Toronto.
www.aaknopf.com

Knopf, Borzoi Books, and the colophon are
registered trademarks of Random House, Inc.

Library of Congress Cataloging-in-Publication Data
Guilfoile, Kevin.
The thousand / Kevin Guilfoile. — 1st ed.
p. cm.
ISBN 978-1-4000-4309-5
1. Mathematics—Fiction. 2. Composers—Fiction. 3. Murder—Fiction.
4. Chicago (Ill.)—Fiction. 5. Psychological fiction. I. Title.
PS3607.U48T57 2010
813'.6—dc 22   2010001606

Manufactured in the United States of America
First Edition

For Mo

We are the most dangerous species of life on the planet, and every other species, even the earth itself, has cause to fear our power to exterminate. But we are also the only species which, when it chooses to do so, will go to great effort to save what it might destroy.

—Wallace Stegner

THE THOUSAND

THINGS CAN GET SO STRANGE SO FAST

SHE WAS SITTING at a kidney-shaped blackjack table, barely glancing at her cards. Her hair was mostly dark, but she wasn't brunette. *What would you call that? Maroon? Venetian? Indian Red? Firebrick?* Wayne had never seen a crayon that color. And her eyes, great big almonds of eyes, even the casino's expensive German cameras couldn't tell him what color her eyes were.

"Here's what you gotta do," Peter said, tossing the remains of his newspaper between their desks. "You gotta bury yourself in mud."

Wayne Jennings recognized this girl on his screen. She was a poker player. A pretty good one. *So why is she playing blackjack in my casino? And for small stakes, too.* The poker pros he knew preferred games where skill could tip the balance in their favor. Even a perfect blackjack player could only draw the odds close to even.

"You gotta bury yourself in mud," Peter said again. He was maybe twenty pounds lighter than Wayne, a barely noticeable amount at their size. Like Wayne, he had played college football, lower on the depth chart and at a smaller school.

"What?"

"I was watching this show on PBS last night. They got these satellites that can detect your heat signature from space. So that means they could do it with a helicopter, too, no problem. When you sleep at night, no matter how thick the tree canopy or whatever, you gotta bury yourself in mud. Eliminate your heat signature."

Peter had a long list of odd interests. One of them was M. C. Escher. He had prints of those crazy drawings all over his apartment. Another was UFOs. The most annoying was disappearing. He thought endlessly about the ways a normal person could erase any trace of himself. To run away and never be found. To scrub the earth of any evidence he still existed. As a result, his casual office conversation was littered with words like *heat signature* and *epithelials* and *tree canopy.* "Bury yourself in mud" was something like Peter Trembley's thirty-seventh rule of disappearing into thin air. *Exiting the grid.*

Wayne clicked his mouse to advance the video and he watched the girl with the big eyes play another methodical hand. "Why would you need to disappear, exactly? Did I miss something on your background check?"

"It's not about what I've done, man," Peter said. "The government is listening to our phone conversations. Reading our e-mails. I mean, look at the shit we can do here at the casino. We can follow people anywhere—into the bathroom, up to their room. It's fucking scary. All I know is that things can get so strange so fast, and the time to be looking this stuff up on the Internet won't be *after* they're already following me."

The redhead, now in one little window on his screen, seemed to be losing about as much as she was winning, playing it exactly according to those color-coded cheat sheets they hand you on the Strip—splitting eights, doubling elevens, holding on bad cards when the dealer was vulnerable. Wayne tapped the keyboard and started an e-mail to his bosses. "Suspicious activity. Name: Canada Gold . . ."

"You have to bury yourself to the neck," Peter said.

Wayne stopped typing. He didn't send the e-mail. Instead, he restored the camera window and watched her play hand after hand after hand.

MONAD

*There is no more obvious expression of power than
the performance of a conductor.*

—Elias Canetti

1

His charcoal suit had been tailored on State Street and drew an intimidating line across his shoulders. It tapered at his thin waist and billowed subtly at his ankles. His left sleeve had been cut just millimeters shorter than his right to better expose his father's heavy platinum watch. In all his suits, he looked tall and confident and independent. But everyone in this warm fifth-floor Chicago courtroom—jury, judge, media, spectators, prosecutors—already knew Reggie Vallentine was smart.

"Regardless of the facts, the state's attorney wants you to believe that convicting my client would achieve some noble result," he told the jury while orbiting the lectern at a radius of six or so feet. "Remember what the prosecution said in its opening statement: 'We cannot have two systems of justice, one for the poor and unknown and another for the rich and famous.' The government's own case, however, has convinced me that two such systems really do exist. The truth is, my client never would have been indicted if not for the fact that he is a celebrity.

"As someone who makes a living at the far table in these courtrooms, I have always had great respect for the state of Illinois. The state of Illinois does not prosecute *unknown* people when it has not a single microbe of physical evidence. The state of Illinois does not prosecute *unknown* people on hearsay. The state of Illinois does not prosecute *unknown* people with uncorroborated testimony from witnesses whose character, as you have seen, compares unfavorably to the accused in every respect."

His client had wanted to wear pinstripes on certain days, but Reggie convinced him that stripes make defendants look guilty. Instead, Reggie selected for him a number of dark suits with brightly colored shirts and patterned ties—a different combination for every day of the sixteen-week trial. An innocent man isn't afraid to stand out in court, Reggie said. It's the guilty man who wants to disappear. The outfits had to be approved by a stable of advisers, consultants, handlers, and hangers-on, but the defendant had made it clear to his people: *We all work for Reggie Vallentine now.* The only element of his appearance that was off-limits to Reggie was the trademark silver hair, which stuck from his head in all directions like a saint's halo in a Byzantine mural.

"So you ask yourself, Why Solomon Gold? I'm not sure I know the answer to that question. Only the state's attorney himself knows why he has mounted so vigorous a crusade for the purpose of sending my client to prison."

On the first day of his defense, Reggie never even mentioned the victim, a twenty-two-year-old cellist in the Chicago Symphony's training orchestra. Instead, he introduced controversial testimony indicating that state's attorney (and gubernatorial candidate) Bradley Spelling had a long record of bringing charges against high-profile defendants and, in advance of this trial, had lobbied hard and successfully to change state law so the proceedings could be televised.

"I speculate about the reason we are all here only because I know the state's attorney to be an intelligent man, and his experienced prosecutors can't possibly look at the evidence they presented in this courtroom and come to the conclusion that my client is guilty. And the only reason I have slept soundly at night throughout months of this Kafkaesque trial is that I know the twelve of you are intelligent, as well. I am certain the only motive *you* will have in your deliberations will be to ascertain the truth. Therefore, I know the only verdict with which you can return is not guilty."

He modulated his rich baritone for the spacious courtroom, which was paneled on all sides by stained oak and attentive reporters, three floors and another world of opulence away from the cramped bench where this same judge dispatched the cases of everyday defendants—drug dealers and addicts and thieves—who weren't so flush with money and fame. Three national cable networks were covering the trial in real time. Reggie wore makeup specially formulated for live-television performers who must look natural both on camera and before an audience. He told his client to wear it, too. The prosecutors wore no makeup at all.

"The state has made a tremendous deal about the cruelty of this crime, and by some transitive property it hopes you will apply that awful quality to my client. The prosecutors organized a parade of experts to testify that Erica Liu continued to be bludgeoned about the head—gouged in the eye—even after she was unconscious. Yet they have not produced a weapon. As you heard from the medical examiner, they aren't even sure what that instrument could have been! How many times did you hear those three words from prosecution witnesses, 'I'm not sure' or 'I'm not certain'? Do you know? *One hundred and forty-seven times.* One hundred and forty-seven times, they weren't sure. Yet somehow they *are* sure that my client is a murderer."

Only in his late thirties, Reggie had been a respected and prominent Chicago litigator before Gold, the Oscar-winning composer and music director of the Chicago Symphony Orchestra, tapped him for this case. Now he was a national star. Late-night comedians constructed terrible punch lines around his name. ("The queen of England was too ill to meet with the president this week and apparently she felt really guilty about that. She felt so guilty, in fact, that she hired Reggie Vallentine.") Sketch comedy shows lampooned him. Glossy periodicals celebrated him. Tabloids shortened his last name to "Valli" for headline convenience. (AIN'T THIS VALLI LOW ENOUGH? read the front-page wood in the *Sun-Times* after his aggressive and effective cross-examinations of the victim's father and twin brother.) *Chicago* magazine had just named him one of the fifty sexiest men in the city, essentially trading him for his own disgraced client, who had dropped off the list from the year before. There was not an African-American publication in the country that had not featured Reggie Vallentine on its cover at least once.

"Solomon Gold had consensual sex with Erica Liu in her apartment and again in his car after a performance in Millennium Park on the night of June fourteenth. That is the *only* thing the prosecution's much-heralded DNA evidence has proved, and it is a point the defense has conceded. Her body was found in an alley, closer to the home of an ex-boyfriend than to Solomon Gold's home in Lincoln Park. You heard detectives testify there was every indication that the crime scene represented a robbery. Erica Liu had no money in her purse, no watch on her wrist, and her own brother testified that a diamond necklace she always wore on performance nights—a gift of affection from the defendant— was missing from around Erica's neck.

"The prosecution wants you to believe that the illicit nature of my client's relationship with Erica constitutes motive. Ladies and gentlemen, if every man who was having an extramarital affair were a murder suspect in Cook County, then the rest of us would have time to do little but sit on their juries." He paused for the laugh, and it arrived as he had hoped, an audible spike in the jury's approval. "What does a famous and successful man like Solomon Gold have to gain by murdering a sweet and talented young woman, a young woman he had mentored, whose talents he had nourished, for more than eight months? Nothing. Nothing at all. What does an ambitious man like Brad Spelling have to gain by prosecuting a famous individual like Solomon Gold? You heard the media consultant, Mr. Carroll, say 'the sky's the limit' for a promising young politician in a world where name recognition and television exposure are more important than sound policies and personal ethics. And despite your unfortunate sequestering, I don't need to remind responsible individuals like yourselves that there's an election on Tuesday."

Reggie used his final minutes to acknowledge the pain felt by Erica Liu's mourning father, and he compared it to the shame felt by Solomon Gold's teenage daughter. "When someone is hurt, it is our instinct to hurt someone in return," Reggie said. "But this courtroom is not about instinct. It is about reason. Reason is the active ingredient in reasonable doubt. And you have not a single good reason to convict Solomon Gold of this crime. All Brad Spelling has given you is a short list of very bad reasons. They are his reasons, not yours."

The jury deliberated for only two days—another forty-eight hours for Reggie behind his inscrutable trial face, another forty-eight hours for Solomon Gold in his jailhouse tans.

Then the surprise verdict, with Brad Spelling himself sitting in the gallery for its reading, graying head between his manicured hands.

"You did great, hon," said Reggie's wife, Steph, over dinner at Spiaggia, their first night out together in almost a year.

He agreed but didn't seem happy.

A dozen important people approached their table with not always sincere congratulations. Reggie and Steph made celebratory love and he tried to fall asleep with his own face all over the muted news glowing at the end of the bed. Undoubtedly, he was now the most famous criminal attorney in America. His fees were about to triple. He had a book contract waiting for his signature. An agent on each coast. Fifteen offers a day to appear on this television show or that one—prime time, daytime, morning, late night.

Life is about to change for all of us, Reggie thought. This verdict would be a ticket to big things. Expensive things. A life unimaginable.

His wife asked why he looked depressed. Reggie told her it was nothing. He said he wasn't getting much sleep. Stress, he said. All the attention. "Don't you ever sometimes feel bad when everything around you is good? Don't you sometimes feel good when everything around you is bad?"

He didn't tell her he couldn't sleep because he knew the Gold trial would be his legacy. Whatever else he accomplished, Reggie would always be famous as the lawyer who successfully defended Solomon Gold. The composer's name would be in the headline of Reggie's obituary, and between this day and that one the long wake of this trial would carry waves of cash and opportunity his way.

Solomon Gold's acquittal would be the best thing that ever happened to Reggie Vallentine.

But Reggie knew something no one else knew. A secret that could be shared, thanks to confidentiality laws and the constitutional principle of double jeopardy, by Reggie and his client alone.

Solomon Gold was guilty as hell.

2

LITTLE ABOUT the girl's demeanor suggested she was giving much thought to the square metal frame that had been screwed onto her head the previous morning, or the dime-size holes that had been drilled into her skull, or the incision that had been opened at the base of her neck, or the long wires that had been pulled from her collarbone to her brain like updated wiring in an old house. She appeared neither brave nor afraid.

Her pale, shaven scalp was hidden under a stocking cap, her bloodred locks having been dispatched to a wig maker, who would refashion them, at the girl's request, for a child in the cancer wing. She wore a hospital gown covered in Donalds and Mickeys. The day nurse was partial to these patterns. She said they made the kids happy. The night nurse, who had two children of her own, thought it insidious that the hospital allowed sick kids to be made into advertising billboards.

And this girl's a little old for Mickey Mouse anyway, the night nurse thought.

"Do you want me to find you a different gown, dear?" she asked.

The girl shrugged, barely.

"Do you even still like Mickey Mouse?"

The girl looked puzzled. She pulled the material away from her abdomen and stared at it. "I hadn't even noticed." Smiling, she added, "These are okay for now. In the morning, I'll change."

The night nurse scribbled a note to the day nurse: "She hates the Mickey Mouse. Says she's too old for that!"

The girl was staring at a West Coast Cubs game on television, but the night nurse couldn't tell if she was watching. The drip from the bag above her bed delivered a slow calm up and down the girl's body, along with one last powerful dose of the drug cocktail that had barely managed her life for the last four years. There were headphones around her thin neck. On the table next to her bed, along with a tall Styrofoam cup of ice water topped with a cap and impaled with a straw, was a rubber mouthpiece in case the seizures recurred, and a CD by a band called Bomb Pop. The nurse even recognized it.

"My daughter likes Bomb Pop, too," the nurse said.

The girl took a moment to respond. A delay, not very long, but almost as if there were a translator whispering in her ear. "Everybody likes them," she said finally and pleasantly. "Not my dad, though. He doesn't like any new music, only music by dead people." She seemed immediately horrified by the implications of what she had said, and with wide eyes and a bitten lip, she appealed for both forgiveness and discretion, which the nurse granted with a smile. Watching the television news over the last few months, the night nurse had developed the impression that Solomon Gold was not someone you spoke frankly about in public—even if you were his only daughter.

The operation had gone well and the night nurse had little to do in the room besides housekeeping. She circled the bed and closed the drapes against the parking-lot halogens outside. Canada was an odd name for a girl, but pretty. "NAH-duh," they sometimes called her. The mother had been to visit only once and very briefly. Rumor was that she had left the state, choosing to abandon her tragic, tabloid life altogether, leaving her troubled daughter as well as her husband—"She's throwing out the baby with the bad father," one of the doctors had punned. The night nurse didn't think that was funny. Daytime visitors were limited mostly to a woman thought to be a nanny and another woman thought to be an aunt. The nurse had seen not a single friend the girl's own age, but then, what parent would really want their kid playing at the Gold house these days?

Solomon Gold, accused killer recently freed by jury, had been here each night since the girl was admitted, avoiding the gawkers and cameras by keeping an odd schedule, after visiting hours, often when Canada was asleep, sometimes singing to her, humming to her, in murmurs and whispers. The nurse saw him arguing with Dr. Falcone, his arms swinging wildly between them, as if the doctor were a flutist in his orchestra, someone he could control like a marionette with his hands. The nurse found

Solomon Gold intimidating, to be sure, and often rude, but like half the population, according to polls, she was happy for his acquittal. Her gut told her he couldn't be a murderer. Despite what joking doctors might say, murderers wouldn't care this much about their daughters.

In fact, he should have been here by now.

The night nurse tried to do her part, always unplugging the phone after 8:00 p.m. The girl was excitable, and this must have been a difficult year for her. She needed a calm environment in which to recover from surgery, and the sound of these hospital phones, calibrated for the near dead and near deaf, was like a hammer to the skull.

"How do you feel?" the nurse asked.

The invisible translator took his time as the girl considered the question. "Dad says it will make things better," she said finally. "He says school will be easier. He says I'll be able to read for hours."

"Do you like to read?"

With exasperation, Canada said, "I *wish* I liked it."

The nurse had a son with the same disorder. Not nearly as bad—her son had never tried to burn their house down—but she was familiar with the symptoms. "Do you have to reread stuff again and again?"

A pause. "It's like I'm reading and suddenly I realize I haven't been thinking about what I've been reading and I have to go back two pages and start over."

"That happens to all of us, dear. But hopefully not for you so much anymore."

"Hopefully." She lifted the sheet and let it settle over her thin legs, circulating the germs and antiseptics to dogfight in the hospital air. "Do you know what it's like?"

"I have some idea," the nurse said. "Then again, no, I suppose not really."

The girl pointed her remote at the television mounted on the wall. She clicked through the short menu of stations provided to the hospital until she landed on a twenty-four-hour news network. "That's what it was like. It was like somebody else had the remote to my brain and they kept changing the channel before I wanted them to."

The nurse turned to a cabinet and removed a small black box about the size and shape of a man's wallet. It had buttons on it like a calculator, and an LCD screen like a digital watch. "Has the doctor shown you this?"

"Turns out there really is a remote to my brain, huh?" Canada smiled, but there wasn't much joy in it.

"Don't worry, dear. It's not like the average Joe can just walk into RadioShack and buy one," the nurse said. "Dr. Falcone turned your device on this afternoon, but she said you might not feel the difference until we transition you off your meds."

"Dad says it's going to make me a brand-new person. A better person."

The nurse nodded. This girl still believed what grown-ups told her. But then Canada's face twisted into a serious pucker, as if she had swallowed something large and sour. "The government won't be able to tell what I'm thinking, will they?"

"Hmm? What? The government? What are you talking about?"

"This boy at school, Dennis. He says neurostimulators are part of a government plot. That they were invented by the Pentagon. That they'll be able to tell where I am all the time. Like a tracking device or something—wherever you go, they can always find you. And that they have computers that will know what I'm thinking."

The nurse leaned on the bed with her palms. "That boy is being silly, dear. No one can know what another person is thinking." She touched the girl on the sternum. "Besides, I happen to think the smartest people do their best thinking not up there, but in here."

The girl nodded and then her eyes froze in the blue aura of the television. The nurse turned her head upward. The volume was low, but the news anchor's image had been replaced by an old picture of Canada's wildly maned father in tails. A caption next to the photo announced "Oscar-Winning Composer Slain; Attorney Wounded." A pair of years five decades apart and separated by a dash materialized under Solomon Gold's face.

The girl's scream shot into the empty corridor beyond the open door, and when the sound bounced around the floor and returned, it seemed even louder than it had coming from her throat.

The night nurse lunged for the television, which was suspended from the ceiling. She stumbled over an empty chair and slapped the face of the TV with her hand, somehow breaking off the old power switch while the anchor continued to report on the still-sketchy details of Solomon Gold's death. *Good Lord, why wouldn't they notify the family first?* She dropped to the floor and unplugged the long black cord from the wall.

Canada had both hands to her face and began gasping for air, drowning between sobs, appealing to the nurse for an explanation. That this program wasn't real. That it was like a reality show where they pretend daddies are dead when they're really not.

The nurse went to Canada and hugged her for a minute or ten minutes or twenty. She couldn't feel time, only helplessness. The other patients on the floor disappeared from her mind and eighteen years of training and experience were reduced to rocking and stroking, rocking and stroking.

The nanny arrived soon, out of breath, desperately worried about the girl. The night nurse put Canada, her face a wet tragedy mask, into the nanny's care and backed from the room. Someone said a counselor had been summoned. A crowd of nurses and doctors had gathered a short distance from the door, and when the night nurse saw them, she burst into tears for the innocent girl whose short life had been hard and whose long life, the life ahead, had just become several magnitudes more difficult.

A decade later, when the devices had become so commonplace that a single hospital might give them to a dozen outpatients in one shift—for back pain and birth control and bulimia and impotence and anxiety and obesity and Parkinson's and plantar fasciitis—the night nurse remembered Canada and wondered how things had worked out for her. With some patients—not all but some—she wished they really could implant a tracking device. And when things were slow, from her computer at the nurses' station, she could drop in on them, quietly and without judgment, just to see what they were thinking now.

DYAD

How're you going to make your way in the world, woman
When you weren't cut out for working
And you just can't concentrate

—Warren Zevon

3

TUESDAY, JULY 13

PHILLIP TRUMAN was twenty-two years old, with hair like indigo silk, black marbles for eyes, and a slim body fitted for thousand-dollar slacks. As of last October 7, when a vacationing Baltimore teenager sneaked out of her family's suite at Mandalay Bay to attend Truman's party on the seventeenth floor, he was also an alleged rapist, which was why Canada Gold, on the afternoon of her otherwise-uncelebrated twenty-fourth birthday, had followed him through the doors of the most expensive French restaurant in downtown Las Vegas.

He sat facing her in an upholstered booth along the wall, maybe twenty yards away. While he waited for the rest of his party, he drummed his thumbs expertly against the face of his BlackBerry, casually answering his e-mail the same way nonrapists would. Nada didn't own a BlackBerry, or even a computer. Her unassisted senses already input as much information as a mind was equipped to handle. Maybe more.

Free on bond with his daddy's cash, Truman was in sexual predator limbo—his sin committed, he now relied on the petitions of others to save him. Since the night of his arrest, Truman's primary advocate had been a Vegas lawyer named English Judson. Fedoraed, mustachioed, only slightly less infamous (and far less handsome) than his client, Judson had a turbulent history with Canada, which would be a kind way of saying they disliked each other profoundly. In reference to Judson, she often used the word *despise,* usually followed by "his ugly, arrogant guts."

She knew many things about Judson—such as the sort of jurors he preferred when his client was guilty, as well as the Vintage Porto he always ordered when one of those grateful, guilty clients had his hand on the check. She could name his least-favorite jazz singers and the poets he loved the best. She knew the brand of fuel additive he put in his Porsche and that behind his back his partners said he looked ridiculous driving it. She could tell you that Judson liked cats better than dogs and both cats and dogs better than children. She knew he adored his wife but hated her friends.

She knew he'd sent someone to break into her apartment and run his hands through her underwear.

Some of this information was important. Most of it was not. But if English Judson were the person Truman was waiting for, as Canada suspected he was, then her stakeout would be over as soon as the valet took temporary custody of that Porsche and Judson glanced around the uncrowded restaurant for confirmation that he was being noticed. If he spotted her, he would take this meeting somewhere else.

After placing a pile of singles next to her half-finished Diet Coke and lemon, she walked to the ladies' room where she washed her hands, counting slowly to ten as the warm water rinsed away liquid soap. She smelled her wet fingertips—*Rosemary*—and looking into the mirror, she assessed the young woman she saw there. She counted that woman's friends, which took less time than washing her hands. She counted her failed romances, which took slightly longer. She counted the one-night stands—longer still. She counted her personal and professional prospects, which took literally no time at all.

"NAH-duh," she whispered.

For all the details Nada's remarkable senses were able to track, the most salient aspect of the world she observed was that she was not in it. For this reason, she often found mirrors comforting. Leaning this close to a big mirror, her breath fogging and refogging the glass, she could make the universe small. In the mirror she could create a world inhabited by no one but Canada Gold.

A small flat screen inside the mirror murmured incessantly, as all televisions had for several weeks now, about the plane crashes in Florida. Two airliners, a United flight destined for Houston and an American flight en route to Boston, leaving within minutes of each other from the Fort Lauderdale airport, had crashed shortly after takeoff, their overlapping debris fields providing shocking panoramas for news helicopters and widespread nightmares for TSA investigators neck-deep in the swamp. Every airport in the nation had been shut down for twenty-four hours and no flights were planned out of Fort Lauderdale until they pieced together the still-smoldering puzzle on the ground. Saturation news stories were a special torture to Nada, the minutiae of tragedy replayed over and over, indelible details scribbled on top of themselves again and again and again.

After her father's murder, she saw a therapist, who had asked about her special gift. Nada replied that it was more like an unforeseen consequence. A side effect. A superpower. Even now, less than a mile away in her new and almost empty apartment, somewhere among her few possessions, was a treasured reprint of *The Amazing Spider-Man #1*. Her own story wasn't unlike that of Peter Parker, who was bitten by a radioactive arachnid and subsequently discovered he possessed odd and useful abilities. She and Peter were both afflicted when they were in their teens, and Nada's spider still had its teeth stuck into the back of her head.

And like Peter, her powers came packaged with complications.

She calculated the time. She had followed Phillip Truman into the restaurant at 11:46, meaning the reservation was probably for noon. Another thing she knew about Judson: He was never late. She had been in this bathroom exactly five and a half minutes, and by now Judson should have taken a seat across from his client, with his back to the bar. She dried her hands with a thick paper towel.

Nada closed the restroom door with a soft click and returned to her chair. Judson was seated as she'd hoped, but he was facing her, settled into the booth next to his client. *Like a lover,* she thought, perhaps only because Judson would find the idea so offensive.

He spotted her and stretched his thin lips into a delighted line as he pulled his napkin from the table and dropped it across his tiny lap. Exposed and defeated, Nada clutched the icy glass that held her drink and raised it to him in sarcastic surrender.

Judson leaned into Truman, his face square to Nada's.

"Have you been talking on the phone since you arrived?"

"No," the rapist replied.

"Good." Judson pointed toward the bar. "You see that attractive young lady with the auburn hair, staring right at us?" Truman sneaked a glance at her and nodded briefly. Judson said, "Her name is Canada Gold, and despite the fact that she has never been to law school—doesn't even have a bachelor's degree—she was, very briefly, one of the most sought-after jury consultants in the state of Nevada. Do you have any idea why? Of course you don't. If you did, you would have sprinted from this restaurant the second you spotted her.

"You see, Phillip, Ms. Gold, who grew up in the same house as a cold-blooded killer, possesses a unique set of abilities. She reads lips in two languages. She can hear conversations from across a crowded room. Allegedly, she has a photographic memory, and I wouldn't be surprised to discover that her idle thoughts can bend spoons. She's a freak of nature, and my firm has been burned by her so many times, we seriously discussed conducting all our business in Navajo."

Truman looked again at her. Nada sipped her Diet Coke, winking at him over the rim of the glass. The rapist jerked his head down, while Judson never took his eyes away from hers.

"These are talents certain unscrupulous attorneys find very useful," Judson was saying. "Some of her associates, perhaps even in the district attorney's office, paid Ms. Gold for information she obtained by spying on opposing lawyers and their clients. For stealing privileged information they couldn't otherwise obtain." Truman opened his mouth silently and wide, like a hungry baby chick. "You don't believe me? Why don't we test her?" Judson reached his arm across the younger man's shoulders and put his mouth very close to the rapist's ear. He whispered, "Ms. Gold, can you understand what I'm saying to my client right now?"

The lawyer's lips moved in exaggerated slow motion: *Canada. Gold. Is. A. Loathsome . . .*

The last word had one syllable, which began with the thick part of Judson's tongue against the rear of his palate and ended with the tongue's bow striking just behind the upper incisors.

Nada grabbed the bartender's pen and scribbled on a napkin, which she then held up with her left hand while extending a middle finger at the end of her outstretched right arm. She didn't know if Judson could read the message from his seat, so she left it on the bar for him to find later and lifted her yellow purse and thanked the bartender, who seemed amused and confused and perhaps aroused in equal parts.

Judson continued, his voice apparently just above a whisper but his opinions still largely for Nada's benefit. "There isn't a Vegas attorney worth a nickel an hour who'd recite the alphabet to his client without first checking to make sure Canada Gold's not within a hundred yards. So the retainers have dried up and she spends her days counting cards at blackjack tables and, it seems, harassing wrongly accused young men such as yourself. Do you know how pathetic you must be to become an outcast even among *poker players*? Nevertheless, if you don't want every goddamn detail of your personal life to get back to the assistant district attorney, then every time you flap your lips in public, you put your *fucking* hand over your *fucking* mouth. Do you understand me?"

Truman looked terrified. *A minor victory,* Nada thought.

As she was escorted to the door, ten new digits encoded into the seemingly limitless bank of recorded facts inside her brain, Nada wondered how it was possible that a cowardly scumbag like Phillip Truman had so many friends willing to protect him.

Once again, Nada counted her own friends in her head. Friends as good as the rapist's friends. *One. Two.*

"Pathetic," she said to the perplexed maître d' as she stepped into the revolving door. "Just pathetic."

4

THE BUILDING WAS an unremarkable rectangle of pale masonry and mortar, with metal doors and small single-paned windows fronted by a thin line of waxy shrubs. Inside were partitioned offices, rehearsal rooms with molded plastic chairs and aluminum music stands, and a gymnasium-size performance space lined with an assortment of donated and used instruments. Still, Chicago's third Solomon Gold Memorial Youth Center represented new construction, which, amid the neglected three flats and bodegas and storefront churches of West Division Street, was unusual enough to warrant a dedication ceremony even the mayor cleared his schedule to make.

The mayor, Reggie thought. *Christ, if only he knew.*

Gold's widow, Elizabeth, was addressing the medium-size crowd of passersby, neighborhood activists, children in yellow prop T-shirts, and television crew persons. "Solomon would be so proud," and so forth. The woman must have loathed her husband at the end of his life but was nevertheless forced to praise him in death.

It was something she and Reggie had in common.

"Solomon would have loved this place," said Elizabeth to the crowd. "He loved children."

Attractive in her advancing age, Elizabeth Gold was a strong woman with broad shoulders and thin ankles and radical curves in between. During the trial, Reggie had often marveled at the physical differences between Solomon Gold's wife and his lover. Erica Liu had been such a tiny thing. In photos, she seemed so small next to her instrument that the cello almost looked like it were playing her. Elizabeth Gold had small eyes and an impossibly small waist, but everything else about her—butt, tits, hands, and hair—was outsize. *And all sexy,* Reggie thought. As she spoke just in front of him and to his left, it took every bit of his concentration not to let his eyes follow the looping S shape that began just under her toned arm and ended at the bottom of her big round ass.

Reggie often wondered why Elizabeth had kept his client's surname through two unsuccessful marriages, given how consuming her hatred of Solomon must once have been. Perhaps she just enjoyed the celebrity attached to the Gold name—the attention in charity boardrooms and the privilege of good tables in restaurants. Or maybe, Reggie realized, in fifteen years with a personality as strong as Solomon's, her transformation into Elizabeth Gold had become irreversible. It would have been as unthinkable for her to become Elizabeth Kennedy again as it would be for a butterfly to go back to being a caterpillar.

And then there was the child they'd had together. As far as Reggie could determine, the Gold name was the only connection Elizabeth and Canada still had.

A founding board member of the Solomon Gold Foundation, Reggie attended half a dozen of these things each year—fund-raisers, tribute concerts, school dedications, and, last year a spelling bee. Despite the always-pressing needs of his wealthy and celebrity clients, Reggie never missed a Gold Foundation event. At every one, seated in a conspicuous position of honor, often next to Elizabeth Gold or his own lovely wife, he hoped his eyes wouldn't hint at the scenes reconstructing in his mind— scenes from the night ten years ago when Reggie had been wounded and his best-known client, the acclaimed conductor and composer and accused killer, Solomon Gold, was murdered in his own home.

The case had been closed the next day when Erica Liu's father, Michael, the primary "person of interest," killed himself without leaving a note. There was no trial, no further investigation. Solomon's murder could have been a crime of passion, or rage, or an assassination, or a revenge killing, or even self-defense. All these years later, Reggie still didn't know for sure.

He knew it wasn't an accident.

Exactly two weeks after the acquittal, the phone had rung in Reggie's LaSalle Street office. It was just before eight and the Polish-speaking cleaning crew, hunchbacked over their vacuums and buckets, had just started their systematic march through the halls. Reggie had spent much of the early evening drinking too quickly from a twelve-year-old bottle of Maker's Mark and staring helplessly at a pile of pink message slips, an accumulating record of calls from a dead girl's father.

"Let's meet," Gold said.

Reggie had no desire to see his client. He knew it would be impossible to look into Gold's face without seeing Erica Liu's lifeless body reflected in his dark eyes. He wouldn't be able to shake Gold's powerful hand without conjuring Erica's long, thin neck squeezed between its fingers. Reggie had represented bad people before, but a case had never affected him this way. Never given him headaches and a temperature and sleepless nights and the chronic shits. Maybe it was the public nature of the trial. More likely, it was the fame and success that were coming to Reggie in its wake, the dividends that would be paid at the cost of one dead girl and one smug and carefree killer. Before Gold, he'd never regretted taking on a guilty client, never been depressed about winning a case. Never felt this combination of shame and guilt and anger and fear.

Never been rewarded so abundantly for helping a murderer walk out of prison.

"The trial is over, Solomon," Reggie said. "You need a divorce lawyer now." He thought about hanging up, but he knew Gold would only call back again and again until he had what he wanted.

"Just to talk," Gold said. "I can't talk to these people. I can't talk to anyone."

Reggie had no idea whom he meant by "these people." Whoever they were, they probably weren't bound by confidentiality. Do enough bad things, keep enough secrets, and eventually you can't hold a decent conversation with anyone but your own lawyer.

"I have one more thing I need to discuss with you," Gold said.

Reggie let a disbelieving snort escape the cavity behind his nose. *One more thing.* The horrible truth about Erica Liu's death would always bind them together. Secrets like that were shackles. Reggie's sworn obligation to his client meant he would never be rid of Solomon Gold, and Gold's acquittal meant he would never be done with Reggie.

Locking his office, Reggie waved good night to a group of young associates pecking at a large take-out carton with chopsticks—their night, like his, was only beginning—and took an elevator to the lobby and another to the parking garage. It was more than half empty, but the echoes of the heavy metal doors and his thick soles against the concrete felt different to Reggie. Duller, less reverberating.

He wasn't alone.

Quickening his stride, Reggie scanned the cars and saw shadows in every one, shadows that disappeared at his glance, only to rematerialize when he turned his head. He heard a cough, a sniff, a swallow, a breath, a single boot step. He smelled onions and garlic, motor oil and urine. When he was within ten yards of his own Audi, he broke into a run, squeezing the car remote five, six, seven times. He started the car and locked the door, then screeched his tires around nine levels of garage as fast as the turns allowed.

He was breathing in gulps. His heart ran laps in his chest. Reggie glanced in his rearview and saw nothing.

Still unbuckled, he worked sweat from his hands into the leather wheel cover. He hated Gold. Hated him for what he had done to Erica Liu and for what he continued to do to Reggie Vallentine. A jury had found his client not guilty, but Reggie's own guilt could not be dismissed as easily. He knew now how mob lawyers felt. Despite what they tell you in law school, with a certain kind of defendant there seems to be little difference between representing him and becoming him.

"Son of a bitch," Reggie said out loud, and as he accelerated north onto nearly empty Lake Shore Drive, his anger was like bubbling pop in a shaken can. For months it had been waiting to explode.

Although he'd accepted his client's guilt midway through trial prep, Reggie had decided to remain as Gold's defense counsel. *A conviction is worthless if it hasn't been challenged by a vigorous defense,* he'd reminded himself. And he couldn't be known as a lawyer who turned against guilty clients, even repugnant ones. *Especially* repugnant ones.

As weeks stretched into months and then a year, he recognized insane rages across Gold's face in short glimpses. Like a shark's, the composer's attention almost always came in the form of attacks—unrelenting verbal assaults that seemed to carry the threat of violence. Other people were invisible to Gold unless they offered a service he required. Reggie wondered if this was what had happened to Erica Liu. When Gold no longer needed her, she just disappeared. Became invisible to him. *Dead to him,* as they say. It must have been very easy for Gold to kill someone who, in his own twisted mind, had already expired.

When he exited the LSD at Fullerton, he was minutes away from a horrible, fateful meeting in Solomon's graystone on the park.

A decade later, after he stepped behind the podium on West Division to enthusiastic applause, Reggie gestured once at the crowd with his good arm and bowed his head respectfully to the dead man's widow and told the audience how much Solomon Gold had treasured Chicago, the city where he had been born, educated, unjustly tried, and tragically murdered.

He told them the work of the Gold Foundation was just a small example of the limitless good that can take root in the barren soil of senseless tragedies like the killings of Erica Liu and of the great composer whose name was being affixed to this building today.

Then Reggie Vallentine, the man who had murdered Solomon Gold, touched the old wound in his right shoulder and told them they were all blessed.

5

"ENGLISH SPOTTED ME. He's a smart little bastard."

Shins folded under her thighs, body straight and stone-still atop Beatrice Beaujon's overstuffed couch, tiny Nada looked almost like origami—delicate, angular, precise. Hair back in a ponytail, she wore jeans and an extra-small gray T-shirt silk-screened with a curvaceous mud-flap silhouette. For long stretches of time, her giant green eyes were the only parts of her that moved. *If you were walking quickly through the room, you could almost mistake her for a cat,* Bea thought.

It was close to 9:00 p.m., but there was just enough light coming through the sliding glass doors to expose the furnished red deck and the swimming pool beyond it. Bea and Donald Beaujon were both attorneys, but the pool and the big house and the mismatched Beamers in the garage were products of Don's partner salary. The mahogany deck all by itself had cost as much as Clark County paid Beatrice in a year.

"What the hell were you thinking?" Bea said, an involuntary and unhelpful laugh punctuating the end of the sentence. What Nada had done was outlandishly stupid, and yet typical at the same time. "*Goddammit,* Nada, you're going to get me fired. Maybe sanctioned, if I'm lucky. Worst case, Phillip Truman gets a new trial because English convinces the judge I sent you to spy on the two of them." She handed Nada a generous goblet of Shiraz and lowered herself to the floor, resting her own glass on the factory-distressed coffee table between them.

"Relax. Did they make it illegal for me to sit down in a nice restaurant now?"

Bea had changed into jeans and removed her jacket, but she still wore the white cotton blouse—now untucked and loosened at the collar—she had worn earlier to court. "Do you really expect anyone, especially a Las Vegas judge, to believe you just happened to be sucking down six-dollar Diet Cokes at Le Papillon when a kid I'm prosecuting for sexual assault was eating there with his attorney? And English Judson, of all people?"

Nada twisted her lips into something that was half pout and half grin. More than a year ago, when Nada was still drawing an occasional free-lance paycheck as a consultant for the Clark County DA's office, English Judson had found an excuse to call Nada as a hostile witness in the assault trial of a city council member. His examination of her, in which he managed to sneak in a cheap reference to her notorious father, was the beginning of the end of Nada's snooping in the hallways of the Regional Justice Center in Las Vegas. The end of the end came when a casino camera caught her paying a little too much attention to the cards.

Bea had barely escaped the taint of the double scandal.

Nada's hair began to free itself of the elastic band and long brownish red bangs now slipped across her forehead one strand at a time. "Truman's guilty as hell and he's going to buy his way out of it with his father's cash. That doesn't piss you off, Boo?" Boo, as in *BOO-john,* one of those nicknames that doesn't abbreviate or tease or illuminate. She apparently liked referring to Bea as Boo simply because no one else did.

"Of course it pisses me off. And I won't let him get away with it. But I've been really careful with this one and I just don't want the . . . the *appearance of impropriety* to fuck up my case."

"Impropriety? Christ." Nada's jaw was tight and the tendons in her neck stuck out like long blades. "He put a beer bottle inside that girl and then wagged a finger in her face and told her she wasn't old enough to drink—"

"We're gonna get him."

"You know your case is weak. And the girl won't be good on the stand."

"There's another witness."

"You don't even know where Kerry Meadows is."

"Jerry will find him. Meadows is a scared twenty-two-year-old trust-fund kid with everything to lose. He'll start talking the second I point out that if he *doesn't* talk, we'll slap him so hard with an accessory charge that he'll be having his midlife crisis up at Ely."

"Yeah, well, I'm a twenty-something trust-fund kid myself. And I say you're not going to find him if you insist on *propriety.* These little monsters don't know shit from propriety, and neither does English Judson."

"Which is why it will feel good when I put Truman away."

Nada took a long swallow. Her little body processed alcohol the way an old car absorbs five-weight oil. "Do you know what he called me today?"

"English? No."

Nada bulged her eyes and puckered her lips and then she whispered it across the room, like a little girl who's just discovered the word *fart*.

Bea giggled. "English's dropped so many C-bombs on me, he oughta have *Boeing* stenciled on his ass. He even called me that in *court* once, although not so the judge could hear it. He's a dinosaur. And a pig. A pigosaurus. *Tyrannosaurus pig*." She scooted forward a few inches on the carpet and lowered her voice in case Don was coming down the stairs for another bowl of pretzels. "Look. Garfield has already warned me about my friendship with you. He says your reputation is jeopardizing my cases. My *career*. I told him it was under control."

"So you don't want my help?"

"Yes, I want your help. I want your help picking out birthday presents for my daughter. I want your help tutoring math down at the Learning Center. I want your help drinking good wine. I want you to come with me to artsy girl movies that Don refuses to go see. But I *don't* want your help on cases anymore. You understand that, right?"

Nada exhaled. She made a brief face—apprehensive but resigned—like Bea's daughter would make when she was about to tell Bea about a bad grade on a test. "English broke into my apartment."

"That's crazy." She tried to use the word sparingly with Nada. "You're obsessed with that guy. English is an asshole lawyer, just like a thousand other asshole lawyers in this town. Nothing else."

"Someone was in my apartment yesterday. While I was out."

"Did they take anything?"

Nada paused her glass at her lips and her answer reverberated inside the bowl. "There's not much to take."

"Did you call the police?"

"And tell them that I know that my drawers had been opened? That my sliding closet doors had been shut the opposite way than I left them? That someone had lifted a knife from my silverware tray and put it back with the forks? That a few revolutions of toilet paper were missing from the roll?"

Nada could be joyful and funny, even scary, the way she could celebrate the present without regard for the next day or even the next hour. There was hardly an offer, a suggestion, a caper that she ever said no to.

Bea once watched her stare at the newspaper for almost fifteen minutes before announcing with a delighted grin that she had finished the crossword in her head. But Nada also possessed a relentless cynicism that sometimes seemed to border on despair. She seemed capable of knowing everything, but Bea was starting to realize that it's mostly the things a person *doesn't* know that make her content. "What makes you think it was English?"

"I don't think it was English personally. It was one of his thugs."

"They're called investigators, Nada, and we use them, too."

"Your Jerry's a pussycat. The ones Judson uses are thugs."

"Well, what makes you think one of English's *thugs* was in your place?"

"Who else would it be?"

"I don't know. David, maybe?"

Nada cackled loudly enough for Donald to hear upstairs. "You think David Amoyo broke into my apartment to sniff my panties? No way. Not his style. If he cared enough about me to do that, we'd still be together."

"But why would English do it?"

"He wants me to leave Phillip Truman alone. Maybe he was hoping to find drugs or pot. Something he could blackmail me with. Too bad for him I'm not that interesting."

Bea could think of a long list of more probable explanations. A stalker still following Nada from the days when she played in televised poker tournaments. Or a frustrated burglar who found nothing of worth in her spartan apartment. Or maybe it was one of those nuts on the Internet who was obsessed with her dead father. All of it creepy, but more plausible than what Nada was suggesting. "I don't know. It sounds—"

"Paranoid?"

"You said it; I didn't."

Nada chuckled and scratched the corner of her eye. "Would it be okay if I crashed here tonight? The whole thing's freaking me out a little."

Every few weeks or so, Nada asked to stay over. Sometimes she'd become buzzed on the Beaujons' expensive Rioja and didn't want to drive. When she was living with David, he'd frequently do something to piss her off and she'd want to stay for a night just to make him wonder where she was. Donald was understanding about these sleepovers, and Bea's daughter, Lori, was usually downright ecstatic.

Nada closed her eyes, nodded once, and relaxed her shoulders an inch or so, which Bea recognized as one of the many subtle ways she said thank you.

A good time to change the subject. "I got a call about you today," Bea said.

"From who?"

"A lawyer in Chicago. Don't know him, but he's with a huge firm. He said he had a client who could use your 'services.' "

"Oh yeah?" Nada lifted one shoulder seductively. "Which services would those be?" She drawled the phrase in a way that sounded intentionally dirty.

"That's the way he put it. He promised the money would be good."

"What's the job?"

"Don't know. Based on your reputation, I can guess."

"Client's desperate and he needs information."

Bea sipped her wine. "Like I said, the firm's respectable."

Nada whispered something inaudible. Something about Chicago. Something "memories." Something "mother." "Corporate" something "espionage."

"What?"

"Nothing." Nada looked through the doors toward the pool, which was illuminated with bright floodlights. "Do you want to make a bet? About whether you can find Kerry Meadows before Truman's trial?" Nada pressed the right side of her head against her own shoulder, like she had a telephone handset pinned there.

Bea chuckled. "A proposition, you mean?" Bea had lived in Vegas long enough to know that gamblers like Nada bet on anything—that the next commercial on TV would be for beer and not razors, that one or the other could lose fifty pounds in a month—and they called these bets "propositions." By habit, a gambler will assign every event a probability, and every probability a value. "I know better than to bet against you."

"Close your eyes."

"Why?"

"Just close them."

A skeptical glare.

"I'm *helping*, Boo, not hurting. Trust me."

Bea shut her eyes. She heard Nada crumpling paper and felt something hit the ground lightly next to her foot.

"Open."

Bea's eyes found the yellow ball of Post-it on the carpet. "What's this?"

"Anonymous tip. Just flew in the window."

"Dammit, Nada."

"Just read it."

Bea unfolded the paper, which Nada had wrapped around a green casino chip to keep it from fluttering when she tossed it. "Twenty-five bucks from the Colossus Casino. Thanks." She read the Post-it. "And a phone number."

"Northern California."

"Where did you get it?"

"I watched Truman key it into his BlackBerry."

"*God*. From your seat at the bar?"

She nodded.

"You watched a man texting into his phone from across an entire restaurant, and you could tell what he was writing?"

"Well, not *every* word. Even when I'm reading lips, I don't get every word. But numbers are easy."

"When did you learn to do this?"

"David had one of those frigging things. That's how I found out about Sandy."

Bea realized she wasn't so surprised.

"I already did the reverse lookup." Nada took another slip of paper from her tiny black purse and held it over her head. "Oh, that's right. You don't want my help." She put it back. "Have Jerry do it. It's a house in Marin County. Kerry Meadows went to Stanford, right? He's probably got friends in that area. It's worth a drive by the place. Maybe a knock on the door. See if Meadows is hiding up there."

Nada either didn't understand the potential trouble facing Bea or she didn't care. Still, the ten digits scribbled on the Post-it felt electric between her fingers. Over the past three years, she'd learned to doubt Nada's judgment but never her abilities. Bea glanced at her cell phone on the coffee table and she just knew that on the other end of this number, Kerry Meadows was slumped into a beanbag chair in some college buddy's condo with a PlayStation and a case of Miller High Life. Kerry Meadows was the difference in her case. The difference between he said/she said and he said/*they* said.

Bea had told Nada on multiple occasions that it could be frustrating to be her friend. But it wasn't only frustrating; it was often exciting. Frequently, it was both.

This was one of those times.

"You might have to testify."

Nada waved away the worry on Bea's face as if it were secondhand smoke. "English won't trace this number to me. You know he spent the afternoon bragging to all his partners at Becker how he outsmarted the despicable Canada Gold. They're probably at Zefferino's right now fellating Cuban cigars over it. Even if he suspected it, he'd never admit I got the better of him. Besides, if English is claiming that he's not hiding Meadows, how can he object if you find him? Tell the judge it was an anonymous tip. English'll blame his client. He'll just figure Truman blabbed too much around a pretty girl." She opened her arms in a parody of modesty. "Which is technically true."

"I just can't believe you're putting me in this position. For Chrissake."

"Yeah, I'm terrible," Nada said. "And by the way, I wouldn't waste my time getting to that address. One of the other words I saw Truman typing in his e-mail was *Cozumel.* I'm pretty sure."

6

WEDNESDAY, JULY 14

AS RESTAURANTS GO, Mr. Beef was even less fancy than it sounded, with no chairs and a narrow, peeling counter at standing height and the best "wet meat" in the city, which was what Bobby Kloska liked to call an Italian beef sandwich. Photos of famous customers, mostly actors formerly of the Goodman or Steppenwolf or Second City, hung along a grease-stained wall in cheap plastic frames. Elbow off the countertop, facing the street, Bobby's old and unlikely acquaintance Reggie Vallentine gripped an overstuffed bun in his left hand and made a pair of false starts before shoving a fat end over his jaw.

"Watch the drip," Kloska said. "What's your suit worth? About five hundred wet meats?"

Reggie mumbled a reply, his mouth full of bread and peppers.

Kloska was the cop who had pulled the Erica Liu murder investigation, and he was one of two detectives who arrested Solomon Gold for the crime. He and Reggie had a sharply adversarial relationship at trial, which softened after Bradley Spelling tried to place much of the public blame for Gold's acquittal on what he alleged was Kloska's sloppy work at the crime scene. "You treat me with more respect than the frigging state's attorney," Kloska had whispered to Reggie in the courthouse halls. "Makes me wonder whose side I'm supposed to be on."

Neither had been to the other man's house. Neither had met the other man's family. Still, Kloska considered Reggie something other than a professional acquaintance. Somehow *friend* didn't exactly describe him, either. Having survived the trial, they were like enemy soldiers who were able to forge an unsteady kinship in the ensuing peace.

Kloska wondered if the truce might be broken before he finished this sandwich.

For the last ten years, Bobby had privately tumbled over and over in his mind the story Reggie told the night of Gold's murder and had come to the conclusion that it never quite dried. It wasn't impossible, but it didn't exactly conform to the evidence or to Kloska's theory of the murder. The killing itself didn't trouble Kloska so much. Solomon Gold had barely enough human inside him to count in a government census, so you could hardly even call his death a murder. More like a misdemeanor cruelty to animals. Every day, Kloska and his fellow cops happily looked the other way while lesser shitheads than Gold were eliminated with drive-by gat fire from this South Side gang or that one.

And anyway, they got their man. Or their man got himself. As officers responded to a desperate 911 call from Erica Liu's mother, Erica's father, Michael Liu, killed himself one day after Liu murdered Gold. Still, it pissed Bobby off to think Reggie might be holding out on him. Reggie had been in the room when it happened, had seen it all from beginning to end, and had even been wounded by Liu himself, suffering such extensive nerve damage that he could now barely move his right arm. Nevertheless, he refused to identify Michael Liu as the killer. Reggie said Liu had been wearing a mask, but after months of depositions and testimony and all the media bullshit around the Gold trial, Reggie should have recognized his voice, his build, his posture. Reggie never said it *wasn't* Liu, but he never said it definitely was, either.

Lawyer crap about confidentiality aside, Kloska couldn't finger a reason Reggie might have lied, but he also thought motive was overrated as a tool of police work. Motive was to a murder investigation what dew point was to the weather forecast. It was probably a useful thing for somebody to know, but Kloska really couldn't give a shit.

He said, "How's the Gullibility Gang these days?" This was Bobby's name for the Believers Project, a group of law students and young attorneys working pro bono under Reggie's direction to help win reversals, or at least reprieves, for convicts on death row.

Reggie was probably making untold numbers of millionaire clients circle his office in chauffeured Town Cars while he and Bobby had lunch.

Nevertheless, he let the conversation proceed at a casual pace. Reggie Vallentine was always the coolest guy in the room. "You like the death penalty, don't you, Bobby?"

Kloska waved a hand and said, "I got no problem sticking bad guys with long needles. But out on the street, most of these shitheads know their life expectancy isn't much past thirty." "Shithead" was what Bobby called anyone with even the slightest taint of criminality. Never "suspect" or "perpetrator" or "defendant." Only "shithead." "When you throw in ten years of appeals, death row starts to sound like a health plan."

Reggie held back a laugh while he swallowed.

"That's a sweet little con you got going," Kloska said, his voice a few decibels lower. "All those hotties with the heart-shaped asses and the flannel skirts who went to law school both to save the world and to worship at the altar of Reggie Vallentine. Like that one intern you got. Della? I tell you what, I don't think my pants could stay up under that kind of temptation. Probably wouldn't even bother to zip them in the morning if I were you. I'd put a rubber on same time I put on my socks."

Married for ten years and divorced for two, Kloska hardly let a woman cross his line of sight without a comment. A lot of the cops Kloska knew were the same way, but a lot of them were just blowing steam before heading home to their wives. Kloska, on the other hand, had been a serial adulterer during his marriage, and the pace of his conquests hadn't slowed now that he was single. For him, every night held the potential for a mad grope in a dark bar with some oversexed Bridgeport girl—usually college age but not enrolled, usually a cop groupie or a chick from a cop family whose cop father never gave her enough approval or attention or hugs or whatever, the kind of girl he knew his own neglected daughter was certainly at high risk of becoming one day. If Bobby were as famous as Reggie, if he could have any woman he wanted, it would ruin him for sure.

CNN had a deep pool of legal pundits, but when a celebrity got in serious trouble, especially the kind of trouble that left a body behind, they always summoned Reggie Vallentine to the studio for a comment. Since the Gold trial, Reggie had been a crossword answer, a *Jeopardy* question, and there had even been a recurring character on a Saturday-night comedy show named Ronnie Sweetheart, a sophisticated black lawyer with a bum arm and a charming smile who represented despicable but famous clients.

"Anyway, I called because I got some news," Bobby said, piercing the lid of his Styrofoam cup with a straw.

"What's that?"

Kloska locked eyes with him. "One of the guns used to shoot your client was used in another homicide last week."

"What client?"

Kloska bounced his chin against his chest. "You've had more than one?"

Reggie set down his sandwich and lifted a paper napkin to his lip to collect a bit of sauce along with— Was it sweat that now appeared there? "I thought you already had the gun that killed Solomon in evidence. Did you lose it?"

"*That* gun is the gun that shot you in the shoulder and him in the leg, and it's still there. But over by Harrison, they got a fifty-six-year-old female corpse, and buried inside that meat the ME found a *bullet* that looks like it blew out the barrel of the same gun Michael Liu used to shoot Solomon Gold between the eyes. Crazy, huh? Victim is known to friends, colleagues, and loved ones as Marlena Falcone. Name mean anything to you?"

Reggie shook his head.

"Marlena Falcone. Neurosurgeon. Pioneer in deep brain stimulation. Those electrodes they put in your skull when you want to quit smoking or overeating or control your seizures or whatever. Had her medical license stripped after a bunch of her patients went psycho following her treatment. Seems she jumped ahead of the FDA in implanting some of these brain things. Obituary in *The New York Times* and everything."

"Of course. I remember now."

"What hasn't been all over the news yet is that this doctor and your client knew each other."

"What are you talking about?"

"This procedure that got her in trouble? These implants? Apparently, she gave one to Gold's daughter. You remember anything like that?"

Reggie commenced a slow, slight nodding of his head. "I do. Canada was actually still in the hospital the night we were shot."

Kloska noticed the passive construction: "the night we were shot." "See, there's one enduring mystery about Solomon Gold's murder. Our shithead, Michael Liu, used two different kinds of ammo. He shot you in the arm with a .357 Magnum. He also shot Gold in the leg with a .357 Mag. But the kill shot, the one to Solomon's face, that bullet was a .38 Special. A day later, we find Liu with the back of his head blown out and a .357 revolver in his hand. Quick ballistics test matches that gun to the

.357 slugs at the crime scene. And since our witness"—he rolled his hand in a royal wave—"the esteemed Reggie Vallentine, mentioned only the one gun, we figured Liu had picked up.a handful of cartridges and mixed some .38s in with the .357s."

"Because you can fire .38 Special ammunition in a .357 revolver," Reggie said.

"Right. Not the other way around, though."

Reggie started to say something, then stopped.

"We never tested the .38 slug that killed Solomon against the gun we had because the suspect was dead, the case was closed, and ballistics was six weeks fucked on active cases already."

"But you compared the bullet you recovered from this new body."

"Oh yeah. We definitely had two guns at Solomon Gold's murder. Funny you didn't mention that."

"I guess I didn't notice."

"Michael Liu comes at you with a gun in each fist like in a goddamn John Woo movie and *you didn't notice?*"

"It was a stressful few minutes. I really thought he was going to kill us both. I'm sorry."

"I appreciate the apology, but the .38 we didn't know about disappeared in the wind, and now it's got another notch in it and I'm up shit creek with the bosses. Normally, I'd guess this gun was ten years and at least that many shitheads removed from the one that did Gold, but this link between Marlena Falcone and your client is a coincidence for fairy tales. It doesn't seem to be a burglary—the doctor's purse was intact and in plain sight, nothing else missing. The killer might have left some barely partial prints at the scene. Not good ones, but we're trying to get them enhanced. We got some trace DNA, too, some hairs and some skin, but until we have a suspect, that's all just dust in an evidence locker. And the gun is still out there."

Kloska grabbed his giant root beer by the lid and sucked on the straw between his ring and middle fingers, all the time studying Reggie's face for a sign of surprise. Nothing he could read. "We're holding back the Canada Gold connection as long as we can, but they're releasing the ballistics today. Apparently, there's a consensus down in Bronzeville"—Bronzeville was the name of the South Side neighborhood that was home to CPD headquarters—"that releasing the information is going to 'stimulate traffic to the TIPS line,' which I think is bullshit, but nobody cares what I think. If I had my way, we wouldn't tell nobody nothing except who dead and who done it. Anyway, I thought you'd want to hear before it shows up on Channel 7."

Reggie nodded. Bobby wiped his hands on his lap and leaned forward for a longer view of a blonde walking past the window. "Anything that puts Gold back in the news is good for your business, right?"

Kloska was trying to rattle Reggie a little, but he couldn't tell if the comment stung. Vallentine was so hard to read. "I'm not quite that cynical, Bobby. Yet." As he spoke, Reggie seemed to go away in his mind. Kloska knew Vallentine was always trying to think six, eight, ten steps ahead.

Bobby leaned closer, his voice assuming a volume preset for professional secrets. "You want to know how many females will be murdered in the city of Chicago the last five months of this year? Because I can give you a number today and I'll bet you my boat slip in Belmont Harbor that I'm right within ten. *Which girls* those will be? That's between God and the Gangster Disciples. But *how many* is not really a variable in the cop's equation. The mayor makes a big deal when the murder rate goes up or down a few ticks, but that's just luck and good weather combined with statistical bullshit. Shuffling budget lines on death's balance sheet. Truth is, people always seem to want each other dead by roughly the same amount. It's like the speed of a penny dropped from the Hancock. It don't change."

"Acceleration."

"What?"

"The speed of a penny dropped from the Hancock would increase on its way down. It's acceleration that's a constant."

Kloska didn't care. "Meantime, you owe me one, and I need your help with something. The connection to Solomon is the only lead I have in the Falcone murder. I was hoping you could help me with a few of the facts from that night, just to get me jump-started." He took out a pocket notebook so warped and frayed, it might have been stored under a dripping faucet for the last decade. "My memory's better than my handwriting, but even my memory isn't what it used to be."

"For crying out loud, Bobby." Reggie demonstrated his skepticism with a straightening of his spine and a high-volume laugh. "You haven't forgotten a damn thing about Solomon's murder. Not a fingerprint, not a bloodstain, not a fiber sample, not a witness statement."

This was true, although Bobby didn't acknowledge it. The perhaps transparent fact was that he had another purpose for this interview. In a file close to his desk, apart from all the other evidence in the case, was Reggie's original statement, and Kloska wanted to compare the lawyer's memory to his impressions at the time. If Vallentine was holding something back out of professional obligation, and if that information was the key to this case, maybe solid and skeptical detective work could nose it out.

Of course, Kloska was holding back information, too. Reggie Vallentine didn't need to know every clue in the Falcone case. Like the index card, folded and unfolded so many times that its edges were frayed and its face had become a map of soft creases. On it Dr. Falcone (or someone) had stacked four numbers in the shape of a pyramid:

$$
\begin{array}{c}
2 \\
1\ 9 \\
3\ 2\ 9 \\
7\ 8\ 8\ 3
\end{array}
$$

It was the only item (except for cash, credit cards, and ID) in the wallet he found inside Marlena Falcone's purse. By comparison, Kloska's wallet was a repository of all kinds of useless scraps of paper—receipts and notes and insurance information and frequent-shopper cards. Why was this piece of scratch paper so special to the victim?

Kloska felt in his shirt for a pen and for the first time in several years he felt like his best arrest was ahead instead of behind him. That there was still a shithead out there who might never be caught if Bobby Kloska wasn't on the case.

AS MUCH OF THE TRUTH

REGGIE LIFTED the mostly deadweight of his right arm onto the counter and took a long breath. There was nothing wrong with Bobby's memory, or with his understanding of the Gold case. Despite the gentle mockery of his fellow detectives, Bobby was a devoted opera fan. He was always making jokes about "my boat," but Kloska didn't really own a boat. He spent his luxury money on a yearly subscription at the Lyric. Reggie knew because two years back he and Steph had borrowed the seats for *La Bohème*. Prior to Kloska's arrest of Solomon Gold, the composer had been something like his hero, a young standard-bearer of classical music, a forward-looking music director who had brought the admiring attention of the classical world to Chicago.

Bobby Kloska was different from most cops Reggie knew. He pretended to be as cynical as the rest, but every case wounded him a little bit. Years ago at this very counter, Kloska had been talking about a little girl who'd been shot in her home in some random gang drive-by misfire and he muttered into his root beer, "This job'll kill ya." Reggie figured that in Bobby's case it was literally true, that the compounding effect of all the shit he'd seen and couldn't forget would finally choke him like a cancer.

The murder of Erica Liu had been a malignancy he couldn't beat. Bobby Kloska had been betrayed by a man he had once admired, and now Bobby, who would never let this case go, wanted to see if Reggie could tell the same story he had told the night of Solomon's murder, something that shouldn't be difficult if he had always been telling the truth. Following the advice he always gave clients and witnesses, Reggie knew he hadn't volunteered much and that he had kept his story simple.

He'd told as much of the truth of that night as he could, right up to the point where the truth became bad for him.

Reggie had parked his blue coupe in an easy forward and back motion just off Lincoln Park West and walked a block toward the lake and three blocks north to Gold's home. To the east, the park was dark and silent except for exotic trilling from the direction of the zoo. Cars hummed up Lake Shore Drive ten miles over the summer speed limit. The air was light and cool in his lungs. He walked quickly, the rush of adrenaline and paranoia still lingering from his scare in the garage. The iron front gate was open an inch, and so was the heavy front door. "Hello!" Reggie called as he pushed inside. He heard a shouted reply from the second-floor office.

Up the crimson carpet of stairs.

In contrast to the rest of the home, which had been decorated by Solomon's soon-to-be ex-wife with straight modern lines and large blocks of bright unbroken color, Gold's office was like a Renaissance hallucination. Mad murals of Italian skylines covered three walls and the ceiling. The carpet was an enormous interbellum Persian. The desk was a massive slab of old European wood, carved on all sides with columns and arches and porticos and cupolas. Books—biographies and music histories but also philosophy and math, much of it in languages other than English—filled wide painted bookshelves on the fourth wall. A baby grand piano dominated one corner; an old violin on a stand was featured in another. The air smelled of sweet pipe tobacco and linseed oil.

Illuminated only by a desk lamp, Gold held his hands behind his back and tilted his head toward the window as he looked down at the street below. His clothes were pressed and clean, as if he had just slipped into them. Reggie had always noticed the great care in Gold's every motion. He did not cross his legs or fold his arms or twist or stretch or bend unnecessarily. When he sat down, he did so in a controlled vertical descent. When his body was at rest, it was always very still. By contrast, when Reggie was in court, he was in constant motion, a preacher of the law. If it was going to be a long day at trial, Reggie might take along three white shirts and a pair of identical suits.

"The buzzer's broken," Gold said in reply to an unasked question.

Anxious, Reggie settled into a club chair ten feet from the desk. "It's a little dicey leaving the front door wide open like that, yeah?"

Gold waved away the suggestion with his big left hand. Taller and broader than Reggie, Gold also carried a slight paunch even after months in county jail. "There are wolves out there, you know that? Here in the city. In the park. Their habitats are being pushed out by all the building in the suburbs. The disappearing woods. Some of the wolves keep moving west. Some go south. But some of them come east. Right down the damn expressway. Toward the water, the tall buildings. The urban forest."

"Coyotes," Reggie said. "It's not wolves that live in the city. It's coyotes."

Gold looked at Reggie's faint reflection in the glass. "I know for a fact that there are wolves in the city." In his right pocket, Solomon's hand fidgeted with something nervously, uncharacteristically. Maybe his keys.

Although he knew his client would never allow him to use it in a plea, Reggie believed Gold had been insane from the start—the bloody crime scene and autopsy photos of Erica's bruised neck and perforated body were evidence of that. She had been stabbed and strangled. Kicked in the head. Her left eye had been gouged with a blunt stick, or maybe the knife handle. Reggie's entire defense was based on a feeling he hoped for in at least one juror's mind—that Solomon Gold just wouldn't have done such a horrible thing—and in the week before closing arguments, Reggie's worst fear was that his client would start acting in sight of the jury like a guy who really would do horrible things.

In retrospect, maybe that would have been the best thing for everyone.

Looking into the big window, south toward the city, Reggie could see the lights of the Hancock Center tapering skyward. Reflected in the glass, he appeared small, legs crossed in the chair, with Gold and the Hancock looming like twin giants above him.

"Sorry to pull you out like this," Gold said. "You got other folks to save, I know."

Reggie's expression didn't argue. "Where's Canada tonight?" He didn't bother to ask about Solomon's wife. According to the papers, she had taken possession of their home in Florida in advance of the presumed divorce battle. Canada was still attending the Latin School just down the street, though. Either Elizabeth Gold was still angry with her daughter for standing by her father or she couldn't find a prep school down south with enough prestige to suit her.

Gold looked surprised. "She had surgery yesterday." He took a breath. "I'm going to see her later tonight."

"A little late for visitors."

"They make exceptions. For exceptional people." Reggie wondered if he was referring to himself or to Canada.

Gold walked to the front of his desk and retrieved a thick sheaf of oversize paper from the leather portfolio and handed it to Reggie. At the center of each page progressed a long handwritten musical composition, too formal and complicated for Reggie to make sense of. The wide margins around the staffs were filled with Gold's handwriting, precise and indecipherable. Words gave way to numbers, which fell away into exclamations. Latin and Italian phrases were formed into blocks, which were, in turn, used to construct geometric designs. Equations seemed to run from one page to another and back again.

"You know how a lot of cons say they discover God in prison?" Gold said.

Reggie put on the face that demonstrated to clients he remained unimpressed.

Gold said, "Many believe God once took the form of man. What if I told you He could take the form of *music?*"

Reggie sniffed. He lifted pages of the manuscript one at a time, only to find more of the same madness underneath.

"I have a story for you." Gold placed himself in front of the dark window again. "In the summer of 1791, a messenger brings a letter to the Viennese home of Wolfgang Amadeus Mozart. The letter is unsigned, but the anonymous correspondent asks Mozart if he would compose a requiem mass. His intention is to have it played every year on the anniversary of the death of his beloved, departed bride."

"Requiem mass?" Reggie asked. "Sorry, I'm a Miles Davis guy. And a Baptist two days a year." The manuscript felt heavy in his lap, as if it had the density of something heavier than paper.

"A Catholic mass honoring the dead," Gold said. "Mozart is intrigued. He's never written a requiem before. He is also in debt. He names a price, which the messenger pays in coin on the spot, and promises to double that amount on the composition's delivery. The courier never names his sponsor.

"Generous as the offer is, Mozart is unable to complete the requiem right away. He has not one but two operas to finish, including the famed *Magic Flute*. He also tells his wife, Constanze, that he's afraid to finish the requiem because he fears he is writing it not for some benefactor, but for himself. So he puts it off in favor of other projects. Do you see where this is going?"

"Constanze is your daughter's middle name." *Canada Constanze Gold*. Reggie was always making tangential connections in his mind, but the adrenaline in his blood combined with the lingering scotch caused him to blurt this one out. Even as he said the name, he noticed it written on the manuscript in Solomon's hand—"Constanze!"—next to his own thumb.

Gold nodded in annoyance. "Mozart finally continues work on the mass late in the year, but a mysterious illness seizes him after he begins and he is unable to finish it. On his deathbed, Mozart summons a minor composer, Franz Süssmayr, and describes to him how the work should be completed. Süssmayr and several other students work as a team to finish, with Süssmayr doing the transcribing, as his handwriting is most similar to the master's. Mozart dies in December, and sometime in January, Constanze, in pursuit of the remaining commission, delivers the completed work to the mysterious client, representing it as Mozart's own. But history knows better. Süssmayr is not a master and the parts written after Mozart's death are obviously inferior."

"Obviously," Reggie said.

"For more than two hundred years, the final composition by history's most brilliant composer has carried the practical equivalent of an asterisk next to a baseball statistic. Some have tried to repair Süssmayr's contributions in a manner more worthy of Mozart, but because the students were presumably operating under instructions from their mentor, the Süssmayr Completion, flawed as it is, has remained the definitive version."

From the title page Reggie read aloud one of the few phrases he could decipher. "Mozart's Requiem in D Minor." He glanced up. "The Gold Completion."

Solomon walked over to Reggie and reached to take the manuscript back with both hands, and as he did, he let an awful animal sound escape his throat, as ominous as a hiss but deeper and more menacing. Reggie tried not to flinch, as he had heard it before. Every time the prosecution scored a point at trial, Reggie had felt Gold lean in, lips to his ear, as if he had a counterpoint to make, but instead he would leave his mouth there so Reggie could hear him breathing in and out, and after fifteen or more seconds of this, Gold would emit a low growl. A horrible purr. Then he would lean back in his chair, poker-faced. Reggie understood it as an attack command. Gold engaged people only through intimidation. His family, his musicians, his staff, his lovers. His lawyers, too.

Wolves in the city indeed.

Gold touched the back of his own head. "There have been celebrated Mozart scholars over the years. They could tell you every detail of his life; they studied every one of his compositions. Perhaps they could recognize a Mozart symphony in the span of a quarter note. Nevertheless, they could never *write* a Mozart symphony. This is because you can't deconstruct genius. You can't re-create it. You can't even understand it. Brilliance is a mysterious current that flows one way from the genius out."

Gold rubbed the fleshy part of his left hand with his right thumb. "And yet I have reconstructed a lost work of Mozart. I have finished the requiem *exactly* the way Mozart was planning to had he lived."

This was the kind of insanity Reggie had tried to keep off the witness stand. After his arrest, Gold had been charged with murder with special circumstances and held without bail in a private cell in Division 9, the maximum-security wing at the Cook County Jail. He wasn't treated much like the other inmates, but County was no golf club. Somehow, he always managed to keep his County tans as unwrinkled as his Armani.

"I discovered that Mozart was following a map." Gold opened his palms in front of his face like a book. "A map of the heavens, you might say. The answer Süssmayr sought was not musical. The answer was *mathematical*."

"Mathematical."

Gold nodded. "Mmmm."

"I don't follow."

Gold seemed unsurprised. "I believe art is a repository of truths. Art is where truth hides from politics and religion and law and history and war and lust and greed and time, anything that seeks to subvert and tarnish and exploit it. Art is a safe in which man keeps his soul." He waited for a reaction and looked disappointed when he didn't get it.

"I listened to the requiem after finding this map and I did it with new ears. The notes that had been Mozart's were suddenly obvious, and the missing notes just as evident. I've never had an experience like it. Religious, I suppose you'd say. In jail, the requiem became my calling."

"And where did you find this map of Mozart's?" Reggie asked.

"The same place he did." Solomon tapped himself above the ear. "But I studied the texts, as well. Plato. Nicomachus. Al-Hasan al-Katib. Giorgio Anselmi. Isaac Newton."

"I've heard of the first one and the last."

"A man of your talents must know of Cicero."

Reggie bobbed his head once. "Roman orator."

" 'The revolutions of the planets produce seven sounds, and this number seven is the bond of well nigh all things.' " When that didn't get a reaction, Gold said, "It's an equation. The requiem is a mathematical equation."

Reggie rubbed his cheek. Solomon had a habit of never explaining himself, as if his genius would be cheapened if he told you what the hell he was talking about.

Solomon said, "I wanted you to be one of the first to see the completed work. If not for your efforts, the debut performance of my masterpiece might have been by some goddamn Stateville jug band. Or maybe at my own funeral."

If not for me, Reggie thought. He felt the bite of an angry tear almost forming in his eye and he turned his head. He saw the violin on a padded instrument stand in the corner. *The Guarneri.* It had been purchased for more than a million dollars as part of a complicated sponsorship agreement, and after Gold's arrest, the Boeing Company tried to force him to return it. Gold sued for breach of contract and the violin sat in safe-deposit purgatory throughout the trial.

"Reg," Gold continued after a pause, "there are people who won't want me to publish this. They'll think it blasphemy. *Dangerous* even. If they knew my intentions to do so, they would do anything to stop me. I don't care. One day everything I have done, and everything I ever will do, will have been forgotten except for this. Years from now, there will be no difference between the requiem and me."

Reggie thought he understood. If lawyering were an art, after all, Reggie Vallentine's masterpiece had been the unjust acquittal of Solomon Gold.

8

REGGIE PAUSED to assemble his thoughts before saying anything more. He never let even his innocent clients be interviewed more than once for just this reason. To this point, he had recounted that night exactly the way it happened, but in a moment Reggie was going to have to repeat a lie he'd told a decade ago, and a whole hell of a lot depended on him getting it exactly right. "You know NBC did a *Dateline* on Gold's murder. You could ask them to send you a copy." He took a breath. "I also wrote a book." Published a year after Gold's death, it was called *An Otherwise Infamous Crime*.

About a third of it was outright fiction.

Kloska looked up from his notes. "Yeah, I got a signed copy. 'Justice needn't be cruel, but it is always unusual.' That's what you inscribed in it."

"It's still true," Reggie said.

Kloska blinked. "Did you see anybody else on the way to Gold's house?"

"No."

"You didn't see anything weird or suspicious?"

"Like I said, the door was open. He said the buzzer was broken, so he'd left it open for me."

"Gold left the door unlocked?"

Reggie raised his hand in a shrug.

"Did you shut it behind you?"

"I'm sure. But I don't know if it locked."

"So he tells you about the requiem. What happened next?"

Reggie rubbed his dead arm. "I got shot."

Kloska licked a bread crumb from his thin lips. "Right. Michael Liu. How did he get in the house?"

"I don't know. The same way I did, I suppose."

"You didn't hear Liu coming up the stairs?"

"No."

"He surprised you?"

"Yes."

"He was wearing a mask."

"A Halloween mask. A monster of some sort. Zombie maybe."

Kloska nodded as he wrote. "You really couldn't tell it was Liu?"

"I know it because you tell me it was him. If I was sure it had been Liu, I would have said so that night when I saw you at the hospital."

Bobby glanced briefly out the window. "We know it was Liu because we had his fingerprints and hair all over Gold's office. Unless they were poker buddies or something."

Reggie laughed through his nose.

"Was there anybody else in the room that night besides the three of you? No? Then our masked man was Michael Liu. See, that's detective work."

"Well done, then."

"What did he want?"

"I don't think he said. I figured it was a robbery. At the time, I thought he might be there for the requiem."

"What would Michael Liu want with Gold's manuscript? How would he even know about it?"

"I know he grabbed the song right out of Solomon's hands."

" 'Rocky Raccoon' is a song, Reggie," Bobby said. "That thing you were holding would have been Mozart's Requiem in D Minor. The Gold Completion."

"Knowing my client, I'd be surprised if he wouldn't have wanted his name to go first." That made Kloska laugh, a welcome break in the tension. Reggie polished his chin with three fingers, trying to distinguish the truth he had observed from the history he subsequently created. "Was anything besides the requiem missing? I don't remember." Reggie did remember actually, but he wanted to establish that his memory wasn't perfect on an inconsequential detail in case he needed to forget a more relevant fact later.

Kloska squinted at his notes. "Gold's watch and his wallet. Which we found in Liu's car after he offed himself."

"Do you think Solomon was killed for his watch?"

"I think we all know why Liu wanted Gold dead. Maybe he wanted to make it look like a robbery. He wears a mask, disguises his voice so you won't recognize him. Takes a few things to make it look like a B and E." Kloska lifted the cuff of Reggie's shirt with his finger. "This big-ass watch of yours. Were you wearing it that night?"

Reggie nodded and stretched his hand beyond the sleeve to show the thick band. "Always show them your watch," Henry Vallentine once told his son. "A man who cares about his watch respects time, and a man who respects time—his time and the time of others—will always have respect."

Bobby continued, "You said Liu—sorry, the guy in the mask—took the requiem. Who else would have known Gold was working on it?"

"I don't know," Reggie said truthfully. "Solomon hadn't mentioned it to me before that night."

"How about his wife?"

"Maybe. Solomon seemed to think he could patch things up with her, but that might have been his ego talking. He probably had a hard time believing that anyone could actually leave him."

"Did you ever ask her?"

"Even if I had, I probably wouldn't discuss it with you."

"Are you her lawyer, too?"

"I am counsel and also a board member for the Gold Foundation, which she runs."

Kloska pressed his teeth together like he was trying to set them with glue. "So we found Solomon's watch and his wallet among Michael Liu's things, but we don't know what happened to the requiem. If it showed up today, that manuscript would be worth a tall pile of cash. Gold is even more famous dead than he was alive. You know how many Web sites are devoted to Solomon Gold's missing masterpiece? Hundreds of them."

After Gold's murder, Reggie had assented to dozens of interviews with the media, and in each one he spoke of the requiem, the lost masterwork that had been wrenched from Solomon Gold's hands as he weakened and died. The story had served to secure Gold's legendary status as an artist, which, in turn, had helped cement Reggie's professional reputation.

Reggie said, "The thief would have a hell of a time selling it. Any expert would recognize Gold's handwriting. I'd know it if I saw it again."

Kloska sniffed. "There's a black market eBay for every damn thing. The guys who steal Picassos don't have any trouble finding buyers, especially if they have the patience to lie low for a while. Remember when a Norman Rockwell ended up in that movie director's collection? He didn't even know it was hot."

"Then maybe it's still out there. I don't know."

"We never found the mask, either." Kloska's voice echoed with the remains of old cigarettes. "I'll be honest. If you were just some witness and not Reggie Vallentine, I'd say you made up this story the night of the murder to protect Michael Liu's identity. And then the next day, when Liu offs himself and we can put him on the murder, you're stuck with a bull-shit story, and you're still stuck with it today. And now I'm stuck with a dead doctor in Andersonville and a bunch of crazy whodunit bullshit that doesn't make sense." He rubbed his thumb against a pain in his forehead, an attempt at do-it-yourself acupressure. "Three things still missing from the scene of Gold's murder—the mask, the gun, and the requiem. Some-time after he left and before he killed himself, Michael Liu stashed them somewhere." The detective gears in Bobby's head were still grinding together. "Canada is really our common denominator, right? We got to find her, maybe to protect her from the shithead that killed Falcone, but also because she's the connection between our corpses. That and your story and the ballistics on this gun."

Reggie didn't like the way Kloska said the word *story*. He scanned his brain for something he should be curious about. On a different day at Mr. Beef, Bobby had told him that when a suspect didn't ask a lot of questions about the crime, he always knew the guy was guilty. "What did you say the doctor was killed with? The .357 or the .38?"

"The .38 Special. Not the one that ended your golf career. The same one he used to poke Gold between the eyes. Liu used the .357 again to kill himself."

A cold twitching in Reggie's abdomen. An untwisting of his intestines. "You said they're going to release it? The news about the gun connecting this new murder and Solomon's death, I mean."

"As we speak, probably. The *Sun-Times* got it on their own somehow, and like I said, it's gonna be a fucking heater. Day and night. Overtime."

Sunlight bounced off the mirror of a passing cab and Reggie deflected it with a blink.

Bobby said, "I might even have to skip mass this Sunday."

9

THURSDAY, JULY 15

HER CHIPS WERE ARRANGED by color and ordered in a tight spiral of towers, from the smaller stacks of blacks and purples winding around to the taller columns of reds and greens and blues. A short glass at Canada Gold's elbow, only as high as it was round, was a third filled with Tanqueray and about an eighth with tonic. The only other player at the table was a round woman named Fran with a Manhattan and a cigarette and a god-awful orange blouse with a flower print. By Wayne Jennings's count, Fran had just lost her seventh hand in a row.

From the pit, Jennings watched Nada push a black chip into the betting circle with the tip of a long unpainted nail. The house responded with a pair of cards. Three and a deuce. *Hit. Hit. Stay.* Manhattan Fran busted. The dealer busted. Another chip added to Nada's black pile. Another one hundred dollars pushed out to bet.

"If you hadn't taken that second hit," Fran muttered.

"If you hadn't taken that third drink," Nada said.

Three busts later, Manhattan Fran retreated to an empty chair at an adjacent table and Nada had the felt to herself. The dealer, a stoic and handsome young fellow named Jimmy, wore a black shirt with a white silhouette of the Colossus of Rhodes on the left breast. Wayne wore an identical shirt, three sizes larger, under his black blazer and ID lanyard. Jimmy had dealt Nada on many evenings in the past and now began sliding cards from the shoe at treble speed—*phhht, phhht, phhht.* Playing three hands at a time, Nada made instantaneous decisions—*hit, stay, split, double down*—indicating each with abbreviated (and barely differentiated) hand gestures.

There had been a lull on the floor for a day or so while the nation's airlines had been grounded and tourists stuck in Vegas for an extra forty-eight hours had mostly been tapped out of cash, but the hotel was almost back to capacity again. A small crowd of players waiting for a chair had gathered at a short distance behind Nada, but none dared interrupt the frantic pace of the deal by taking a seat at the table. "It's like watching a computer play," one said. Even in a crowded casino, Nada Gold had managed to get what she wanted most: time alone.

I almost hate to break things up, Wayne thought.

Before leaving the pit, he let her play another ten minutes—maybe thirty hands, of which Nada collected on better than half. Watching her shoulders stiffen as he approached from behind, he wondered what detail had tipped her to his proximity. His measured footfalls on the thin carpet? The smell of his cologne? The sound of his inseams rubbing together? She didn't look up, nor did she interrupt the barely audible and tuneful humming that often accompanied her play.

"Hey, Nada." He sat next to her, his big scarred knees almost touching her chair.

"Hey, Wayne," she said without looking. "Are you cutting me off already? That would really harsh my Zen."

"Did I say that?"

"Do you ever come by just to say hello?"

"Would you like me to?"

"Sure."

"I don't want to be a distraction."

"I'm undistractable, lover," she said.

Wayne swallowed. Four months ago, nearly a year after he first spotted her on a security camera, after beers and martinis at one of Club Nikita's tiny, tall round tables, Wayne and Nada had driven in separate cars to his apartment, where she stayed the night for the first time. He hadn't forgotten a second of it and he was damn certain Nada remembered it all, if only because he was pretty sure Canada Gold didn't forget.

Specifically, he remembered how small she was, how light in his arms, as if she were hollow inside the tan skin and tight sinew. He handled her gently, conscious of the difference in their sizes, but from the moment they were behind the door of his apartment, her vulnerability evaporated. Her eyes drilled through his, changing focus as she examined each layer inside him. Her teeth bit into his swollen lower lip, a small drop of sweat appeared at the end of her nose, and in the places they touched—her hands on his shoulders, her legs wrapped around his thighs, her hips tight against his—their bodies adhered as if a mighty external force were pressing them together.

"Are you kidding me, Nada?" he said afterward, exhaling into the dark. It felt good to make her laugh.

The occasion was repeated only twice. She and Wayne soon arrived at a business arrangement, and that's when Nada explained to Wayne her immutable rules of sex.

She preferred to call it a "philosophy of sex," one that made future intercourse with Wayne Jennings impossible. "I can have sex if it's truly meaningful, and I can have sex if it's entirely meaningless," she said. "But I always avoid the area in between." Wayne would have quickly rescinded the business offer in order to be with her even once again, but he knew he couldn't bear it if Nada had to spell out the subtext that she'd rather come to his casino than return to his bed.

Now once-banished Nada Gold played blackjack at the Steve Rhodes Colossus Casino and Hotel eight times a month, and when Wayne Jennings, associate director of security, walked over for a visit, she occasionally called him "lover." No doubt she was teasing, but he still liked hearing her say it.

"Okay, next time," Wayne said to her now. "I'll come over just to say hi."

"I'd like that."

"But right now, I'm cutting you off."

For the first time, she looked up from her cards and gave him a wide smile. "*I knew it*. Liar."

"I wasn't lying. You've probably played three dozen hands since I sat down."

"Forty-two." Nada reached over and tugged hard on his ID. "It figures you'd cut me off just when the count got to plus twelve. . . ." She winked and let him free.

"I thought you didn't count cards," Wayne said.

"I don't. It's beneath me," Nada said. "But that doesn't mean I don't know what the count *is*." She puckered her lips into a red circle smaller than a dime.

Wayne straightened the cords on his lanyard. "Give me a break. This is the last decent casino that lets you play at all."

"Fair enough," she said, but absent another signal, Jimmy continued to deal. "It doesn't matter. I was going to quit in twenty minutes."

One at a time, Wayne cracked the knuckles on his left hand with the palm of his right. "How do you even know what time it is? You don't have a watch. No cell phone. There aren't any clocks on this entire floor."

"It's nine-thirty-seven," she said without looking up from her cards.

He pulled his sleeve off his Timex and adjusted the minute hand by three ticks.

"I'm meeting somebody at ten."

Wayne couldn't be sure what his reaction looked like. Nada touched him warmly, but also chastely and briefly.

"At the bar." There were eleven bars and nightclubs at the Colossus, but she didn't have to specify which one. "Relax, he's not a surfboard model. It sounds like a job. I'm pretty sure he's a geezer. Name is Jameson."

"What kind of job?"

Nada shrugged. "I'm not so picky these days."

"Maybe I should go with you."

"Um"—she laughed now—"*no.*"

"He could be a perv or something."

"Would you even know a perv if you saw him?"

"I don't know. Would you?"

"From miles away, lover. Heck, that's how I first spotted *you.*"

The bug clipped over his ear squawked and Wayne adjusted the volume in his pocket. Every moment of the working night, Wayne was plugged into a wireless network that included voice, Internet, text, and video, all coordinated through a device in his jacket barely bigger than a pack of ladies' cigarettes. He called it his "phone" because he didn't have another word for it, but his mother wouldn't recognize it as a phone any more than her great-grandparents would have recognized his Ford Mustang as a horse. Wayne's entire professional life was inside this device. Every note he made, every address, every appointment, every colleague, every gambler, every single bit of minutiae pertaining to this casino, this hotel, or any other aspect of his job was accessible through his phone.

As Nada continued to play, Wayne looked to one side and tuned in to the chorus of voices that followed him through the casino. One of his colleagues was asking for him. He acknowledged the call and then turned the volume all the way down. "Kelvin's pouring at Nikita tonight. Stay near the bar and he'll have your back." Wayne unfolded a long pocketknife, one he kept in his desk but often carried around the casino for opening boxes or tucking loose felt, and cut a fraying string from the fabric of Nada's chair. "Peter just hollered anyway. I need to check out a situation in the high-limit room."

Jimmy whisked cards in front of Nada and she continued to conduct the play with her hands. Kings and fives and aces appeared and disappeared. Bets were collected and paid. None of these decisions caused even a pause in her attention. "High-limit room?" She sighed. "Sounds nice."

"It is nice. But I'd be fired if I let Canada Gold play a hand of blackjack against this casino for five thousand bucks. It'd be different if you wanted to play poker again and the house could have a piece while you took somebody else's money. I understand you were once good at Hold 'Em." He wanted the last bit to come off with some sort of sexy double meaning, but it didn't.

"I was *great* at Texas Hold 'Em," she said. "But I can't even get in a cash game anymore, thanks to the rumors. You hear the one where I'm some kind of *robot*? Nobody wants me at their table. And tournament poker is dead. It's all for amateurs now."

"Isn't *amateur* just another word for sucker?"

As Jimmy shuffled, Nada leaned backward, found the waitress, and ordered another drink with her eyes. "The thing that makes Hold 'Em a beautiful game, the thing that makes it a worthy test of skill, is that I know the cards inside out. And at a table of good players, I have faith that *everyone else* knows the cards almost as well. Every hand, I say to myself, *I know that they know that I know that they know.* . . . But at a table of amateurs, what do I know except that *they* don't know *shit*? If I'm heads-up with a pro, by fourth street I can usually tell that he's got one of two hands. And I figure he's sized me up the same way. So we're each trying to put on like we've got the hand we don't, and that we think the other guy has a hand we know he doesn't. Now that's gambling. That's a dance. That's *art*. But an amateur might push his chips in for God knows what reason. He'll fold the nuts because he has to take a piss. There's no play against that. Amateurs turn poker into lotto. It's like going hunting with blind men—somebody's gonna shoot you eventually; you just don't know which direction the bullet's coming from." She paused. "What's going on in the high-limit room?"

Wayne said, "Rhodes is playing host to this Saudi building contractor." Wayne had seen him in the casino before. "Hospitality calls him 'the Concrete Sheik.' Loves the baccarat. Saudis all think they're Sean Connery."

"Steve Rhodes is here tonight?"

"Yeah."

Nada said, "What does he know about our little arrangement here?"

Wayne leaned close and whispered into the back of her ear. Her hair smelled like hotel conditioner. "He had to approve it."

"Do you talk to him a lot?"

"I basically speak to Steve Rhodes when spoken to, which happens pretty much never." He smiled. "Two years ago he asked me what I thought about the Rebels quarterback playing with the flu. Maybe he had a number on the game."

Nada busted and muttered something foul. Wayne thought he must have misheard it.

"What?" He stood up.

The end of Nada's lip turned. "A name I got called yesterday. I've been swearing like a ship's whore lately. Dad would have killed me if he'd heard me talk like that." She covered her mouth and laughed loudly, as if that joke, black as a rattlesnake hole, had really been unintentional.

"Dad would have killed me," she had said, and now all the family details Nada had whispered into Wayne's pillow—gory details in every sense—were suspended in the awkward silence between them. Wayne reached out and touched her on the arm, but she pulled away by polite millimeters.

During their three nights together, before and after, Nada told him many things. She told him about the operation when she was thirteen. The tiny device they planted under the skin at her collarbone and the wires, like a spider's legs, to the meat of her brain, all of which had been orphaned there after her father's death. She told him about the powers it bestowed, along with the troubles that had arrived in the same package. She told him about her bad relationship with David Amoyo, whose face and name were now known to every casino professional in Vegas.

She told him about her infamous father and her distant mother, but she did it with the smallest, oddest details. How in better times they always wore some combination of black and red so it would be easier for strangers to recognize them. How her mother sometimes called her father "Mo," after Mozart, and how he sometimes called her "Loopa." How her father, Chicago's advocate general for high culture, had a secret collection of Edgar Rice Burroughs paperbacks. Each time, when she was done talking, Nada would kiss Wayne on the lips and tell him she was going to sleep. And she just did, in his arms, like a light on a dimmer. She fell asleep almost before she was done closing her eyes.

Wayne had never seen anything like it. But just as quickly, Wayne had done something even more remarkable.

He had fallen in love.

Now at the blackjack table, he asked Nada, "Can you really count cards and talk to me at the same time?" As Wayne had explained to a trainee just that afternoon, *the count* tracks the number of face cards still in the shoe. A positive count means there are more face cards than average and the advantage shifts slightly to the player. Card counters track these numbers in their head and use the count to determine the size of their bets. Counting isn't illegal, but the ones who get caught are banned from the casino.

Or anyway, the ones Wayne wasn't in love with.

"For the last time, I *don't count cards.*" Silent Jimmy tossed out six more—*three, four, seven, jack, king, deuce, seven.* "I know the cards. I remember their names. I'm intimate with them. I don't count cards any more than an Irish mother counts her children. I can just tell which ones are missing." Her chip spiral now reached as high as the butterfly tattoo on her right biceps, the one Wayne had traced with his thumb while she slept.

Wayne nodded at Jimmy, who waved his hands over the felt. Game over. "Before you go, give me a status report," Wayne said.

She expelled a sarcastic sigh. "You stop me from doing *my job* and now you want me to do yours?" Everything normal again.

Wayne reached across her body, brushing against her with his arm, and thumbed a tall stack of her chips. "You want me to add these up? You know our deal."

She turned her body and drew tiny circles across her sternum like a child in a playground huddle sketching out a long pass. "Three o'clock. Caribbean poker. Cowboy is pissed off that his barely legal girlfriend there spent three bills on a massage. Nothing major yet, but I'd keep an eye on his liquor. From what she says, he's a mean drunk."

"Okay."

"Shooting crap. Guy in the Knicks jersey's fond of the racist joke and says the word *titties* a lot. Not a crime, I guess, but it pisses me off. Feel free to roll him as a personal favor to me. And you see that NASCAR slot machine, third one from the end? Guy in the red hat is playing it." Wayne found it. "It's not random. There's a pattern. In fact, it'll pay a small jackpot in six more pulls. Watch." They counted together. It did.

Nada pointed out three other potential trouble spots on the casino floor. Bits of conversation she'd picked up. Unpleasant details she'd observed from afar. Wayne assessed each one in his head. He'd make notes after she was gone.

"Uh-huh. Anything else?"

For fun, she identified five prostitutes, a famous movie actor in disguise, and one exceptionally attractive transsexual. "Also, you got a counting crew that's been working the room for about an hour."

Card counters frequently descend on casinos in teams. The person tracking the count never changes the amount of her bet, which is how most counters get caught. Instead, when the count gets high, she signals her partner, "the whale," and he walks over to the table and throws down the big money only when the odds have swung in the players' favor. Despite Nada's insistence that she didn't actually count cards, the consensus on the Strip was that, for a brief time, Nada and David Amoyo had perfected the art.

"You didn't think that was worth mentioning before?" Wayne asked.

She sniffed. "You don't have anything to worry about. They suck. It's like it's their first day. You got Blondie, Pizza Face, and Reverend Moon there. Blondie and Pizza are doing the counting. She's in way over her head. Moon's your whale."

"Yeah, I've had my eye on him."

She touched her chin to her chest, hiding her expression. "Bullshit." Nada handed her stacks of five- and ten-dollar chips to Jimmy so he could exchange them for higher denominations.

"I did. He's been . . ." Wayne paused for the word. "Conspicuous."

"You're a regular one-man Interpol, Wayne. That's why you need me in here twice a week."

"My eyes aren't as good as yours, that's true."

"It's not my eyes, lover." She tapped her forehead. "You don't see with your eyes any more than you screw with your hips."

Wayne took a breath and rapped the table with his knuckle. "I remember," he whispered to her. Out of the corner of his eye he saw Jimmy waiting for an instruction, and Wayne gave it with a nod. Before paying them out, Jimmy passed a few high-denomination chips under the table, a barely perceptible motion that any player could mistake for one of the many practiced gestures—the knocking and waving and showing of palms—always incorporated into a Vegas deal.

Most people never noticed. Nada almost certainly did. Whether she knew its significance—or if she cared—Wayne didn't know.

Standing, Nada tipped Silent Jim with a black chip and dropped the rest in her yellow purse as six waiting players pressed forward to occupy the table. She squeezed Wayne's hand awkwardly and he marveled again at how weightless she seemed. The first night they were together, when she turned the switch in her head and fell asleep in his arms, he felt the mass return to her body, and that's when he understood what it was: balance.

A trainer for his college football team had explained it to him once. "When your body has balance, it's in harmony with gravity and you can move like someone half your size." The trainer tested all the players and calculated what he called their "moon weight." He told them a player whose balance was good enough—his moon weight low enough—could almost defy gravity. He could change directions in a blink, leap a wall of tall linemen in a single bound. According to the test, Wayne's balance was so poor that his moon weight turned out to be twenty-five pounds *heavier* than the one assessed by the locker room scale. The other players got a laugh out of that.

Wayne figured Nada's moon weight was next to nothing. But he also knew that on top of that perfectly balanced body was a head full of worry.

Nada's mind was a hell of a lot heavier than most.

10

KERRY MEADOWS was right where Nada had said he would be—lying on the couch, watching baseball on a plasma TV in a pair of drawstring pajama bottoms and a Stanford T-shirt. All Jerry had to do was knock on the door. Kid didn't try to rabbit or anything.

"That's the thing about rich kids," Jerry told Bea on the phone. "When you got so much to lose, you can't run very far away from it."

Meadows said he didn't know anybody was looking for him, if you can believe that. Said he didn't even know his best buddy, Phillip, had been charged with a crime, even though the story made page three of the *San Francisco Chronicle*, rich as Truman's daddy was. Guess it was true what they said about young people not reading the papers. Didn't offer any reason he'd been crashing on a couch in Marin, but he said he'd be happy to cooperate. Said he wanted to make a phone call first. Jerry told him to go ahead. The police wouldn't be there for another ten minutes.

The police. That made his eyes sweat.

Kid made two calls. The first was probably to Phillip Truman—he was that stupid. The second was probably to his own rich daddy. By the time the police arrived, he'd lawyered up, but Jerry was sure he'd talk once they dragged him back to Vegas. That is, if his attorney was anyone but English Judson.

"I've seen a lot of kids like him," Jerry said. Jerry Gaiter had been a high school physics teacher before he became an investigator for the Clark County DA's office. "They're all the same, as predictable as math. Most rich folks never surprise you at all."

Bea tried to call Nada to tell her about Meadows. They hadn't spoken since the previous morning, the day after Bea opened her eyes and found the folded paper with the twenty-five-dollar chip inside and the phone number that led Jerry the investigator right to Kerry Meadows's hidey-hole.

She also wanted to pass along a message from a Chicago cop named Kloska, who claimed he was looking for Nada and that it was important, something to do with an investigation. Bea remembered that Nada'd said someone was following her, that she even thought someone had been in her apartment, and after talking with Detective Kloska in Chicago, Bea convinced the LVPD to send a cruiser by her building every few hours.

Rubbing Nada's chip with her fingers, following a little scratch across its surface with her thumb, Bea was sick and sleepless with worry.

Nada's phone rang and rang and rang and rang.

11

NOT FOR the first time in his life, Bobby Kloska felt older than he was.

The naked body in the bed next to him was to blame. Carrie was a student at Columbia College, maybe twenty-two or twenty-three. Her skin was smooth and uniformly untanned all over and she wore hardly any makeup, because there were no imperfections to mask, nor was there a single favored feature to highlight. She was pretty in an entirely unmemorable way. In the bar, he had started talking about the heat and the sun and he told her he hoped that she wore big hats during the day, because her face was like a priceless painting in a museum that needed to be placed away from windows and shielded from UV rays. Later, when he was fucking her, his feet apart, standing beside her raised bed, she on her back, calves around his waist, he placed his hands on top of her and noted the contrast between the skin on her belly, which had performed little work except as a medium for navel piercings, and the skin on his hands, which had seen one tour of battle after another, skin that had been scraped and scarred and twisted and bitten. Skin that had been punched and that had punched back harder. Skin that had swelled and tanned and calloused itself around his fingers until it had formed a pair of natural gloves. The armored hands of a good cop.

He held her gently, fearing his old, rough mitts might scuff her like heavy shoes on a new floor.

But that wasn't even what made him feel old.

Posters were what made him feel old. She had posters on her wall. Not even in frames, just tacked and taped and pasted to the wall. Posters for movies he didn't know, bands he'd never heard of. Pictures of kittens, for Chrissakes. HANG IN THERE! one cat poster urged as Bobby thrust against her and she crossed her ankles behind his back and shrieked and moaned—sincerely or not—underneath him.

Hang in there. Fuck you, fucking cat.

The pyramid of numbers on the card from Marlena Falcone's wallet were almost all he'd thought about for two days. Well, that wasn't true. He'd thought about sex and gin and cigarettes and the scorching heat and the White Sox's wounded rotation and his kids and pieces of half a dozen open cases he and his partner were actively working. There was Marlena Falcone, but also a Juan Doe who had washed up on Oak Street Beach and a badly burned body in a Dumpster arson in Wrigleyville. Kloska had asked the private clinic where Falcone worked—Executive Concierge—for any files relating to Canada Gold, and they had been, as Kloska put it to his lieutenant, "communicative but uncooperative." Some muckety over there said they needed to take doctor-patient confidentiality seriously under all circumstances, even this one, and she assured Kloska that they were conferring with their lawyers. Kloska asked the state's attorney to get him a warrant, but he hadn't heard back.

In the meantime, with the bodies of Marlena Falcone and Solomon Gold heavy in his mind, Kloska worried they might find Canada Gold dead, too. She had been just a teenager holding her daddy's hand from the car to the courthouse metal detector back when he started hating Solomon Gold. Canada showed up on the poker tour a few years later, and the media noted it briefly before she abruptly quit playing. She'd since been forgotten again—even coming up with her name would be a head-knocking challenge for trivia buffs—but when they found her body and made the connection back to Kloska's heater, it would get front-page treatment all over the country and the feds would be on the Falcone case like flies on—he thought darkly—*Dr. Falcone.*

He needed to close this case fast, and so those four numbers were always in his head: 2, 19, 329, and 7,883. In the last forty-eight hours, he'd spoken on the phone with a dozen friends and former colleagues of the victim. The numbers meant nothing to them.

Along with the newspapers, Kloska had been poking at the connection between Gold and Falcone. Neither he nor the press had come up with much new. Kloska had spoken to a nurse who had lost her license in the same scandal that had tainted Falcone. Canada's procedure had been part of that mess, but the nurse couldn't give him anything except that Solomon Gold had seemed like a decent father.

His date was asleep and Kloska was bored, so he reached a hand blindly across her nightstand and grabbed a handful of papers and Chap Sticks, looking for some hint about this chick. Some people liked to smoke after sex. Since he'd quit smoking for the eleventh time, Kloska preferred to snoop.

He found an ATM receipt showing a twenty-dollar withdrawal and a pitifully low balance. He found a prescription for something that sounded like birth control. A ballpoint pen. A warranty for a recently purchased television. *Maybe the first new television she ever purchased on her own,* Kloska thought. He found an index card with a man's name—probably more like a boy's name—and what must have been a phone number: 312 365 9078.

His cell was in his pants somewhere, so Kloska picked up the girl's pink phone and dialed a 773 number—in the city but not downtown. After the seventh ring, his ex-wife answered.

"Are the kids up?" Kloska said with a slur.

"Hell, Bobby, it's the middle of the night."

"I know. I just haven't talked to them in a long time and things are crazy. I'm working this case, Dr. Falcone—"

"Where are you calling from?"

"My desk," he said.

"No you're not."

Bobby rubbed his eyes. "When did you get caller ID?"

She hung up.

What had he been thinking? Not about the time, that's for sure. There was something about that card with the phone number, so much like the note on his desk reminding him to call his kids. Sometime. Anytime. He looked at the index card again: 312 365 9078. Except she hadn't written it that way.

Detective Kloska tried to imagine it. The phone was on the left side of the bed. She had picked up the phone and needed to write a number, so she grabbed a piece of paper and with her right hand jotted down the digits. From an especially creative bit of foreplay, Kloska remembered that the girl was left-handed, so when taking down this number with her right hand, she had done the best she could: 31236 5 90 78.

I'm an idiot, Kloska thought. *It's not four numbers. It's ten.*

He picked up the girl's pink phone and dialed 1, followed by 219-329-7883. He listened to a recording and wrote six letters on his palm: C-E-P-E-D-A.

The girl's apartment already smelled like an herbal cocktail of cumin, tobacco, and weed, so Kloska didn't feel as if a lit Newport would be noticed. He borrowed a cigarette, lit up for the first time in a month, and called Jim Traden.

"Christ, Bobby, it's two in the morning." There was a pause while his partner apparently checked the display on his phone. "Who's Carrie Donleavy?"

"I'm picking you up at four." Bobby still felt a little drunk, but in another couple hours he'd be okay to drive.

"Why?"

"I want to beat traffic on the Skyway."

"The Skyway? What's in Indiana?"

Kloska blew smoke from one side of his mouth, away from his sleeping date. "Just wear your pledge pin, college boy. You're going back to campus."

12

THE THIRD-LARGEST BAR at the Colossus Casino and Hotel had a Soviet theme—crimson walls and black carpet and mural-size photos of missile tests and military parades and yellow hammers paired everywhere with sickles. Club Nikita served 107 different brands of vodka, the names of which, on her first evening here and for no reason, Nada had quietly memorized and alphabetized and also sorted according to price. For atmosphere (although there was some unlikely explanation on the drink menu about the proper environment for the enjoyment of Russian spirits), the temperature was maintained at just below sixty degrees.

Ducking through the crowd, Nada used the toggle in her head—her "spider"—to block out the thumping German disco, and as she brushed past the other patrons, she tuned in bits of random conversation—narcissistic small talk and exaggerated gambling adventures, most of it. After a minute or so, she blocked those out, too. Sometimes it was important to go silent, to shut the whole operation down for a while. Unwind. *Unfocus.*

Noticing every damn thing, she knew, could make a girl crazy.

Peering through white and odorless smoke piped in for aesthetics, she finally made it to within a few tightly packed bodies of the bar and, after catching Kelvin's eye, stretched her arms high into the hyperoxygenated air and turned her hands helplessly. Kelvin nodded and waved her past the far turn of the bar, where it was dark and there was an empty chair. A man—probably the oldest person in the room by twenty years—was meditating there with his drink, and when Kelvin motioned to him, he looked about and, seeing Nada, smiled and stood and shook her hand, giving a short bow.

Courtesy, Nada thought. She had almost stopped missing it.

Jameson wore a lime cotton shirt—heavy starch—with long sleeves and pressed khakis. Between his feet sat a soft leather briefcase, the kind that might hold a laptop computer. He was fit and had broad, strong hands, and his thick, graying hair had been massaged with expensive hair product. More than twice her age—late into his fifties, she assessed—he was still taut and strong, and possessed the dignified ruins of a once-handsome face. Nada searched for a surgeon's signature in front of his ears and around his eyes but saw nothing. Dozens of times she had casually nodded at an attractive man old enough to be her father and said to Bea for a laugh, "I'd fuck him on a bet," and she wasn't always kidding. Jameson was in that category.

Following an earlier direction, Kelvin brought them a pair of Rodnik rocks with the slightest bit of tonic. Nada tilted her head at the drink. "Thanks."

"Gary Jameson," he said, shouting a bit. Nada almost told him that as long as she could see his lips, there was no reason to raise his voice at all.

With his carefully arranged hair, buffed shoes, and business school manner, Jameson couldn't have seemed less like her father. Solomon Gold might have been American nobility, but he was also a wild-haired nonconformist who, in spite of his young daughter's disability, taught her to aim and fire a handgun at their Michigan summer home when she was only nine. Still, she detected a subversive resemblance around the eyes. Her therapist once claimed that Nada looked for traces of her father in all men of a certain age. Self-awareness did not stop her from finding such markers attractive.

"I know a great deal about you," Jameson said. "I want you to know that up front. I don't want you to think that it's creepy."

"Too late," Nada said.

"I always do my homework, Ms. Gold. That has been the secret to whatever success I've enjoyed. My attorney described you as having 'extraordinary powers.' I needed to see for myself what he meant by that."

"It pretty much is what it is," Nada said.

Jameson straightened and began reciting details from memory, like a professor extemporizing on his favorite subject in front of a class. Or else like a man trying to impress a girl with near-photographic memory.

"When you were a child growing up in Chicago, you suffered from severe attention deficit/hyperactivity disorder. You were literally bouncing off the walls of your Lincoln Park home. Screaming at parents and teachers and classmates. You couldn't sit still, even had frequent seizures. On the polo grounds of Oak Brook, you once punched your mother's horse in the jaw. The horse was more levelheaded, thank goodness."

Nada felt the same chill she'd encountered when she realized someone had been in her apartment.

"Drugs were the common treatment at the time, but prescription medication in any combination seemed only to make your behavior worse. The side effects were unbearable. Several times you ran away from home, only to resurface after days spent on the streets. Friendships were few and didn't last. After many consultations, your father found a specialist who recommended deep brain stimulation in the form of a neurostimulator—basically a pacemaker for your nervous system, a device that was initially developed as a treatment for Parkinson's. The FDA had a warning out against configuring the device for ADHD, but your behavior had become so unmanageable that your father gave the go-ahead and the doctor falsified the diagnosis."

Nada tried not to appear startled. "You have my attention, Gary Jameson."

"*Chicago Reader.* A lengthy article dated about eight years ago. I uncovered it during a LexisNexis search."

Right. The article. "Okay." She gestured for him to go on.

"Deep brain stimulation soon became a huge success, a drug-free treatment for all kinds of neurological disorders and maladies, from depression and obsessive-compulsive disorder to chronic pain and obesity."

"Last year the FDA approved one for boners," Nada said with a half smile. "I guess I can take a little bit of credit for that." Jameson acknowledged the joke with a deferential nod and turned his drink like a dial on top of its cardboard coaster—back and forth, like a safecracker. Not so much as an extra tick in the man's pulse rate.

He continued, "But for the treatment of ADHD, the results were mixed, to say the least. In fact, Dr. Falcone quickly stopped using the device as treatment for that disorder. The few neurostimulators that had been activated as part of Dr. Falcone's trial were immediately recalled. There was a scandal. She lost her license to practice medicine."

What the hell? "Your point?"

"From your abilities, at least as they have been described to me, it would seem that yours is still operating. At least you no longer seem to be struggling with the effects of your disorder. Before we go any further, I'm curious why."

"What is this?" she said. "You're dressed too well to be a reporter."

He enjoyed that. "I should hope so."

She considered the question. "I still have the neurostimulator because there's nothing wrong with mine. They still write to me every once in a while, asking me to come in so they can slice it out. I just ignore them."

"Deep brain stimulation is supposed to treat only the illness and have no side effects. But I understand many ADHD patients had an extreme reaction to the pacemaker."

"You mean they went nuts."

"Several committed suicide."

"They tried to come up with different names for it. Acute sensory integration disorder. Neural stimuli incapacitation. Some of the kids just went batshit. Two jumped off bridges. One crashed his plane into an office building during a flying lesson. One kid almost died trying to cut it out himself."

"But you were unaffected?"

"I didn't say that. I went through a rough period."

"You almost burned down your parents' house."

"*Summer* house," she said, correcting him. "And that was *before* the operation. No, I just learned to cope."

"And how did you do that?"

Nada looked down at the black marble bar top and her eyes followed a rivulet of red paint baked into the surface. As Kelvin poured a drink, he pressed against the bar with his large hand, which was a dark maple color on top and a pale yellow across the palm. It transferred a ghostly impression that evaporated into the cold, dry air. Quietly and involuntarily, she classified the vanished fingerprints—*four loops and a whorl.*

"You ask a lot of personal questions for a man who hasn't even told me why we're talking," she said.

"It's all very relevant to me, Ms. Gold."

She scratched with one finger behind her right ear. "You know what it was for a lot of them, I bet?"

"I don't."

"Appliances."

Jameson frowned, confused.

She said, "There are dozens, even hundreds of electrical appliances everywhere we go. At home, at work, at the store, at the doctor's. And they are all *humming.* You don't notice it because your brain has learned to tune it all out. But the neurostimulator tries to make sense of all that humming. Maybe because it's a machine itself, it organizes all that low unnatural ambient noise into songs and choruses. That's my persistent Muzak. All day, every day. Can you imagine being sad because your blender and your humidifier and your computer printer all combine into a depressing minor chord?"

Nada made a slight gesture with her head and pouting lips. Her eyes directed Jameson some fifteen feet around the turn of the bar. "There's a girl sitting behind you and to your right. In a bright yellow top. Study her face for ten seconds."

Jameson turned and stared. The girl noticed him after five beats and brusquely turned away.

"Now look at me. What do you remember?" Nada asked.

"Pretty. Brunette. Ribbon in her hair. Long nose. Thin lips. Large bosom."

Nada leaned forward an inch. "During the day, she wears glasses that pinch her just a little bit here. She's wearing blue-tinted contacts over hazel eyes. Her shade of lipstick is Plum Berry. She cut her own bangs this morning. Her name is Gwen. She whitens her teeth with one of those home kits. Although she tries to cover the scar with makeup, she's had some sort of surgery in the area of her thyroid, probably as a child. She's left-handed but plays tennis with her right. Her friend in the pink is Shelley."

"You picked up all that since you sat down?"

Nada made a circle in the air with her finger, indicating the rest of the room. "Now multiply that by a hundred."

"There's so much information coming in, some brains don't have the ability to handle it."

"Between you and me, I think the real issue for most of the others was just . . . *knowing*. Knowing too much stuff. Knowledge can be a burden, especially if you feel compelled to do something with it."

Jameson rubbed his neck. "Most would say knowledge is power."

She scoffed with a squint. "Selective knowledge, *intelligence,* is power. Unfiltered knowledge is just noise." Jameson was listening, but he still wasn't getting it. "Look, blue and yellow make green, and that's simple, elegant. But you mix all the colors together and you get black. When you see everything at once, you can't make it add up to anything, and that's depressing. That's what the world looks like to me—hopelessly compli-cated. I see so much stuff that the world's not green; it's black."

"So what do you do?"

"Like I said, I've learned to deal."

"Why you and not the others?"

"I don't know. Lucky. What I do know is that the neurostimulator is a part of me," she said. "It might not have been with me when I was born, but taking it out now would be like giving me a lobotomy. That little spi-der *is* who I am. It is me. I'm it." She turned her head toward the dance floor and said, "Take this out of me and I'm nobody."

Unembarrassed, Jameson said, "Before your father's legal difficulties, what was your relationship with him?"

"What do you care?"

"I'll answer that question. But I asked first."

"I loved him."

"How about your mother?"

"I haven't spoken to her since I was a teenager."

The long months of the televised trial strained the family in every direction. Nada had always been closer to her father than to her mother—he had been the one who played with her, who read with her, who was patient with her—and with Solomon gone and their last name on the front page every morning, Elizabeth and Nada had become bitter adversaries. Awful words that could never be taken back were spoken by both mother and daughter. Rich girl Nada spent long days and entire nights in a Dunkin' Donuts parking lot trading family secrets and angst with runaways and prostitutes even younger than she was. She got her first tattoo the same night she lost her virginity between packed coatracks in a massive Belmont Avenue thrift store to a kid without hope or money, a kid she knew to be gay even if he didn't yet, a kid whose picture was probably plastered by his frantic parents in every Barrington shop window, a kid who was just a few desperate weeks away from finally approaching the open window of one of those slowing cars and nodding at the much older married man inside. It was the last good story she ever shared with her mother, and she told it only to horrify her.

Jameson looked like he was making calculations in his head. "For the record, Ms. Gold, I believe your father was one of the great geniuses of history. Aristotle. Galileo. Leonardo. Michelangelo. Caravaggio. Newton. Pascal. Leibniz. Van Gogh. Mozart. Frank Lloyd Wright. *Solomon Gold.*"

She smirked. "His film score for *NeedleBots Two* was that good?"

"Actually, it's excellent. Perhaps it's not the requiem, but how could it be?"

No, she thought. *How could it?* The Gold Completion of Mozart's Requiem in D Minor was a myth, a legendary composition. The only person known to have seen it was her father's lawyer, who said it had been stolen from Solomon's hands by the man who murdered him. Nada knew only that it was the most important achievement in her father's life and he never even mentioned it once to her while he was alive. Now it seemed like she was constantly trying to avoid the endless discussion and debate about it, which she often heard acutely in the background.

"Who's Leibniz?" she asked.

"What?"

"Your list of geniuses. There was one I don't know. Leibniz."

Jameson nodded. "Leibniz was a philosopher and mathematician, among other things. He's best known, along with Isaac Newton, as the inventor of the calculus. Or maybe it's better to say they were the *discoverers* of the calculus. Leibniz saw the entire universe as a giant system that was both an expression and an instrument of God's plan. Asian migration into Persia, the Mongols' invasion of Europe, Magellan's death on Mactan, kangaroos, the fur trade, Charlie Chaplin, the Eisenhower administration, Vietnam, the Gold Completion, you, me . . ."

"Leave me out of it, if you can." She said it pleasantly.

He drew a breath. "Do you believe your father killed Erica Liu?"

She answered without conviction, as if she were just ejecting another random fact from her head. "Yes."

"As an admirer, I've always held out hope that he might have been innocent."

She waved. "People say I have a photographic memory, but I don't remember everything with pictures, or words. Sometimes I remember detailed abstractions—shapes that represent ideas. They're more like charts than photographs. The chart of my father I keep in my head tells me he's guilty, but it's nothing like proof. It's more like faith."

"Most people reserve the word *faith* for beliefs that are more inspiring."

Nada said, "The next time I see you, I might recognize your face or I might recognize your chart. It's all data that's in my head. Converting that data into the things I believe takes an act of faith."

"But you will recognize me."

"If I want to. Actually, I'm almost as good at forgetting as I am at remembering. It's not even forgetting really. It's more like *deleting*."

"How much of your father have you *deleted*?" he asked.

"None of him."

There were a lot of people dancing suddenly, as if the DJ had put on a popular song. She turned the music off in her head and now she watched the young couples hop and weave and nod and wave in silence. Some of them danced as if they couldn't hear the music, either. Maybe they had no rhythm. Maybe they were so in love with their partners that everything else in the room had fallen away. Maybe, like Nada, they were just lonely in crowded places.

Jameson said, "In the first ten seconds you were sitting here, what did you observe about me?"

Nada said, "I never tell anyone the things I notice about them."

"Why is that?"

"Because no one *really* wants to know how other people see them. And I don't see what just one person sees. I'm more like a *whole team* of people studying you. Taking notes. Gossiping. Making judgments. Do you really want to hear their summation?"

"Fair enough."

"I have too few friends as it is," she said.

The couples, now bathed in different lights—reds and yellows and purples and blues—continued stepping to different beats.

"Nevertheless, a person of your abilities should have many opportunities," Jameson said.

Nada had worked two real jobs in her life, both for weekend poker warriors whom she had busted and impressed at the table. One was the CEO of an insurance company. The other ran a public-relations firm. Neither job lasted a month.

She said, "I came to Vegas to play cards and I stayed here because I like it. This place can be all the way on or all the way off, you know. The Strip and the desert. I'm like that, too."

Jameson smiled. "You didn't only play cards here."

She shook her head. "Some attorneys paid me for jury consulting. But I could also offer them the truth. Sometimes they paid me what the truth was worth. Sometimes they didn't, but I gave it to them anyway, if it was the right thing to do."

"And how did you determine when it was the right thing to do?"

She noticed more than a few of the girls along the bar admiring Kelvin, as she often did when he reached for a bottle. "Half the time, the prosecution and the defense are both peddling stories to the jury that they know are bullshit, because the truth isn't so good for either of them. They don't want to give the jury all the facts. They want the court to see only blue and yellow so the jury can make green. I was there to make sure the system got it right every once in a while, and I did a better job of figuring out who was guilty and who wasn't than any jury ever could." The vodka had left a sting in her nose and she pinched it away with her fingers. "Hell, there were more than a couple innocent guys whom Clark County would have charged if I hadn't stopped them."

Jameson paused for a very long time. He made a tent with his right hand over his left and tapped a large gold ring with his platinum wedding band from underneath. The gold ring had a triangle of diamonds on its face. "I'm a very lucky man, Canada. I have a lovely wife of thirty-five years. Two grown children, both very successful. This is all information you can look up for yourself."

"I will," she said as her drink arrived. Then she noticed something at a table to her right, just a blur of it, but . . . "Damn."

"What?"

"Did he put something in that girl's drink?"

"Who?"

The kid might have turned twenty-one yesterday. He had close black hair and a short-sleeved shirt with a tropical print. Nada could see tiny hairs on his bare arms standing on end, from cold air, from nerves. He was sitting across from a ponytailed blonde whose WASPy features had been elongated by upper-class inbreeding but more recently slackened by Long Island iced tea. Jameson turned quickly and Nada put a hand on his arm to restrain him. "In the blue shirt," she said. "He's here with three other guys."

"You saw him put something in her drink?"

"I didn't *see it* exactly. I wasn't looking at him. I mean, I think he put something in her glass when she checked her purse under the table."

"Like what?"

"Don't know. What does a douchebag like that put in a party girl's glass?"

"What exactly did he do?"

"It happened fast." She looked Jameson in the eyes and began running her words together, getting them out of her mouth as quickly as she was able. "Sometimes it's like I remember things—I have the *chart,* a record of having seen them—but I have no memory of actually seeing." She tapped her head. "I just know that when I think I've seen something, I'm not wrong a lot."

Nada knew there was no more foolish pursuit than trying to convince another person you weren't crazy. She peered through the dark and smoke for Kelvin at the other end of the bar and called for him voicelessly into the din.

To her surprise, Jameson wore a serious frown, as if he understood. "There's a nomadic tribe called the Moken that lives on and between islands near Thailand and Burma. They are true Gypsies of the sea. Just before the deadly tsunami a few years back, a number of Moken fishermen sensed something was wrong, that the ocean was threatening. They headed for the safety of deeper water. Nearby, Burmese fishermen did nothing. When asked why they survived and the Burmese had not, the Moken said, 'They don't know how to look.'" He glared into Nada's eyes for a moment; then he stood and pushed into the dense crowd. Nada lifted herself up so she could see. Jameson approached the table where the douchebag was leaning in toward the party girl and reached slowly between them with his right hand—*gracefully,* Nada thought—and pushed her drink off the table. The heavy glass thudded as it hit the carpet and splashed tequila and vodka and triple sec on their shoes. He made no effort to pretend it was an accident.

With her toggle, Nada silenced everything else in the room. There was a tunnel between her eyes and ears and that table.

"Hey!" the girl said, lifting her arms and examining the front of her tight blouse for stains. The boy rose from his chair tentatively. Jameson, half a head taller, reached into his pocket, removed a thick silver clip, and tossed a fifty onto the table. "Sorry," he said, not looking away until the boy sat down.

Nada watched the girl say "Asshole."

Jameson turned away without a word and returned to the bar. Douchebag studied the puddle on the floor. Party Girl snatched the fifty and slipped it into her purse.

As Jameson sat down again, Nada smiled at him and touched his sleeve. Now *that* was something like Solomon Gold would do. Nada asked herself if David Amoyo had ever shown that much faith in her. Not once, she realized, in their eighteen months together. And Jameson had known her for what? Twenty minutes?

She kept Douchebag in range of her senses. He was walking away from the table now, away from the girl. Jameson had earned her attention. "You were about to tell me what you wanted. At least I think you were."

"As I was saying, I've made a lot of money and—"

"How?"

Jameson's mouth hung open. He said, "Do you know what Eurodollars are?"

"No."

"They are U.S. dollars deposited in foreign banks."

"And you had a lot of these?"

"I never had any. I traded Eurodollar *futures*."

"Which means?"

"I doubt you really want to know. Basically, I made bets on whether U.S. interest rates would go up or down."

"So you're a gambler?"

"In a manner of speaking, and a rather good one."

She brought her glass to her lips, allowing him to continue.

"Anyway, I made enough money to retire and follow my true love."

"Which is?"

"Art. As the daughter of an artist, you will understand the importance of this assignment." He leaned closer. "The pieces I collect are not by trained artists. I'm mostly interested in intuitive art. 'Outsider art' some call it, although I'm afraid the phrase has become associated more with Grandma Moses than with Basquiat or Henry Darger."

"Who?"

Jameson shook his head. Explanation was irrelevant. "There is a man in Chicago. He *was* homeless. Some say schizophrenic, although I'm not a psychiatrist. His name is Patrick Blackburn, but he calls himself 'Burning Patrick,' or at least that's the name tattooed across his forearm. For a long time he made small amounts of cash painting objects that he'd found on the street or in the garbage. Some of these pieces were quite remarkable. A few years ago, Blackburn was 'adopted,' you might call it, by a group of rock musicians. They paid for his health insurance, tried to procure the treatment and medication he needed. They acted as his publicists, his managers. They got him a show in a prestigious gallery. Even had him sing a few songs at their shows—and by 'sing,' I mean shout his poetry into a microphone while they made a lot of noise behind it. Some people must like it, because every few months they perform sold-out shows with Burning Patrick. They call themselves the Bat Wing Vortex."

"They're exploiting him."

"Not necessarily. Historically, benefactors have been every bit as important to art as paint. No doubt these young men provided Patrick with an income and a roof and access to some kind of health care. In fact, Burning Patrick's legend grew very quickly. I and others began collecting his work. Prices skyrocketed. I continue to pay them because, while I might not think much of him as a singer, I think he's a stunning artist."

There was something about the way Jameson pronounced that phrase. "You're not sure he's for real, are you?" Nada said.

Jameson paused to bite his lip. "After he joined the rock band, Blackburn's output changed. He now paints almost exclusively on six-inch square tiles—like you might find in a public restroom—maybe a hundred of them each year."

"What are the images like?"

"At first glance, they seem like typical folk art. Almost a parody of folk art. Animals, portraits, rural and urban landscapes. At first glance."

"What do you mean?"

"If you consider the tiles as a whole, it appears Blackburn is painting a mural on a massive scale. But he's not doing it in order."

"What do you mean, not in order?"

Jameson reached into the bag at his feet and pulled out a blue folder. "Here are some photos of Burning Patrick's tiles. I own seventeen of them, but I have photographs of another several dozen owned by acquaintances."

"If you're so rich and so fond of these tiles, why don't you buy more of them?"

"There are other people who want them just as much as I do. Also, there's almost no secondary market. Collectors who own them aren't selling."

"Burning Patrick is no longer homeless, I take it."

"He lives in a modest home in a relatively modest neighborhood. Apparently, he barely touches the money, except when he gives chunks of it away to charities."

"Is that why the rich folks call him crazy?"

Jameson acknowledged the joke with a pretend wince but didn't respond. "The finished tiles themselves, as you can see, are interesting. Disturbing, passionate, original. But what has become apparent to the community of collectors is that each of these tiles seems to be a part of a larger work. Many of the tiles fit together. Look here, and here. The sides match up perfectly. And although the individual tiles appear to be unrelated and somewhat crude, when you get three of them that fit, you start to get a separate image that is almost photorealistic. Here's part of the iris of a human eye. Can you see it?"

She could. By themselves, the tiles seemed to her as sophisticated as a fifth grader's crayon drawing. But looking at these three together after blinking and refocusing, an intense bloodshot eye appeared. The effect was like cold water poured down her back.

"But here's the thing. He's painting the tiles *out of sequence*. So let's say Blackburn painted this one on Tuesday"—Jameson pointed to a tile in a different picture—"and then this one over here on Wednesday. He might not have painted the tiles that fit next to each of these until months later, maybe after he had already sold the first ones to collectors. Still, when he finished, they fit together perfectly. Can you imagine?" He pulled out three photos and set them on the bar. "Look at these. Adjacent pairs. The holy grail for Burning Patrick collectors. If you have two tiles that fit together, their value goes up by a factor of ten."

Nada examined the pairs closely. The tiles matched perfectly along their sides, consistent lines of crimson and indigo extending from one tile to the next. She peered again at the eye. The left eye of a man possibly in his last moments stretched over three tiles, its red veins meeting exactly at the edges like sections of a torn map. "Maybe he's already painted the whole thing and he's just *selling* them out of order?"

"His interlocutors say he does not. They claim to sell them as he paints them, numbered in exactly the order in which they are produced. And they claim not to know exactly what Patrick's vision is, or what he's ultimately trying to accomplish. That could be a lie, of course, but in any case, it would have been almost impossible to paint the entire thing at once."

"Why?"

"Because as more of the tiles are released, we're starting to get an idea of the size of this thing. It would have to be gigantic."

"How gigantic?"

"Bigger than Times Square in New York. Bigger than Grant Park in Chicago." He lifted his arms up. "Bigger than the Colossus Hotel. At this rate, he'll never finish it in his lifetime. He'll never finish it in three life-times."

"Maybe he's doing it in sections?"

"No, he's doing a tile here and a tile way over there. As far as we can tell, he's painted only fourteen adjacent pairs and five triples."

"You could do this on a computer."

"Maybe. Maybe everything about Burning Patrick is a lie."

"In which case?"

"In which case, obviously, my tiles would be worth considerably less than I paid for them."

"Well, how else could he do it?"

"Some of us want to believe that Patrick possesses a genius we don't understand." He added, "Your father had that kind of intelligence."

She turned up one corner of her mouth. "What do you want me to do?"

"I'd like you to prove it one way or the other."

"How?"

"I want you to follow him. I want you to eavesdrop on his conversa-tions and on the conversations of his managers. Whatever it takes. I want to know how he's doing it."

"You mean go to Chicago?"

"You can stay on my estate very close to downtown. It's gated and guarded and comfortable. You will have access to my home, my kitchen, my staff for as long as you need. Months if necessary. In return for your time and effort, I will pay you two hundred and fifty thousand dollars."

Nada studied him for a tell, for any sign of disingenuousness. "You want to pay me a quarter million to find out your art isn't worth as much as you paid for it?"

"I'm hoping you'll discover the opposite. Of course, if you discover that Burning Patrick is not the genius I believe him to be, I have a nondisclosure agreement prepared, and the penalty for violating it would be severe."

"Until you can unload your tiles at present market value."

Jameson stopped short of laughing. "I believe Burning Patrick is a singular genius—a visionary, perhaps divinely inspired. If I didn't believe that, I wouldn't be spending a fortune on his art. But I spent a working lifetime dealing in hard currency—euros and drams and dollars and yen. Faith is not good enough for me. I need to know. I need confirmation. Years from now I don't want it revealed that Burning Patrick has been perpetrating an elaborate hoax and watch a significant investment shrink to nothing."

Finally, a motive she understood.

She turned toward the room and found the douchebag. He was talking to one of his friends, hand on his left hip, weight on his left leg, leaning toward the door. She couldn't see his lips.

Jameson said, "So, Canada, I'm very interested to know what you say to my . . ."

Nada knew the word he was going to use even before he said it: *proposition.*

13

WAYNE WAS RUNNING, bouncing, spinning all over the casino. Cowboy Hat's girlfriend turned out to be his sixteen-year-old stepniece. Dealing with that mess and with the counting crew at the same time took the attention of the entire staff. Meanwhile, he separated the card counters and sweated each of them in different conference rooms and took their photos and typed a report. He e-mailed their mug shots to his counterparts at other casinos. Their features would be programmed into facial-

recognition software and, Wayne promised, if the Colossus security cameras ever caught their cheating mugs, an alarm would ring in the bug in
his ear and their next parting wouldn't be so cordial.

The official policy of the Colossus stated that the staff should treat
suspected cheaters firmly but with respect. But the rumor around town—
the legend—was that in the back rooms of the Colossus, the burly security staff would kick your ass just for rocking a slot machine. The truth
was somewhere in the gray between. Cheaters usually got away with a
scare and a warning and a ban. Thieves, on the other hand, met a different fate.

About a year after he started working at the Colossus, Wayne caught a
dealer conspiring with a gambler to cheat the casino. In blackjack, the
players' cards are dealt faceup. The dealer gives himself one card up and
one card facedown. If the dealer is showing an ace, he offers insurance
to each of the players—a smaller side bet that the dealer has an unbeat-
able hand of twenty-one. Wayne caught one dealer tipping a friend when
he had blackjack so that the gambler would know when to take the insurance.

That night, Steve Rhodes had met Wayne outside the conference
room where he was sweating the dealer. "I don't want the cops to find out
about this," Rhodes said.

Wayne didn't understand. "You want me to let him go?"

Rhodes shook his head. "I want you to take care of it." When Wayne
didn't respond, he leaned into Wayne as if for a kiss. "I want you to fuck
him up." He stood straight again. "He won't press charges. Hell, he'll
think himself lucky to have it behind him. He'll also be a walking bill-
board that you don't fuck with Steve Rhodes." Rhodes started to walk
away, stopping to pound twice on the door of the adjoining room. He
turned back to Wayne. "Make sure his friend in there sees the result."

Wayne had been in fights, sloppy, drunken four-on-six bar fights where
nobody really connected and everybody walked away bloodied and mad
but with most of their pride. Before that night, he'd never punched a
man—much less a man he knew and liked—handcuffed to a chair.

But he'd done it twice since.

Tonight, shuttling between rooms, Wayne would check his phone
often, just glance at it as if acknowledging an e-mail. Before Jimmy, the
dealer, let Nada go, he had attached her name to the serial numbers on
her chips, which could now be tracked anywhere in the hotel—from table
to table to restaurant to gift shop to room. This allowed the hotel to follow

the play and spending of its best customers. The more the casino learned about the behavior of their biggest spenders, the better they could serve them, please them, and keep them coming back. Wayne didn't know exactly how it worked—some geek from the manufacturer had given a PowerPoint show, something about low-frequency radio broadcasts and thousands of receivers placed throughout the casino—but the specifics hadn't seemed important, so he'd tuned them out.

What was important to Wayne was a little green dot in his palm that, until she either left the casino or traded those chips for cash, showed him the whereabouts of Canada Gold.

Every time he checked his phone, she appeared to be sitting at the bar in Club Nikita. For one hour. For two.

Thirty minutes ago, he had passed Steve Rhodes on the floor. Rhodes was leading the Concrete Sheik to the private elevators, probably up to his office to show him an item from one of his expensive and oddball collections—maybe a fifty-million-dollar Picasso, or a ceremonial ax alleged to have been wielded by Genghis Khan, or even a clown rug latch-hooked in prison by an Oregon serial killer. Wayne was walking quickly back to the room where they were holding the Cowboy and he was muttering into his ear bug at Peter Trembley with more urgency than needed, the stress more to do with the increasing unlikelihood of a relationship with Nada than with the cheats and perverts filling up his incident logs. Behind the Sheik's back, Rhodes gave Wayne a look that asked if any of this was something he should be worried about, and Wayne shook his head once. Rhodes paused and smiled and motioned for Wayne to follow them.

Wayne recalled one of the few (and very first) conversations he'd ever had with Steve Rhodes. It was the final stop in the final round of interviews for his job. They met in a foyer in Rhodes's executive suite. The casino mogul, dressed for golf in some other state, was waiting for an elevator to take him to a helicopter. They shook hands and Rhodes asked Wayne if he had a philosophy that he would apply to the job; then he looked up at the lights over the elevator, making it clear that he had no time for the answer. But Wayne was prepared and he told Rhodes that in football everyone on the offensive line has an assignment. If every player concentrates on making his assigned block, then the offense is successful. He also said linemen are noticed only when they screw up. At the Colossus, he planned on being as nameless and invisible as a left tackle.

Rhodes nodded at Wayne and gripped him firmly on the biceps, then stepped on the elevator without a word. Before Wayne had returned downstairs for what he assumed would be handshakes and promises to be in touch, Rhodes had called from the rooftop to say "Hire that kid."

Wayne liked to believe that he and the boss had had so few conversations since because he had earned his confidence. Rhodes trusted Wayne to take care of his assignment and took him at his word that he would remain invisible, so invisible that Rhodes never even needed to call his name.

But he was calling it tonight.

Wayne followed Rhodes and the Sheik through a metal door guarded by a man not under Wayne's supervision. A burly ex-cop with a real gun, a heavy black thing at his belt that made Wayne self-conscious about the closest thing he had to a weapon—the long folding knife in his pocket. They walked down a long corridor lit like an airport, around a corner and past another set of guards, and then into the vault. Casinos required a lot of cash—more cash than most banks. It was in shiny metal drawers and loaded up on wheeled carts, either coming or going from the cages. Cash never stayed out on the floor very long. Cash on the floor could go missing.

Wayne had been in this room only three times in seven years.

Rhodes said to Wayne, "I wanted to show our guest something, and I thought you might be interested in it as well, seeing as you're local law enforcement." The Sheik didn't react, and Wayne guessed he didn't speak much English. Maybe Rhodes had brought Wayne back here just so he'd have a person to talk to.

Someone had placed a small wooden box, about the size of an oversize Bible, on a cart in the center of the room. The box was in the exact center of the top tray. The preciseness of it all led Wayne to believe it had been placed here specifically at Rhodes's instruction. Everyone carried out his direct requests that much more carefully.

Rhodes slid the top off the box and swept aside some brown packing material that looked like straw. He tilted the box so Wayne could see what was inside.

A gun. Wayne didn't know much about guns except what he'd picked up in a few hours training at a range, but he knew from the cylinder at its center that it was a revolver. It looked like it had some age on it, but it wasn't antique.

Wayne tilted his head at Rhodes.

"My newest acquisition," Rhodes said. "This gun was used in the kidnapping of Patty Hearst."

The Sheik must have understood that part, because he nodded, impressed. Rhodes presented it to him, but the Sheik shook his head and waved his hands. Rhodes turned to Wayne. "Go ahead. Feel it."

Wayne wasn't as interested in the gun as he was in keeping Rhodes happy. He lifted it into his hand. It wasn't as heavy as he'd expected. "It's not loaded, is it?" Wayne asked. Rhodes shook his head. Wayne turned it over, not really sure what he was supposed to be looking for. It was cold and a little bit oily. At the bottom of the stock were three engraved letters: *EKG*.

"What's that? Like a cardiac thing? A heart attack?" Wayne said.

"Those Symbionese were fucked up, huh?" Rhodes laughed, and the Concrete Sheik laughed, too. "I don't know what it means yet, but it's a personal touch that makes this particular gun ten grand more expensive than the other one I was looking at."

Wayne smiled and wished he could leave. This was probably supposed to be some kind of honor, alone time with the billionaire boss and his billionaire Saudi client and this souvenir from a long-ago billionaire's kidnapping. But Wayne had an urgent assignment, and it didn't involve Patty Hearst or cheaters or thieves or any of a dozen situations that might be unfolding at the casino.

His number-one assignment was a stationary dot on a gray screen, a dot representing a beautiful woman sitting in a bar, talking to a man who wasn't him.

14

FRIDAY, JULY 16

KLOSKA WAS EXPECTING more from the office of a tenured math professor at an exclusive private school like Sampson University—maybe oak paneling and leaded windows and a cathedral ceiling with a chandelier. He was certainly expecting books, even a great big wall of them, with volumes stacked so high that you'd need a ladder to reach the dustiest ones at the top.

Instead, Professor Cepeda's office was the size of a typical cell at county lockup and it contained about as many scholarly books. One short laminate shelf held half a dozen paperback bindings with inscrutable titles and Cepeda's name along the spines. The rest of the office was covered in paper—faxes and printouts and scribbled calculations. Some of them were in Spanish and the rest of them, as far as Kloska was concerned, might as well have been. Cepeda's desk was a banged-up old thing, a sorry twin to the dented and undignified piece of scrap in the cubicle Kloska shared with a second-watch detective back at Area 3. The only difference was Cepeda's double-wide platinum flat-panel monitor growing out of the mulch of paper at its base.

The whole place was small enough that during the interview, Traden had to stand, arms folded, back against the gray metal door. Kloska sat in a narrow straight-backed chair with a torn upholstered seat, making preliminary scribbles in his tiny cell phone–size notebook, which he pressed against the top of his crossed thigh.

Professor Cepeda was examining the card found in Marlena Falcone's wallet.

"Clever," he said almost inaudibly.

"What's clever about it?" Kloska asked.

"It's my phone number." Cepeda had been born in San Juan, but his American accent was so good that it made Kloska self-conscious about his nasally Chicagoese.

"I know. I'm wondering why she wrote it in a little pyramid like that."

Professor Cepeda laughed, as if he was just teasing out the obvious questions. "It's not a pyramid. That's a *tetra-CAH-tus.*" He spelled it out on a random corner of a paper on his desk: T-E-T-R-A-K-T-Y-S.

"What's a *tetraktys*?" He tried unsuccessfully to pronounce it like Cepeda had as he copied it into his notes.

"It was a sacred symbol to the followers of Pythagoras."

"Pythagoras?"

"Greek mathematician. You know, the Pythagorean theorem? The formula for determining the dimensions of a right triangle. The sum of the squares of the sides equals the square of the hypotenuse. *A* squared plus *B* squared equals *C* squared."

"Yeah, I remember." *Barely.* Kloska looked through his Falcone notes for anything he'd heard about Pythagoras, or triangles.

"Funny, but the real Pythagoras probably had little to do with the theorem named after him. He was far more interesting and complicated than that. He wasn't only a brilliant mathematician; he was a philosopher, a theologian, a teacher, a political svengali, a cult leader, a mystic. He eventually settled in a Mediterranean city called Croton, in what is now Italy, and set up an important school called the Semicircle. You might even call it a cult more than a school. Some of his followers thought he was descended from the god Apollo." Cepeda took a pen and re-created Dr. Falcone's pyramid on another corner of the paper on his desk. Instead of numbers, he drew black circles. "Ten dots. *The decad*—the number ten—had special significance for Pythagoreans."

Kloska studied the revised drawing. It reminded him of a gang symbol. One chapter of the 14K Triad in Chinatown used a triangle for a tag, but not like this. "What significance?"

"Well, Pythagoras believed that everything in nature—this desk, the buttons on your shirt, the grass and trees on the quad outside—was made up of numbers. Not just that everything could be *described* by numbers, but that numbers were the basic building blocks of everything in creation.

"Pythagoras taught that some of those numbers had specific attributes. The *decad* represented the sum of everything. Perfection. The power of all things. You and me and all the gods together. The consciousness of man in perfect harmony with the cosmos."

Kloska hadn't the slightest idea what he was talking about.

Cepeda's hair was graying and cropped close to his oblate head. He wasn't large—"fun-sized" was how Kloska would describe him later to other detectives in an Ashland Avenue cop bar—but looking at Cepeda's tight, pressed dress shirt, he sensed the definition of a once-serious athlete. "To an ordinary person, it's complicated."

An ordinary person. That had to be an insult. Kloska asked, "Why didn't she just write your name next to your number the way everyone else would do it?"

"Who knows. Maybe she wanted to remind herself that it was my number but put it in a code." He leaned forward. "Didn't you ever keep a secret phone number? For your bookie." His voice dropped to a whisper. "Or maybe your mistress."

Kloska flinched, a lifetime of girls' phone numbers disguised as the digits of sources and snitches flashed across the inside of his skull. "Were you having an affair with Marlena Falcone, Dr. Cepeda?"

"Goodness no." Behind his glistening eyes, he seemed to be considering the idea for the first time.

"Then what?"

Cepeda glanced skyward. "Dr. Falcone called me several times over the past few years to ask questions about a project she was working on."

"Dr. Falcone? I thought she lost her medical license."

"She went back to school to get her Ph.D."

"In what field?"

His smile turned satisfied. "Mathematics. She was one of my students."

He could feel Traden deflate behind him. The only clue they had, the *tetraktys*, was looking like nothing more than a scribbled shorthand between teacher and former student. The whole fucking day wasted.

As long as they were there, though. "What project was she working on?"

"She never said. Her inquiries were very narrow. Carefully posed. Marlena was circumspect. It makes sense that she'd draw a *tetraktys*, actually. In my class, we spoke a great deal about Pythagoras. About the history of mathematics. The intersections between math and physics and nature. About *harmonia*."

Kloska had never gone to college, but he was as uncomfortable as one of Cepeda's students on quiz day. "What's *harmonia*?"

"It's an old-fashioned name for an ancient proposition, but modern physicists would probably call it 'the theory of everything.' See, today we have theories like relativity, which explains the role of gravity in the universe, and then we have quantum theory, which explains how electrons and protons and subatomic particles behave. Both make perfect sense, but they don't agree. Many scientists have searched for an explanation that unifies these theories. Well, Pythagoras recognized similar contradictions in nature twenty-five hundred years ago. He thought nature resolved this tension mathematically through something called *harmonia*."

"You're going to need to back this up for me a little," Bobby said.

Cepeda straightened, cracking every vertebra up his spine. "Pythagoras was especially interested in the connection between music and math. Pythagoreans believed that the harmonic ratios in music—the numerical relationships between pleasing musical notes and chords—were the mathematical fundamentals, the organizing principle, of the entire universe. Did you know Pythagoras secretly taught a heliocentric view of the solar system? This was *two thousand years* before Copernicus."

"Yeah." Kloska felt the discussion lurching to a complete stop. "*Harmonia*?"

"Pythagoreans believed that the motion of the planets could be translated into music: a perfect symphony composed by the universe itself.

The Harmony of the Spheres, some called it. They believed that the key to understanding the complicated mathematical infrastructure of the universe might be found in *music*."

Symphony? That word got Kloska's attention, but he had too many questions to start following the many assumptions leaping through his head. "So this *tetraktys*. What's that about? Why would she want to keep her communication with you a secret?"

"I didn't suspect it was a secret until now." He rubbed his scalp. "Maybe she didn't want her medical colleagues to know she was working on such an oddball, romantic project. Maybe she didn't want them to know she'd been contacting me."

"She was working for an outfit called Executive Concierge. Why would they care?"

"Mathematicians are an odd lot," he said. "Did you know we are statistically more likely than any other classification of scientist to believe in heaven? And do you know why that is? Because we *see* it. Every day. A world so perfect, so logical, that in comparison our actual existence seems like a confusing dream. An illusion. Perfection exists in our notebooks and on our whiteboards and our computer models. Ask any mathematician which world seems more real—the perfect world of numbers or the disordered, incoherent mess all around us"—Cepeda waved his hands at the room—"the universe revealed to us by our eyes and ears—and almost to a man we will vote for the numbers. What most people call reality is just the overmatched mind trying to make sense of a universe too vast for it to understand. As the world appears more and more complex, we find ways to deny its complexity and make it simpler. Our brains fill the huge gaps in our knowledge with myths and delusions in order to create a world through which we can navigate. A world in which we can feel secure. Numbers are up to the task by themselves, however. You and I are blind and deaf, but numbers can see and hear."

"Hm-hmm," Kloska said.

"Tell me, Detective. What is real to you?"

Kloska didn't try to hide the sideways look he passed to Traden. "Um, I guess real would be a Verdi opera and women in stretchy skirts, and a steak sandwich with peppers and provolone, and a cold beer. Anything I can see and hear and touch and smell and taste. What I can know. What I can prove and confirm. It's not complicated."

Cepeda said, "Einstein predicted the existence of black holes, years before anybody had observed one, using only math. One of the most vexing problems in all of physics today is dark matter, a mysterious, invisible substance that accounts for over 95 percent of the mass in the universe. We know it's there because the math says it must be. The fact that we can't see it is meaningless. If humans didn't have ears, we wouldn't know about sound or pitch until math could prove it. Scientists trust the math. Call it faith if you like."

Cepeda blinked his eyes and made a motion with fingers against his lips, a sign one makes when looking for a cigarette. Reaching for a smoke in his drawer, he asked, "Do you mind? Not supposed to in the office. Sometimes I wonder if I should put a wet towel under my door, but what are they going to do?"

With a nod from the professor, Kloska took a cigarette for himself as Traden fanned his face with a hand. Bobby was becoming frustrated by Cepeda's tangents. He wanted to know what any of this had to do with Marlena Falcone and whadidjacallit—*harmonia*. "So Pythagoras was into celestial harmony or whatever. Why would a modern-day former neuro-surgeon be interested?"

Cepeda considered the red tip of his cigarette as if the answer might appear there. "Numbers were originally abstractions, invented just to quantify things, to count rocks or people or grapes or whatever. The fact that dust floating in the air and the price of stock options behave accord-ing to the same mathematical principles, the fact that everything in the universe apparently can be described or predicted with a mathematical equation—a radical idea when Pythagoras suggested it—is probably the most startling coincidence in the history of mankind." He snatched a piece of paper, one among thousands, turned it over, and slapped it against the pile on his desk. With his other hand, he reached into a drawer and pulled out a cheap ballpoint pen, snapping it in two with his thumb. From his pocket he retrieved a pair of cuticle scissors and cut into the refill cartridge. Kloska jerked backward to avoid the splash of ink, which landed mostly, but not entirely, in a sloppy pattern across the scrap paper on Cepeda's desk. "We have here a seemingly random series of splotches, but if we wanted, we could figure out an equation for a curve that ran through every one of these dots. These random dots, in other words, can be described with math. This is also true of the physical uni-verse, and this is where you have the chicken and egg question of cre-ation. Which came first? The dots or the math that describes them?"

Kloska sensed the onset of a patronizing tone as well as a minor smirk across the professor's lips. This time, he felt like he deserved it.

"In a modern context, the Pythagorean concept of *harmonia* could represent a mathematical description of creation," Cepeda said. "A theory of everything, with applications across all the sciences, and the humanities, as well. Pythagoras symbolized it with the number ten. The *decad*." He tapped the ten dots of the *tetraktys* he'd drawn. *"The sum of everything. You and me and the universe and all the gods together."*

"The gods?" Kloska said.

Cepeda paused and drew a satisfied breath. "What is religion except for a layperson's theory of everything? In fact, some call Pythagorean thought the 'religion of science.' That's because Pythagoras was the first to claim that numbers were infallible. That two plus two always equals four. But we can't prove that. It's *faith*, based on observation. I can calculate the exact location of Venus relative to the sun. I can calculate its orbit and its speed and tell you exactly where Venus will be three days from now. Three months from now. All of science depends on such calculations, done properly, always providing an accurate result."

"And don't they?" Kloska said.

"Almost always." Cepeda took a long draw on his cigarette. "The math I use to explain the forces holding together the planets in galaxies can't be used to explain the forces holding together protons and neutrons in atoms. Little tiny objects act very differently from big ones—the math just doesn't sync—and we don't know why. As a result, physicists are desperate to find their own theory of everything, something that would explain both heavens and atoms together. Einstein was obsessed with it. Because to admit that numbers are fallible is for a scientist to have a crisis of faith.

"In fact, some say scientists are often no better than creationists who just ignore the fossil record because the Bible tells them the earth is only six thousand years old. Some say that when confronted with evidence that challenges the basic tenets of our blind, Pythagorean faith in numbers, we scientists simply ignore it. We say it can't be or insist that someday someone will figure it out. That someday someone will bring those pesky neutrons and electrons and quarks back in line." He laughed. "Truth is, up until the point that science becomes predictive, science *is* religion."

"And that's what Marlena Falcone was after? Proof of God?"

Cepeda made an uncertain gesture with his hand. "I might argue that the *only* way to prove or disprove the existence of God is through math. Some Pythagoreans believed the discovery of *harmonia* would help them achieve immortality of the soul. But God or no, a theory of everything would produce a thunderstorm of practical applications, not just theological ones. Medical science. Physics. Robotics. Cryptography. The military applications alone are enough to keep me up at night. Whether you think it has anything to do with the afterlife or not, whether you think this is just an academic, intellectual exercise, a great financial windfall awaits the person who can unite the whole universe—large and small, macro and micro—using math."

Bobby still didn't understand what any of this was about exactly, but at least Cepeda was finally talking about money. *That* he could understand. "You mentioned music. Is there any way Solomon Gold fits into all this?"

Kloska thought he saw the professor twitch. "Of course. The Gold Completion of Mozart's requiem is legendary among mathematicians. A piece of music alleged to have been written from *divine equations.* We talk about it in class. Why?"

"You don't read the Chicago papers every day, do you, Professor?"

Cepeda shook his head.

"Dr. Falcone was killed with the same gun used to murder Solomon Gold."

Cepeda's eyes became white circles with tiny black bull's-eyes. He started to say something and stopped. Started and stopped again. Picked up the paper on which Dr. Falcone had written his phone number. It was so quiet, Kloska could hear a mini-fridge door slamming shut in the next office and Traden pursuing an itch on his right arch by squeaking his foot inside his shoe.

"My God," Cepeda said finally.

And then he whispered, "You have to leave."

15

EVEN IN THE MIDDLE of the busiest days, when he was trying one case at Twenty-sixth and California, filing a motion in another at the Dirksen Federal Building downtown, and prepping a third case to be tried later in L.A., Reggie would always make a few minutes to be alone with the manuscript, a few minutes behind his locked office door, his assistant, Kate, left to wonder if he were napping or lighting a joint or meditating or "psyching up" or looking at pornography or playing solitaire on the computer or phoning a mistress (or some "quality law school skirt" in the similarly active imagination of Bobby Kloska). Reggie explained everything in his schedule to Kate except for what he did when he locked that door, and as a result, she suspected Reggie of keeping an untold number of secrets. Suspicious but always loyal, the most desirable skill set on a secretary's CV.

On the other side of the wall, Kate was no doubt speaking calmly into her phone. "Mr. Vallentine isn't taking new clients right now. . . . No, you cannot speak with him. . . . Do not come down to this office; you will not be permitted to meet with him. . . ." The desperate and accused petitioned Reggie night and day, by phone and e-mail and courier. Kate protected him. She was his moat, his pikeman, a pot of boiling oil poised over his castle wall. She kept the world outside from getting in.

Kate didn't know it, but the most precious thing she protected was under his desk in a safe, along with Reggie's will and insurance papers and ten thousand dollars in cash. Although Reggie managed a dozen different accounts—checking and savings and brokerage and mutual funds and IRA—the stacks of fifty-dollar bills were a tribute to his parents, who trusted no one, not even banks, to be caretakers of their hard-earned money.

A safe protects but also conceals, and this safe concealed one thing in particular. One thing from Kate and from Steph and especially from Bobby Kloska.

Reggie should have destroyed it years ago. But to a man who had been taught to respect history, the fact that it might incriminate him in a murder seemed like a poor reason to run something so precious through a shredder, even as the attorney part of him had whispered urgently in his ear every day for ten years to do just that.

"Many believe God once took the form of man," Solomon had said. "What if I told you He could take the form of music?"

Ten years after his client's death, the Gold Completion had become a legend in classical circles, a lost masterpiece that, for many critics, was a metaphor for every problem that plagued the industry.

"Classical music has been dying for years because we are the only community in all the arts that assumes our golden age is in our past and not our future," a *Chicago Tribune* critic declared on the five-year anniversary of Solomon's death. "Attendance at classical performances declines each year, and why should anyone be surprised? We who are supposed to be experts are always telling the public there's no longer any reason to pay attention because every great symphony has already been written. Like Luddites working for technology companies, we are our own worst enemies.

"Throughout his career, Solomon Gold challenged this self-fulfilling prophecy by writing vibrant themes and symphonies that were modestly celebrated but still underappreciated in his lifetime. It is a tragedy that what might have been his masterpiece—evidence that the classical form can build a bridge between the glorious past and an even more glorious future—could be lost to us forever."

There had also been plenty of skepticism. "On what basis can we describe the Gold Completion as a lost masterpiece?" asked another critic at *The New Yorker* magazine. "We have only Gold's word for it, relayed to us as hearsay by his attorney. And these secondhand pronouncements about divine equations sound like madness far more than genius. Of course, a poseur is someone who thinks brilliance is anything he can't understand, and that genius often sounds like madness. In reality it rarely does, fanciful an idea as that may be."

Although the requiem had never been heard, there had been dozens of attempts to re-create the Gold Completion. A cottage industry of Solomon Gold scholarship had made great sport from the dissection and reinterpretation of every word and note Solomon Gold had ever committed to paper. A forgery of the manuscript had been published with blustering hype and modest sales. As the only person known to have seen the original, Reggie issued a statement that the new work, allegedly discovered in Indianapolis among the effects of a notoriously disreputable dealer in rare books, "does not conform to my memory of the one shown to me by Solomon Gold." The publisher advanced the possibility that the manuscript could be authentic, even as music critics decried the result as hackwork. Years later, the fake composition had been performed dozens of times by orchestras all over the world, including at the funerals of a European king and a celebrated film director.

Other than his initial deauthentication, Reggie refused to comment on the matter, allowing the mystery to persist. Truth was, the disappearance of the Gold Completion had been good for Reggie Vallentine's business.

He removed the top six pages of the score—he had never been certain he had reassembled them in exactly the right order—and spread them across his desk. He ran the fingers of his left hand up and down the staffs, caressing the ridges of ink that formed the notes. The dots and lines and squiggles and circles undulating across the page were like Cyrillic to him. Reggie had just a few moments to dedicate to the Gold Completion each day and he was doomed to spend those moments only glaring at it in wonder and frustration.

He recalled Solomon's invocation of God when he referred to the requiem. Reggie had always thought it curious that killers so often became religious in prison. Wouldn't the best hope for a murderer like Solomon be no God at all? No final judgment? No one to say definitively that what he had done unto others had been wrong?

He supposed the guilty and the faithful were always looking for one more appeal.

In fact, since Reggie had become a murderer, he found time nearly every afternoon to run his hands over these pages, and what was he looking for if not God? In the presence of misfortune, the everyday bad—an illness in his family or an unsympathetic jury in deliberation—agnostic Reggie had nothing to pray to except for the mystery perhaps locked inside this score.

Sometimes, headphones on, he would listen to a performance of the original requiem—the Süssmayr Completion—while he tried to follow along with Solomon's revised script, frequently relying on the Latin lyrics as place markers. He had even acquired a Süssmayr manuscript and tried to compare the places where Süssmayr and Gold parted ways on the page, but the differences meant nothing to him.

Of course, Solomon had claimed the manuscript's real value was in the margins, but the composer's notes were equally indecipherable. There were numbers and letters and sentences without verbs and elaborate doodles—frequently of wolves or dogs—and even messages to himself, which sometimes took on the form of banal affirmations like "This is the key!" and "Brilliant!" There were a few citations to other works—to symphonies and composers and to books—but even if he had shown the requiem to a musician or a historian or any other kind of expert, Reggie doubted they would have been able to translate it. It was an odd and confusing and thrilling mess.

Looking through the window, he stared down LaSalle Street, across three blocks of early-twentieth-century skyscrapers, toward the magnificent Deco façade of the Chicago Board of Trade. *Futures market to the world.* Inside that building, traders were paying today's prices for tomorrow's corn, placing bets whose outcomes depended on so many variables—supply, demand, rain, drought, oil prices, trade with China, whatever.

The week before, the hour before, the minute before he shot Gold, Reggie never would have bet he was capable of doing it. As he sat in Gold's leather chair holding the requiem manuscript for the first time, the idea that he would soon hold a gun in his hands and fire a bullet into Solomon Gold's face was, like the prospects of war in a distant galaxy, too alien and remote for sane men to consider. And so long as it never occurred to anyone that Gold's own attorney might have fired the shot that killed him, Reggie's secret was safe. But there were variables that needed to be accounted for.

The private line on Reggie's phone blinked and he recognized his home number on the caller ID. He didn't pick up. His wife didn't know about the requiem, either. Reggie knew he had become a different man the night he killed Gold, and he wondered if Steph had a right to know that. If he had an obligation to tell her. He often wondered, *Is a murderer someone who has killed, or is a murderer someone who might kill again?*

Reggie returned the requiem to the safe and then stood and unlocked his door with a turn of the handle and stuck his head outside to let Kate know he was available. Sitting on a small chair next to Kate's desk was one of the few people Kate would let inside his sanctum unannounced.

"Hey, boss," she said as she stood.

"Della." Reggie nodded at the containers and blue folders she had stacked on a wheeled catalog case—a "lawyer bag," Reggie called it— with a long handle and a bungee for holding document boxes. "Got anything good?" He waved her inside his office.

Della Dickey said, "Nope. Every single one of them guilty." She sat down again and lifted a folder off the top and waved it in the air. "If they asked me, I'd stick the needle in this one myself."

Reggie laughed. He had known Della for only eighteen months and yet he saw a potential in her he couldn't describe. A confidence without arrogance. A wisdom that remained curious. An earnestness that retained a sense of fun. He trusted her so completely that he often let her study alone at night in his office after they were through working on the Believers Project. He wouldn't even let half of the firm's senior partners into his office when he wasn't there.

"I thought you were a pacifist," Reggie said.

"Screw that," Della said. "I'd buy a ticket from a scalper to poke this guy with pancuronium bromide. I'd stick it right in his eye."

Della was one of those law student sirens Kloska was always going on about. The second-year DePaul student was plenty young and pleasant to look at and she knew how to dress. *Textures,* Reggie thought. *Sexy dress is all about textures, about wearing clothes that not only flatter the body but make you want to touch.* Still, he never imagined sex with Della except in the fleeting Darwinian way in which men consider all women a potential mate.

Not until Kloska kept bringing it up anyway.

Reggie noticed the safe at his feet hadn't shut all the way. Della couldn't see it from the other side of the desk, but when he kicked the door with his foot, it locked with a loud clang. "We have some new petitions. Some drafted by attorneys, and a few more interesting ones written by the inmates themselves. About half of them from Texas. You want to start on a new batch?"

"Always."

Reggie handed her a slip of paper, the only one on his immaculate desk.

"Any of these especially promising?"

"All pretty guilty," he said. Della replied with a stare. "I said a few of them were *interesting,* not necessarily innocent," Reggie said.

Della sighed ironically. "I hoped to dedicate my summer to freeing the oppressed victims of our flawed legal system, you know."

"We get to do that sometimes. This week just freeing them from my in-box will have to be enough." Reggie remembered something, another piece of the ongoing deception. "Bobby Kloska has a file for me, but I need to get it discreetly. Could you drop by Area Three and pick it up?"

Della nodded. "Let me guess. Info on that doctor's murder up in Andersonville?"

"On the advice of counsel, et cetera," Reggie said.

"Give him my cell and have him tell me when I can get it." Della stood and volunteered her plans for the weekend—study, a rock show, study some more—as she packed her files and loaded them on her cart.

"You forgot one," Reggie said, pointing to a small box, the kind in which you might expect to find an expensive fountain pen, on the edge of his desk.

"That's not mine," Della said.

"It's not?"

"Kate handed it to me just before I came in here. It's got your name on it."

Reggie stood up and walked around his desk. It was taped shut and hand-addressed. It had a Chicago postmark. No zip code. No return. Only:

MR. REGGIE VALLENTINE, ESQ.
VALLENTINE, SISSMAN, HOLLY AND CARLIN
CHICAGO
PRIVATE AND CONFIDENTIAL!

He pinned it under his bad arm and sliced into it with a barely used letter opener.

"Don't you have people who open suspicious packages for you?" Della asked, halfway out the door. "You know, first-year associates. Expendable ones."

"Har," Reggie said without looking up. Della said good-bye and walked out of his office suite, toward the elevator.

He lifted the lid. A necklace that was immediately familiar even after ten years and a half sheet of paper, torn by hand. He lifted it, started to read it.

What the hell? "Kate!"

The narrow face of his assistant appeared in the open door.

"Yes, Reg?"

"Where did this come from?"

"Reception said it came in the mail," she said without eye contact. "No return address. The label said it was personal. I didn't think I should open it." As usual, Kate had made herself his accomplice in an affair he wasn't having.

Reggie nodded. "Thanks." Kate returned to her cube. Reggie read the note again.

It began: "The police have been here. If I have to, I will tell them what you really are."

He didn't know right away who had written it, but he knew exactly what it meant. *Is a murderer a man who has killed, or a man who might kill again?* Reggie did not panic. Panic was not in his repertoire.

He only swallowed through a dry mouth and thought, *Variables. God-damn fucking variables.*

16

MONDAY, JULY 19

THE PROFESSOR backed into the room, arms full of books and papers and an old leather bag with a soft handle hanging by a few stubborn threads. He didn't see them until he turned around, and then the high-pitched sound from his mouth and the frightened expression on his face and the way all those books and papers and the satchel dropped into a messy pile on the floor made the detectives laugh out loud.

"Jesus Christ," Cepeda said as Kloska and Traden bent down to help restore some order to his day's work. "What are you doing here?"

"I didn't like the way our last meeting ended, Professor," Kloska said. "I usually decide when these interviews are over."

"How did you get in here?"

Kloska smiled. "Your janitor has apparently done some things he regrets. Some people cooperate with the police a little too eagerly."

"I told you I have nothing else to add about Marlena."

"That didn't strike me as being exactly true," Kloska said. When he had assembled the dozens of papers and blue books into a rough stack in his arms, Bobby transferred them to Cepeda's already-overwhelmed desk.

"I don't know what else to tell you." Cepeda was a nervous perspirer, Kloska noted, and dark, wet clouds spread under his arms and across his back with unusual swiftness, even in this heat.

Bobby said, "Your wife likes to shop, doesn't she?"

"What are you talking about?"

"What she doesn't like to do is pay her parking tickets." Traden produced a more or less official-looking printout that he had manufactured on his computer. The tickets were real—most of them anyway—but the documentation was strictly for drama. "I bet you don't even know about some of these. Out-of-state folks, they get a ticket in Chicago, they usually just pluck it off the windshield and drop it on the street. Some days it looks like the curb is painted orange. Anyway, Lorena was very lucky she didn't get the Denver boot the last couple times. Must not have been one available."

"What is your point, Detective?"

"My point is that the tickets can go away and your wife can drive in Chicago again without looking over her shoulder for the tow truck." There was a knock, and before Cepeda could move, Bobby answered it. A student with a thick wave of moussed hair, textbook in one hand and an iPod in the other, started to open his mouth but stiffened when Kloska shoved his badge into the hallway.

"You get an A," Kloska said to him. "Go play on the quad." He slammed the door.

Cepeda clenched his teeth. "Do not talk to my students like that."

"Yeah, he'll probably go blog about that, won't he? Maybe post it to one of those teacher-rating Web sites. Wait until you see what I tell the next one."

Cepeda rubbed his face. "I really don't know anything. It's all speculation—"

"Then speculate."

"The ramifications of my talking about this could be far more serious than a few parking tickets."

"Convince me," Kloska said.

Bobby watched the professor's body language as he came to the conclusion that he was going to lose this battle of wills eventually. It was an old cop trick. You don't really have to threaten to do anything, just get the subject to understand you're capable of pushing a lot harder than he is, if it comes to pushing.

"The Thousand," Cepeda said, more to the room than to Kloska.

"What?"

"The Thousand. Pythagoreans."

Pythagoreans? Kloska groaned. He had been ready to move the questioning in an entirely different direction. "I thought you said Pythagoras lived before Jesus."

"That's right."

"But there are still Pythagoreans?"

"There are still Christians, yeah? The followers of Pythagoras were exiled from Croton in a political coup and they spread out across the Mediterranean. They had incredible influence on art and religion and science and math. But most people thought the cult itself had basically disbanded, or been absorbed by other secret societies like the Freemasons. However, in 1738, a handful of students at Yale formed a debating society. Membership was extremely exclusive. It was the first secret society at that university."

"You mean like Skull and Bones?"

"Skull and Bones, Scroll and Key, dozens of others. They are all just copies of Yale's original secret society. And do you know what it was called, Detective?"

Kloska didn't even bother to shake his head.

"It was called Crotonia."

Bobby looked helplessly through his notes.

"Like Croton," Traden said over Kloska's shoulder. "Where Pythagoras started his school."

Cepeda nodded, acknowledging Traden for the first time. "By the 1760s, Crotonia had basically disappeared from Yale without a trace. Nothing about the group except for the name is known. But some believe Crotonia was a clue to an ancient mystery, a rare visible manifestation of a wildly successful conspiracy of silence—an ancient brotherhood known as the Thousand. Unlike the groups Crotonia spawned—*so-called* secret societies with prominent placement on their members' résumés and giant houses in the middle of campus, ridiculous tombs even—the Thousand might actually have a secret worth protecting."

"Which is?"

Cepeda stood and ran his fingers over a number of old volumes on the dusty and drooping shelf above his desk. He removed one and scanned the table of contents. "This is from a second-century biography of Pythagoras by Nicomachus of Gerasa. Only fragments of it still exist." In a moment he had a page bent back and he cleared his throat. " 'Thus they composed some sketchy and symbolic commentaries collecting the writings of the older men and what they themselves remembered, and left them behind where they happened to die, instructing their sons or daughters or wives not to give them to anyone outside the household. And their families observed this custom for a very long time, handing down the same order from generation to generation.' "

Cepeda looked up, apparently waiting for Kloska and Traden to appear impressed, and when he saw no reaction, he said, "Pythagoras didn't allow his students to write down any of his teachings, so most of what he taught was lost to us. We can only guess from the work of his disciples what he must have said. But what if his ideas really had been passed down secretly from generation to generation on through the millennia?"

"What would be the point?"

"We can assume the most practical teachings of Pythagoras were taught and applied immediately by his students and became common knowledge. But what if Pythagoras had made abstract mathematical discoveries so far ahead of his time that for centuries, even millennia, they remained just esoteric musings—in the ignorance of the past, they must have seemed more like astrology than math. The Pythagoreans never put them to work or revealed them to others because they had no practical use.

"But then comes the twenty-first century. Our cars have computers. So do our blenders and our shoes and our timepieces and our ice cream makers, as well as our thermostats and our smoke detectors, our pacemakers and our baby monitors. Numbers play a far more critical role in our lives than they did in the time of Pythagoras.

"Suppose, then, that this once esoteric and useless mathematical knowledge, passed from the ancients down to a small group of modern minds, is suddenly very useful. Powerful even. Perhaps this knowledge is now being used in secret, to build better washing machines and laptop computers and vacuum cleaners. Perhaps they're using it to design better weapons and surveillance devices and tracking software, to develop methods of cryptography and financial instruments. Machines that think like people. People who think like machines. Perhaps the modern-day descendants of the disciples of Pythagoras—'the Thousand' is what they allegedly call themselves—have become wealthy and powerful because they possess information no one else does."

"That sounds like urban-legend bullshit to me, Professor," Kloska said.

"You're the one who insisted on hearing it." Cepeda bit his lip. "But just imagine if you lived in the time of Christ and you knew something as elementary as Newton's laws of motion."

"I'm not sure I know what those are now," Kloska said. Traden laughed.

"Okay, but what if even today the Thousand knows mathematical principles that might not be generally accepted for five hundred years?"

Kloska said, "So, what, you think Marlena Falcone was getting close to one of their secrets?"

Cepeda was suddenly very still. A pearl of sweat rolled along his chin. "I'm suggesting she must have been one of them."

"Oh Christ," Kloska said out loud.

Cepeda told them, "From almost the very beginning the Thousand have been rumored to be at war with themselves. A secret civil war that has been raging for millennia and is still going on right under our noses, right across our front pages. After what you've told me, I think Dr. Falcone might have been one of the casualties." He walked to his desk and looked in vain for a piece of paper among hundreds. "Shortly after Pythagoras died, there was a schism among his closest followers. One group called themselves 'acusmatici.' They were basically Pythagorean fundamentalists. They believed that Pythagoras had been a prophet or a god and that his teachings were divine truth. But they also believed the truth ended with his word and that trying to expand upon his teaching was heresy. Think of them like Christian fundamentalists who perceive the Bible as literal truth. The other group called themselves 'mathematici.' They believed Pythagoras possessed great wisdom but that he had given them only a starting point. They believed they had a right to build upon Pythagoras's teachings to enrich themselves, but also had an obligation to pursue the unifying truth of the universe—*harmonia*."

Bobby caught his partner's eye with a skeptical glare. Traden suppressed a laugh.

Cepeda apparently found what he was looking for and turned to face them. "When those planes crashed last month and the authorities were unable to find a direct cause right away, I started thinking about the coincidence of it. Coincidence can be explained by math, of course. The person who reads the Lotto numbers knows somebody's gonna win, but the person who wins always thinks, *Christ, what are the odds?* When you hit a golf ball onto a fairway, there's a 100 percent chance that the ball will land on a blade of grass, but that particular blade of grass must think it's been chosen by divine intervention. Still, this time I thought there might be another explanation.

"The weekend before the crashes, there had been a conference on private-wealth management at an extremely exclusive hotel called the Boca Raton Resort and Spa. The invitees included wealthy families and powerful individuals from all over the world." He pulled a folder from a shelf and handed Kloska a sheet of paper with a list of names; a couple dozen of them were highlighted.

"These don't register much with me." He handed it to Traden for a look.

Cepeda said, "Many of them are CEOs in high-tech industries and aerospace, or banking and Wall Street."

"I've heard of this guy," Traden said, stabbing the paper. "He owns casinos."

Kloska asked, "So what?"

"Have you ever been to Boca Raton, detectives?"

They shook their heads.

"Do you know what airport you fly out of when you're leaving Boca?"

Traden guessed: "Miami."

"That's one option. Do you know the other?"

The answer came to Kloska quickly. *Fort Lauderdale*. It took Bobby a moment to believe Cepeda was really making the accusation. "You think that conference was really a meeting of the Thousand and you think *they* crashed those planes."

"It crossed my mind."

"Why would they do that?"

"Acusmatici and mathematici consider themselves Pythagorean brothers, but they are still opposed on many issues. Think of them like Democrats and Republicans. They share a common interest in preserving the secret knowledge of Pythagoras, but they disagree vehemently over what should be done with it. I think it's possible that one or two people on those planes were being targeted by the mathematici. Let's say the intended victims were acusmatici attending the conference along with everyone else. Maybe something happened at that meeting and the mathematici wanted them dead."

"Why crash planes?"

"Legend has it that the mathematici like to use big disasters to disguise small crimes. Do an Internet search for the Thousand and 9/11. Or the Thousand and Katrina. You don't leave any evidence. You don't create any suspicion. You kill innocent people as well, so it's not even clear who the intended victims were, or even that there were intended victims at all. And by making the wildly improbable occur—causing two planes from the same airport to crash within minutes of each other—you send a message to your adversaries. It's a demonstration of your power and a devastating calling card that only other members of the Thousand would recognize."

"They didn't find any bombs in the wreckage. Black boxes turned up nothing."

"Do you know how many computers are on board an airplane? In the cockpit. In the main cabin. In passenger luggage. In electric shavers. In pants pockets. On wrists. If you have the power to manipulate numbers, you can make *anything* happen."

"Did you tell anyone about this theory? The police? The FBI?"

"Of course not."

"Why not? If true, this would be critical information." Kloska tried to say it with a skeptical lilt, mocking the professor with two quick jabs: *If true.*

Cepeda breathed and then he jerked his head toward the window as if he thought he had seen something out there, something that frightened him. "I'm just thinking out loud here. Nobody knows for sure that the Thousand still exist. And I didn't tell anyone, because if I'm wrong, I'm a crackpot. A joke. My career is over." When he turned around, Kloska thought the mathematician looked suddenly tired. "And if I'm right, I've just pissed off people who know how to make planes fall from the sky."

Kloska felt a little twinge in his gut. He almost wished he wasn't hearing this. "So which side was Marlena Falcone on?"

"Marlena would definitely have been one of the mathematici. She was always on a search for something."

"*Harmonia*. A theory of everything."

Cepeda bobbed his head. "Maybe. Yeah."

"And what does that have to do with her murder? What's any of it got to do with Solomon Gold?"

"I could only guess. The Thousand would be obsessed with Solomon Gold. The requiem, an alleged marriage of music and mathematics, comes up a lot in neo-Pythagorean discussion. If you were on the acusmatici side and wanted to kill Marlena—either in retaliation for the deaths on those planes or because you thought her research was somehow dangerous or blasphemous—and you wanted to let the mathematici know it was you, then using the gun that killed Gold would be a sneaky way to send a message. It would be very acusmatici to go low-tech and just shoot somebody. They wouldn't be in favor of using numbers to crash planes, to kill civilians. That's the kind of ostentatious use of their secrets acusmatici are rebelling against."

"If any of these people even exist," Kloska said.

Cepeda admitted as much with a blush.

Later on the toll road, the thrum of pavement underneath them and the monotony of roadside mile markers passing them once a minute, as regular as clock hands, Traden said, "Shit is spooky."

"Bullshit is what it is," Kloska said. *A-kooz-mah-tee-chee. Math-ah-mah-tee-chee.*

"I don't know what to think."

Kloska rapped his head against the window until it hurt. "I think we wasted our time coming back." Traden didn't answer, perhaps waiting for an apology from Kloska for dragging him twice to Indiana, but Kloska wasn't going to give it to him. Until Traden had a few more years as a homicide detective, Kloska wasn't going to apologize to him for anything short of an accidental slug in his ass.

As they passed the Gary exit, Traden tried to clear the window of bugs, but the empty washing-fluid reservoir just moaned under the hood and the wipers spread dry white smudges in a wide arc. "We got the same doer for Falcone and Gold, you think?"

"You mean Solomon Gold killed by a triangle-worshipping cult? No, I still like Michael Liu for Gold. That other thing Cepeda said is feeling true to me, though."

"What other thing?"

"About how nothing in the real world makes any sense."

Traden's phone rang and he fished it out of his coat pocket without taking his eyes off the road. Kloska straightened in his seat. "Talking on the phone while you're driving, that's illegal in the city. I'll write you a ticket when we cross the Skyway."

Traden, into the mouthpiece: "What did you find out?" He nodded several times. Kloska hated that. *Why the hell does anybody nod when they're on the phone?*

"You ready for it?" Traden closed the silver clamshell and dropped it between the seats.

"Just tell me already."

"The weekend before those planes crashed, Marlena Falcone flew to Miami. When the airports were still closed on Wednesday, she rented a car to drive back to Chicago."

"I probably don't have to ask you where she was staying down there."

"Probably not."

Kloska made a face and punched the recirc button on the dash, closing the vents of the car to the Gary factory stench. "Bullshit is what it is," he said, but this time the words were mumbled and agnostic.

17

IF HE HAD BEEN a common guest of the hotel, ordering off a sommelier's secret wine list, the four ounces of cognac in the Concrete Sheik's glass would have cost him more than four thousand dollars. These grapes had been harvested over a century ago, had aged for a hundred years in an oak barrel, which itself had been specifically prepared and dried for over a decade by expert winemakers from another century who understood that value from their labor wouldn't be assessed for five generations. The Sheik was wealthy enough to afford this luxury, but he was also powerful enough to expect he shouldn't pay for it.

He accepted the glass without compliment or thanks, palming the bowl of the tulip-shaped crystal and glancing at the big watch under his cuff. He warmed the brandy for a time, never looking at it, waiting for the precise minute, calculated over years of trial and error, at which the cognac would achieve the perfect temperature.

"You look unhappy."

"I'm figuring out how much that cognac costs by the sip," Steve Rhodes said. The Sheik understood English but spoke Arabic and the syntax often seemed formal when Rhodes translated inside his head.

"That's not it."

"No?"

A recording of the Vienna Philharmonic's presentation of Bach's Cantata No. 82 played from invisible speakers. They paused at times to listen, as if Bach were a third participant in the conversation.

"Have I ever told you the story of my ancestor and Johannes Kepler?" the Sheik asked.

"Who's Johannes Kepler?"

"You possess knowledge that would make a NASA scientist weep with envy, and you've never heard of Kepler?"

"Who was he?"

"Maybe I'll give you the parts that aren't in his Wikipedia entry."

"Please."

"He came close to uncovering something."

"What?"

"One of the divine teachings. A teaching that has since been revealed by science. It doesn't matter what. But the tradition was concerned at the time. They sent my ancestor to take care of it."

"To kill him. When was this?"

"Early seventeenth century."

"How did he do it?"

"Smallpox."

"Jesus." Rhodes paused as he considered that. "We created smallpox."

"You are not a student of our history, are you, Stephen? We did not create smallpox. My ancestor left a man's coat at Kepler's door. A fine coat, infested with the disease. He assumed Kepler would wear it."

"I suppose the brotherhood was pleased."

"Not at first. Kepler survived."

"Maybe I should just let you tell it."

"His wife took the coat and cut the fabric and made it into a vest for their six-year-old son. Kepler's wife and child died instead, along with seven of the son's playmates."

"Christ."

"Kepler's grief set back his research a decade. It was enough to put him off the discovery forever."

"Someone else discovered it, though."

"Three centuries later."

"Because of a father's grief."

"Yes."

"How is that any better than what they are doing now? You call *them* terrorists."

"They are putting our secrets at risk when, like us, they should be protecting them. Think how different the world would be if Kepler had made the discovery in the 1600s? How much closer we would be to annihilation."

Rhodes understood, but he didn't like it. The Sheik was clever like that, good at climbing inside your head. Of course, he had heard similar stories. His own father had told him about Hippasus, who revealed the existence of irrational numbers to people outside the Semicircle. Some say Pythagoras himself ordered Hippasus's execution, but Rhodes didn't know if that was true. He knew much about the Sheik was false. For instance, he was wearing a tailored Western suit, one of a dozen he kept at the casino. They were always waiting for him in his suite, and as soon as he arrived he would trade his robe, embroidered with the colors of his branch of the royal family, for the duration of his visit. When it was time to leave, he would change back into his traditional garb.

"I think I would know if the mathematici were planning something imminent."

"They didn't tell you about the airplanes. That's because they're suspicious of you. Of our meetings together."

"You and I have known each other a long time, and you have other friends across the aisle, too. You do business with dozens of mathematici."

"It doesn't mean I trust them. It doesn't mean I trust you. It doesn't mean you should trust me."

Steve frowned. "Then why are we having this conversation?"

"There's only one reason to do anything. Because you know it's right."

Rhodes's office was large and divided into sections. There was his desk, with a wide, thin monitor on top and a huge Rothko behind it. There was another area with a treadmill and a television. The third was a sitting area large enough for a dozen people, occupied for now by only Rhodes and his Saudi guest. There were artifacts from Stephen's odd collections, and books all around, the sum of their knowledge not amounting to a nickel's worth of the wisdom he and the Concrete Sheik kept locked inside their heads.

"My father said everything we know will be discovered in time."

"We protect an ever-dwindling number of secrets. One day the tradition will be irrelevant."

"And in the meantime we kill each other. And other people, too. For what? To preserve our *relevance*?"

"To preserve our existence. And not just ours. Everyone's. When everyone knows what we know, our species will cease to exist."

"So I've heard."

"You already know what I think is coming next."

"You already know I think you're crazy."

"When was the last time you saw her?"

"She was supposed to be here tonight."

"And?"

Rhodes shook his head.

The Sheik shifted in his chair. "Has she ever been late before?"

"Sure. She's a flake."

The Sheik gave his cognac a gentle spin in its glass. He was down $200,000 to the house just in baccarat the last two days. When his losses reached a million, probably toward the end of this year, he would wire the Colossus the money. Or he'd offer Steve Rhodes a horse from some royal racing bloodline. Because of their sworn allegiance to the Thousand, Rhodes was unable to pressure the Sheik to pay. For the same reason, the Sheik would never let his debt to Rhodes go bad. Such arrangements were how secrets and civility had coexisted among warring factions for 2,500 years.

"She's a flake who can beat your casino."

"She's a cheat."

"Is she so different from you and the other mathematici? You use the divine teachings to gain the slightest advantage in your games, to move the odds a few tenths of a percentage point in your favor. You cheat pennies and dollars from thousands of tourists every day. I even know how you're doing it, and I can't beat this casino at cards. And yet she . . ."

Rhodes didn't reply.

"You need to find her. Tonight."

"I already have my people looking. But not because I think they've taken her. I'm more afraid of Elizabeth than I am of you."

"You should be. She thinks you're looking after her daughter."

"The mathematici won't go after Canada. Elizabeth would never allow it."

The Sheik ignored him. "Where would they take Canada Gold?"

"It's not conceivable."

"Where would they take her?"

"Miami. New York. Chicago. Rio. Mumbai. London. Someplace where we have a good surgeon."

"They could bring a doctor in from anywhere. What about Montana? Upstate New York?"

Rhodes shook his head. "They would stay away from a hospital, but they would do it in a city where there are good facilities and expertise. Where they could gather without drawing a lot of attention. If something went wrong—if she tried to run away or something—they'd want other people around. Variables. Distractions. The ability to create a diversion."

"To hide their crimes behind the chaos, as usual."

"But they won't touch that girl."

"You don't give your mathematici brothers enough credit."

"And once I find her?"

"Retrieve it. Smash it. Crush it under the big heel of that boot. There will be nothing left for them then."

If it had been anybody but the Sheik talking to him this way, or Elizabeth Gold, he'd be on his feet, arms waving, launching the kind of tirade that made him one of the most feared men in Las Vegas. Quietly, he said, "How am I supposed to do that? I'm not a fucking brain surgeon."

After the Sheik left, Rhodes was alone in his office with a joint and a glass of scotch. He paged through surveillance screens on his computer and then made a call. No sign of Canada Gold at her apartment. It was past midnight. She wasn't coming.

He phoned his wife, waking her, and said good night. He envied her.

Steve Rhodes had been twenty-five years old when his father told him the universe wasn't anything like he thought. Far more was known about its mechanisms than Steve's Yale professors even knew. And yet there were also mysteries that went deeper than anyone imagined. His father, his father's father, his father's father's father had all been keepers of these ancient confidences.

Their biggest secret of all was how and when the world would end.

It would end when everyone in the world knew the last of their secrets.

Steve realized soon after his ceremonial indoctrination that there were great benefits to being caretakers of such valuable knowledge. Steve began to suspect the real purpose of the Thousand—or at least the mathematici faction, to which his family belonged—was not to save the world from itself, but to profit from the gap between what they knew and what everyone else knew.

For a time he had believed they were the good guys. Soon he realized there were no good guys, just bad guys and worse guys. There was his father's mathematici, who would kill for the right to use the knowledge, and the Sheik's acusmatici, who would kill to keep it under wraps. The moral difference between them wasn't clear to Stephen.

His parents encouraged him to marry another mathematici, as they each had, keeping the secrets and allegiances within families. Every time he saw a familiar name of someone engaged to a distant cousin on *The New York Times* wedding pages, he could feel his parents smiling. Rhodes, though, had no plans to pass his burden on to his own son.

It was the plane crashes—the appalling murders of 374 people—that finally turned him. The Sheik had been calling him for months, ever since the mathematici had declared their intentions to go ahead with "the Beijing Development," as the Sheik called it. "The acusmatici need your vote in Boca," the Sheik said. "A vote to stop the mathematici from risking not just what we have but everything." Could Rhodes imagine what would happen if the knowledge and power entrusted to them were leaked to the outside?

The Sheik had told him, "The act of self-destruction, murder and suicide, is accounted for in God's human equation. It is written in the same hand both in our DNA and in the laws of probability."

Rhodes had voted with the rest of the mathematici in Boca Raton, but the Sheik's words were in his head when he saw the helicopter shots of the Florida accident site on the news. *What if everyone knew how to crash a plane with a calculator?* Two acusmatici and one mathematici—the last a traitor who had voted against the Beijing Development—were dead in the wreckage. The mathematici had the votes to proceed, but their actions had turned Steve Rhodes into a double agent, his sympathies having secretly shifted from mathematici to acusmatici.

Yet since he'd thrown in his lot with the Sheik and his allies, the acusmatici had done nothing but ask him to commit one horrible act after another. The expertise to carry out the Beijing Development was supposed to have died with Marlena Falcone. But now the Sheik suspected the mathematici had found another way, and now more people would have to die. He wondered, *Am I a better man as a spectator to one side's atrocities, or as a participant to the other side's crimes?* Now he was stuck, an adherent to a religion he didn't believe in.

The Sheik was a pious man. He believed the Thousand were keepers of the word of God, passed to them by the prophet Pythagoras, a testament that preceded the Gospels and the Koran by centuries, a glorious, if incomplete, peek at creation's divine order. Most of Rhodes's colleagues among the mathematici, on the other hand, thought the testament was simply a scientific revelation from a brilliant man, millennia ahead of his time. There might or might not be a God, but what Pythagoras had discovered and passed along to his disciples were simply the gears of the universe waiting to be manipulated for their benefit, even if (as their acusmatici rivals believed) the use of these secrets would make them vulnerable to discovery, accelerating the self-extermination of mankind.

Canada Gold's father—one of the mathematici but also a man of faith—had been a bridge between factions, a man who believed in building discreetly on the ancient knowledge in order to better know God. Since his death, relations between mathematici and acusmatici had gone from cordial to bad to very bad. The casualties were mounting, and the Sheik feared Solomon's innocent daughter might be part of the next mathematici scheme.

Rhodes was no bridge. He didn't believe in anything anymore. For him, there was only stumbling, stumbling, trying to find his way. Trying to do the least worst thing.

Now they wanted him to find a little box hidden inside Canada Gold.

"How am I supposed to do that?" he'd asked the Sheik. "I'm not a fucking brain surgeon."

The Sheik had finally taken a sip of his cognac. He assumed a smile that clenched Rhodes's stomach like a fist.

"What we want done," the Sheik said, "is nothing as elegant as that."

TRIAD

But take heart for men are descended from the gods, and nature generously reveals to them everything holy.

—The Golden Verses of Pythagoras

18

WAYNE HAD HOPED to enter this apartment under different circumstances: late at night, maybe a little bit drunk, his hand running down her back to the low, round swell of her behind and then up her left side as she fumbled with the keys and swatted him away playfully. Once inside with the door closed behind them, she would turn and kiss him and let his hands drift where they wanted and rip his shirttail from under his belt and, without ever breaking their embrace, back him slowly toward the bedroom.

Ideally, it wouldn't have been like this, with a bleeding cut on his hand and shattered glass from the little window next to the door embedding itself in the carpet around his feet.

At least it was late at night. And he *was* drunk.

From the outside, the complex had the charm of a community college. Eight identical buildings of cinder block connected by narrow concrete pathways and a landscaped quilt of grass and pea gravel. There was a small overchlorinated swimming pool, an adjoining hot tub, and covered but not enclosed parking where the tenants' cars baked like Toll House cookies in the daytime.

The apartment itself was a box made up of three smaller boxes—living room, bedroom, and kitchen/dining room—each of roughly equal size. The bathroom was large, and one of the closets was the walk-in kind. The living room included a fireplace that was mostly for show but usable on those December and January nights when the temperature dipped into the thirties. There was a balcony just big enough for a romantic breakfast, Wayne mused, early in the morning, before the sun was desert hot.

It was nearly empty, absent any trace of Nada at all. Not even a tack hole in the wall. Not a single size-five shoe print in the vacuumed carpet. Wayne was a lifelong resident of the desert, and by his expert estimate the air-conditioning had been off for at least a day, probably more. He forced a breath of hot, stale air into his lungs and checked his watch. Four a.m., breaking and entering. Not that there was anything for a burglar to take. He was just so worried. Worried that he hadn't seen or heard from her.

Worried that he'd find her body, five days decomposed, after she'd slipped from a wobbly stool while changing a lightbulb and cracked her head on the kitchen counter. He couldn't admit it to himself, but he was almost as worried that he would find exactly this—an empty apartment and every indication she'd simply split town without saying good-bye.

Wayne scanned the living room—beige carpet, beige sofa, beige chair—hoping that whatever he had come for would announce itself through the Heineken haze. It didn't. The entire contents of the apartment could be cataloged in a handful of seconds.

The last time he had seen her was at the Colossus. It was close to one in the morning and he had slipped down a long, empty hallway leading to some out-of-the-way restrooms to peek again—for the twentieth, thirtieth time—at her location. The little green dot representing her whereabouts was no longer at Club Nikita. It was moving.

He walked toward the casino floor, trying to regain his bearings. Nada was still in the building, but she was walking quickly, and from the coordinates on the screen, Wayne was having a difficult time pinning down where. He hadn't gotten the hang of this device the way Peter had. Peter was only four or five years younger than Wayne, but in technology years Peter might as well have been from the future.

Head down in concentration, Wayne took small steps forward, past rows and rows of busy blackjack tables, with the flat-screen quilt of the sports book just beyond them. He lost the dot on the screen and found it again. "Where are you?" he said out loud just as Nada grabbed his arm.

Startled, he could only imagine the ridiculous look on his face. He knew he had expelled a silly noise, high-pitched and involuntary, and then an embarrassed heat bubbled up from below his skin, reddening his cheeks and ears and neck. He saw Nada kill the first spark of a laugh with a hand to her mouth, and Wayne wanted to die.

He tried to recover with a mumbled explanation, something about how he had been thinking of her, wondering how her meeting had gone. He was hopeful that she might still leave him with one of those promising "Good-bye, lover!" comments, but instead she pointed to a guy across the floor and said, "Search that asshat. He's got something in his pocket." As soon as Wayne locked on to the man, Nada had disappeared.

From the way she had said it, Wayne thought the guy might have a gun or a knife. He muttered into his ear bug for backup and followed the kid and three of his buddies as they drifted from blackjack to video poker to craps table to roulette wheel. Peter Trembley and a security guard, Eddie, had now formed a posse behind him, the three of them more than seven hundred pounds together, and they moved in formation to intercept the group, like linebackers pursuing a rusher and his blockers. His embarrassment moments before had been flushed by adrenaline, and they made the confrontation near the entrance to the Rhodes Theater, where a famous but aging magician/impressionist still packed the house with two shows every night. Cornered, the kid acted perplexed, demanding unspecified rights in a loud voice. When he tried to push away, Wayne muscled him to his knees and he and Peter and Eddie helped him toward one of the hot, windowless, and infamous "conference rooms." As soon as he went to the carpet, the kid's friends had backed away, disappearing into the tourists and poker machines, not offering even a word of support. Wayne guessed they had bad somethings in their own pockets, but he let them go.

While they walked and stumbled and dragged, the kid flipped a plastic vial of something behind his back at a trash can. Peter picked it up off the floor, covering his fingers with his shirt cuff. When he held it up, Wayne could see a few small white tablets, about the size and shape of the pills he sometimes took for acid reflux.

They sweated him for an hour, but they didn't touch him, and he didn't say much. The cops came and took the kid and the plastic tube with the tablets. A few days later, Wayne called to follow up.

"Rohypnol," a detective acquaintance named Maxwell told him. "Date-rape drug. And the generic kind. Colorless, odorless. Dissolves like sugar into a drink. Anybody who's got generic rope is up to no good. Have you got a victim? Or a witness? I'd sure like to talk to her."

Me, too, Wayne thought. He told the cop it was an anonymous tip.

"With what we got, the DA charged him with possession," Maxwell said. "But first offense with a club drug like that will hardly get him a spanking from the judge's granny. If it goes to trial, which it won't, they'll want you to testify you saw him drop the stuff. I doubt you'll see him at the Colossus again, though. You scared him good."

Wayne had become expert at scaring people.

Now he stepped into Nada's kitchen. The green countertops shined. No chocolate-smudged prints or wine stains anywhere. A white cabinet door creaked from disuse. Empty inside. There were no crumbs at the bottom of the toaster oven, no yellowing inside the microwave, no soap scum ringing the dishwasher.

The only thing that set the place apart from a showroom sample was a small pile of envelopes on the counter that marked the border of the kitchen and the dining area. Nada must have brought the stack in from the mailbox with a plan to go through it later, Wayne realized.

He sifted through the envelopes. Junk. Nothing personal. No handwritten letters or cards. Nada didn't have e-mail, or a cell phone. At least that's what she said. If someone wanted to get hold of her, presumably they might write, but there was no evidence of that here.

Most of it looked like advertising flyers and coupons. A few fast-food menus. A packet of stickers from the Humane Society. An envelope from something called Executive Concierge. The name meant nothing to him. He tilted the envelope toward the streetlight outside and checked the postmark.

Chicago. July 13. Two days before he last saw her.

Wayne tossed the letter back on the pile; then he turned and walked toward the bedroom.

The bedroom.

His phone vibrated in his pocket. A message maybe. An incoming call. He wished he'd turned the damn thing off. The casino might be open twenty-four hours, but Wayne Jennings wasn't. Right now, Wayne Jennings was closed. Closed and drunk.

He looked at the screen, but it was out of focus. He held the device at arm's length.

What the hell?

CANADA GOLD.

Wayne tapped the bug at his ear several times to answer before he realized it wasn't an incoming call.

The touch screen had turned to a blank grid and a green dot was beeping at him. A green dot labeled CANADA GOLD. Clumsily, he tried to orient himself. With the Heineken in his bloodstream and without the digital map of the casino to guide him, Wayne was lost. But there was only one place the signal could be coming from.

He had a horrible vision of Nada on the other side of the bedroom door, her body twisted on the carpet, lips slightly parted in a final breath, the circle outline of a stray chip from the Colossus Casino—Wayne's casino—just visible through the tight fabric of her jeans pocket. With sadness and rage and anger, he was already promising to avenge her, vowing to track down the bastard, the burglar, the rapist, the serial murderer, whoever had chosen to make a target of the woman Wayne Jennings loved.

He pushed on the door. A bare queen-size mattress and a box spring. A side table and lamp and an old-fashioned Princess phone. A cheap linen chest and dresser. More beige carpet. He flipped the bathroom light. This room was as antiseptic and unsmudged as the kitchen.

He exhaled, expelling the fear he would discover Nada's inert body in the bathtub or bed. Just as quickly as that terrible thought departed, however, it was replaced by regrets of what could have been. About the nights he had imagined himself between her sheets the way, three times, she had been between his.

Wayne allowed himself a few moments to wonder what it would be like to be her boyfriend. To have his toothbrush in a holder behind the faucet, his brand of deodorant next to hers in the medicine cabinet, a second bottle of shampoo in the shower. One entire wall of the bedroom was composed of mirrored closet doors, and he imagined what it would be like to sneak glimpses of himself making love to her. There was an all-day breakfast place just down the street from the apartment, close enough to walk for a tall stack of blueberry pancakes, Wayne reading the Sunday sports, Nada picking through the style section or the police beat or whatever it was she liked to read, while under the table her bare foot, free of her sandal, tickled the back of his calf.

He washed his face in the bleached sink, picking up her scent in the soap, and decided to go home. Work tomorrow. Another long, late, lonely night. Leaving the bedroom, he stopped and opened the wooden linen chest with his foot. Maybe five feet long and three feet deep and two feet wide, the inside was lined with white fabric but contained only an understuffed pillow. He dropped the lid and walked again to her closet. Maybe because it was the one place he hadn't looked and maybe because he wanted to see the rods and shelves where his imaginary boyfriend clothes would have been kept. Some shorts, a sweatshirt, a pair of jeans, a couple of good shirts in case they wanted to shower after a day on their bikes and head out to dinner. Someplace nice, where Wayne's standing at the Colossus would earn them respect from the maître d'.

He slid the door aside. Empty except for two shoe boxes. Wayne lifted one of the lids. Stacks of chips she'd never cashed in. Some from the Colossus—these were the source of his phone's vibrations—some from casinos she was no longer allowed to walk inside. Thousands of dollars' worth. He wondered if this meant she was coming back or if it meant she didn't care.

Wayne sat on the bed and remembered the last conversation he and

Nada had had between his sheets, her toned, curved flesh pressed lightly against his muscle and fat. They were talking about her name, and she wanted to know what people had called him besides Wayne. He told her he had been a pretty decent offensive lineman, a good-enough pass protector that the quarterback had given him the nickname "Fort Wayne," which never really caught on. He played some tackle but usually offensive guard, and on the depth charts he was listed by position and name: G. Wayne Jennings. His teammates started calling him "G.W." or "Gee-Wayne," and when they were giving him a hard time, the way good teammates do, they sometimes called him "Guh-Wayne," and when he made a rare mistake, when he missed a block or flinched before the snap, it sometimes became "Duh-Wayne." He often thought it funny—and he remembered telling Nada this—that his football career was long over and yet he was still a guard. He was still G.W. He was still Gee-Wayne.

"I like Gawain," Nada said with a satisfied smile, her hand raking across his big chest. "Like the knight."

Wayne couldn't admit he had no idea what she was talking about, so he went to the library the next day and discovered a book about the Round Table. Since then he'd read everything he could about Arthurian legend. He'd found T. H. White's *The Once and Future King* tough going at first, but he loved it now, absorbing it in his car at lunch hour. The musical *Camelot* became his secret guilty pleasure. He never told her any of this. That a word from her could change him so much.

Her phone.

Beside the bed was a red phone, a corded model his own mother had in her bedroom. It rang a second time. A third. For some reason, he thought of a line from the King Arthur novel: "Yet, with her prescience, she was aware of dooms and sorrows outside her lover's purview."

A fourth ring. A fifth.

That was Canada Gold all right.

A sixth. A seventh.

Aware of all kinds of dooms and sorrows.

Eight. Nine.

He'd had to look up *purview.*

Ten. "Hello."

There was no acknowledgment from the other end, but there wasn't silence, either. Breathing. A background cough. A television.

"Hello? Nada?"

Five seconds of nothing and then a soft *click.*

Wayne sat on the bed for another hour, but the phone didn't ring again.

19

MONDAY, JULY 26

ONE FRIDAY a year ago, after seventeen hours counting cards for David Amoyo at the tightly packed blackjack tables of New York New York, Nada pushed through the glass doors out onto the Strip and, surprised to find herself in daylight, drove to a dealership in Henderson, where she traded her Subaru and nineteen thousand dollars in cash for a loaded yellow Miata convertible off the lot. Twelve months and twenty thousand miles later, she found it a perfect fit for the rare remaindered parking spaces of Chicago. Despite an adult life lived mostly in the wide-open West, Nada could squeeze this car into a too-small parallel spot like a cat wedging herself into a shoe box.

Nada stepped from the Miata and locked the door, leaving the top down. Tightly packed brownstones to her left. Tightly packed graystones to her right. Condos here and there, some carved out of century-old mansions. This was an old-money neighborhood. "The Gold Coast," they called it, adjacent to the lake as well as to the tony Oak Street boutiques and the Magnificent Mile of Michigan Avenue beyond that. Perhaps some of the residents of the new glass high-rises had notched their first millions only recently, but if you were an actual landowner on this block, Nada knew, your cash had likely compounded more than a couple generations of interest.

Walking north on Astor, Nada admired the homes in the unfiltered midday sunlight. Each house was fronted by a secure iron fence, usually with a crest or cryptic scroll. The tiny square gardens behind the gates were geometric and professionally tended, frequently accented with an expensive-looking sculpture. Looking between open curtains, Nada cataloged the grand pianos, giant plasma televisions, Erté figures, antique sideboards, and oversize hanging original oils. The whole neighborhood was like a museum open to the public twenty-four hours a day. Parking was scarce, but there was little moving traffic. Permanent Jersey barriers ordered by political clouts meant these streets were convenient routes to nowhere else in the city. An aluminum ladder struck a dull tone as a pair of Latino workmen lifted it from the top of a double-parked van. Nearly every person she passed on the sidewalk was walking a baby or a dog, although Nada guessed that none of these pets or children belonged to the youthful, casual, and foreign-sounding women tethered to them.

She felt a shiver, an ominous sensation in the heat. Nada had always been sensitive to the slightest changes in barometric pressure. She was often more accurate than the TV meteorologists when it came to predicting the weather, but the price was frequent and uncomfortable changes in her equilibrium—dizziness, sinus pain, chills. She remembered now this was one reason she had settled in Las Vegas, a city where the weather hardly ever changes.

Nada approached the end of the block and a fence like the others, but longer and half again as tall. Between the leaves and fence pikes the Victorian mansion came into slow focus. Stories of red brick were separated by stripes of stone, layered like a cake. Towers and bays and juts created dozens of exterior sides and semicircles. Gables and dormers and caps were repeated in triangles across the enormous slate roof. Every surface seemed to have its own window and every window seemed to be a different size and variation.

And then there were the chimneys—she stopped counting when she got to fourteen—each a different height, like medieval spikes protecting the house from an aerial assault.

The property wasn't big by Vegas standards, and in terms of its footprint the house was an old-fashioned idea of a mansion, practically a bungalow compared to the outsize modern castles the wealthy and even near wealthy built in the suburbs and exurbs these days. But it was more than four times the size of the luxurious home in which she had been raised, and she recognized the lot as relatively massive, considering its location was only blocks from downtown Chicago. Large enough to be bordered on three sides by named streets—State and Astor and North—a dozen of the expensive brownstones she had just walked past could fit easily within this fence. The elaborately landscaped grounds were big enough to dig the foundation for a high-rise, like the towering condos just steps to the east. For a front yard, the house had the shaded lawns and softball fields of Lincoln Park stretching as far north as Nada could see. Lake Michigan was to her right, just beyond the six lanes of Lake Shore Drive. Close enough to hear the water's breath against the shore.

God, what's the land alone worth? Tens of millions? More?

As she turned the corner onto North Avenue and made her way

around to the gate on State Street, eight-armed elms waved their limbs and giant maples leaned into her line of vision. She could see an arching brick carport (probably a porte cochere for carriages when this thing was built). Several sets of exterior stairs led to multiple entrances, with a large porch in back. She found it difficult to see all of the building at once and had to assemble it again and again from glances and memory.

The house refused to look her in the eyes.

She pressed a buzzer at the gate. In a moment, the gate buzzed back and she pushed herself onto the Jameson estate.

"On the clock now, I guess," she said.

Nada was sick about the way she'd left Las Vegas. She really couldn't have botched it worse. She thought about the last night there, slipping from sheets she no longer owned, padding to the black and chrome galley kitchen in David's sweatpant shorts and oversize T-shirt, pouring cereal from a cardboard box. Like an alcoholic the morning after a relapse, she hated herself for coming back to Amoyo's apartment—at one time *their* apartment—and feared he might mistake intimacy for forgiveness. Amoyo could be charming and relentless, and she had, too many times, surrendered to his white smile and persistence.

Peering through the kitchen window, Nada could just make out the uppermost details of the Strip—the towering Stratosphere, the half-scale Eiffel Tower of Paris Las Vegas, the faux Chrysler Building of New York New York, the reflective gold edifice of Mandalay Bay. For a time, those places had been both a playground and office to them, and for a time David and Nada took cash away from the casinos, not in wallets and purses but in duffel bags and wheeled luggage.

The casinos had put a stop to that life eventually, and Nada's personal relationship with David also ended with an inquiry of sorts when Nada finally pieced together the life Amoyo was enjoying away from their bed.

Like all bad relationships, this one survived as long as it had because memory convinced her it hadn't always been so terrible, and Nada's good memories were measurably more detailed than most. She could replay their early dates with the toggle in her head and she could repeat every touch and smell and taste from those nights: the fine sandpaper starch of the restaurant tablecloth, the cold melon in the wine, the shiver all the way to the top of her thigh when David's foot touched hers under the table. Earlier that night in the Ghost Bar at the Palms, with the blinking Strip out the windows both CinemaScope wide and Technicolor bright, she had allowed herself to replay such a date from months ago, and it was sense memory that triggered her desire, nostalgia that led her back to his bed. No doubt she was also staying clear of her own apartment, where English Judson's revolting thugs had pawed through her drawers and pissed in her toilet. Still, there had been a time when she had been so certain of her love for David. That life now seemed long enough ago that it must have been lived by another person, one of many different people who had worn Nada's skin in succession.

She'd had an epiphany two nights before. Gary Jameson, a man she had just met, had shown more trust in her than David ever had. Would David have slapped that girl's drink to the ground only on her say-so? The idea was a joke. In that moment, she'd realized how much more David was like the drunk frat boy, dispensing knockout poison in the form of hollow charisma, than he was like Gary Jameson, who'd had the strength and trust to snatch that poison away.

The bad sex with David Amoyo established the fact that she no longer loved him. Nada could have sex if it were meaningful, and she could have sex if it were meaningless. Since David had made it clear that it was no longer the former, her willingness to sleep with him one last time proved that he meant nothing to her.

The tunnel out of David's prison, she'd rationalized, just happened to run under his sheets.

She had sighed as she ran her fingers over the back of the white couch. Even when they were happiest, she knew David had been going to the strip clubs. She hadn't liked it, but she'd dismissed it with the rest of his odious lifestyle. After days of his pathetic pleading, she'd even accompanied him once to such a place. A humiliating mistake. Positioned uncomfortably in a leather chair as David and his friends cackled and threw fifties at the freakishly bosomed entertainment, Nada had tried not to cause a scene when Amoyo, fueled by tequila and testosterone, assaulted her right there with his fondling hands and open mouth. She'd pushed him away and taken a cab home, and now she wondered if it had been later that night, perhaps in one of those tiny curtained rooms where the strippers periodically led their best customers, that David first met Sandy.

Even before she began surveilling his BlackBerry, the clues that gave away his afternoon affairs had been subtle: an extra dirty water glass in the dishwasher, an unfamiliar divot in the couch cushions. David's voice, when lying, raised a quarter note in pitch. He began scheduling his underwear, donning his favorite silk boxers on days when he and Nada would be apart. There were unexplained withdrawals from the tank of David's Jaguar, only half a gallon once or twice a week, but to Nada's special eyes—the eyes that had brought them together in the first place—the millimeters lost by the gas gauge were like telltale anomalies in lie-detector ink.

That last night, thirsty Nada hoped to find unexpired milk in the harsh refrigerator light. She didn't. On the top shelf, however, was a bucket of soy margarine. She flipped open the butter tray. Empty. She pulled on the drawer labeled MEATS. Nothing. That pole-dancing vegan slut had emptied omnivore David's fridge (with its B-flat drone) of all animal products.

Amoyo had never changed a thing for Nada. Not his fishy cologne or his oily mousse or the Nagel prints in their bedroom. Yet after one month with this whore—*a literal whore*—he'd given up meat? And, for Chrissakes, *butter?*

Funny, then, that they first met in a steak house at the Monte Carlo. Nada was collecting on a meal she'd won in a prop bet with a poker pro named Yeager. It had taken almost no effort from Nada—repeating verbatim the first ten minutes of dialogue from a newly released movie he paid for. At dinner, as Yeager tried to impress her with nonstop chatter (an unpleasant departure from his silent persona at the felt), she pushed the lever in her mind and muted him, eliminating all sound from his direction. Cutting Chicago-style into a thick rib eye, blood crimson on the inside, glancing indifferently past Yeager's silent, flapping lips, she first spotted David, first noticed his unlined skin like fired clay, his deeply inset cat's eyes, his undersized mouth with the thick lower lip and the thin upper that opened again and again into perfect dark ovals when he spoke. She observed the grooming about his eyebrows, the diligent maintenance around his sideburns, the round and white manicured tips of his fingernails. She noted the fit of his shirt, brick red silk and long-sleeved, which surely had been tailored for him, unless (she allowed herself to imagine) he maintained the sort of torso underneath—thin and tapered and fit—to which an unaltered, one-size-too-small shirt loves to cling.

On the street, Nada banished the image with a shiver. She hadn't even said good-bye to Bea because Nada knew she wouldn't be able to lie. She would have to tell Bea about her night with David, and she was just so tired of people being disappointed in her. As for Wayne, how could she look him in the eyes after, well, everything.

For many years, she had avoided returning to Chicago, the city where she had been raised. She had avoided watching even movies or TV shows that had been filmed there. For a long time, the thought of seeing its streets had paralyzed her. To Nada, this city was just another of her father's old things, things she had abandoned long ago. They weren't just reminders of him; they were evidence. Evidence of his love for her, and of his betrayal. Of his brilliance and his madness. A representative of all the things Nada had to reconcile if she were going to acknowledge that all of her father was half of her.

After arriving, she'd checked into a modern minimalist hotel and spent one day at the beach and one day at the Harold Washington Library, reading up on Jameson. Multiple degrees from prestigious schools: Yale, Duke, Harvard. Named one of *Forbes* magazine's "Fifteen Smartest Tycoons." Married, with handsome children. One was in real estate in New York; another was a fledgling producer in Hollywood. His wife, Myra, was active with local charities, especially animal ones. Their name was on a primate house at one Chicago zoo and a dolphin facility at the other. He'd made a fortune trading Eurodollars (which Nada'd tried to study up on before declaring the topic both boring and irrelevant). In addition to trading, he'd made good money buying real estate in neglected city neighborhoods. In one article, Jameson remembered his first major purchase decades ago: an entire block of Halsted Street just east of Wrigley Field. "I bought when the Germans were moving out and the gays were moving in," he was reported to have said with a laugh. *"Follow the gays. That's been my MO ever since."*

With her feet, Nada traced a curving walk of new bricks around an impressive garden built in vertical steps leading to a large fountain. Half a dozen men were working the grounds—mowing and weeding and trimming—and the blades from their instruments chirped from the hedges like hungry starlings. No one paid any attention to her.

Dressed for golf in short sleeves and creased khakis, Jameson emerged from behind the screened front door and stepped out onto the porch to meet her.

"Ms. Gold," he shouted as she approached.

Nada walked up the steps and extended her hand, which Jameson accepted in a chivalrous manner. A wind forced itself along the building's eccentric curves and corners like soft breath through a woodwind, and to Nada's ears it sounded like the house was greeting her with a low moan. She twisted her body to observe it at close range. From so near, she could see the door and the narrow columns to each side and the bricks just above her head, but nothing of the upper stories.

Across the porch and through the heavy doors, Nada followed Jameson into a large foyer. Probably thirty feet wide and a hundred feet long, the floor was covered with enormous old carpets from Central Asia. To her left was a fireplace taller than she was by a head. Given its location by the door, it had no doubt been a source of welcome warmth to long-ago winter visitors, but today Nada was met by the chill and low thrum of retrofitted central air. *F-sharp,* she thought. To her right were large mahogany panels carved with what looked like New Testament scenes—apostles and such. Five women her size could have stood on one another's shoulders and they still wouldn't have been able to touch the checkerboard of expensive wood squares that constituted the ceiling. Antiques lined the wall to her right—chests and chairs and bureaus and tables—and above the furniture were old portraits of unfamiliar old men. Including the door and the paintings and more carving on the furniture, she counted seventeen crosses.

Opposite the crosses were tiny paintings or pictures in frames that looked to Nada like square rivets in steel. Further distorting her sense of scale were wooden double doors, two stories high, leaning against the wall and carved with repeating patterns of circles stacked on one another like pyramids. The wood had an inky grain, like it had been painted black at one time and restored.

"I always wondered what the inside of this house was like," she said.

Jameson nodded. "You lived nearby, I know."

She tossed her index finger over her shoulder. "Just on the west edge of the park. You could see this property from our roof in the winter. I liked to count those chimneys. The bishop used to live here, right?"

"The cardinal's residence," Jameson said. "I bought this home from the Catholic Church."

Nada didn't believe in ghosts, but a long, slow chill went through her, beginning at her toes, and like water filling a tub, the tingling rose up her back to the bottom of her neck. It bothered her that she might be affected by the suggestion, as if the superstitions of the previous occupants—devils and evil spirits and demonic possessions—might somehow be visited on her. Her mother had no religion at all, not that Nada could ever discern. Her father had believed in something he called the Unity or, sometimes, the One. When her mother wasn't around, he would sometimes try to explain it, to pass along his passion for it. The One was something like the God her Christian and Jewish friends worshipped, a creator anyway, except that He didn't, or maybe couldn't, intervene in people's lives.

Nonetheless, her father said, everyone was connected to the One—all living things together making up the Unity—and the goal of this life was to one day be reunited with the One. Or something like that. Her mother would become annoyed when she heard him talking about it. It was just another of her father's idiosyncrasies, and she hardly paid attention. Nada never saw much sense in hoping for a God that didn't care about her.

"I suppose the Church decided at some point that the Cardinal's home needn't be so conspicuous," Jameson said. "Best piece of property in the city—by the lake, on the park, at the edge of downtown. We did a lot of interior renovations, as you can see. When we started, there were thirty-five rooms, and now it's more like twenty-five. We kept the chapel and we bring in ensembles to play for special guests every few months. I wouldn't say we gutted the place, but we performed invasive surgery for sure. Still, we tried to preserve the soul of the residence, you know what I mean?"

"A soul." *Is that what I'm feeling?*

He nodded reverently. "Buildings get new lives, just the way people do. Buildings leave traces. Memories. You should never try to erase them."

Quietly, Nada decided what she thought about buildings with souls. She doubted it. But then she doubted that people had them, either. Her mind briefly conjured the image of Phillip Truman. *Soulless prick.*

Footsteps echoed from beyond the far end of the foyer. A thin woman appeared at one of two doors framing a large old grandfather clock and walked quickly toward them. Nada recognized her wide grin and bright eyes and carefully styled white hair from society pages she'd reviewed in the library.

"Myra!" Jameson said, pleased. "Come meet Canada Gold."

Handsome Myra Jameson wore her hair short, a white shirt tucked neatly inside a checked skirt, high heels, and enough jewelry to trade straight up for Nada's car and all its contents.

"It's a pleasure," Myra said, blushing as she shook hands. "To be honest, I've been terrified of meeting you, Canada. It kept me up all last night." She glanced at her husband and winked. "You see, Gary has told me about the trick you do. How you know everything about a person in the first instant that you meet them? Here it's only been a few seconds and I'm horrified just imagining what you know about me!" Her laugh was loud, distinctive as a signature. When Myra Jameson started to laugh, everyone in a room would know it instantly, and they would also want to know what had so amused her.

Nada made the rest of her assessment quietly. When she walked, Myra held herself straight up and down, stiff, like new paper money. Like she'd been told all her life that she wasn't just a person, but a symbol. To the world, she represented her family, her family's name, her husband's name, her alma mater, her sorority, her friends, her country club, her neighborhood, her city, her country, her hemisphere.

And despite her insistence to the contrary, Myra Jameson was not in any way terrified of Canada Gold.

Nada instantly liked her. "No worries, Mrs. Jameson. I love that skirt."

She beamed and held the hem out for display. "Oh dear, it's *Myra*." Then turning to her husband: "Have you shown her?"

"Of course not, hon. I was waiting for you."

"Fantastic!"

Nada bent her neck.

"Come," Myra said, taking her hand. "I can't wait to show you your room."

They walked past the clock, through the door, and then turned right through another hallway, recently painted. Nada peeked through a large arch into a dining room, holding the impression in her head for examination later: *Another fireplace, more portraits, fussy chairs.* Myra's cold, thin fingers intersected comfortably with Nada's, as if the two were old girl-friends, and the chunky, colorful bracelets on Myra's other hand made a clicking sound with every step. With Jameson tailing, they walked into the kitchen—painted a deep red and accented in white, with three Viking ovens, a dozen gas burners, and a Sub-Zero refrigerator as large as a two-person submarine and with the same polished steel surface. It smelled good here, like cinnamon and char. Afternoon talk mumbled low from a cheap radio. She had a glimpse at the corner of a large pantry and a small room with a window where a short, round woman in white polyester was playing rummy with a tall, thin man in a white shirt and black pants. They were both well into their sixties.

Myra waved at them. "That's Molly and Hugh. You'll meet them soon enough. In a week, you'll believe they're your own grandparents, I promise."

Several turns later, they emerged into a bright atrium twenty yards wide and three generous stories high. At the center of it was a spiral staircase made of black steel and maple that twisted its way to the ceiling in wide, sensual turns. The railings were simple but elegant, like long ribbons suspended in air.

Nada was stunned by it.

"Isn't it fantastic?" Myra Jameson said.

If she could have spoken at that moment, Nada might have said it was the most beautiful thing she had ever seen.

"I don't know if you're into design, Canada, but Wes Woodward stairs are coveted from Hollywood to the Hamptons. Woodwards have made nine appearances in *Architectural Digest* and I personally know half a dozen people who ordered a Woodward spiral specifically to increase their chances of landing on the cover of that magazine. To Myra and me, it's worth more than an ocean view."

Nada nodded slowly.

Jameson continued, "Now Wes Woodward passed years ago. Way too young. Probably your age. Horrible tragedy. Killed himself." He put his finger against the roof of his mouth to demonstrate and Myra batted it away. "Nasty stuff. But I found this twister—the term Woodward preferred—at an estate sale in Kentucky just as we were meeting with the architects about this place. A fellow down there died and left six heirs who couldn't agree which one of them owned the house, so they decided to sell it off piece by piece. Clearly, the children didn't know what it was. I had it brought to Chicago on a train car, but it was well worth the trouble. It's a masterpiece. As pretty as a Renoir."

Myra leaned close to her ear. "But this isn't what we wanted to show you."

As they ascended the staircase, Nada toed each step gently, as if trying to avoid leaving marks. The empty room below them turned, degrees at a time. They passed a short bridge to the second floor and continued skyward, floating toward the ceiling.

They alighted in a spacious hall painted gallery white, with large canvases on either side. Myra led the way to one of five tall oak doors on the left, turned the brass knob, and waved Nada inside.

Stepping into the room was like walking into light. White carpet, white linens, white walls, and white ceiling. White drapes framed a white windowsill and white hardware was attached to the doors and drawers. A large bathroom—white tile and porcelain and fixtures and towels. The fireplace bricks were painted white inside and out, and on the white mantel was a white box of fireplace matches. The only color in the whole room was a long and beautiful green reed tucked among white lilies in a white vase atop a white table.

"It's beautiful," Nada whispered.

Myra's voice was low with satisfaction. "Gary gave me the article about you. When you were a girl. You described your perfect room. I wanted to make it for you."

Jameson added, "She spent three weeks getting it just right."

"A room of light and nothing else. A room of night and nothing else." Nada had been a teenager, obsessed with poetry but not very good at composing it, when she read those words to a reporter from the *Chicago Reader*. She now imagined the team of painters and decorators and contractors working under Myra's direction to make it happen.

"Wait," Myra said, stepping toward the large window. "Close the door, Gary." She turned something under the sill—a knob or a switch—and a shade descended from inside the white silk valance. In seconds, daylight had been sucked from the room, along with the breath from Nada's lungs. She was surrounded by almost total darkness.

"My God," she said.

Myra must have turned the switch again, as the blackout shades reversed direction and the room reflected the light again. Nada walked to the window and scanned the green-and-red gardens below and the towering black Hancock above. Nada never trembled. She never cried when she didn't want to.

She wanted to now, though. "Thank you," she said.

Myra's long fingers wrapped Nada's wrists. "I know this must be strange for you. But it means so much to my husband. In the meantime, I wanted this place to be perfect. A *sanctuary*."

Myra quickly went over house procedures. Laundry and housekeeping. Dinner in the dining room each night at 7:00 p.m. Nada was free to attend or not, but Myra encouraged her not to miss too many of Molly's "deliciously creative meals." The kitchen was available anytime. Nada could help herself or Molly would fix her something.

"If you need to use the phone—" Myra began.

"I won't," Nada said. Myra told her where it was anyway.

Jameson asked where her car was parked and said he would have it moved off the street and into the garage beneath the grounds. Her luggage would be brought to her room.

"There's not much," she said.

"I'll show you the tiles in the morning and we can talk about next steps," Jameson said. "But I hope you can make dinner tonight."

Nada told him she had nowhere else to be and then waited for them to leave so she could turn the switch on the wall that would bring back the night.

20

IT FELT MORE like a country club lounge than a waiting room, with wide leather chairs and heavy briefcase-size art books instead of news and gossip magazines. Footsteps on the new carpet left impressions that slowly evaporated like breath on a window. Hanging on the walls was real art, abstract and probably expensive, although Kloska was no expert. The receptionist was attractive and wore a designer dress and mid-high heels and expensive glasses, possibly for show. She wore her brown hair up and sat at a narrow desk, polished clean except for a small laptop. There was no sign to indicate the nature of the business or even its name, Executive Concierge, which still wouldn't hint to passersby that this was a medical clinic. Not that there would be many passersby eighteen floors above Michigan Avenue.

Nice as it was, Kloska didn't think the patients of Executive Concierge spent much time sitting in the waiting room. They paid a lot of money to do away with the small and large inconveniences of health care. This waiting room was for other people. Like cops.

Dr. Russo eventually appeared with an apology and a smile and waved Kloska and Traden back to his office, which was as plush as the waiting room, if slightly more cluttered. It had medical books at least, and a few triathlon medals, and a monitor that silently flashed and scrolled the day's business news. The detectives settled into another set of leather chairs and the doctor asked what he could do for them.

"We have some questions about Marlena Falcone."

Russo shut his eyes reverently and then opened them. "Yes. We're still a mess over that. Any idea yet who might have done it?"

Kloska shook his head. "Nothing to talk about. I'm still trying to get my head around her professional life. I mean, what did she do, exactly? I thought she lost her medical license seven years ago."

"Marlena didn't see patients. But she was a brilliant scientist and innovator. We helped fund her work and we shared her patents, and our patients saw the benefits." He looked down at his desk and then up again at Kloska. "Do you think her murder might have been related to her work here?"

Kloska shook his head, but not in a way that necessarily meant *no.* "I think her murder might be related to Solomon Gold." Russo didn't reply. "Did Dr. Falcone ever mention him? Or his daughter?"

"Have you asked the Gold family to waive confidentiality?"

Yeah, right. Jesus. Kloska said, "I'm not after any secrets," which wasn't true.

"I'm sorry. I'm assuming since you didn't bring a warrant that the state's attorney has explained our position. I'm happy to cooperate any way I can, within ethical limits. To be honest, I thought you had come here to discuss the threats Marlena had been receiving."

"Threats?"

"Dozens of them." Russo spun his chair and plucked a thick folder from a credenza behind him. "Marlena had been keeping a file. She told us that if anything ever happened to her, we should turn these over to the police."

"Why didn't you call us?"

Russo looked surprised. "I did. The 311 nonemergency number. The day she was killed."

Kloska would check on that. He grabbed the folder with two hands.

"All anonymous of course. Most in e-mails. But Marlena had spent a lot of time and effort and money trying to track the bastards down. She figured out that seven of them originated in the offices of two large pharmaceutical companies."

"Why drug companies?"

Russo snickered the way Kloska used to when one of his kids asked why water is wet. "Marlena's passion for brain stimulation came from her belief that the medical establishment, at the urging of the pharmaceutical industry, overprescribes powerful medicines for its patients. That these chemicals running through our bodies in different combinations do more long-term harm than good. She was outspoken on the subject and, with the success of neurostimulators, certain drug companies have taken a hit."

Kloska slid into a skeptical slouch. "But why would they kill her? That horse's already left the barn, hasn't it? You see commercials for nerve stimulation on TV every night. My ex-brother-in-law got one to quit smoking."

"Do you own any pharmaceutical stock?"

"My money's all tied up in alimony."

"There are a lot of angry shareholders out there. Hundreds of physicians perform this procedure, but Marlena was unquestionably the public face of it. She was a cheerleader and an inventor. She wrote extensively on the subject. Her overenthusiasm, of course, is what lost Marlena her practice."

"Do you think a drug company killed her?"

Russo put his hands behind his head. "I'm not a detective, Detective. I'm just handing over the file."

"But only *this* file."

Russo snorted once.

"All right," Kloska said. "What *can* you tell me about this place?"

Dennis Russo was probably better-looking at fifty than he had been at thirty. His face wasn't classically handsome, but he was fit and his hair was largely intact and he wore an expensive suit well. It was more like he had outlasted his once more attractive contemporaries and he knew it. "We provide concierge medical services. Our patients pay an annual retainer and we provide them with twenty-four-hour care, three hundred and sixty-five days a year. If you're feeling sick, we see you today. If you're away from home, we will tend to your needs long-distance. Last week one of our clients broke his arm rock climbing in Guangxi Province. I found the best doctor in Guilin. I arranged transportation, as well as a translator who met my client at the hospital. I e-mailed his medical records and consulted with the physicians by phone. Our client list is short, so we can provide the most attentive care possible."

"What does all this attention cost?"

"Our services begin at twenty thousand dollars a year and go on up from there."

Kloska looked at Traden, for whom twenty grand was about one-half his take-home pay. "That's just the retainer, yeah? That doesn't include doctor's visits, medication, surgical fees, and so forth."

"Correct."

Kloska's thoughts returned to the doctor's suit. Walking down the hall, it seemed like all the doctors in this office dressed like lawyers. Not a lab coat in sight.

"Did Marlena ever mention the word *harmonia* to you?"

Russo shook his head.

"Something called the Thousand?"

"The Thousand *what*?"

"She had a doctorate in math, right? She ever talk about the ancient Greeks?" Kloska, who couldn't believe he was asking this, choked a little on the words. "Maybe Pythagoras? Like that?"

The doctor's brow arched high over his left eye. He looked at Kloska and then at Traden. "Actually, I saw that name just last night."

A hopeful lean forward. "Where?"

"In my son's eighth-grade homework."

Five minutes later, with the interview at a stalemate and the excuse of a patient ascending in the elevator, Russo walked Kloska and Traden toward the lobby.

Casually, Kloska asked, "Have you replaced Dr. Falcone yet?"

Russo shook his head. "Her skills were unique, I'm sad to say."

An exam room door, thick and paneled and stained, was open about six inches, and Kloska peered through it. How different was a visit to the doctor when you paid more than twenty grand for it? Did they still force you to submit to the usual humiliations? The poking and probing, the nudity and embarrassment. Kloska hated doctors and saw them only when he was extremely sick. He was certain that whatever killed him eventually would have been preventable had he only gone to see a doctor regularly, and still that threat was not severe enough to prod him into yearly checkups.

Looking through the door, he glimpsed a mahogany sideboard and a framed print hanging on the wall—some prewar British poster promoting weekend rail travel to the seashore. Reflected in the glass was a desk and on the desk he saw—

Kloska stopped. "Was that Marlena's office?"

Russo appeared startled. "No. And anyway, we've already removed her things."

Kloska studied Russo for a long second. The doctor was leaning forward, eyes down, hand gently on Bobby's arm. He wanted the cops out of his clinic. "Can I look in there?" Kloska tapped the door with his finger, pushing it open a few extra millimeters.

Russo reached for the brass knob and shut it. "No, you can't."

"Why not?"

Russo took a long breath, trying to remain composed. "The men and women who come to see us are important people. They are CEOs, presidents, corporate board members, celebrities. If leaked to the public, information about their health could have broad ramifications for stock prices, consumer confidence, politics. Doctor-patient confidentiality is always sacred, but in here its importance takes on another dimension."

"I'm not asking permission to rummage through your patients' files," Kloska said. "I just want to see something in plain sight on the other side of that door."

"Whatever's on the other side of that door is confidential. In plain sight or not."

Kloska said, "Are you really going to make me get a warrant just to look at something sitting on a table inside that room? I'm trying to be friendly."

Tall Dr. Russo leaned down, his face now inches above Kloska's. He whispered, "If you think you can get a warrant for this office, I invite you to try. *A third time.*"

Bobby was stone-still, determined to maintain his best cop stare. This was exactly what he hated about doctors. They demanded submission. Kloska never submitted, not to shitheads on the street, not to lovers in his bed, and certainly not to rich doctors in their posh clinics. Bobby put a hand on the doctor's sternum and pushed, not hard enough to move a triathlete like Russo, but hard enough to insult him.

Russo reacted with a sweep of his arm, which caught Kloska on the wrist. Bone on bone, it stung more than it should have, and Kloska's reaction, the instinctive reaction of any cop to aggression, was swift. Then Russo was doubled forward and then he was on his back, his face twisted in pain and his left hand examining his ribs for the source, the exact place where Kloska's fist had landed.

A crowd gathered—doctors, nurses, receptionists, at Executive Concierge they all dressed with similar refinement—and Kloska waited until Russo was looking at him again before placing his still-vibrating right hand on the disputed office door. He didn't push it open, but invited Traden to follow him out instead.

21

TUESDAY, JULY 27

WALKING DISTANCE to Chinatown, under a concrete knot of expressway exchanging east and west for north and south, was a racially mixed neighborhood of folks with just enough money saved to own a home here and not enough leftover to fix it up. That's where Reggie Vallentine found the man who had sent him the note, in a house with splitting gray shingles and cracked windowsills and a small square yard of hard soil and burned grass. Reggie stepped over the crumbling walk to the door as if it were a shallow stream, gingerly placing each toe.

He'd always wondered. Reggie guessed that in the twenty-four hours between Solomon's death and Michael Liu's, there might have been someone Liu had confided in. He figured there could be someone out there who was keeping his secret.

Now he knew who it was.

The Lius had been a comfortably middle-class family when Erica was growing up. Michael Liu had a good job as an engineer for a bottle-manufacturing company in the suburbs. His wife had been an elementary school teacher. Erica's murder and Michael's suicide had been tough on the family bank accounts. Linda Liu pursued a lengthy civil wrongful-death lawsuit against Solomon Gold's estate, a case she would lose. It would cost her tens of thousands of dollars.

Linda moved to San Francisco, leaving behind her only surviving child, Erica's twin brother, Derek. Derek Liu had unsuccessful careers as an artist and graphic designer, some minor scrapes with the law. He accepted work as a barista for a big coffee chain, mostly for the health insurance. A few years back, the *Sun-Times* had filed an update on his personal tragedy and Reggie had quietly followed the story.

In ten years, Reggie had never contacted Derek Liu. Never phoned. Never even passed by the coffee shop, even though he had been in the neighborhood several times.

Derek Liu answered the door and stared at Reggie for a long time, squinting as if at a mirage. Then, his head making sense of it, he nodded.

The living room was a collage of unread newspapers and take-out containers. The house smelled like it hadn't been opened in weeks. A soap opera mumbled on a newish television, the sleeve of a dirty shirt obscuring a portion of the screen. An undersized air conditioner rattled in the window like a pocketful of keys. The home was so hot and thick with despair that, except for the lack of light, the place reminded Reggie of a prison.

Derek Liu, in his early thirties but looking much older, sat on a cluttered couch without offering Reggie a seat. Reggie picked up a days-old newspaper, still rolled up in blue delivery plastic. "You said the police have been here."

Derek nodded. "Enough detectives for a poker game, including that Kloska. The one who thinks my dad was a murderer. You and I know better, though, right?"

"I never said your dad killed Solomon."

"You haven't really gone out of your way to set them straight, though, have you?"

Reggie answered by not answering. "What did they ask you?"

Derek sank into the mildewed couch. "They wanted to know what happened to the gun that killed Solomon Gold. And to that, um, *song*. The requiem."

"What did you say?"

"I told them I didn't know." He laughed. "Which is *half* true anyway."

This kid hated him, but he'd kept his mouth shut for a long time. Reggie wondered why. "What happened to the gun?"

"I didn't know you cared so much." Reggie let the silence answer for him. Silence is your best friend when you want the truth. Derek said, "I needed money." On the soap opera, two men were planning the burglary of some small-town politician's office. "A man came to me at the coffee shop about three years ago. A collectibles dealer. He said there was a market for items related to famous murders—especially Solomon Gold's—and he wondered if I had any. 'Bad memories,' he called them. He wanted clothes that Erica might have worn while performing. Or jewelry. He said he would be discreet."

Derek turned toward the television for a long time, as if he had been waiting for this scene. "I couldn't give him the clothes, or anything of Erica's. But the gun. That wasn't an artifact from her life or from Dad's. That was an artifact from *Gold's* life. From yours. I didn't want it."

Reggie said, "What did you sell it for?"

"He gave me twenty thousand dollars."

"Did you tell him? What the gun was?"

"I didn't have to."

"Where's the money?"

"Gone. I fixed the back steps. Paid off my credit card bill. That television. Some went to my mom. She thought I'd finally sold one of my paintings." He laughed.

"No one asked you where it came from? What about the IRS?"

"He paid cash. It never even passed through a bank."

"What was his name?"

"I didn't care."

"If that gun were ever traced back to you, you could be in a lot of trouble. The cops will have more questions."

Derek Liu held out a hand for something to pull himself up, finding the arm of the worn and understuffed sofa. "My dad told me he was grateful to you. But if you hadn't kept Gold out of jail, my father would still be alive." He licked his chapped lip. "Your job is to help bad people get away with being bad."

Reggie had an easy reply to that old argument. His job was to equalize the power of the state by giving power to the individual. He cared only that his clients were accused, not whether they were guilty. He didn't give that speech now.

"What did the *EKG* stand for?" Derek asked.

For a moment, Reggie had no idea what he meant.

"The *EKG* inscribed on the gun."

Reggie scanned for a recording device. "Why have you kept quiet all this time?"

Derek's hands were shaking. "I know a lot of stuff about a lot of people. Stuff I wish I didn't know. Some of it my dad told me before he died." He nodded at Reggie. "Some of it Erica told me before she was killed. She was scared, man. I don't think Gold killed her because she was his lover. I think he killed her because she overheard something. Or because Gold told her something he wasn't supposed to tell her. And I don't want anyone to know that I know it, too." He dropped onto the couch.

"Why are you telling me this now?"

"I never called you. I almost did, a couple times when I was arrested. I wanted to keep what I know hidden in my pocket for when I really needed you. Now this shit looks serious, and if it all comes back on me—this doctor who was killed—I'm gonna need help and I need you to know that I know. So you'll help me."

"What did Erica tell you, Derek? What did she find out that got her killed?"

"Uh-uh," he said. "You just let them know that I'm keeping my mouth shut. You keep me from getting desperate, no one will ever hear a peep from me."

Reggie took a step forward, pinning Derek Liu to the sofa. In court, he was a master of shrinking and expanding the distance between himself and a juror whose attention he wanted. "Who am I supposed to tell that to, Derek? Who are these people?"

Derek didn't even look up as Reggie reached into his pocket and set Erica's necklace on top of the television.

22

WAYNE DIDN'T WANT to admit he was intimidated by David Amoyo, but as he pulled his Mustang into the vast lot of the Puma Lounge, there were butterflies in his stomach and bees in his intestine and a whole gaggle of geese pushing their way into his colon.

At least the bathrooms in the high-end strip clubs were usually clean.

Amoyo was a minor star among Vegas players, his digital assistant reportedly loaded with celebrity numbers. Even before he started counting cards with Canada Gold, he was famous for being modestly famous. For always having an invite. For always leaving the party early because he knew of a better one across the Strip. His notoriety ended up being the perfect cover for his con. No pit boss or casino dick thought twice when David Amoyo sat down at a table with this movie actor or that Los Angeles Laker and started throwing around money he shouldn't have. And when Amoyo was at the table—making a scene, exhorting the crowd, flirting with dealers and waitresses—no one noticed the tiny girl several chairs to his right with the minimum bets and the innocent small talk and the subtle but meaningful hand gestures.

Wayne noticed her, though. Before anyone else.

The bouncer waived the fifty-dollar cover after Wayne announced his business and then he found a seat on the main floor near the exit on a small sofa covered with paisley. Hundreds of directional spotlights, some covered with colored gels, lit the floor selectively, leaving most of the chairs in darkness or shadow. Across from him, a pair of empty chairs were separated by a shiny black cube. Maybe twenty customers were spread throughout the club, but the room was big enough to look empty. The music—some mash-up between Aerosmith and an old disco hit— seemed loud compared to the number of ears tuned to it.

Two topless women in G-strings were dancing, indifferent to each other, in the blue light on a stage some twenty yards to Wayne's left. Others were floating about the room, stopping occasionally to let a customer buy them a club soda and a chat. After a brief prologue, the dancer would do a four-minute wriggle between the man's knees that wasn't supposed to approximate a sex act so much as ambiguously suggest one, firing the same synapses in the brain, releasing the same chemicals and adrenaline, without ever assuming the actual shape or mechanics of real intercourse. *The lap dance*, Wayne thought, recalling an art history course from college, *is postmodernism brought to sex. Or maybe Impressionism. Expressionism. One of those.*

"You don't see with your eyes any more than you screw with your hips," Nada had said. Strippers also seemed to know that was true. Sex happens all in the head.

Wayne hadn't been seated a minute when a short blonde dropped down beside him on the couch. In addition to her pink thong, she wore a red half shirt that quarter-covered a pair of breasts as large and round as bocce balls.

"Do you mind if I take a break and sit here? I hate this song," she said.

Wayne nodded once.

"What's your name?"

"I thought you were on break."

She threw up her hands, but the bocce balls on her chest didn't move, as if the surgeon had attached them to her frame with bolts. "Just talking."

"I'm Wayne."

"I'm Anya. What do you do?"

"Security at the Colossus."

"That sounds interesting."

"Really?"

"I sometimes think about getting a hostess job, but the money is so good here."

"A casino hostess can make good money."

"Any of your hostesses drive a 335i?"

Wayne conceded with a laugh.

"I know a girl here who flies to Houston to work during the week—" Her big lids opened until the exposed eyeballs were almost higher than they were wide. "Oh, this song is awesome, but it's so *short.*"

"Eagles of Death Metal," Wayne said.

She seemed impressed but might have been faking. "You know it? Do you want a dance? I'll give you the rest of this song and the next one, too. Because it's so short."

"That's all right. I'm meeting David."

Break over, she jumped to her feet, bocce balls steady as gyroscopes.

"Okay, see you, Wayne." He waved. She lip-synched the chorus at him: "Don't waste your time cause the boy's bad news."

But Wayne already knew that.

A waitress stepped in and Wayne ordered a Heineken. It was just before 9:00 p.m. He guessed that in two hours there would be two hundred men in here with folds of ATM twenties in each fist and Anya would have few opportunities to sit out a song and chat up the awesomeness of the Eagles of Death Metal. Wayne had no moral objection to stripping. To his mind, much more demeaning than the nudity and even the discrete and cursory sexual activity exchanged on this busy trading floor were the dozens of monitors everywhere tuned to ESPN. As humiliating as some might think it was for a woman to dance naked in front of men for money, it had to be far worse to have to compete with the Arizona Cardinals for their attention.

When he'd arrived at the Colossus that afternoon, he'd walked the length of the executive offices and taken the elevator up three floors to a large room where the techs worked at wide tabletops, their heads hidden behind three or four flat panels. They were responsible for all the office IT, as well as for the simple maintenance of electronic games—video poker and keno and slots. Wayne let himself in with his magnetic key card, and three or four faces leaned around screens to evaluate the visitor. They were used to being summoned to other people's offices, not being visited themselves.

Wayne pointed at a programmer, thin and athletic, in a designer T-shirt and long, baggy shorts. The man waved and then ducked behind his monitor. Wayne circumnavigated the wall of screens. "Hassan."

Hassan pushed himself away from a homemade turkey sandwich. He had long wavy hair tied back loosely behind his head and a vintage Pixies sticker on a skateboard under his desk. Most of these guys preferred to eat in a hurry and spend the rest of their break skating in one of the huge unused sections of the underground parking garage.

Wayne held his phone out. "How does this work?"

Hassan smiled. "You mean computers or telephones?" Hassan was a child of both Iran and Beverly Hills, and he observed everyone and everything with a friendly detachment, as if to say that he might have been born in this country and he might love American music and American movies and date American girls and live and work in the most aggressively American of all cities, but the culture did not own him the way it owned everyone around him. Hassan understood more about surfing and rap music and Tarantino films than anyone Wayne knew, but if tomorrow he found out Hassan had packed up his things and moved to Costa Rica or Bangkok or Dublin or Dubai, it wouldn't surprise Wayne a bit.

"I mean this software," Wayne said. "This program we use to track chips."

"You've been using it for two years," Hassan said with a chuckle. Wayne pushed it forward a few inches. Hassan was a hard guy to be pissed at, mostly because he was smart enough to back up his talk and because he was the only guy who worked in IT whom Wayne could regularly understand.

Hassan took the phone and with his mayo-tipped pinkie pointed to a stationary green dot representing some high roller currently sitting at the baccarat tables. Type at the top of the screen identified him as MITCHELL CRANE. "Radio-frequency identification. It's like a tiny antenna we put in each chip. The dealer can scan a handful of them when he pays out a big player and the pit boss can assign the guy's name to that ID number—in this case, Mr. Crane here. Then you can see what games he's playing, where he's eating, what time he retires to his room with a hooker and a bottle of Cristal. Basically, you can follow him around until he cashes out at the end of the weekend."

"So the chips are transmitters, then?"

"It's a passive tag. There's no power source. We have readers all over the casino—in all the gaming tables and poker machines and slots and sports-book tables and security cameras and elevators—and *they* transmit a signal and the antenna in the chip just bounces it back."

"Could I locate someone outside the casino with this?"

Hassan poked curiously into Wayne's eyes with his own. "You could, I guess." He held up Wayne's phone. "This thingamajob is a reader, as well. It can detect a chip at maybe fifteen meters. Between the fixed readers at the tables and the employees walking all over with these suckers in their coat pockets, we have almost every public area in the hotel covered. Eighty-five percent maybe."

"But if I activated the program outside the hotel?"

Hassan frowned, as if the question had never come up. "We have the Colossus floor plan mapped to a GPS system. On the street, you wouldn't have the same precision. There's no map of Nevada programmed in there. But the tags never die, so if someone walked out of here with his chips and you passed him on the sidewalk, it would vibrate and beep at you, yeah." Hassan asked, "Why? Did you lose one in your couch?"

"Kind of," Wayne said. "And by the way—undo the hack you put in that NASCAR slot before you get your ass fired." Hassan grinned.

An hour later, Wayne had popped into Club Nikita. It was only seven o'clock, so the club was mostly empty and the music was set at a third of prime-time volume and the lights were still up and Kelvin was restocking the bar, humming some tune out of his head. Although Wayne knew his preoccupation with Nada was a whispered joke around the casino, he said without a hello, "The last night you saw Canada Gold."

Kelvin turned with a cool look, arched brow, and a knowing half smile, then nodded. "Hey, Wayne. Yeah. A couple weeks ago. She was in here talking to some old dude."

"Guy's name was something like Jameson, right?"

"I don't remember."

"How did he pay?"

"Cash. Lots of it. Big tip."

"Do you know where he was from?"

"Aw, man. It was late and it was loud."

"Was he staying in this hotel?"

"People staying here usually just sign for their tab, right? So no, probably."

"Shit." Wayne tried to think. He tried to imagine what a real detective, not a half-assed amateur like himself, would do. What question he could ask. "Did he mention another hotel? Make small talk? Ask about the score of some game? Anything?"

Kelvin said, "Wait a minute. No, he was *definitely* staying here. Because when he sat down, he was shivering and complaining about the heat out there and the cold in here. He said he wasn't going outside again until his flight the next day. And then he said it was practically this hot back in Chicago already."

Chicago. There were more than a hundred Jamesons who had stayed at the hotel since it opened, and three just last week, but it took Wayne only five minutes on his computer, searching the hotel's billing records, to find a home address for Gary Jameson of Chicago: 1555 North State Parkway.

At the Puma Lounge, the beer and Amoyo arrived at the same time and Amoyo waved off Wayne's attempt to pay. "First one's on me," Amoyo said. Wayne thanked him with a duck of his head and then forced the ten into the waitress's hand as a tip.

Amoyo was handsome in an unqualified way. Wayne had heard his mother was Filipino, but his father might have been from Saharan Africa or Sicily or the Basque area of Spain. Whatever the ethnic ratio, it was a perfect aesthetic blend, unidentifiable but pleasantly toned and exactly proportioned. Wayne liked to believe his own face would be considered handsome if it weren't so fleshy and oversize, and when he was younger, he had spent hours in front of a mirror trying to substantiate that fact. A generous woman might have found Wayne attractive, but Amoyo was the kind of good-looking everyone agreed on. You could hate his guts and still find him handsome.

"Wayne Jennings," Amoyo said. "What in the world could I have done to make one of Steve Rhodes's musclemen pay me a visit at my office? For the record, I swear I haven't set foot in your hotel since the *unpleasantness.*"

Wayne absorbed the mockery and took his first sip of cold beer. "I'm not here representing the casino."

"Not working tonight?"

"Went home sick."

"Interesting." Squinting, Amoyo tried to discern Wayne's intentions. "Maybe you want out of the hotel dick business and into something with a little more upside. Huh? Maybe you've saved up some money. Looking to make an investment? Or find a friendlier work environment? How'm I doing?"

"Nope," Wayne said. "This is about Canada. She's missing."

A noise in Amoyo's throat. "Missing? When?"

"At least a week."

"I heard you guys were letting her play blackjack again. In exchange for . . ." He paused to see if Wayne would betray some secret. "You better keep her on a short leash around cards. That girl could take you down hard if you turned your back. But you know that. And you probably know she's not greedy like me."

Wayne nodded. "Any idea where she is?"

"Nope. I saw her Friday before last, so she hasn't been gone longer than that."

"Where did you see her?"

"In my bed." If he knew that information would hurt Wayne, he didn't seem to take pleasure in it. "She was gone in the morning and I haven't heard from her since."

Wayne tried to betray no feeling at all. "Any idea where she would go?"

"She doesn't have any family, or none that she likes anyway. And friends to her are mostly just whoever's around at the time. She leases *everything,* you know. Friends, apartments, cars, boyfriends. No long-term commitments."

"As I understand it, she was pretty committed to you for a while."

Amoyo said, "Why do you care so much, Wayne? Is she really such a valued employee at the Colossus these days? That would be funny after so many months of being public enemy number two? And I say that as public enemy number *one.*"

"She's a friend."

"Yeah. You probably think she's special."

To Wayne, it sounded like Amoyo was insulting both him and Nada, and the next thing just came out of his mouth. "I do. In fact, I'm still wondering what she saw in you."

Amoyo sniffed indifferently and accepted a clear, lime-garnished drink in a highball glass from the waitress. "When I met her, she wasn't special at all. She was okay-looking, I guess—maybe not *dancer hot*—but she had these crazy, unfocused abilities. Imagine if Tiger Woods had never played golf. Nada was moody and bored and lonely and agitated. *Depressed.* I taught her it was okay to be happy. Okay to laugh. Smile every once in a while. Have fun. You know, she'd never even played blackjack before me. She thought blackjack was all about luck. That it was beneath her. But when I showed her how to beat a casino, I showed her that she had power. I *made* her special. That's what she sees in me. She knows that whatever it is you or anybody else finds attractive in her now, David Amoyo put it there."

"So why did you let her go?"

"It's not clear I have, based on the other night." Amoyo paused to think about that, then seemed to disregard the notion. "Blackjack was all we had in common. When we got busted and banned from the Strip, there wasn't much else holding us together."

"And by then you were holding Sandy, right?"

"She told you about Sandy? That's interesting." Amoyo set his drink down on the black cube. "Are you fucking her?"

Wayne was quick to deflect. "You mean Sandy?"

A flash of jealousy came and went on either side of a blink. "Sandy also has great abilities. Actually, that's not true. What Sandy has is *charisma,* which is another word for sexy, and that could take her far, when you combine it with her legs and her tits and everything else. Between here and here"—Amoyo put one hand at his collarbone and another just above his knees—"that girl is world-class. I'll have her in *Playboy* by the end of next year. Maybe a reality show the year after that." He picked up his drink. "She introduced me to the owner here and now I manage the place and run an event-planning business, as well. Celebs fly in to celebrate this or that and they want to throw a bash. I cut a deal with a hotel. I make sure the right people are there, call the media, find a sponsor. I can put the Colossus on my preferred list if you guys cut me some slack."

"You mean let you back inside the casino?"

"That would be for starters. I see it wasn't off the table as far as Nada was concerned. This ban is a drag on business, and I'm talking lots of money here. Great PR. Rock stars, movie stars, athletes. All making the Colossus their Vegas home."

"Not for me to decide, David. As far as I'm concerned, you can do whatever you want in the hotel as long as you stay away from the tables. If you give me a card, I'll pass it along to the marketing and catering folks."

"With your endorsement?"

"Okay."

"Great."

Wayne wasn't going to pass along any endorsement of Amoyo. It was something of a miracle that Steve Rhodes had agreed to let Nada back in the Colossus, and now that Wayne knew Nada was sleeping with David again—or had at least once—he wasn't going to let Amoyo six steps into the casino before he kicked his ass back into the desert.

"Did she talk about a guy she met at the Colossus that week? An old guy?"

"No. She rarely mentioned anybody except a friend in the DA's office. I think her name was Bea."

"Is there any reason Nada would go back to Chicago?"

Amoyo thought about it. "Her mom is still there, as far as I know. At least part of the year. But they never even spoke as long as we were together. Why?"

Wayne hesitated, but if he wanted information, he'd also have to give it. "She was talking to a guy at the casino. His name was Gary Jameson. I think he was offering her a job in Chicago."

Laughing, Amoyo said, "Well, there you go. Mystery solved, right?"

"You think she'd just pack up and move to the Midwest?"

"They got blackjack there?"

"Kind of. Riverboats."

"Then hell yeah. Places don't mean anything to her. The world in her head is so much bigger than the world outside. Las Vegas, Montana, Chicago, Pittsburgh, Istanbul—they're all the same place. It's all just *outside* to her. And she doesn't really say good-bye like other people you know." Wayne thought he almost looked nostalgic for a second. "Maybe the other night was her way of saying good-bye to me."

Wayne wanted to punch him.

23

BEA BEAUJON had prosecuted maybe a dozen cases of home invasion, and twice that many rapes (including a satisfying guilty plea from Phillip Truman just that afternoon). She'd put away abusive husbands and identity thieves. She'd been the lead prosecutor in three murder trials and the second chair in seven more, all convictions. Frequently, one of the obstacles to conviction was what she called "the stupid effect." She couldn't count the number of times, when debriefing a jury, she'd heard one of them say about the victim, "I know it wasn't her fault, but how could she be that stupid?"

Bea didn't always have a good answer.

In her own case, when she came home in the early-morning dark and saw a broken window in the side of the garage and debris scattered across the painted concrete as if someone had cleared Donald's workbench with a dramatic sweep of his arm, she didn't run back down the driveway to a neighbor's house, as a meditative juror might expect her to have done, or even dial 911 on her cell phone. She kept walking farther and farther into her home, examining the damage, trying to make sense of it, calling out to her husband, "Do-nald? Don? Don? Do-nald?"

She extracted Nada's twenty-five-dollar Colossus chip from her purse, her new good-luck charm, and rubbed the scratch on it for comfort. She'd last spoken to Canada on the phone three days ago. She'd taken the job in Chicago and Bea begged her to get a cell phone, even one of those drugstore throwaways so popular with the drug dealers Bea put away. "The police are looking for you," Bea had said. Nada joked that was exactly why she didn't have a cell phone. There were too many people she didn't want to talk to. The chip now reminded Bea, fleetingly, that she hadn't returned the call to that detective in Chicago.

Bea followed the light bleeding down the stairs, calling out "Donald" again and again, as if repeating the name of the person she loved most in the world would somehow ward off the thing she most feared. As a hypothetical juror might have pointed out, a prudent person (especially one who had just lectured her friend on the subject) might have taken the cell phone from her purse and dialed 911, but Bea did not.

The stairs led straight up to a small square landing and a wall with a light switch and a photo of their daughter, Lori. Bea froze, then recalled that Lori was at a friend's house for the night. She pushed aside her fear and pressed her feet slowly against each of the last four steps to the second floor.

"Don?"

He was in their bedroom, kneeling on the floor, head bowed, hands tied behind his back. His shirt was torn, a bruise painted a third of his face purple, and one eye was swollen shut. Blood and dirt formed a gory paste in his thin blond-gray hair. His lips moved.

Bea screamed, loud and long, a horror movie scream that was full of fright and surprise and despair and loss. Fear controlled her now. Fear of the inescapable. The fear a passenger must feel on a crashing airplane's rapid descent. The fear that life has given you no more choices.

Only when he spoke did Bea notice the man sitting behind Don on the big plush chair she used for reading and for slipping on her shoes. He was tall and broad and dressed in a black sweatshirt and new jeans. A stocking mask that must have covered his face earlier had been lifted up to his hairline. He had an angular nose, full lips, a boxy jaw, and small, intense eyes. He had muscles in his neck that must have been developed on some specialty machine at the gym.

He said, "Where is Canada Gold?"

24

WEDNESDAY, JULY 28

"THREE DAYS. No pay."

Kloska was wearing a green softball jersey. Although it was a size too tight and soaking with sweat, he thought it still looked decent on him. Coach Reggie's team of lawyers, the Nolo Contenderes, was playing a team from the *Chicago Reader*. The Nolo Contenderes were short a few players—Reggie's seventeen-year-old son, Louis, was even playing left field, although you wouldn't know they were related by the number of words they exchanged. Della had asked Kloska to sub for a first-year associate who couldn't make the game, and while they waited for their turns to bat, Bobby was explaining to Reggie why he had time to be playing softball even though he had a long month of paperwork bottlenecked on his desk and a heater like the Falcone murder was still screaming through the newspapers.

Reggie spit sunflower-seed shells between his feet. "Suspension? You must have really whacked the guy."

"There's this software—they call it 'the Brain'—and it keeps track of all the complaints against cops, every single one, whether it's bullshit or not, and it assigns each one a score, and they add up over time. When they put this one in, I guess it and all the other crap the Brain has on me spit out three days. I could get a hearing, but what the hell. I pushed the guy. With my *fist*. Probably harder than I should have. Not harder than he deserved, but harder than I should have."

Despite the heat, the softball diamonds just south of Grant Park were completely occupied with sixteen-inch Wednesday night league play—coed, no gloves. Beyond the outfields, the city seemed to have been built in layers—the grass and low leafy trees of the park and the concrete and steel of downtown and above it all the ceilingless blue sky under which they'd all been baking alive for two straight weeks. Some of them were still alive anyway. According to the news, twenty-six elderly and homeless had been killed by the heat. And it was still only July.

"Did you get anything from the doctor before you slugged him?" Reggie asked.

Bobby shook his head. "It seems weird to me that someone with Marlena Falcone's résumé would go to work at a place like that. One of her neighbors told me they thought it was strange, too. Executive Concierge is where doctors go to semiretire. They see a couple patients in the morning and then go work on their putting. Falcone was a lab rat. She was all about the research. She had twenty-three patents."

Kloska shut up as Della Dickey stepped into the batter's box. In her ill-fitting jersey, she looked a little shapeless from the back, but a better indicator of the body underneath was the way the script of her jersey was contoured over her breasts. He'd been flirting with her since she dropped by Area 3 for a copy of much of what, but not everything, he had on the

Falcone murder. She hadn't yet told him to go to hell, and the invitation to today's game had been promising.

"Your gal has gotten me some good stuff," he told Reggie.

"Oh yeah?"

"She tracked down a whole bunch of crap on the Internet about this group the math professor was telling me about. The Thousand." Kloska waited for a visible reaction from Reggie and got none. "Crazy stuff, most of it bullshit. Hardly any mention of it in legit news sources. She found these videos of protests, people with signs with that symbol—the *tetraktys*—showing up at Fortune Five Hundred shareholder meetings, and the G-Twenty summit last year." Della fouled off a pitch. "You ever hear of these things called numbers stations? . . ." Reggie barely shook his head. "Me, neither. They're these shortwave radio broadcasts that can be heard all over the world. It's just like an automated voice, like a robot, reciting a series of numbers over and over. Or sometimes words. Or Morse code. Most people figure they're a way for spies to communicate, but some people think the Thousand are using these broadcasts to talk to each other. You know, in *number language* or something. Probably all of it bullshit. Professor's probably full of shit, too. I gave it to Traden, see if he could find out how much of it's for real. But all the people who are interested in these guys, these *Pythagoreans,* they also have a real hard-on for Solomon Gold. All that crap he told you about his music being an equation and whatnot."

Reggie said, "Della's told me the Gold trial is what got her interested in the law."

Vallentine smiled with the half of his mouth nearest Kloska and added quietly, "Which is funny, because that was the trial that almost made me *lose* interest in the law."

Della smashed a line drive right at the Aon Center, the ball dipping into the grass just before the left fielder. *Girl can hit,* Kloska thought with an immodest amount of arousal.

Bobby's head was a jumble of clues, none of them more significant than the others. There was the gun and Pythagoras and ancient religious cults and *harmonia* and doctors who wore suits and computer chips that gave you boners and so forth and like that and so on. The itch he couldn't scratch was that Russo acted like he'd hardly ever heard of Pythagoras, but when Bobby peered through that office door and looked at the reflection of the desk in the glass hanging on the wall, he saw a *tetraktys.* It looked like it could be a Lucite slab, maybe six inches square, with the circles etched into it. If that didn't belong to Dr. Falcone, then somebody else at Executive Concierge was into this Pythagoras business, and either way, Russo was lying when he said he'd never heard of it.

Della advanced to second on a single. "Christ it's hot," Kloska said. Between fields, a Middle Eastern guy had the misfortune to be selling Vienna Beef franks from an aluminum cart instead of ice cream. He'd sold out of cold Pepsi. Even the usually reliable Lake Michigan, just a hundred or so yards to the east, was unable to produce a breeze. Bobby recognized Reggie's wife, who was wearing a pressed white T-shirt and khaki shorts, sitting in a folding lawn chair behind the backstop. Not that they'd ever met, but he knew her handsome face from the pictures the *Trib* was always printing of charity balls and whatnot. It seemed clear Reggie wasn't going to introduce them today, and Kloska resented that a little bit. He'd heard Reggie say he liked to "compartmentalize" his life. Maybe keeping Kloska and Stephanie separate was just his way.

Nevertheless, for Kloska it remained a source of suspicion. Reggie was holding something back, even as Kloska was mostly spilling his guts. Vallentine had an angle on this business that he wasn't telling. *That's the advantage defense attorneys always have in court. They never have to tell you exactly what they're up to.*

Della scored on a double. Kloska watched her run around third, short arms pumping and hips turning and ponytail bouncing out the back of her cap and big white teeth clenched and grinning all the way. She crossed home plate and walked right to them, and as Kloska and Reggie clapped their congratulations, she pushed her ass in between them on the bench, and now Kloska's thigh was pressed right up against hers.

"Boys," she said, hardly out of breath.

"Nice hit," Kloska said.

She smiled and straightened her cap. "What are you two talking about?"

Kloska tried to contain his excitement. He was up in two batters.

"Mostly how Detective Kloska here won't play by anybody's rules," Reggie said.

Della rolled her eyes, but then she smiled. She'd been listening to Bobby whine about the Brain and his suspension all afternoon.

"You want to go to a show Friday night?" Della asked.

Bobby's imagination projected a montage of possibilities onto the inside of his skull. "What kind of show?" he asked coolly.

"Well, Solomon Gold isn't the only local artist Marlena has a connection to, apparently. There's this guy called Burning Patrick. You ever hear of him?"

Bobby shook his head. Reggie was watching the game.

"He used to be homeless. But now he's an artist and his paintings go for thousands of dollars. He's also a singer in this band called the Bat Wing Vortex. Most important, this Burning Patrick—real name Patrick Blackburn—was also once a patient of Marlena Falcone."

"Oh yeah?" Bobby didn't really care, except for the fact that Della was saying it.

"Marlena lost her medical license because she altered the neurostimulators to treat ADHD despite a warning from the FDA. Canada Gold got one, but a bunch of other kids who got the procedure went crazy, right? They had to have them removed. This Patrick Blackburn—Burning Patrick—he was one of them. Marlena even wrote a paper about him for a medical journal. I guess she kept track of him even after he had the device removed and collected a big settlement."

"And how is that related to her murder?"

"I don't have any idea. I just want *someone* to take me to a rock show."

The part of Bobby's brain that was in charge of pleasure—the dominant part, no doubt—was parsing the invitation a million ways. He accepted casually and then changed the subject before his imagination made an ass of itself. "Speaking of, you heard from Canada Gold?" he asked Reggie, who shook his head.

Whatever thrill Kloska got from the thought of a date with Della was suddenly tempered by a big ball of sick in the bottom of his stomach. No word on Canada's whereabouts. That prosecutor in Clark County hadn't returned his calls, either. If Canada Gold really was the common denominator in these murders, he had to catch this shithead before her body was found half-buried in the Mojave, because once that happened, whoever was warming his seat at Area 3 could count on a call from the feds.

Reggie stood to cheer a bases-loaded walk, and Kloska rubbed his leg subtly against Della's. She didn't reciprocate.

Federal prosecutors didn't usually want jurisdiction unless the connection between crimes was rock-solid—there were ambitious feds and lazy feds, same as cops—but once you had bodies in two different states and both of them had connections to one of the most infamous murders of the decade, there was no way they'd be able to keep their manicured hands off his case. Bobby was really working two fronts here—trying to solve it on one side and trying not to attract interest from the G on the other.

And he had to work them both while officially off the job.

25

IT WAS HER FATHER'S DESK, although Solomon Gold had almost certainly never sat behind it the way she did now, with a purpose, a project, a job. Her father had never worked sitting down. His private work spaces had all been at standing height, like a podium, and when he wrote music, he leaned against the furniture as if he were pushing a car, his feet in front of each other, waist forward, his shoulders hunched over the paper, his arms surrounding his pencil like a fence. After a few minutes, he would step away and play his piano or even his beautiful violin, fingering the strings of the Guarneri folk-style, and then return to write down what he had experienced with his hands. When he began using computers, he always had the monitors on stands above his head, with the keyboard at shoulder height, and she remembered watching him type with one hand while the other paged through a book or drew lines across the paper, as if the calculations from the computer were traveling across his right arm and through his head and then down his left arm, where his wrist translated it into an idea. A melody. A note. A theme.

This was a desk Solomon Gold had purchased to intimidate other people. It was broad and arrogant, same as he had been. When someone sat on one side of it and Solomon Gold stood on the other, her father, already a giant, tripled in size.

She remembered that feeling from experience.

"I bought it at an auction of your father's things," Jameson said. "I suppose your mother didn't want it in her house."

"Something this desk and I have in common," Canada said.

On the desk was a legal pad in a leather portfolio, along with a selection of pens, two pencils, and a sharpener. (A computer had been offered, but Nada'd made a face and sent it away.) More of her father's possessions were displayed around her—books on shelves and paintings on walls. "I'm something of a Solomon Gold collector," Jameson admitted.

She recognized the carpet as having come from his office. The space wasn't an exact replica, but Jameson had enough original stuff for an imitation of Solomon's office, which, to Nada, was mostly just the place where her father had died.

"I thought you'd like to be surrounded by your father's things," Jameson said.

He's not as smart as I thought, she said to her spider.

Across from the desk, where in her father's real office had been a mural of Florence, were seventeen tiles painted by Patrick Blackburn. *Burning Patrick.* Each had been mounted on a thin rod and pushed out about six inches from the plaster. Jameson explained that the spatial relationship between the tiles was nothing close to scale—even this enormous house could not contain Burning Patrick's vision—but he had guessed where each might belong in relation to the others.

Canada had spent almost the entire morning with a cup of coffee, staring blankly at the fragmented mural. She attributed the loud ringing and sharp pain to the previous night's good red wine—better even than Bea and Donald's old Bordeaux.

Nada thought about calling Bea again, but she didn't. She was anxious to get news about Phillip Truman but still wasn't ready to be scolded. Nada planned to go back. She'd even left some of those chips in the closet for her building super, casino chips being something like Las Vegas city scrip. Ten grand would cover her rent for a few months, with a tip generous enough that he'd keep an eye on the place and sweep the grit and sand from her vestibule. More chips went into storage off Boulder Highway. The chips were her "out button," the little disk they put at your chair when you want to sit out a poker hand but remain in the game. She thought maybe they could hold her place in Las Vegas until she put herself together.

The night before, over Molly's stuffed chicken, Nada had politely responded to Gary's and Myra's questions about her father's work and made her own inquiries about Burning Patrick. Jameson related gossip and legend and amusing tales of the lengths collectors would go for a particular tile or adjacent pair.

"Do you know what they say about the musically inclined?" Jameson asked, perhaps about her father, perhaps about Patrick Blackburn, perhaps about both.

Nada lifted her eyebrows. *Obviously no.*

"They say if you look at the MRIs—the brain scans of randomly selected individuals—an expert eye can tell you which of those people are musicians. Just by looking at their brains. Isn't that remarkable?"

Myra said, "In a few years you won't need an MRI. Everyone will have a computer in his head eventually. You want to know something about a person, you just download it to your laptop. Or your phone."

Jameson laughed. "Like diagnostics on a car."

Now Nada looked back across the room at the seventeen tiles and from this distance, maybe forty feet, her mind began filling in the missing squares—thousands of them, even tens of thousands, by Jameson's estimation, most of which had yet to be painted, probably never would be painted. The images that came to her were horrible; each one was more fantastical than the last—dragons and bombs and bullets and soldiers and sea monsters and yeti and gargoyles and trolls and tanks and tsunamis and zombies and demons—but she let them come and go, eventually turning them off with her toggle. *Sitting here is pointless.*

Nada stood and browsed through her father's old things. A shelf of old books—math and music, mostly. A few awards, although not his Oscar. *That,* her mother had kept. She'd kept the Guarneri, too, even fighting Boeing over it before the airline manufacturer, in a desperate miscalculation, allowed her to purchase it at a discount, figuring Gold's infamy would devalue the instrument, rather than the other way around. Most of the rest of his things had been auctioned off when her mother sold the house.

The room had hardwood floors, just like her father's office, narrow boards with the tinted varnish of a basketball court, and she suddenly had one of those memories from before the chip, before the spider had been placed in her head. They were never as sure, as sharp, or as satisfying as the ones she retained after—Nada's memory was much like that of a scrapbooker who hadn't been given a camera until her thirteenth birthday—but they occasionally bubbled to the surface, usually for a reason, she liked to think. Recollections of her childhood only came to her when she needed to know.

An exclamation mark. A black scuff on her father's floor shaped like an exclamation point. It had come from her mother's high-heeled shoe, right around the time the troubles started in Nada's head. There had been a fight in the office. She heard some of it and understood none of it. Nada now assumed her mother had found out about an affair, not Erica Liu, who was later, but maybe another. She had made the mark by stamping her foot, and Nada saw it the next day when she sneaked into her father's office to play with the books and the globes and the instruments he displayed along one windowless wall.

Her mother. *God.* That woman was all exclamations. Nada wondered if she was in Chicago or if she had fled somewhere from the heat— Europe or Australia or South America. Hell, the Caribbean was cooler than Chicago right now. She knew she should call her. Even a bad daughter would call her bad mother after being away for so long.

Later.

She turned once more to the tiles, flipping the switch in her head again, and imaginary missing tiles returned, filling every blank space with a bad memory. This time, she saw Erica Liu's lifeless body, her mouth slightly parted and filling with blood, an image taken by a police photographer from a height and angle that must have been similar to the height and angle at which her father had last glimpsed his lover, before he turned and walked away.

Nada remembered visiting her dad in jail. She hated that. Even before the spider was in and all her senses were heightened, the smell of the place was just about unbearable. She remembered asking him directly if he had done it. And he leaned forward and told her, "The wolf killed her. I just couldn't stop the wolf."

She figured it must be how he coped with what he'd done. How he cut away the part of himself that was capable of killing Erica Liu and gave it a name, as if it were a part of somebody else.

Horrible images came and went on the wall, and a long-dormant fear returned—that the crazy that had once consumed her father, *the wolf,* was finally coming for her.

26

THURSDAY, JULY 29

PETER TREMBLEY PICKED UP a *Review-Journal* every day on the way to work, so Wayne usually saved fifty cents and a tree farm conifer and read Peter's copy before heading out to the casino floor. Mostly, he did it to annoy Peter, who every day wished out loud Wayne would just buy his own. Peter had two rules. Wayne couldn't do the crossword, which Peter saved for his break. Also, Wayne was forbidden from reading any section until Peter had read it first. "Just give me the sports while you're reading that," Wayne would say, but Peter would insist that Wayne was going to "ruin it." Peter seemed to think of real life as if it were a movie or mystery novel and so he kept the unread sections in a stack under his forearm, rationing them out when he was through.

Wayne could get the news on his computer, of course. Hell, he could get it along with stock quotes and sports scores and daily Sudoku puzzles on his tricked-out superphone. But it wasn't the news he wanted so much as the ritual—picking up his coffee and turning the page and setting his cup down again. It was a habit he'd picked up in junior high from his father, who loved newspapers and who also read each day's like a book, front to back.

Wayne got to work an hour early and worked out at the hotel gym on the thirty-second floor. He showered and settled behind his desk and Peter had handed him the sports and the business and the living sections in that order.

There were minutes in the day when Wayne didn't think about Nada—while scrutinizing a Dodgers box score, for instance—but they were few. Out in the casino, in addition to everything else he was looking for—drunks, cheaters, and general unruliness—he was always scanning the tables for her tiny shape, checking every hour for her little green dot on his screen, convinced that she wouldn't call first but would just show up one day when her troubles had passed, assuming she was in any trouble at all.

Amoyo was right. Nada was exactly the sort of person who might disappear on a whim. Like a loose balloon, it was her lack of attachment that made him want to hold her so close. Nada could take care of herself far better than Wayne could take care of her, which was just one reason, he knew, she would never settle for him.

Peter tossed the front section of the paper over the narrow gap between their desks and, turning it right side up, Wayne winced at the above-the-fold headline, two lines of large type with a grisly report:

SPR. VALLEY MASSACRE LEAVES
ASST. DA, HUSBAND DEAD

According to the article, the bodies had been mutilated with a knife and police were exploring the possibility that the murders were the work of an individual (or individuals) whom Beatrice Beaujon had prosecuted in the past. The murder came on the same day Beaujon had extracted a surprise guilty plea from the son of billionaire shopping mall developer Danny Truman.

The description of the slayings unbalanced Wayne. He felt his moon weight rising. Even though his title was associate director of security, stories like this proved that security was mythical. Like with snuff films and hangover cures, there was no such thing as security. Any *security* can be circumvented by somebody who wants what you have more than you want to protect it.

Nothing seemed to have been taken from the Beaujons' home, and both victims had been stabbed multiple times. "Carved" was the way the DA had put it. Donald Beaujon was a lawyer as well, and his case list would be examined for the potentially disgruntled, but between the lines, it was clear that the police thought Beatrice was the real target. They'd refused to comment when asked if they thought the killings might be related to any of the cases she had recently prosecuted.

Wayne wondered what it would be like to be murdered. Ambushed in your own home. He figured his size would give him an advantage over most attackers, but then, if someone really wanted you dead, if someone was angry enough because you had put him in prison, where he had wasted away for half a dozen years and maybe been gang-raped or gotten AIDS or all the horrible stuff you always heard went on in there, if someone wanted you dead as badly as that, there was probably no stopping him. If an unstoppable force was pissed off enough, Wayne would take it over an immovable object any day.

Wayne folded the paper and returned it to Peter's desk. Peter's computer was running its SETI screen saver, a dancing graph of greens and blues and purples and reds. SETI stood for Search for Extraterrestrial Intelligence, a project with which Steve Rhodes was famously obsessed. He had given the University of California over a million dollars to help fund radio telescopes pointed at the stars, scanning the white noise for intelligent patterns that hadn't originated on Earth. Colossus employees were encouraged, though not required, to install these screen savers. The software enlisted the computing power of thousands of idle CPUs all across the country to process the telescope data, trying to discover even a hint of mathematical order in the cacophony of the universe. Peter was also a bit of a UFO nut, having made several trips to Roswell, New Mexico. He liked to talk about UFO lore, or rather, *UAP* lore—Peter frequently had to correct Wayne, pointing out that the preferred term was *unidentified aerial phenomenon.* He was always going on about Betty Hill and Kenneth Arnold and especially the secret terminal at McCarran Airport, from which unmarked planes allegedly shuttled workers back and forth each day to Area 51. "Every time a decent witness sees a UAP, governments and scientists always call it a weather balloon," Peter liked to say. "How many fucking weather balloons have you seen in your life? Zero, right? Why should I believe in weather balloons more than aliens? They tell us if we can't explain it, it can't exist. That's just stupid. The truth is, they don't want us even to know about anything they can't explain, because then people would lose confidence in the status quo."

A common interest in little green men had granted Peter some extra face time with the boss over the years. Enough that Wayne noticed, but not enough to make him feel threatened. When Rhodes wanted to show someone his new toy—the Patty Hearst gun—he'd chosen Wayne, after all.

Coffee depleted, Wayne picked up his phone and walked out onto the floor. He could hear waitresses and dealers talking in whispers about the murders the night before. He realized, with a little bit of guilt, that he was glad he didn't know these Beaujons. He hated funerals, even when they came at the end of a long illness and nobody was especially shocked or sad. He couldn't imagine what you'd say to the family of someone who'd been brutally stabbed to death on page one of the *Journal-Review.*

Then, as he was picking up a plastic cup that someone had dropped on the carpet outside the theater, he had the horrible feeling that maybe he *did* know Beatrice Beaujon. The Phillip Truman rape case had been a sustained source of conversation and gossip as well as schadenfreude in the office, since the crime had happened in a nearby hotel. Wayne thought he might have heard the name in passing or on the news. Nada'd even mentioned Truman a couple of times. She was pretty worked up about the crime.

Had Nada mentioned her? Had she been working with Beatrice Beaujon? He tapped through the contact list in his phone. Searched his e-mails. No mention of that name. Nothing triggered a memory.

Wandering out by the pool, where an army of men and women in black polo shirts were setting up tables on the slate tile for a private party, he ran the name through a loop in his head, hoping the repetition would solve the mystery. *Beatrice Beaujon what? Beatrice Beaujon where? Beatrice Beaujon who?*

He watched a party planner chattering into his wireless headset, the man's legs covered in white linen pants and moving quick as a coastal bird's. Wayne quickly and indifferently assessed him as gay. He wondered if the aggressively heterosexual David Amoyo was a rarity in that business and he recalled Amoyo's plea to put in a word with the catering department, which Wayne, of course, hadn't done.

"She rarely mentioned anybody except a friend in the DA's office." Amoyo had said that at the Puma. "I think her name was Bea."

27

SHE HAD TAKEN A WALK down hazy and hot Michigan Avenue, clearing her head of the awful images she'd imagined on the tiles, trying to replace them with window displays—Gucci and Tiffany and Ralph Lauren. It frightened her to have thoughts that didn't seem to originate in her head. She couldn't imagine where such awful images had come from.

I'm not going crazy. I'm not going crazy.

Nada had an ache in the middle of her forehead that she assumed was from caffeine withdrawal, so she picked up a free *Chicago Reader* in a coffee shop and scanned the club ads over an iced latte. Jameson had said he thought Burning Patrick's band, Bat Wing Vortex, was playing this weekend. She noted the particulars and her spider filed them away.

She idly tuned in and out of half a dozen conversations around the shop. In many cases she could only monitor half the discussion because one or more participants were turned away from her. An elderly woman was near tears because she had to move her sixty-year-old son into a nursing home. A woman in nurse's scrubs was trying to convince her friend to try Botox. Two men in polos and khakis were discussing printer ink and the Cubs. There was a man sitting alone, reading a magazine. He was dressed like a lawyer, but his hands were very clean and rubbed white around the cuticles, and he had a yellow pen-size flashlight in his shirt pocket. Nada guessed he might be a doctor and tried to remember if there was a hospital close to Michigan Avenue. A young woman sitting along the wall was leaning across the table, talking to her companion. She occasionally moved her hand in front of her mouth and frequently scanned the room with her eyes. She was in her twenties. A dyed blonde. Slightly pudgy, but not unattractively so. She had seven piercings in her left ear but was trying to fill in three of them. When she moved her arm,

Nada could see a slight discoloration under her collarbone. It wasn't a birthmark. More like a tan line. Like she'd been wearing a necklace in the sun and had recently removed it.

It was a pattern of dots. Nada had seen it before. High up on one of the big oak doors in Jameson's foyer. Like bowling pins seen from above.

"You think he's *automatic* now." Nada wasn't sure about the second-to-last word. *Automatic* didn't make any sense.

Her companion said something. His back was to Nada, but she could see part of his face in the reflection of a framed poster on the wall. Lip flap is never perfectly symmetrical and so she had to focus to try to make sense of it. Something about a "religious freak"?

"I hear the Sheik's been to his place a bunch the last six months," the girl said.

The man said something about how this Sheik, or the religious freak, if they weren't the same person, liked gambling too much.

Nada was never very good with coincidences. She saw far too many of them. People who think the world makes sense are surprised by coincidence, but Nada found it everywhere. She knew if she sat in this coffee shop and continued eavesdropping on conversations, she could identify some connection between every single person there—shared dermatologists and ailments, alma maters, favorite books.

Occasionally, she would give in to the paranoia. Bea liked to say that Nada was good at obtaining information but not so good at making sense of it. Here she had a girl who used to wear a necklace with the same pattern she'd seen in Jameson's house. That could be nothing. Probably was nothing. But they were also talking about a Sheik who liked to gamble, and hadn't Wayne mentioned somebody called the Concrete Sheik who was visiting the Colossus casino last time she was there?

This couple had stood in line behind her, which meant they could have followed her inside.

"It seems like there's gotta be a much easier way," the girl was saying now. "It's so crazy over the top."

He said something about its being only a couple of days. That it happened almost every summer anyway. This was just (something—"controlling" maybe?) the timing.

They started talking about personal things—boyfriends (the man was gay, it turned out), jobs. Nada decided they had nothing to do with her. Just one of those moments when her spider wanted to stir up trouble.

She left the coffee shop and walked three doors north, stopping at the entrance of a Japanese luxury electronics showroom. She waited there until the dyed blonde and the gay man left the shop and turned south, walking away from her into the heat.

28

IN THE PANELED DINING ROOM with the big Rauschenberg on the windowless north wall, Reggie Vallentine was having, but not enjoying, a late and mostly silent dinner of pumpkin ravioli with his wife, his son, and the widow of the man he had murdered.

Elizabeth Gold, tall and straight in the Vallentines' Stickley chair, wore expensive clothes and expertly applied makeup and had a few sandbags against the tide of aging in the form of recent surgical improvements around the eyes and ears. She wore a small silver pendant around her neck—some kind of animal, a horse maybe—which drew his attention involuntarily to her chest when he should have been looking her in the eyes. She smiled easily, Reggie noticed, but not always sincerely.

"What should I do?" she asked him after a long and tense period of quiet.

"You're doing it," Reggie said. "Cooperate when they ask. And if you think of something later that might be helpful to them, call me."

"Call you or the police?"

"Call me."

"I don't want to bother you, Valli."

Without a change of expression, he said, "You were the estranged wife of a murdered man. I don't care if his killer has been dead for ten years. You never speak about Solomon's death to a reporter or a cop or a prosecutor or anyone in government higher than the cashier at the DMV without me present."

Since police had zeroed in quickly on Michael Liu, Elizabeth Gold had never been a serious person of interest in Solomon's murder. Whatever they wanted now was no doubt related to the Marlena Falcone investigation. But as long as they were asking, Reggie wanted to be there, and not just for Elizabeth's sake. He wanted to know everything about this inquiry. As long as no one raised the question of whether Reggie Vallentine might have killed Solomon Gold, no one could ever contemplate the answer.

Which was why he had to take seriously Derek Liu's threat about talking to the cops. Once he raised the possibility, the possibility would exist.

He counted the things that would dissolve in that mixture of indictment and innuendo. His reputation, his marriage, his way of life, his freedom—everything he possessed would be gone. Everyone he knew—his wife, his son, his friends, his partners, Bobby Kloska, his brother and sister—all betrayed.

Reggie even considered, privately and with uncharacteristic immodesty, that he'd be forced to hire a lawyer who wouldn't be as good as he was.

And although it was the least of his many worries, Reggie wondered how the widow Gold would react if she knew his secret. Would she despise him or quietly and huskily thank him for the favor?

The chandelier lights were dimmed, but to Reggie's mind, they couldn't be dim enough. As the subject changed and his wife and Elizabeth began to debrief each other about Gold Coast gossip, he wished they could eat in total darkness.

The Vallentine residence occupied half of the fifty-third floor of the Clarion Building, a solid blue monolith seventy-five stories high, which was a highlight of the architectural boat tour that motored up and down the Chicago River each summer between the lake and the Michigan Avenue Bridge. Its subtle curve along the water reflected a generous sample of adjacent skyline. In other cities, it would be the kind of building populated by celebrities—film actors and network anchormen and media moguls. In Chicago, a city that raised healthy crops of celebrities for export but rarely for domestic consumption, the residents of such buildings had acquired their wealth more stealthily.

Most of them anyhow.

Below their condo were thirty more luxury condos and below that was a boutique hotel and below that was an upscale shopping mall with thousand-dollar sunglasses and baby strollers that cost more than Reggie's parents ever paid for a car. You had to own at least a quarter of a floor if you wanted a key card to the gym and the pool on sixty, which, in the odd hours that Reggie worked out, had always been empty.

The phone rang. Stephanie looked to Reggie to see if he was going to answer it. After a pause, he stood and walked to the phone in the kitchen.

"Sorry to bother you, Mr. Vallentine," said Thomas, the doorman to whom Reggie gave a bottle of cask-proof scotch every Christmas. "It's a police detective named Bobby Kloska. He says he knows you and that he has to see you right away."

"Yeah, Thomas. I know him."

Reggie returned to the table and excused himself without explanation, and his son, Louis, took the opportunity to do the same, retreating immediately to his room, leaving Steph and Elizabeth to trade freely in other people's embarrassments. Reggie grabbed his wallet and stepped into the hallway outside the apartment, closing the door behind him.

Kloska emerged from the elevator, angry and liquored up. His lower lip was tucked under his teeth and his hand was clenched above his head, index finger extended into an accusation.

Reggie shook his head. *Not here.* In two long leaps, he caught the elevator door before it closed and held it for Bobby.

"Something ain't right, Reggie, and you need to come clean with me. *Right now.*"

Reggie pushed a button for the sixtieth floor—gym and pool. "Hello, Bobby."

Whiskey, thick on Kloska's breath, dispersed in an oaky mist when he spoke. "You're a piece of work, I tell you what."

The doors opened into a narrow hall with a glass and metal door at the end. Reggie inserted a key card and the door clicked open onto the wide tile deck surrounding the pool, which included four lanes for laps and a small hot tub for aching muscles or cuddling lovers. Pairs of wood and canvas lounge chairs were arranged at equidistant intervals, but the deck was otherwise uncluttered. At one end, behind a glass wall, was a handful of treadmills and StairMasters and elliptical machines. Across the east and north walls were breathtaking views of the lake and downtown, although at this hour they reflected only a dim image of Bobby Kloska and Reggie Vallentine, who right now felt as if his metaphorical head was barely above water.

Bobby looked around the empty room until his eyes settled on Reggie's. Reggie nodded, and then Bobby said something entirely unexpected: "Are you one of them?"

"What?"

"The Thousand. This creepy group of math freaks that, until a couple hours ago, I wasn't even sure really existed. You're one of them. It explains everything."

Reggie was relieved that Bobby had come to ask him something he could comfortably deny, but he knew not to deny it right away. Reggie was always and consistently noncommittal, in anticipation of the day when he would be confronted with a truth he *couldn't* deny. "What would that explain, Bobby?"

"You've been covering for them, right? They killed Gold for the requiem. They killed Marlena Falcone for God knows why, some kind of internal power struggle. You're one of them. Or else they've hired you to cover their tracks. They'd need a guy like you to help them stay secret for so long. Cepeda says they like to do things big and out in the open, and you're as big and in the open as any lawyer around."

"Slow down a minute."

"Three weeks. That's my new suspension. And now the Independent Police Review Authority is involved. You know when a cop usually hears from the IPRA? When he shoots somebody or he beats his wife. I haven't shot anybody in eight years and I hit my wife never. Cops always look after cops, but this Russo, this fucking doctor, is one of them, one of the Thousand, and he's pulling some thick strings to get me off this case, and he's pointing the investigation toward some drug company conspiracy, which the brass is buying because it's just slightly less crazy than what I think. And you know what? I think you're in on it, too. I think you've been quietly leading me down the wrong path for ten years, starting the night of Gold's murder, and I want the truth right now. Because this isn't just about a case anymore. This is about my reputation. My career. It's about being your asshole. You've fucked with me for long enough." Reggie noticed Bobby's gun, unholstered and wedged comically between his belt and his abdomen.

"Just calm down."

"Fuck you," Bobby said. "Did Michael Liu kill Solomon Gold?"

"That's what you keep telling me."

"Bullshit. You were there. Who did it?"

Reggie said nothing.

"What really happened that night?"

"I have always given my full cooperation to this investigation, except when your inquiry has conflicted with my respons—"

"Shut up." Bobby's phone rang. He glanced at the number, probably hoping he could ignore it, but then he flapped his arms in frustration. "Stay there a minute."

He turned his back and listened to the call, frozen, silent, his head down. To Reggie, he looked decapitated. After less than a minute, his left hand dropped to his side and he folded the phone shut with a finger and turned slowly back to Reggie. With his right hand, he had drawn the gun, and now he lifted the barrel to Reggie's eyes.

"Tell me the truth right now."

It had been ten years since Reggie last looked into the barrel of a gun.

"Last chance to tell me what it all means. I want to know everything that happened that night. The truth this time. Not what you wrote in your bullshit book. Not what you told the TV reporters. Not what you told me ten years ago. Or last week. For the sake of my job. For the sake of your conscience. For the sake of our friendship. Tell me the truth. And it better be the truth, because Traden's sitting with a guy right now who might be able to tell me if you can't."

Reggie raised his arm. "I don't know what else I can tell you, Bobby."

Kloska brought the gun down and returned it indelicately to his waistband. He blinked a few times and then held up his phone. He said, "Erica Liu's twin brother has just been arrested for obstruction of justice.

"And fuck all if he isn't asking for you."

29

FRIDAY, JULY 30

THE COFFINS WERE ARRANGED at slight angles to one another, forming a flat V at one end of the Vernon Drake Funeral Home's heavily curtained Mojave Room. Caked in makeup, their heads met at the center, and there was a small kneeler in front of each coffin, at which friends and families offered prayers and paid tearful respects.

Gentle, nostalgic laughter occasionally broke the hush, as did a spontaneous sob. In yesterday's newspaper, Wayne had read that the Beaujons left a young daughter, but she was absent for the moment. Maybe an aunt or uncle had taken her across the street to McDonald's. As Wayne had pulled into the parking lot, he considered how often that restaurant must be filled with tired and hungry mourners. *It's a respectable calling,* he'd thought, *making cheeseburgers for the bereaved.*

According to the news, great violence had been done to each body, but the killer (or killers) had apparently contained the assault mostly below the chin. Wayne thought he could see some evidence of a blow around Donald Beaujon's left eye, but all in all, the couple looked pretty good for murdered people, not that Wayne had much experience kneeling this close to days-old butchered corpses. He prayed as best as he remembered how, then stood up and backed away from Donald's body.

The large gathering had convened in smaller groups—her friends and family segregated from his friends and family, and their mutual friends, people they had met after marriage, separated in another huddle of folding chairs. There were subsets of cousins and work friends and neighbors, as well as parents of their daughter's friends. He didn't spot the one person he was hoping to see, and he wondered how long he should wait. It might be less awkward to watch from across the street with a couple of those cheeseburgers.

He stood in line to look at a triptych of easels that had been set up with pictures of the Beaujons and their friends. Wayne scanned them methodically until he finally found it—a photo taken in someone's backyard, Bea and Canada Gold with glasses of sangria in their hands and smiling Bea's head on Nada's bare shoulder and Nada looking off to the left into the woods or another backyard or whatever scene was there out of frame, her perfect profile revealing one half of an inscrutable smile.

He found another one, a photo clipped from *Las Vegas Magazine*'s coverage of a breast cancer charity event, according to the caption. She was standing next to Bea and on the other side of a smiling Nada was a grinning Amoyo, his left arm around her back, his left hand not visible. A flash grenade of jealousy exploded inside him. His face went hot. It drove him crazy not knowing where that hand was. Was it inside the waistband of her skirt? Cupped over her ass? It made him nuts to see her looking so happy with a jerk like Amoyo, made him nuts when he could imagine their life together so vividly. How crazy good it would be for both of them together.

Wayne stared at the photo. Three people in it. In the past week, one of them had been murdered, another had gone missing, and the third, according to a Puma employee Wayne had been hounding with phone calls, hadn't shown up for work in twenty-four hours.

Wayne turned and walked out of the Mojave Room and into the foyer, where he double-checked the guest book. Canada hadn't been here and she wasn't coming. That meant wherever she was, she either couldn't leave or she hadn't heard about Bea's murder. He knew Nada would do anything to get back for the funeral of a friend. Anxious and bored at the same time, he wondered if this was what soldiers felt—both the weight of tedium and the fear of the unknown crushing him from both sides. He had to do something, but whatever *something* was, he couldn't do it here.

He moved through the foyer and out into the parking lot, passing three unrelated smokers clinging to the asphalt nearest the building. Wayne pulled out his phone and dialed the Puma Lounge and got the same, flat story he had the last three times. "David isn't here. I haven't seen him. I don't know when he'll be in." Four one one again. Amoyo's home number was unlisted. If he still had the apartment he shared with Nada, then he lived in a newish high-rise condo building downtown. She had enjoyed the health club, she'd told Wayne, and she liked having a doorman.

Traffic wasn't too bad yet—or at least it wasn't at a dead stop like it would be on the Boulevard in another hour—and Wayne called Peter from the car to tell him he'd be gone just a little longer, which was certainly understating it, but fuck 'em. It all sounded crazy, but if Amoyo knew who Bea was, then maybe he knew why she was dead. Maybe he knew without even knowing it. Maybe Amoyo had noticed something else in the last couple of days. Someone suspicious around the club.

Maybe he would remember something about the day they took that picture for the magazine. Anything.

He pulled into a visitor space at the apartments and the middle-aged doorman—a career hospitality guy, all shoe shine and hair gel and straight back and creased pants—buzzed him in. Wayne told him he was there to see David Amoyo, and with a nod the doorman deferred to a touch-screen kiosk in the wall. The doorman had a round face and a bad toupee with a part in it. Wayne scrolled through only three names before he found Amoyo/Chester—*Sandy's last name*—and he laughed quietly at that and wondered if her name was as fake as those tits Nada used to bitch about, and when there wasn't any answer, he went back to the doorman and pleaded with him to let him go upstairs.

"Is Mr. Amoyo expecting you?" He cleared his teeth of the remains of a Subway club sandwich with his tongue.

"No."

"I can't let you up, then, sir."

"I think something might be wrong with him."

"Why's that?"

"I just do. He didn't show up for work today."

"As I understand it, Mr. Amoyo spends many days working away from the office." He said the word *office* in an ironic way, perhaps to indicate he understood it was a strip club.

Wayne said, "Please. It's a well-being check. You do those, don't you?"

"With our elderly tenants. When the situation warrants."

"It warrants. It warrants." Wayne removed his lanyard and showed the doorman his casino ID and then pointed to the plastic name tag on the doorman's blazer, which looked to be the closest thing the man had to a badge, and as he handed over his ID for inspection, he passed a pair of twenties underneath it with his thumb. Wayne said, "Come on. One security professional to another."

The doorman puckered and then nodded slowly. He called someone from maintenance to watch his station and when the much younger and more casually dressed replacement arrived, Wayne and the doorman rode the elevator together.

"What kind of trouble do you think Mr. Amoyo is in?" His name tag read HOOVER.

"How many kinds of trouble are there?" Wayne said, and as Hoover fingered his keys, Wayne started to worry that they were going to catch Amoyo and Sandy Chester fucking on the living room carpet and Hoover was going to get his ass fired and all Wayne would have by way of explanation was a not very credible story about some innocent photo in a magazine six months ago.

I'll give him a job, Wayne thought. *I'll find Hoover a job at the Colossus if he gets fired for this.*

At the door to the apartment, Hoover knocked several times housekeeping style with the end of the key and then he unlocked the door and pushed it open. "Miss Chester is out of town on an engagement." Wayne nodded and Hoover backed nervously down the hall, in the direction of the elevators, no doubt worried he'd be spotted and reported for letting a stranger into one of the apartments. "Anybody asks, I had nothing to do with this," he said. "I got your name. Gonna know, you take anything."

The apartment was clean for a guy's place. Uncluttered. Lots of blacks and whites and reds and tans. Expensive numbered prints in frames. Glass and metal sculptures on shelves instead of books. A large plasma TV and a couch wide enough for a couple to stretch out on it end to end.

Amoyo was lying shirtless on his back in a nest of crusted blood and bone and brains and beige carpeting, a dry black hole in his forehead. Bloody tears in his shirt everywhere. Stab wounds.

Oh God. One photo of three people. Two of them dead, one of them missing.

Wayne found Amoyo's phone and dialed 911, and as he described the scene to the dispatcher, he wondered how long he'd be tied up here with the cops sorting through this mess. Hours? All day? Into the night? He'd never been part of a homicide investigation.

The countdown of police response time provided Wayne a few moments alone with a fresh murder scene. This was the realm of the real detective. A real cop's office and laboratory. Wayne folded his arms so he wouldn't touch anything and knelt beside Amoyo's head. He breathed hesitantly, but the corpse didn't smell like anything much besides dry cologne. The hole in Amoyo's head was small and it looked like it had been filled with tar. He noticed other wounds now, including a narrow bruise across his neck.

A bat? A forearm?

The observation excited him. The thrill of a real detective. Wayne suddenly felt like a fantasy baseball player taking batting practice at Chávez Ravine. He leaned forward, touching nothing, anxious to absorb as much as he could on his own before the cops kicked him out.

Amoyo's palms had long cuts from the fingers to the wrists and in the carpet around his torso were markings in blood, too deliberate to be splatter. Wayne turned his head, seeing them as Amoyo would. There was something that looked like a lowercase *y*, and near it, an uppercase *N*. Around each letter were small dark ovals of blood. Six or seven smudges around the *y* and three or four around the *N*.

N *for Nada?* North? Y *for what?*

Wayne heard footsteps and hacking and the *ding* of an approaching elevator down the hall. He had only minutes before the police would come and shoo him away.

Yes, it came to him shortly. Y *for yes.* N *for no.*

He glanced again at the bruise on Amoyo's neck and a story came to him at once. The attacker had stabbed Amoyo. Beaten him. Stepped or leaned on his larynx so he couldn't scream.

But still, he had interrogated him.

The killer had written the letters in the white carpet with his victim's blood and then David had pointed to them. Y for *yes,* N for *no.*

Wayne stood up and took a step backward. Widening his field of vision, he saw more letters at an arm's radius from David's shoulder. What could he have been telling his killer? What did he know?

These letters were harder to make out—all different sizes and some pressed together and smudged. But he didn't find just letters. Wayne could make out words.

PLEASE said one. *DONT* said another. Wayne wondered if they were supposed to go together. *Please. Don't.*

Sirens from a distance.

Amoyo had written something else.

CNIO8CO.

Wayne tried to imagine what that could be. *A license plate? A computer password?* As the sirens grew louder, he tried to translate it into a real word, something he could decipher.

CNIO8CO.

What could Amoyo have known that would be worth torturing and killing him for?

CHIO8CO.

Something about Nada.

CHIOACO.

About where she might have gone?

CHIGACO.

Oh hell.

Wayne took a step backward toward the door. He needed to get the cops to listen. He needed to tell them everything. It would be uncomfortable. They would be suspicious of his story. But Wayne had to keep a clear head. The police would need to move quickly. *David Amoyo was a coward and now whoever did this is on his way to—*

The smooth sole of his clunky right shoe slipped out from under him and his big ass hit the floor with a sound like a gong, reverberating in Amoyo's lamps and his flat-panel television and in glass all around. Wayne put his hand down and felt something wet, and then with a horrible sensation he held up his palm. *Blood.*

He stood up, carefully this time, and looked with horror at the red stain on the carpet that had now been transferred to the seat of his pants.

Sirens closer now.

He took a breath. This would be bad, but he could explain it. The cops would be unhappy, but he had information that could help them. David Amoyo's killer, and Bea Beaujon's, too, was really after Canada Gold.

As he waited, he looked at the body again. There was an object he hadn't seen before. A knife. A long, folding knife.

It looked like Wayne's knife.

He patted the front of his pants, spreading Amoyo's blood to the fabric. His knife wasn't there. Had it fallen out when he knelt over the body?

Had he even been carrying it today? He couldn't remember the last time he'd used it.

When he slipped, hadn't he felt something hard under his foot? Maybe he had slipped on the knife. Maybe it had been there all along. Maybe it was just a knife that looked like his. Or maybe somebody had taken it from his desk. If it was his knife—whether it had slipped out of his pocket or been stolen from his office and planted in this apartment— it had his fingerprints and Amoyo's blood all over it.

"Once the cops have reason to suspect you, they never unsuspect you," Peter had once told him. And when Wayne considered what would turn up in even a cursory search of his desk and computer, waves of panic radiated out to his fingers and toes.

Wayne scooped up the bloody knife and was at the elevator in steps, pressing the button a dozen futile times, in the process transferring more blood and fingerprints, which he tried to wipe off. Two cars arrived simultaneously, and as he leapt onto one, Hoover's replacement, the kid from maintenance, stepped off the other. Wayne supposed Hoover had sent the kid to check on him.

Downstairs, Hoover had a handkerchief in one hand and was wiping his chin. Wayne pushed against the revolving door and mumbled, "Getting something from my car. Be right back," and Hoover opened his mouth to protest but couldn't say anything before Wayne was gone.

As he rushed to his car, Wayne tried to make himself small, holding the Mustang's remote close to his hip. He just had to get out of this parking lot. He had to get out of the lot and then decide what to do next.

Wayne dived behind the wheel, wincing as he turned the ignition. He rolled calmly onto Fifth Street just as three police cruisers pulled into the lot in a line.

Amoyo had been killed and tortured in his living room. The Beaujons had met the same fate in their bedroom. A bloody knife in Wayne's pocket, his bloody ass print on Amoyo's carpet. His bloody fingerprints everywhere, and now all over his car, as well.

He couldn't go home. Couldn't go to work. His arms were numb, his face hot with fear.

Wayne glanced at his quarter-full gas tank. He knew where he had to go next, and this car couldn't take him there.

30

"THE THING that made him a freak is what made him a genius. The same thing. Genetics. Or maybe it's chemical. Or maybe his oversize skull put pressure on parts of the brain. Anyway, when it happens to most people, it just makes them retarded."

The guy who said this was standing across the room from Nada, who had her back to the south end of the long bar. Like his date, he was over-dressed, wearing a suit with thin stripes, a paisley-patterned thrift store tie, and newly polished shoes. Before she met Jameson, the only guys Nada knew who still even wore shoes that needed polishing were lawyers or musicians. This guy was neither. The date, who was barely listening, was wearing tight blue jeans and a tighter white top. Layers of blond hair reached the zippered pocket of a tiny black backpack, which hung on long, thin straps, like a daddy longlegs clinging to her shoulders. She had small breasts and her thin arms had bony bulges at the elbow and wrist, like Tinkertoys.

The bar was hot and loud, the heat intensified and the noise amplified by the weird configuration of the room. Darcy's was on the North Side, across the el tracks from an allegedly straight-friendly lesbian joint called the Bar and Grrl, in a neighborhood with high-rent shotgun apartments and low-rent attic-space theaters. The room's tin ceiling was very high— probably four stories—and there was a narrow horseshoe balcony about halfway up, with the open end closest to the stage. A small bar served the balcony, which might have held seventy-five people, while the downstairs was dominated by a larger, more traditional bar, perpendicular to the stage, from which Nada scanned the room. Ventilation was poor, a fact testified to by the unchanging bolus of smoke that hung, in defiance of city ordinances, a few feet above everyone's heads. Nada wondered if it had been there since before the smoking ban. Despite the occasional pre-sumed fire inspection, there was only one obvious entrance or exit, a door currently fortified by an elite squad of bouncers who spoke almost exclu-sively to the tiny bugs in their ears.

The bouncers reminded her of Wayne.

Thinking about Wayne made her ribs hurt because Wayne loved her so much. What she felt for him was more complicated than love, a gray area of affection and annoyance and tenderness and, for a few nights, even passion. What was the difference between that and love? Was it only his size? She had asked herself that in the days since their first night together. Was she really so bothered that he was so much bigger than she was, bothered by the not entirely unattractive amalgam of muscle and fat that he carried with, she had to admit, a surprising amount of grace? If Wayne were a normal size, would she like him more? Would she love him?

Or was it just that she found it possible to imagine a life without him?

The buzz of conversation took a dip with the lights and a moment later the hush was splintered by cheers when a guitarist, a bassist, and a drummer walked onstage, heads down, coolly oblivious to the affection all around. A pair of female violinists joined them, as well as a trio of backup singers. After a beat, a big ball of a man walked out to another roar, also unacknowledged, but less self-consciously. Burning Patrick was large, larger than Wayne (maybe not taller, but at least heavier), and he was wearing a ripped black parka, even in the heat, and a dirty green backpack. He gripped a wire-bound notebook tightly with both hands, the way you might hold a steering wheel in mid-skid. His dilated eyes were unfocused and independent of each other, the result of a detached retina. He approached the microphone and began to sing without preamble, and the band tried to catch up to him with a rushed intro.

A few dozen fans of the Bat Wing Vortex had taken positions on the floor in front of the stage and even through the opening acts had sat cross-legged in circles, drinking bottled water or beer. When the band appeared, they jumped to their feet and started yelling, and when the Bat Wing Vortex began playing, they started moshing, some spinning in great repeated leaps, carelessly throwing their fists and elbows in all directions. Others preferred a charging style, running toward the tightly packed group and then hurling themselves backward into the spinners. With every new assault, a few kids were thrown to the ground, but they were up again in a second, as unaffected by their bruises as the band seemed to be by their presence.

Burning Patrick stood very close to the microphone and in a barely intelligible but not entirely tuneless voice started shouting as much as singing:

Sex is money! Sex is bank!
Sex for dollars, pounds and francs!
Sex for savings, your college fund stash!
Fuck me thirty days same as cash!

Nada had to angle herself to a position from where she could watch his lips move above the notebook and mike—it was the only way she could understand what he was saying. The violinists seemed to be playing a tune of some sort, but the other musicians obscured those efforts with a dense wall of reverb and noise. *This is Jameson's genius?*

Nada wasn't a music snob like her father. In fact, classical music was too distracting for her. There was too much depth to it. Too many layers. Too many strings, too many valves. What was that famous line—"too many notes"? Too much to notice. Solomon Gold had always taught her that music was part of the Unity, one of the delicate strands that connect everyone to the One, her father's uncaring God. He once told her that music—some perfect composition—could one day make those transparent bonds visible. Music was the common language of mankind and the One, the only thing man and God experienced exactly the same way, which was why he didn't pray. Music was the only thing man could share directly with God, he said.

Whatever. When she listened to music for pleasure, which wasn't often, she listened almost exclusively to three-chord rock and dumb pop songs—the dumber and catchier and more repetitive, the better. She liked music she could understand at first listen. Nothing that wouldn't leave her head when she wanted it to go away. Nevertheless, she liked melody, which seemed to be an object of scorn for the Bat Wing Vortex. The whole enterprise seemed a cruel joke at melody's expense.

She tuned out the stage and began walking the room, hoping to drop in on an informed conversation. Band girlfriends or maybe coconspirators. The computer geek who mapped out Burning Patrick's mural and who spit out the template for each tile. The art dealer who conceived the fraud. She picked up little except gossip and odd theories concerning Patrick Blackburn's alleged genius.

"The mental illness is an act. He has an M.B.A. from Northwestern."

"He can start a Toyota car engine just by touching the hood."

"Ronnie says he's gay but that the gays won't claim him 'cause he's fat."

There was something off about the crowd, she realized as she weaved through it. Next to the stairs was a cluster of unshaven, unshowered men in long, tattered coats—perhaps acquaintances of Blackburn from his days on the street. There was another bunch, this one of too many beautiful women huddled around too few ordinary men. Nada recognized one of the males as a modestly famous sitcom actor who seemed to have made it his goal to be seen at this show. She spotted an older man, black and built like a bowling pin on its head, with a barrel chest and skinny legs and these big ugly feet shoved into old sandals. The hundred or so closest to the stage seemed about right—between twenty-one and twenty-five, mostly male, mostly earringed, comprehensively tattooed. A handful of men and at least one woman, not apparently together, stood along the back wall, looking like they knew they were too old for the club. They had uncomfortable postures and their attempts at casual dress were undermined by tucks in their shirts, parts in their hair, and creases in their pants. Nada studied them, her back to the stage, for two entire songs. They did not sway or tap or nod or dance or spin. They seemed transfixed by Blackburn's presence.

She wondered if these were Burning Patrick collectors, Jameson's rivals for the precious tiles. Perhaps they were each here independently on the same mission as she was—to find out if Burning Patrick was for real.

They wouldn't find out from the back of the room, and neither would Nada, who had been to enough rock shows and made out with enough guitar players to know how to improve her seat.

She pushed her way back up front and assessed the men onstage one at a time. The drummer had a wedding ring. The guitar player had a photo taped to the back of his ax. It might have been a girlfriend or it might have been a daughter—Nada wasn't close enough to see—but either one was a deal killer. She slid over and squared herself with the bass player, looking into his eyes, never letting her irises leave his, and when he moved onstage, she moved with him. He noticed her almost immediately and, song after song, Nada caught him sneaking glances at her, tracking her position. He nodded. She didn't reciprocate. She never smiled. She just never took her eyes off him.

When they broke at the end of the first set, the bassist tried to make her react with a wink, but she refused, only staring, staring, staring. He laughed and turned to walk offstage, but he looked back at her, which was all the confirmation Nada needed.

31

ON SEVERAL OCCASIONS, Wayne had pushed the eight cylinders of his Mustang past one hundred miles per hour over this stretch of I-15. Now he edged his powerful car through the desert at barely half that, an excruciating slow-motion getaway. Getting pulled over now would mean something a lot worse than a ticket.

He had panicked. Eventually, they would piece things together back in Amoyo's apartment. Old Hoover wouldn't remember how many minutes Wayne had been in the apartment, but he would remember Wayne's name, or at least his Colossus badge, and some tech would compare the fingerprints in the apartment with the ones in his HR file, and that same file had this car and license plate registered for his employee parking tag. It wouldn't be long before the NHP was looking specifically for red Mustangs, which weren't known for their stealth. They would find him covered in the victim's blood and still carrying the knife that helped torture Amoyo.

The hours were going to rat him out for sure.

In his wallet, he had about sixty dollars in cash. "Once you're on the run, you can never use your credit or ATM cards," Peter once said during one of his unsolicited tutorials on disappearing. "Not even once. Cut 'em up. Even if they haven't frozen your accounts yet, credit cards will tip them to your direction. They can narrow the search. Concentrate their resources. It's just about the worst mistake you can make."

Cars carrying people with far less on their minds passed him on the left. Wayne used to smile over the difference between cars leaving Vegas and cars headed for it. The same with planes landing at McCarran and planes departing. People on the way to Las Vegas were all kinetic anticipation, their wallets and suitcases filled with cash and condoms and multiple bathing suits and e-mailed spa appointments and paperback books and high hopes. All this in contrast to the tourists leaving the city, tanned and tired and beaten up good by the slots and the dice and the cards, making the return trip home from Sin City, dreading their depleted bank statements and their first, endless hours back in the office. Wayne saw it every day in the lobby of the Colossus—Peter once joked that an optimist is a person checking into a Vegas hotel and a pessimist is a person checking out.

Wayne was certainly driving in the pessimist lane now. Things were bad and they were going to get worse.

Across the median, a state cop on a motorcycle was headed in the other direction. Glancing in the rearview, Wayne saw brake lights. *Shit.* Were they looking for him already?

A road sign marked twenty miles to the town of Tornillo. He had been there once for a high school football game. *The Tornillo Bulldogs.* He didn't know the geography of the place, barely remembered what the field looked like, but he knew the town because he'd grown up in a border town just like it. Ten to fifteen thousand people settled along a river. Used to be a farming village. Gambling arrived to serve day-trippers from Arizona. Now the town fed off a single casino along the interstate, an enterprise that supplied the town with paychecks, only to have the slots suck all that money back in.

He drove toward the exit with one eye on the rearview, his right foot gently pushing the accelerator past the legal limit. He didn't really know if they were after him yet, but it felt like seconds counted. The mile markers rolled past him in slow motion.

Finally, down the ramp, an old-fashioned sign for the Tornillo Blue Chip Casino begging visitors to stop for the "Hottest Slots East of Vegas." Even small casinos were oases of anonymity, and he needed to disappear quick. "You don't want to just abandon your car on the side of the road," Peter had told him. "That's giving them a clue. A direction. Even setting it on fire to get rid of evidence is a bad idea because it attracts the authorities. If you can, leave it in a bad neighborhood. With the keys in it. Let someone else strip it or drive it away, hopefully in a direction away from you."

Wayne didn't know if Tornillo was big enough to have a neighborhood constantly patrolled by car thieves. In Wayne's hometown, hardly anyone locked their doors, and you could leave car keys in the ignition for a month without anyone noticing.

He figured Tornillo was small enough to employ only a handful of cops, though.

It was coming up on dusk and he maneuvered toward the lights of downtown, really a long four-lane strip of hotels, restaurants, car dealers, and fast-food joints. Fed by the Virgin River, trees and shrubs and grass decorated the roadside, and all around were the red hills of the desert. At a stoplight, cars were overloaded with teens, boys at the wheel, girls in the passenger seats, painted toes out the window. He remembered summer nights just like this, cruising up and down the streets, asking bored girls if they wanted a ride to no place just so you could spend a few minutes sitting next to them. His gearhead friends would pass all day fixing up their cars, installing the loudest speakers, the plushest interiors, the freshest paint.

Wayne's best fortunes with women had not been in high school, but college. Football had made available a class of women that he otherwise would have had no chance with. Good looks are currency for the young and unattached, and there were women on campus who were willing to spend it. To "trade up." Dating a football player meant joining the most exclusive sorority on campus. It meant being envied and talked about. It meant good parties. It meant hanging out with the temporarily famous.

Some girls had been mercenary. They were often the ones who knew football best, who studied it and even, like sports magazines, ranked the prospects and determined which players had a shot at an NFL career. The best of them were clever. They didn't look twice at the quarterbacks—there were only a couple dozen starting quarterbacks in the pros and the competition for their affection was fierce. A pro quarterback was much more likely to leave his college sweetheart for this actress or that country singer. Smart girls played the odds. Linemen. Offensive linemen, defensive linemen. Big men, even *fat* men, whom the other girls ignored. Those boys were easier to get, easier to please, easier to hold on to, and they were an even better ticket to a glamorous postgraduate life.

The longest relationship Wayne had ever had was his five-semester one with Evelyn Burdett. She was impossibly cute, with short, layered brown hair and a tiny athletic body, even though her exercise was limited to a mostly social version of Pilates. She was so small, smaller even than Nada, that they became something like campus celebrities. The cartoonist at the school paper even created a pair of characters modeled after them—an enormous football lineman named Walt, whose body could hardly be contained in the strip's frame, and his demanding girlfriend, Stacey, whom Walt carried about campus under his arm like a football.

A knee injury and his rising moon weight deflated his pro stock senior year and Evelyn started thinking about a future without him. Many college romances fade around that time, and perhaps it was merely a coincidence that Evie's attentions began to disintegrate along with Wayne's ACL. Nevertheless, that was when he stopped believing he had a chance with the best-looking girl in the room. The best-looking girl in the room, in college or in Las Vegas, was always thinking about trading up.

Sitting at the stoplight, having fled his home and his job and his family in a panic, Wayne wondered what he had been thinking, chasing after a girl like Canada Gold, who was frequently, at least to his eyes, the best-looking girl in the room.

He followed the teenagers another mile down the strip and watched them turn into the large, empty parking lot of a chain grocery store. Sitting on the hoods of half a dozen old cars were all the kids Wayne knew from his own high school days—the gearheads and the bad girls and the bored girls—stuck in a town built to entertain people older than they were. One kid was changing his oil. Another, who had a mustache and a muscle shirt, was waving a broken radio antenna, chasing a giggling pony-tailed girl around an old green Impala.

Wayne parked a nonthreatening distance away, across thirty or so faded diagonal parking lines. He grabbed the entire contents of the glove compartment and stepped out of the car. He opened the trunk to see if it contained anything useful or incriminating. A baseball cap and glove and bat from a softball game several months ago. "You have to change everything," Peter had said. "If you always eat Arby's, stop eating Arby's. If you don't have a beard, grow one. If you have a beard, shave it. If you never wear hats, start wearing them."

He put on the cap but ignored the bat, which could be useful but also menacing. Then he backed away from his beloved Mustang, driver's door open, car running. When he knew the kids were watching, he threw up his hands and backed away slowly, into the darkness, under the overpass, toward the highway.

32

BOBBY'S FINGERS were cramped into talons and it felt like the seat of the ancient copper-colored Caprice with the muni plates had grown a malicious knuckle just to press it into his back. He'd started a cigarette south of Madison Street, finally admitting to himself that he'd never really quit in the first place. Cigarettes and he just needed a little time away from each other and now he discovered that making up with them was one of the most intensely pleasurable things he had ever done. Out of the corner of his eye he watched the enabler of his habit pull on her niche-brand Camel from a hot-pink pack, and as her smoke kissed his in the air between them he wondered if any decision concerning this evening's sleeping arrangements had already been made in her head.

"Sorry about the car."

"Yeah, it is kind of *coppy*," she said, picking up the mouthpiece to the nonfunctioning old radio that a force-employed mechanic hadn't yet uninstalled from the dash. The car had no air-conditioning and the wet night air was north of eighty degrees. He could feel the sweat pooling uncomfortably between his back and the vinyl seat.

"My ex-wife has my truck. Her car needs brakes and she has to get the kids to school and practice and lessons. Of course she has it for only ten minutes before she calls to complain that the battery light is going on and off."

Della made it right with a smile.

They were headed to see this Burning Patrick guy play up in Lakeview. Bobby wore blue jeans and a tight blue golf shirt that properly displayed the topography of an upper body he had forged in the gym with a dabble of protein supplements. Bobby liked to take the streets, even though there was probably a quicker route from downtown on the Kennedy or Lake Shore Drive. Highways were for troopers. Streets were for cops.

Bobby liked being alone with her and he was in no hurry to get to the bar. He tapped the brakes at yellow lights instead of gunning through them. As a result, he and Della were more than an hour late and trapped at an endless red on Halsted when the lights went out with a long sigh, the blackout traveling north block by block—Armitage, Dickens, Webster, Belden. A loud groan passed through the windows of a line of DePaul bars, and a cheer washed over the rooftops to the east, from somewhere around Oz Park.

"Oh *shit*," Kloska said. The street ahead was black, with only headlights and car batteries to illuminate it. "You want to turn around?"

Della shook her head. "No way. Lights might come back on. And they might have power farther up north. It's probably one of those rolling blackouts."

He loved that she was always game. The cop part of Kloska wanted to press ahead through the darkness. To stay on unofficial patrol. To dare the bad guys to use the city's misfortune as their cover. Of course, within seconds of the lights powering down on either side of the road, the noncop part of him was already thinking about blackout sex, which he just now realized he had never had.

After long consideration he had chosen Gilbert and Sullivan to play in the car, not because he cared for it, but because he'd heard a lot of college kids did. Now Bobby felt especially ridiculous navigating through the dark with *The Mikado* playing through the police department's cheap speakers.

> *Our great Mikado, virtuous man,*
> *When he to rule our land began,*
> *Resolved to try*
> *A plan whereby*
> *Young men might best be steadied.*
> *So he decreed, in words succinct,*
> *That all who flirted, leered or winked*
> *(Unless connubially linked),*
> *Should forthwith be beheaded . . .*

He turned the volume low and they advanced slowly, the dark pierced by flashes of Della's cigarette and the silence interrupted by her silly jokes and law firm gossip.

With lights out and heavy traffic, it took them another hour to get even within the neighborhood of the club, where Kloska parked his ticketproof Caprice in a yellow zone under the el. It was all black up here, too, and when he caught a glimpse of the buildings downtown, he saw their shapes were ghosted by backup generators powering emergency hall lights. A brighter glow formed a halo around the skyline farther south, which led Kloska to think they still had juice on the other side of the Congress Expressway. It gave him hope his own condo was still lit.

And maybe a good excuse for a North Sider like Della Dickey to come spend the night down south of Roosevelt.

In front of the club, hundreds of people were packed so densely together that the last line of them had trouble keeping their toes on the curb. Others had started using parked cars as benches. Some remained just inside the door, demanding refunds for a half-finished show. Young people spilled into the street, plastic cups of beer in their hands, assuming, perhaps correctly, that the least of the city's laws had been suspended for the blackout. Dozens of tattooed and provocatively dressed kids, weaving between the headlights of crawling cars, looked underage to Kloska, although it had been a long time since he'd been able to consistently tell the often critical difference between a girl who was seventeen and a woman who was twenty-two.

A white van pulled in front of the main doors, displacing a dozen loiterers and fans and causing an enthused commotion. Kloska watched a hulk of a man, head down in a black parka—*a parka in this heat!*—straight-arm his way to the passenger seat.

"That's Burning Patrick!" Della clenched Bobby's arm with surprised delight and Kloska wished, not for the first time, that he had used even a fraction of the idle time of his youth to learn to play the guitar. Even a glimpse of this mope was disgusting—fat, hairy, and ungroomed, the distant sight of him almost giving up an odor—and yet the look on Della's face and on the faces of fans Burning Patrick had indifferently manhandled on the way to his ride was undeniably worshipful.

For the first time, Bobby let his thumb graze the back of Della's hand, and with her long nails she stroked the face of it lightly in reply.

They pressed forward, Della anxious to get a more intimate look at the man. Another guy, apparently also a musician—based on the similar, if more muted, reaction—led a young woman through the same gauntlet from bar to car.

"Omigod," Della said.

"Huh?"

"I think that was Canada Gold."

The girl was gone, having disappeared into the windowless back of the van, which was in gear now and inching forward.

"There's no way."

"I don't know. I think so." Della looked Bobby in the eyes.

"Would you even know what she looked like?" he asked.

Della nodded and then shook her head and then nodded again. "I studied the Gold case before I even went to work for Reggie. And I've handled a lot of Solomon Gold crap since, as a favor. Media requests and foundation paperwork and stuff. I've never met her, but I've seen a lot of pictures. That sure looked like her."

Bobby bit his lip. "You just got Solomon Gold on the brain."

"Okay. Probably," Della agreed. "But what if it *was* her? What does that mean?"

What *did* it mean? If he knew why Canada Gold was hanging out with another former patient of Marlena Falcone, the answer would probably connect a lot of his dots.

"It means she's not dead," Bobby said, adding quickly, "which is good."

33

SATURDAY, JULY 31

NADA WOKE the next morning on a strange and damp mattress with a hangover on top of a headache that wouldn't go away. She frisked herself, hand-checking her blouse and jeans, which seemed attached to her body much the same way they had been the night before. Nada knew she would notice had there been any attempt to re-dress her. Her body felt unmolested except for her brain, which was using the right side of her skull as a gong, and her stomach, which felt at sea.

She hadn't had *that* much wine, had she?

It was still hot, and from the dead silence—no televisions or radios or electrical hums of any kind—she determined the power was still out. From the inside, her ears rang an irritating and painful *natural C*. She closed her eyes and tried to remember where she might be.

The Bat Wing Vortex. I'm at Burning Patrick's house.

She opened her eyes. The sheets smelled like candles and nicotine, a scent that nearly provoked a rebellion from her gut. She sat up. The walls were painted red and black and yellow. The ceiling was shellacked with a collage of torn pages from magazines and newspapers—refugees in Africa, fires in California, CEOs headed for prison, distant galaxies photographed from space telescopes, topless women. She sat up.

Burning Patrick was watching her from a chair. "Good dawning," he said, holding a lit cigarette near his face. His words lacked perfect elocution. In fact, they should have been impossible to understand. When her spider replayed the noise that came from his mouth, it sounded more like a creaking door than words. As she had first discovered when he was onstage the previous night, his lips opened and closed in slow, exaggerated motions that were easy to read, if not to make sense of.

Nada wasn't sure whether to be angry, so she said nothing.

"I slept here," Burning Patrick said. "In this chair. It's all right. I do it sometimes even when I don't have"—he paused—"*visitants.*"

She didn't want to thank him for not raping her. "When was the last time you washed your sheets?"

"Never," he said, then as a polite afterthought, he added, "Brian does. Sometimes. When he *cogitates* on it."

"I should go," Nada said, hoping her shoes were nearby.

"You haven't yet seen my *atelier.*"

"*What?*" Nada wondered if now he was making some crude advance.

He laughed. "My studio."

She had forgotten that she had come here with a purpose and not just followed a bass player home after a gig, something she had done more than once in her life.

Burning Patrick stood. He was wearing the same bear-like costume he'd worn at the show—oversize and tattered, black and wrinkled. As he struggled to his feet, in pain and out of breath, Nada caught a glimpse of hairy fat between his untucked T-shirt and his unbelted jeans. His backpack was still attached to his shoulders. He walked out the door.

"Wait!" Nada said. She was on her feet, putting down a revolt in her throat. She felt around for her shoes, found one with her hands and then the other, and chased after him barefoot into the hall, which was empty.

The seduction of Jude, the Bat Wing Vortex's bassist, the night before had been effortless, or it would have been if Canada had had any intention of actually following through. When the power went out, everyone began shuffling about, spinning in confusion, lighting each other's faces with opened cell phones. The little squares of light turned throughout the club, as if stirred by a giant unseen spoon. Nada stood her ground. After ten minutes, Jude stepped out onstage and shouted that the show was over and people should go home. Amid the boos, he found her with his narrow brown eyes and extended a long arm and a calloused hand and helped her onto the stage.

Nada said almost nothing, only smiled and nodded and listened, and yet she received a series of invitations—backstage, into their van, and up to a darkened Ethiopian restaurant in Edgewater that was somehow still serving, then to a hot dog stand called Weasel Pup that was practically giving away salty chips and pop in the heat. At every stop, Burning Patrick was greeted by fans celebrating in the darkness, and he answered each by reaching out with his left hand and pulling down on the fan's right ear, sometimes gently and sometimes hard. Those who couldn't get close enough to him tugged their own ears in salute. He didn't speak to Nada directly, but she caught him staring at her over and over again. Every time he waited a beat and then looked away, unembarrassed.

Eventually, she accepted a ride in a van packed with musicians and instruments to the house the band shared on Ravenswood, just off Lincoln Avenue.

It was a typical North Side house, wood-shingled and one room wide, three rooms deep, and four stories tall. From the ghostly outlines of old mailboxes in the front entranceway, it had probably been built as a single-family home and then converted to apartments and then rehabbed back again, according to real estate market whims.

Jude opened windows and lit candles and went to find some red wine. The drummer and guitar player were unloading the van, leaving Nada alone with Burning Patrick for a minute or more. They stared at each other in dim, comfortable silence. Nada, who had barely spoken the entire evening, never felt like she needed to engage him.

Jude returned with a bottle and three glasses and sat down close to Nada. As he did, Burning Patrick mumbled, "Go to bed, Jude."

The bassist tried to engineer what had happened in his absence—how he had lost his place, what had happened to his sure thing. "What are you talking about, Pat?"

"She was never . . . *seeking* you."

Nada felt a chill as he said it, because it sounded ominous and cruel and even threatening in that otherworldly impediment of the artist's, but also because it was true.

"Pat—"

"Retire now."

"What are you going to do, Patrick?"

"Go to bed."

Jude looked at Nada. "I can drive you home, if you want."

Nada shook her head. "I'll be okay."

Jude disappeared up a creaking set of stairs Nada couldn't see. Patrick let Nada pour herself a glass of wine, and then he took the bottle and curled up with it in his chair, not drinking from it, but cradling it, fondling it like a blind man afraid of misplacing his cane. After a long time he said, "Are you to call on your mother?"

"What?"

Lips moving without noise: *Have you been to see your mother?*

She shivered. "What are you talking about?"

He changed the subject, speaking now to her as if for the first time, like he'd forgotten the odd, inappropriate question he'd just asked. Maybe he had. Or maybe Nada had just imagined he'd asked it. "You've come to see me paint."

"Yes."

"I know who you are."

She swallowed. "Who am I?"

"We have something in common," he said. "Or we did. Once."

"What's that?" she asked.

Patrick rubbed his eyes and then smacked himself hard on the back of the head, once, twice, three times, a fourth. He sniffed the neck of the bottle but still didn't put it to his mouth. "I followed your father closely." Patrick said something else she couldn't understand because his face was turned into the shadows between his coat and the wing of his chair, muffling his voice and hiding his lips.

In a few minutes, he was asleep.

Nada gently removed the bottle from his hands and set it on the coffee table, already inscribed with the ghostly rings of old bottles and glasses, and walked through the first floor of the home. A dining room with a pool table. A dirty kitchen that smelled of curry. A small TV room that smelled like pot and patchouli. Eclectic furniture, as if merged from several different apartments. Eccentric colors on the walls. Lots of posters for Asian films and European bands. Garbage overflowed from trash cans.

I know who you are. Somewhere in her head Nada acknowledged that she had a certain amount of minor fame—from her father, from her card playing—but she was recognized almost never, especially outside of Las Vegas, so she could be in denial about it most of the time.

She considered going upstairs to look around, but *going upstairs,* even as a spy, was an intimate gesture. Nada didn't want Jude to interpret it as an invitation. She could call a cab, but then the evening's observations would have added to naught.

She was getting paid for this investigation, after all.

Back in the living room (or front room or parlor or whatever it must have been called back when this old house had been built), Burning Patrick struggled to breathe through a staccato snore. Nada tucked herself into a ball on the couch, finished her wine, and, with a switch of her toggle, fell into a sweaty sleep.

Now in the hall outside his bedroom, she wondered, *Did Patrick carry me up the stairs to his room? Did he watch me sleep all night?*

The wall to her right looked as if it had been untouched since the 1920s. Green paint peeled in places wallpaper didn't. Baseboards abused by dogs. Old molding warped into arcs pulled long, thin nails from the plaster.

The opposite wall was covered by a mural. Dark and ominous tsunamis of black and red and brown and orange paint started in stripes by the stairs and built, layer upon layer, spilling into a violent collision across Burning Patrick's door. Nada walked along the opposite side, the Victorian side, the better to see it, but also almost afraid to get too close.

"Up here," came his voice.

She found stairs behind a closed door and climbed the painted wooden steps to the large attic, emerging into a surprising explosion of light. It was by far the sunniest room in the home, thanks to six large sky-lights cut into the roof. It was also the hottest, nearly as hot as outside. Burning Patrick squatted over a page of newspaper, his back to Nada, four inches of ass crack visible to her. Not only bright, the room was unclut-tered. The floorboards were whitewashed. There were no chairs, no tables. Opened cans and jars with tears of paint spilling down their labels stood along one wall. Brushes of all kinds hung on a freestanding Peg-Board. A chest—a toy box almost—was filled with sponges and wire and other objects, dabbled with color. A ventilation fan was frozen impotently overhead. On the opposite wall, boxes and boxes of tile—in seconds, she counted eighty-seven—were stacked, many of them opened.

She approached him from behind and he stopped her, holding up a hand. She now saw three open cans of paint and a cardboard box for a mixing palette on the floor, a brush in his hand. His arm barely moved, dripping and dabbing and stroking paint onto a tile between his feet.

He made a noise that sounded like *Wait.*

When he was done, he stood and stared down at the tile, as if it were changing while he watched it, as if his mind could will the smallest adjustments without lowering his brush, which dripped forest green paint onto a newspaper opened on the floor. Two minutes, three minutes, four. In the silence, the ringing in her head took on volume. An interested gull landed on the skylight and watched from above. Patrick stepped away and over to a window that looked out onto the street and jerked his hand, indi-cating he wanted her to join him. "Look," he said, pointing.

Across the street were three homes, two bungalows on either side of a house almost identical to his own. "What?" she asked.

"Thirty-four fourteen North Ravenswood," he said, indicating the twin directly across the way.

"What about it."

"June tenth, 1980, Ted Kaczynski mailed a bomb to United Airlines."

"The Unabomber," Nada said.

"On the package—on the *return to address*—he wrote Thirty-four fourteen North Ravenswood, Chicago, Illinois six oh six five seven."

"Kaczynski used to live across the street?"

Patrick shook his head. "He grew up South Side. So all the time I want to know, Why Thirty-four fourteen North Ravenswood? Did that number just *pop* into his head? Was it random? Was it meaningful? I sit here and look at Thirty-four fourteen North Ravenswood and I wait for something to happen. As long as it doesn't, I paint." He cackled, like a child. "His brother turned him in. The Unabomber. How terrible to find your brother kills."

"Or your father." Nada put some sting in her voice in case he was taunting her.

Patrick put his head against the glass. "Fathers are never who they seem to be. A mother with a secret is the scariest thing of all."

"My mother can keep all the secrets she wants, as far as I'm concerned," Nada said. She wasn't yet used to the rhythm of the conversation—which information was relevant, which wasn't.

"I wasn't *always* Coca-Cola," he said turning around, his head bobbing.

"Always what?"

He laughed again and his eyes, or one of them anyway, drifted south and he stared at Nada's chest until she became uncomfortable and bothered, and then he pointed a finger and advanced it toward her. She was scared, but she didn't move. The tip of his finger met her collarbone and he pressed it there, hard and hurtful.

And suddenly she knew.

"The spider," she whispered. "You have a spider. Like mine."

He removed his finger and touched his own collarbone and then spread his long fingers, like wires that crept up his neck and across his face and gathered up his hair and then clutched the top of his skull.

"I used to," he said.

"It made some people crazy," she said, unafraid of offending him. "There was a recall. They took yours out."

He backed away, stopping over the tile he had just painted. "Can you still see it?"

"See what?"

He shook his hands at the tile and then raised them above his head. He had a big yellow-toothed grin that seemed unconnected to their conversation. "It! Everything!"

"I don't know what you mean." She added, "I'm sorry."

He studied her, still grinning, and then bent over the tile again, like he was about to shit on it. *Like a bear shitting in the woods,* she thought.

He lifted the tile from the newspaper and brought it to her on his fingertips. "I miss it," he said. Then he reached deep into a torn pocket of his parka and produced a heavy, unruly set of keys, four or five full key chains all linked together. "You drive."

Nada's car was still in a lot by the bar, or it would be if the predatory trucks of North Side Towing, a virtual private police force once much despised by her father, hadn't yet circled it. She followed him down through the empty house to the band's van in the leaning garage and tried to follow the directions he mumbled to her, which was difficult because, eyes on the road, sitting next to him on the bench seat, she couldn't get a straight look at his lips. She adjusted the rearview so she could see his face and tried to compensate for the reverse image of his mouth flap.

The mercy? Diversity? Diversey.

Right on Diversey and then a long, silent drive, the tile balanced on his knee, thirty blocks or more until he stopped her with a grunt and pointed to a large warehouse parking lot. She stopped at the locked gate and Patrick leaned over her lap to undo a key dangling from the ignition. He smelled like tar and he labored to breathe, producing a wheezing sound that caused her to imagine his parka as being like a portable iron lung.

The padlock undone, they drove to the building, to a door Patrick singled out with a series of waves. On the brick Nada saw the ghosted outlines of a long-ago sign reading MARSHALL FIELD. Some of Nada's good memories of her mother involved Christmastime at that department store—elaborate window decorations, Sunday brunch under the big tree.

Another key, and then they walked through a door and into a massive space, forty feet high and nearly a block long on every side. Patrick paced the room, staring at the floor and occasionally looking up to get his bearings. Nada followed steps behind, falling off balance every time he reversed direction. Guided by some internal sextant, he at last found the spot and set the tile on the floor and gestured for her to follow.

Up a set of open aluminum stairs to a small office where some fore-man once monitored the trucks and forklifts and long stacks of merchan-dise. He pointed. *"See it."*

The tile was a speck on the concrete below, barely differentiated from the countless oil stains and sinkholes and pockmarks. "See what? The tile?"

He shook his head in a wide berth and spread his hands. "It!"

She understood. "The whole thing. The mural. You see it here. On the floor."

He nodded.

"You put one tile on the floor and you can see the whole thing. Where every tile fits and will fit."

He nodded. "Do you?"

She looked again. She did not. Burning Patrick nodded, disappointed. "I thought maybe you could still see it. I can only remember it." Nada was afraid he might cry, and then, studying his dirty, hairy, pinched face, she wasn't sure she'd be able to tell if he did.

"That's what you're painting. Something you saw when you had the spider."

"Everything I saw." It sounded like a correction.

They walked back down to the empty floor, to the tile he had painted that morning. He lifted it up and presented it to her again.

It's beautiful, she thought. A tiny head covered in hair like black wire. Hundreds of strands, each differentiated by subtle light and expert brush-work. Hair on edge, hair coarsened in anger, hardened in fear. *The hair of what?* In one corner were three beautifully scripted letters in lowercase: *a s s.* Patrick clearly liked to juxtapose the vulgar and the sublime.

"I can't," Nada said. "It's too valuable."

From inside his parka he produced the newspaper he'd been using to protect the floor of his studio and he slipped the newsprint between the tile and the palm of her hand.

34

SOMETHING ABOUT the configuration of bodies in the front and back seats told Wayne not to climb inside the old maroon Cadillac. A black guy and a white guy in the front seat. A white girl and a black guy in the back. *I'm not a racist,* he kept telling his exhausted, hallucinatory self, and he knew it was true. Still, something told him not to get in.

Except it was the only car that had stopped in hours, so Wayne thanked them and pushed the thumb button on the door handle.

"We got room," the girl said with a grin.

With some effort, Wayne wedged his sunburned, tired body into the backseat. The guy and the girl pressed themselves against the windows, forcing Wayne's large frame absurdly into the middle. "You look like hell," the black guy in the front seat said.

"I'm Ginny," the girl said. She looked about mid-twenties but could have been younger. She was tall and skinny. Wayne was carrying his wrinkled blazer—his phone and earpiece having been transferred to his pants pocket. He had tossed his tie and ID badge into the roadside brush. His black Colossus golf shirt—which he only now realized was a dead giveaway, one of those mistakes Peter would never forgive—was smudged with red clay handprints. His khakis and shoes were covered in dust and Amoyo's dried blood. He pulled his hat down over his eyes.

"And you stink," said the black guy in the backseat, who hadn't given his name. "That's all right, though. So does James." He laughed.

"What happened?" Ginny asked. She was wearing a sundress and had a lot of stuff in her blond hair—barrettes and plastic butterflies and toy jewels.

"Long story," Wayne said. He coughed.

The white guy in the front passenger seat laughed. "Oh yeah. I got those. I know all about long stories."

Wayne looked at his phone. As he'd squatted or walked along the road-side, backward and thumb out whenever he heard the distant sigh of an eastbound engine, his phone had buzzed him four times. Twice the screen identified the call as PETER'S CELL and once it said COLOSSUS HOT & CAS. The last time was a number he didn't recognize. PRIVATE CALLER the screen read.

"You know what makes me feel better when I have a bad day?" Ginny said, touching him on his sleeve, handing him a half-gone bottle of fla-vored water. Her eyes were glassy and unfocused. Wayne concentrated on the left one, which seemed to be looking at him. "That none of this mat-ters. The world. It's not real. It can't be real."

The car accelerated to sixty, seventy, eighty miles per hour. Wayne was still trying to guess how much the cops in Vegas knew about him. He

asked himself if it was too soon for some detective or tech to have compared the fingerprints at Amoyo's to the ones in his file. Or the DNA and
fibers and whatnot he'd left at Nada's, the blood when he'd nicked his
hand smashing her window. *Jesus.* "Could you slow down?"

The white guy up front said, "Are you scared? Of what? Crashing?
There's nothing to crash into for miles." He leaned into the back and
stared at Wayne from up close, then flopped back into the passenger seat.
"Don't worry. James is an excellent driver." He said it again: "Excellent
driver." He giggled. "What's that from? A movie."

"*Rain Man,*" said the driver.

"Yeah, that's right! *Rain Man!*" He slapped James on the arm. "I'm
going to call you Rain Man."

Without taking his eyes off the road, James said, "No, *you* would be
Rain Man."

"What?"

"Rain Man was the one who said 'I'm an excellent driver.'"

"I didn't say *I* was an excellent driver; I said *you* were an excellent
driver." Without warning, his head spasmed and he hit it accidentally
and hard against the window. "Fuck it. That's okay. I want to be Rain
Man."

They drove another ten minutes or so in silence, across the Arizona
state line. Wayne was nervous and wary, but every mile farther away from
Vegas brought relief. Rain Man twisted the rearview so he could see
Wayne's face. "What are you afraid of?"

"Cops," said the black guy in the backseat.

Rain Man and Ginny both gasped. "Is that right? Are you afraid of the
cops? You never did tell us where you were going. Maybe that's because
you're not going anywhere. You're running away, aren't you?" Rain Man
put his feet on the dashboard and tapped his knees. He jerked his head
around. "Is there a reward?"

"Nobody gives a shit about me." Wayne tried to sound convincing.

"Oh, I doubt that," Ginny said. "You know what I was just telling these
guys? Okay, life—it's like a video game. Nothing that happens in it really
matters. There aren't any true consequences for anything we do. But
when you're playing the game, you care about it very much, right? You
play like it's really life or death." She reached in her pocket and took out a
little round tin and opened it. There were half a dozen small pills inside,
red and black and green. "You know what these are? These are like little
cheat codes. They let you change the program. When things are really

sucking, you can't figure life out, these get you through." She reached up and stroked Wayne's cheek.

"Do you want to take one?" she asked him. "Do you need a cheat?"

He felt it sliding out, although he hadn't felt it enter. A dull pain in his side that became sharper as the blade was withdrawn. *What the hell?* He reached over with his left hand and felt something wet. When he brought it back in front of his face, the tips of two fingers were painted red, like he had stuck them in jam. Wayne's clothes were already damp with filth and sweat, but the blood that now leaked onto his shirt felt different. It felt thick and burned cool, like Bengay on an aching muscle.

"What the hell, Hale?" Ginny said.

Hale was holding a kitchen knife in his lap. The tip of it, about an inch and a half of blade, was dark and wet. Wayne grabbed the wrist holding the knife and the pain shot up and down his side. He elbowed Hale in the face, bloodying his nose. Hale hardly reacted, but he wouldn't let go of the knife.

Ginny screamed and Rain Man told her to calm down and then James swerved into the desert, away from the road, bouncing over sand and brush. He cut the lights.

Wayne felt two hard blows on the side of his head. The following moments blurred—the pain, especially at his temple, stealing his attention from the assault in progress. James stopped the car. Hale dragged him into the dust, over some prickly grass and mesquite. He was curled in a ball, holding his blazer to his side, not sure how badly he was bleeding there. Strange hands in his pockets. "Sixty fucking bucks. Are you kidding?" Someone said, "What did you expect? He looks like a fucking hobo. And leave the change, goddammit. I'm not so low-class to be robbing nobody for pennies."

He felt some coins drop on the ground next to him. Then he heard Rain Man: "He's got a knife. And check it out, check it out. It's a phone. One of those tricked-out phones with the e-mail and shit. Worth a couple hundred, right?"

"Drop it." That was James.

"Why?"

" 'Cause it's got a goddamn GPS in it. They'll fucking track you with a satellite."

"Who?"

"Whoever it is that's looking for him. Cops. Whatever. Just turn it off and drop it."

The phone hit Wayne on the hip and bounced into the sand.

He listened as they walked back to the car. James started the engine, but then he heard Ginny say "Wait a minute," and in an instant she was whispering in his ear, which, Wayne only realized now, was also bleeding from the blow in the car.

"Don't worry. They'll find you," she said, and she picked up the phone and turned it back on and placed it next to Wayne's head. She picked up the coins lying in the sand and stuffed them gently into his pocket. He felt her finger under his tongue and then he tasted something sweet she had left there. She covered him with his blazer and then she left him in the sandy soil. He heard the car speed away.

In a moment, Wayne could no longer feel the ground under him. He didn't know if he was on his back or his front or his side. He was floating in space, his moon weight down to zero. When he opened his eyes, everything was warped, as if somebody had folded and twisted and painted the floor of the desert, as if the sky were close, descending on top of him, and he was certain, just as Ginny had said, that none of it was real.

"It's got a goddamn GPS in it," he heard James say again.

He reached up with one hand until he found his phone, and he turned the power off.

TETRAD

The world would perish were all men learned.

—Thomas Fuller, MD

35

NADA PASSED THEM on the way to her room, men carrying chairs, fine teak chairs with padded seats and backs and a thin piece of black Velcro around the perimeter of each for a drape to be attached. She pressed herself against the wall as half a dozen large men pushed by carrying three chairs each. None acknowledged they had even displaced her.

Dozens of workers on the Jameson estate had seen her emerge midmorning from Jameson's cavern of a garage wearing two hours' sleep and last night's clothes. No one even raised an eyebrow in her direction. She wondered how many of these landscapers and handymen and maids and laundresses even knew what she was doing there.

After last night, Nada was beginning to wonder herself.

She went to her room and shut the blinds from day to night and showered and scrubbed and dressed. The headache continued to slice through her brain. The ringing, when she wasn't suppressing it with effort, still battered her eardrums from the inside. The blackout had affected the area all around Jameson's house, but inside here everything was normal—somehow he still had power and lights and air-conditioning. God, she loved air-conditioning. Nada wanted to lie down, but she didn't.

She walked back down the Woodward stairs and spent an hour in the re-created office with the tile Burning Patrick had presented her, trying to match it against the ones in Jameson's collection and comparing its edges to the photos of tiles from other collections he had arranged for her in a binder. She couldn't find its place.

Nada blew hot breath at her bangs. She set the new tile on her father's old desk and flattened the creased newspaper all around it. How did Burning Patrick know who she was? And if he painted the tile specifically for her, what meaning did it have?

She wrapped it in the newsprint again, mostly to keep Jameson from seeing it. If he saw it, he would want it. He might even claim it was rightfully his, given that she had acquired it while on his retainer. Nada had no intention of giving it up.

At lunchtime in the kitchen, Nada asked Molly what was going on.

"Where, dear?"

"Big men with chairs," Nada explained. "I passed them in the hall."

"Concert," Molly replied, and she began arranging an elaborate plate of crab cakes and salad and frites for Nada without asking for her order.

On her second day, Myra had taken Nada on a proper tour of the house, and except for the master suite, which Myra had designed herself, the part of the renovation of which she was proudest was clearly the second-floor chapel. It was nearly two stories high and on either side of its narrow aisle were eight rows of tiny pews. It was a scaled-down version of a real church, but it was just large enough for a small ensemble at the altar and, with a few extra chairs, a modest audience. Myra boasted of the beautiful sounds shaped by the peculiarities of the room as well as acoustic innovations engineered specifically at her husband's request, and she even demonstrated with a note from her throat, a competent, tuneful sustained D.

"What kind of concert?" Nada asked.

Molly said, "Mr. Jameson does this sometimes. Brings in musicians for a private concert, invites his friends. They usually pick some obscure piece of music—sometimes it's modern; sometimes it's a long-forgotten piece the commercial orchestras no longer play. I make a fancy buffet based on a recipe he finds in an old book someplace. Usually with game nobody actually thinks of as food anymore." Molly made a face and held up a photocopy for Nada to see, but trying to decipher the elegant web of calligraphy twisted the knife in her head. She used to be able to turn off physical pain just by thinking about it. She could isolate a headache and her spider would zap it, make the pain go away. She had been a teenager the last time she'd had pain so persistent.

"What's the music this time?" Nada was no expert, but she knew a modest amount about classical music from childhood osmosis.

Molly consulted a piece of paper. "*The Viola in My Life Two*, by Morton Feldman." She shook her head. "I wouldn't know a symphony from a rap song. Woody Guthrie, that's the people's music. This nonsense"—she waved her hands, presumably at the workmen setting up the chapel or maybe at serious art in general—"is no different from sports cars and yachts. Just rich people showing how much money they can spend without it hurting. But then, Mr. Jameson gives enough of his money to people who need it that I suppose he should be allowed an indulgence or two." She garnished the plate and set it at the small painted table in the room off the kitchen where she and Hugh played cards and read newspapers and ate meals and otherwise passed their days. "Sit. Eat."

Nada took a napkin and a fork and knife and sat and rubbed her right eye.

"Headache, dear? You should tell Mr. Jameson you're not feeling well."

Nada said, "Yeah. It's weird."

"When I hurt my back, Mr. Jameson took me to the best doctor. Dr. Huang. He was wonderful. Fixed me right up."

"I think it's just the heat."

"Oh, this blackout is terrible. We're so lucky Mr. Jameson owns a generator. And solar panels and whatever. These poor people all around us, though. Let's hope they get it straightened out soon."

"Are you staying here tonight, then?" Nada asked. The Jamesons kept a servant's suite made up for nights when Molly and Hugh were working late.

"No reason to go home. Our apartment is hotter than that Thermador oven."

Hugh appeared in the door. "Are you talking about me?"

Molly frowned. "Hotter than an oven? Don't we both wish."

"Hell no, before that. When you said Mr. Jameson gives enough of his money to people who need it."

"Shush. Eat." Molly reached for another plate.

As Myra Jameson predicted, Nada had become fond of Molly and Hugh. She had grown up with help in the Gold household, and she had adored many of her caretakers—Nada spent many more hours with a series of nannies than she had with her parents—but being with Molly and Hugh the last few days, sharing meals with them and stories and sometimes beating them at cards, sizing them up with her spider, she began to appreciate the dignity of their work. Their complete dedication to making one person happy. Of course, Gary Jameson wrote them checks for their trouble, but in Molly and Hugh's world, that was almost beside the point. They lived comfortably but humbly so that another person could live in luxury. And although they described themselves as "Johnson liberals" (and at other times "confirmed socialists"), whether or not their lifelong vocations had been fair or just or equitable never entered their minds. Nada had heard Molly say it: "No chef at a fancy restaurant is better than me just because he cooks for more rich people than I do." She and Hugh did honest work and they were extremely good at it, and a man they admired, in spite of his wealth, was happier because of them. Doing a difficult job well was the most honorable thing Molly and Hugh could imagine.

Hugh took a pair of crab cakes and, with a flourish of linen napkin, sat opposite Nada, who tried to offer him sauce from her plate. "I'm sorry. I took it all. All the—"

"Rémoulade, dear," Molly said.

"All the rémoulade," Nada said.

Hugh stopped her advancing fork with the palm of his hand. "My wife is an expert saucier, but I like 'em dry, the same way I like my arteries *unclogged*."

Molly said, "You've lived long enough, Hugh. Eat some damn mayonnaise."

They all laughed. Then just as the mirth had subsided, just in that pause after a good joke when the conversation resets, the breath that lets more serious subjects take shape, the room lurched hard to the right and Nada grabbed the table to keep herself from falling. Plate and silverware and crabmeat and rémoulade were tossed by the force of her hand and she watched them tumble to the ground in slow motion. Molly asked, "Are you all right, dear," and Nada tried to say "I'm fine; it's just the heat," but the words, so clear in her head, never assembled in her throat, and soon the floor, like the deck of a ship in a storm, tossed her again, the other way this time, and she folded forward, head speeding toward the table's beveled edge, her hands not quick enough to stop the impact.

36

AFTER A FEW HOURS Wayne woke up, sand in his mouth and in his hair and stuck to one side of his face with drool. The pain in his side and the other one in his head didn't hurt too much if he didn't move. The bleeding had stopped—the cut hadn't been deep enough to penetrate the thick layer of fat and muscle around Wayne's midsection—but his stab wound screamed at him every time he twisted. He was a long way from Chicago and broke except for a few pennies. He stood carefully and surveyed the dusty landscape in every direction until the sound of a truck directed him toward the road.

He was so far from anywhere, it was pointless even to bother walking. He sat by the side of the highway. It was hot now, but still only morning hot. By 2:00 p.m., it would be 110 degrees. Twenty minutes passed before another vehicle came in sight. Wayne stood and waved as desperately as the pain would allow, but it flew by without even a tap of the brake.

If he'd looked like hell before Rain Man and the others picked him up, he tried to imagine what he looked like now. Every inch of his shirt and pants was filthy from the inside out with clay and dirty sweat and dried blood—his own and Amoyo's. Two days of beard had forested his face. He smelled bad. He was hungry. The blood had turned the fabric of his shirt to crust, but the black color disguised the nature of the stain. He tucked it in. He couldn't look respectable, but he tried hard not to look frightening.

He wondered what they must be saying about him back home. He was tempted to turn the phone on and call somebody, anybody—his mother, his brother, Peter (*Peter's from a family of lawyers, isn't he? Back east? People who could help?*)—and just tell them he hadn't done it. *That's what an innocent person would do, right?* Somewhere his mother was hearing the news—from the paper, from friends, from the cops. No doubt she would be protesting his innocence to anyone who would listen, telling everyone what a good boy Wayne had always been. But for Mrs. Jennings, Wayne's lack of contact would carry with it the slightest, barely conscious, nagging doubt.

Right now his own mother was considering the possibility that her youngest son was a murderer.

By noon, he had fashioned his blazer into a tent to cover his exposed parts. The heat underneath was intense, but it was preferable to the desert sun, which attacked like breath from a dragon. Around two, a car pulled over, carrying a middle-aged woman, alone. She cracked her window an inch, and as Wayne approached he felt the cool conditioned air rushing out across his face. He tried to say he'd been robbed. The woman studied him until the concern and empathy on her face were flushed away by fear. Before pulling away, she squeezed a large bottled water, three-quarters full, through the gap and promised to send help from the next exit, over Wayne's desperate protests.

She meant help in the form of cops, which was help he didn't need.

Three times he spotted the Mars lights and blue stripe of an Arizona Highway Patrol car, a sight that sent him scrambling behind a large rock. When night came without a ride, he felt despair, but also relief. At least the sun was gone.

He found the outline of his bed from this morning and settled into it. Sleeping seemed both impossible and necessary. He'd conserved the water and still had about a quarter bottle for the next day, but he was starving and exhausted.

He heard a helicopter in the distance and checked again to make sure his phone was turned off. "They got these satellites that can detect your heat signature from space," Peter had said. Wayne tried to cover himself with sand, but digging with his hands was useless and he suspected the sand was hotter than his body was anyway. Instead, he curled up into the smallest ball he could, and wondered if there was any possibility at all— maybe if he had another of Ginny's little pills—that the sun would stay down for a whole day.

37

FAINTING WAS ALL IT WAS, she tried to explain when she was able. Just the heat.

Myra Jameson, who answered Molly's cries from the kitchen, wouldn't let her return to her room like she wanted. "Sleep is all I need," Nada said. "A nap."

"Keep her awake," Myra said to Molly.

Within ten minutes, she was prone across a settee in the library, with Hugh holding her hand and a doctor on the way—Jameson's personal physician. Apparently, if you were a man as important as Gary Jameson, you could get a house call from a doctor at any old time, even on a Saturday, even in a blackout. In another twenty minutes, Nada was looking at a slim middle-aged man who had a bit of a gimp and a tailored brown suit. He told her she could call him Dennis, or Dr. Russo if she preferred.

The exam consisted mostly of questions and some gentle probing into her ears and her eyes. Using an old coatrack, Jameson helped the doctor run an IV to her arm and asked her to sit and wait a few minutes. Then Russo disappeared for maybe an hour, during which the pain and ringing in her head crescendoed and subsided. When he returned, Russo set down a thick green envelope and probed her again, after which he said he didn't think the bump on her forehead looked serious enough to have caused a concussion and that she wasn't showing signs of brain swelling. The fall hadn't caused any additional injuries, or not serious ones anyway.

"Additional?" Nada asked.

Russo smiled without showing teeth. "You're dehydrated. Diarrhea, headaches, dizziness, mild hallucinations. But it's a good thing you weren't trying to get into an ER right now. Not with the power outage. It could have become severe while you waited."

"Thanks, I guess."

He performed an involuntary half shake, half nod with his head. "But that's not the most interesting thing I discovered. When I stopped in my office to start a file on you, I got a bit of a shock. Ms. Gold, our office *already* has a file on you."

"What do you mean?" Besides her gynecologist in Vegas, Nada hadn't been to a doctor, or even filled out medical paperwork, since the time she'd lived with her mother.

"Until very recently, we had a neurologist named Marlena Falcone working in our clinic. You might remember—actually, I'm sure you do— that she was the physician who recommended and implanted your neurostimulator." He tapped his head.

She remembered the name but only glimpses of the doctor herself. Most of their contact had been before the implant. "Why would she still have a file on me?"

"Dr. Falcone kept meticulous tabs on all her patients." He picked up the folder and peered into it. "It seems Marlena had been trying to contact you. Three letters here over the past year, one sent just recently. From what I can see, you never responded."

Nada hardly ever opened mail from people she didn't know. If the sender had been a hospital or clinic, she would have thrown it in the garbage. "Executive Concierge," she repeated, her spider searching for the name and finding it. "I figured that was junk."

Russo shook his head. "As you know, the patients with ADHD who had neurostimulators implanted had to have them removed. There was a recall, and yours was supposed to come out years ago, although I can't figure out from the file why that procedure never took place. I'm sure she was just trying to follow up with you."

Nada saw mumbling Burning Patrick, all dirty parka and ass crack, dripping paint so precisely on a little six-inch ceramic tile, made crazy and a genius by this tiny misfiring device, the same device as hers. His had come out, but both the crazy and genius remained somehow. Nada still had hers, but she hadn't painted any masterpieces and it hadn't made her insane.

Nada said, "Can I speak to Dr. Falcone?"

Russo put a hand to his face. "I'm afraid Dr. Falcone has left us."

"I know you said that, but if I could just talk to her—"

"I'm sorry. What I meant was that she has recently passed away."

It felt to Nada like someone was inflating a balloon inside her head. "I'm sorry." She rubbed her arm near the IV. "I don't have any insurance."

"I've already talked to Gary. He's going to cover the cost. After this IV runs out, I'm going to leave you an oral hydration solution. Just dissolve it in water, drink it up. Stay away from caffeine for a couple of days. No fruit juice."

She looked around at the serious decor of Jameson's library. It felt weird having a needle in her arm without the alcohol and soap smell of a doctor's office. It smelled like leather and furniture wax and potpourri. She was drowsy.

"Don't worry about Blackburn," Jameson said as he led her upstairs. "Just stay in your room and rest up."

"I almost forgot," Nada said. "I have something to tell you. About Burning Patrick." *I think he's for real.*

"You can tell me later," he said, and as they marched slowly up the Woodward stairs, around and around, she assessed the strange feelings she had for this man. Fatherly. Fatherish. One bad hangover aside, she'd grown very comfortable in Gary Jameson's old house, with Molly cooking her meals and a maid named Esperanza changing her linens and Hugh anticipating everything else she might need. Since Solomon's death, she hadn't had anyone to take care of her—certainly her mother wasn't up to the role. And maybe that's why she had been able to hold it together all these years while most everyone else with a spider like hers had gone nuts. Maybe out of necessity she'd just learned to do whatever it took.

Myra and Molly helped her into bed. Molly promised to send up a pitcher of water and comfort food. Nada didn't say that she couldn't eat.

She shut the door and was about to close the blinds to make it night when she saw the bit of newsprint caught in the zipper of her purse. The spider tingled in her dry and shrunken head. She pulled out the tile and unfolded the newspaper and stared again at the image. Whatever Burning Patrick was trying to tell her, she still wasn't getting it.

She threw the tile on the bed and picked up the newspaper. The drips of paint had stiffened it like cardboard. Random drips of paint, seven different colors, dots and streams and globs, all coalesced in an imperfect, distended orbit around a single article.

An article about the recent unsolved murder of Marlena Falcone.

She read it and put the paper down on the bed. She picked it up and read it again.

Then she walked to the bathroom and mixed the solution Dr. Russo had given her and swallowed it in gulps.

38

SUNDAY, AUGUST 1

WAYNE HAD so little hope left, he hadn't even stood when the car approached, but remained folded, elbows on his knees. Nevertheless, they pulled over and, with hardly a word, helped Wayne into the front seat of the yellow Subaru with Nebraska plates.

Cynthia was probably nineteen. Will must have been north of that—maybe twenty-two or twenty-three. They gave him water and a peanut butter sandwich from a small blue cooler in back. He was so dry, the sandwich mixed like cement in his mouth, but it felt good going down.

"What's your name?" Cynthia asked. The gears in his tired mind creaked as it tried to come up with a false answer. Looking behind her, he saw a faded sticker on the hatch window for a failed presidential candidate known for his pro-environment stance. Wayne once had an employee named Dan with the same sticker on the side of his desk.

"Daniel," Wayne said.

"What happened to you?" Will asked.

That was a more complicated lie, so he tried to tell the truth. "I got beat up."

"By who?"

Wayne put up a hand, indicating that he didn't want to talk about it.

"Should we take you to an emergency room?"

"No."

"The cops?"

"No," he said too quickly. He could feel their nervousness building. They had chosen to help, but now they were second-guessing themselves. Wayne was big and he was a mess—blistered with sunburn and filthy and more than a little bit incoherent and surly from more than twenty-four hours in the desert and the lingering effects of that pill Ginny had given him. He knew he needed to tell a good story if he wanted to stay in this car.

A good one came to him, one cobbled together from his memory of a newspaper article from a few years back and gossip he'd heard at a high school reunion about one of his old classmates, who'd become an anarchist and pot farmer.

"You know the nuclear power plant down in Palo Verde?" Wayne wasn't exactly sure where they were, but they still couldn't be too far from the Nevada-Arizona border.

"Heard of it," Will said. "Biggest reactor in the country, right?"

Wayne liked the way Will said that, with a tiny trace of disgust. He said, "We were trying to pull off a monkey-wrench operation. Get over the fence and spray some tags. If we could show vulnerability in their security, we figured we might be able to shut it down for a while. Generate some bad publicity. Maybe even gin up support for solar and wind."

"Hard to blow up a wind farm." Will laughed. "We need cheap, clean energy in this country, not obvious targets for terrorists."

"That's right. Anyway, it turns out breaking into a nuclear power plant is harder than we thought. Security, not so *vulnerable*." He laughed and then winced as the infected scab pulled at his side. "They beat us up good. Dumped us in the desert."

"They didn't call the cops?"

"We got far enough inside, they probably didn't want the publicity, like I said. And they know we can't go to the cops, because they'll just arrest us. Probably on terrorism charges."

"Damn," Cynthia said, leaning in from the backseat. "You said 'we.' Where are your friends?"

"I don't know. They didn't drop us off together."

"Palo Verde's pretty far south of here."

"I've been hitching my way back to the interstate for a couple days."

"Jesus? In this heat? Where are you going?" Will asked.

"I'm from Chicago. But right now, I'll go anywhere you're going."

"Not as far as that," Will said. "But we can get you to Lincoln."

"Lincoln would be good." Wayne smiled his thanks. "They took my wallet. I got no money for gas. Or food."

"Don't worry about it."

"When I get home, I'll send you some."

"Don't worry about it."

They talked politics for a while, and tried to ask about other "monkey-wrench operations" Wayne might have been a part of. When appropriate, he substituted his old classmate's biography for his, but Wayne soon fell asleep, his blazer folded into a pillow between his head and the window. He dreamed he was back at the Colossus, watching Nada play roulette, which she never did.

"Red or black?" Nada asked him.

"Green," he said, and the wheel kept spinning and spinning and spinning.

When he woke up, they were stopped at a campground. Looking through the car window, he watched Cynthia and Will struggling with a tent. From the close orbits they made around each other, he could tell they were lovers. When Wayne was standing close to Nada, he longed to touch her casually, the way Will touched Cynthia, gently with a finger to her bony elbow or shoulder or sometimes the subtle curve of her ass, signifying nothing, just letting her know he was there.

"How long was I out?" Wayne asked as he approached.

"Long time." Cynthia smiled. "We're not so far from Denver."

As the three of them fiddled with the tent, they gossiped, traded in rumors. Cynthia and Will had been stuck in Seattle after the plane crashes. It took them two weeks to get to their car, which was at her sister's house in L.A. and that was why they stopped to help him. Wayne admired their comfort together, the small unspoken gestures of affection, the way Will did her some kindness every time he stood—fetching her water, or straightening her flip-flops, or just rubbing her shoulder.

They ate dinner on an unsteady picnic table—more sandwiches and water. Wayne felt good enough to drink half a beer. Will and Cynthia then retired to the tent and Will offered to let Wayne sleep in the Subaru. When Wayne was settled into the bucket passenger seat and had thanked them several times, Will locked it with a double beep, taking the keys with him.

Wayne pulled out his dark phone and wondered again if he should risk a call to Peter, or to his own brother, just to say "I didn't do it." Just to get that on the record. Just so the cop who finally did arrest him wouldn't throw that in his face, wouldn't put a finger in his eye and ask "How come you never denied that you did it?"

How long would it take them to track the GPS signal to his phone anyway? He had seen them track a cell phone on a TV show once. *Triangulation* was the word they used. Triangulation sounded like it might take a long time. This phone was more sophisticated than most and so maybe they wouldn't have to triangulate to find it or whatever, but he could risk it, couldn't he? Risk a few minutes on the phone just to tell his mom or Peter or at least Peter's voice mail that he was innocent.

He was still debating with himself, phone in hand, thumb poised over the buttons, when he fell back asleep.

39

THE HOUSE was city narrow, with a front yard about the size of a badminton court and a narrow concrete walk where the net would be. Like all the other homes for blocks and blocks and miles in any direction, it was dark inside. Yellow police tape had been ripped down in quick pulls, but a few hopeless ribbons of it remained wrapped around tree trunks and light poles, the neighbors either too spooked by a murder on their block or too distracted by the blackout, now in its third day, to sensibly tidy up after the cops. Nada walked up the steps through a hard, hot rain and rang the bell, but it, like nearly everything else, had been silenced by the outage.

She pushed on the front door, which was locked, and then stepped back to the sidewalk to take the house in.

Three stories of new stone and brick. No signs of life.

Nada had slipped out the French doors of Jameson's library, the room where Russo had treated her the day before, without a sound. The nice thing about a big house, she knew from her childhood, is that it's easy to be lost. Once outside, in the dark, in the rain, walking north through the neighborhoods—Lincoln Park, Lakeview, Boystown, Andersonville—the people in the streets sluggish from the heat, she felt alone and alert. Although she had a hollow pain in her stomach from not eating, she had no headache. No cramps. Whatever was in Dr. Russo's bitter powder— electrolytes mostly, he'd said—had her feeling almost normal in less than twenty-four hours.

Forearms over her soaking head, she followed a narrow walk between the house and a chain fence that separated this property from the one next to it. Unlike the well-groomed front, the backyard was overgrown with weeds and grass gone to seed. A cover from the rusted propane grill was caught against a corner of the fence. Rows of tomato plants withered from neglect in the heat. Flowers dead and colorless. Nada stepped up onto the small square deck and tried the back door. Also locked.

Drifting backward again, examining the house from the rear, she saw a basement window inset with a piece of plywood. There were striations in the dusty concrete below where someone had tried to sweep away broken glass, and tiny grains of crystal still glimmered among the raindrops. Nada pressed on the board with a finger. It moved. She pushed with a palm and it lurched backward with a splintering crack. She glanced at the empty house behind her, kicked with her foot, and the board disappeared into the darkness beyond, smashing and tumbling to the floor below.

This was the way Dr. Falcone's killer had entered, and to know it gave Nada a horrible thrill. *What was he looking for? What am I supposed to be looking for?*

Clutching her purse tight to her ribs, she lowered herself into the basement. It was surprisingly cool. She wrung water from her shirt and removed from her bag a small flashlight, borrowed from Hugh, who had asked no questions.

The basement was square and unfinished. A clean metal workbench. A Peg-Board with hooks but no tools. Washer and dryer, a freezer—all unplugged. Empty wine rack. Metal shelves with gardening supplies, household chemicals, pesticides, lightbulbs.

She found the stairs.

The intense antiseptic smell in the kitchen started her gagging. She remembered the masked crew that had come after her father's murder, a private outfit specializing in crime-scene cleanup, which even young Nada understood to mean they were experts in blood, jumpsuited vampires who sucked the stuff from carpets and crevices instead of veins. When she finally sneaked back into her father's office, weeks after his death, she was met by this same sting in her nose. The smell that killed every microorganism in the wake of a messy murder. The smell that meant no life remained.

In seconds she had found the spot where Dr. Falcone must have died, or at least the spot where she had done the most bleeding. The lingering odor of bleach was strongest here, the tile dull where the scrubbing had been intense. She scanned the room, which was ringed with shining stainless-steel appliances, each twice as wide as ones in an ordinary kitchen. The countertops were uncluttered, the stovetop unmarred. Cabinets and drawers had been emptied of Marlena's pots and pans and silverware and aprons. There was nothing to indicate why this woman had been killed or what it had to do with Nada.

It had to have *something* to do with her. Otherwise, Burning Patrick wouldn't have given her the newspaper. Otherwise, Jameson wouldn't have taken her to, of all the doctors in Chicago, the one who'd worked across the hall from Marlena. Nada was wary of coincidences, but this one was making her spider tremble and ring like an old phone.

Room by empty room, dull light flooding in through open shades, she looked for clues only she would recognize. She sat in every corner, studied each space from every angle, methodically working her way front to back and then up the stairs into the stifling heat of the guest bedroom and the country decor of the second bath and finally into the master suite—fireplace, lush carpet, crimson walls—immaculate, dusted and vacuumed since the murder. *Ready for a buyer who won't suspect the horror that happened here,* she thought.

There were round indentations where rubber coasters under the bedposts had been. She walked into the bathroom, tapped on the wall. She peeked in the large closet. Her spider calculated the angles, tried to imagine the upstairs like a blueprint, seen from above. There was a space behind this. Another room.

On her knees, it took her only a moment to find a keypad behind a piece of loose molding. Turning the flashlight to an off angle, she could see wear—a slight rubbing—on the four even digits: 2, 4, 6, 8. She began trying them in combinations, her fingers flying over the keypad, hoping the answer was as simple as a PIN, and in just about ten minutes, a section of wall popped two inches toward her.

She moved a shoe rack and opened it wide.

The room was black and, unlike the rest of the house, she discovered with a sweep of Hugh's flashlight, not empty. An intercom hung on the wall next to a telephone just above a small refrigerator with six bottles of warm water. An impotent glass light fixture sat like a beetle on the ceiling. Feeling about in the dim residual light leaking from the bedroom, she discovered boxes—the name Blackburn on some of them, Woodward on others, another with her name: Gold. She stopped breathing. Patrick, of course. And Wes Woodward, the stair builder. Jameson's twin obsessions. Nada found a light switch, which obviously didn't work, then peered into the containers, which were stuffed with loose papers and expensive notebooks bound with faux-leather covers.

She dragged the boxes in pairs out to the bedroom and parted the curtains as much as she dared. Then she organized the dated notebooks into chronological order and, after a wary peek out into the street, crossed her legs and sat down on the floor.

She opened the heaviest box first. On top were a number of text-books—medicine, math, history. She lifted them out and pushed them aside.

Tiles. More than a dozen painted tiles. Unmistakably Burning Patrick's tiles.

Trembling, Nada removed several from the box and placed them one by one on top of the piles of papers on the floor. Her spider spun them in her head, rearranged them. She studied them up close with Hugh's flashlight shaking in her hands.

Holy God.

Nada dug deep into her purse and retrieved her own tile, still wrapped in newspaper. She removed it carefully and placed it on the carpet, positioning it near the other tiles in the room's best light. She began moving them like puzzle pieces, one just to the right of another or just below another, and then she rotated them and flipped their positions, one just to the left of this one or just above that one, and finally, she noticed one other tile with an image like hers, letters like hers, and, buried in the wiry lines, the hairs, the blacks and the reds, the same letters, in fact—*a s s*— and on the eighth or ninth or tenth rotation, she saw where the two fit together.

Perfectly. "An adjacent pair," Jameson would call it.

She studied the precise strokes and drips and dabs and now she could start to see what Burning Patrick had been painting, could see the animal shape the figure was taking when the pieces were placed together.

Nada placed those tiles in her bag and examined the others for any connection to one another, for any other letters. Finding none, she placed them back in the carton and replaced the textbooks and turned her attention to the other boxes.

Fragments of personal journals, research notes, receipts, memos, printed e-mails, photographs, letters, some postcards. A nonlinear record of Marlena Falcone's life's work. Nada could find no order to it, no indication why she had kept this stuff, or why she had been hiding it. Perhaps she'd been planning on writing a book one day. Maybe she'd planned on organizing it all in the future.

Nada decided she would do it for her now.

In the heat and low light, she began sorting, her spider assigning each document to one of more than a dozen categories. There were piles and subpiles, arranged in a wide circle around her, growing and multiplying by the second. The general theme was chronological, moving clockwise, but there were other references, too, by type, by subject, by name, smaller arcs of relevance inside the main circle. As she scanned each page, the lines between this document and that one were drawn instantly, the papers neatly filed in their exact places with a roll of her hand.

When the boxes were empty, she settled in and began to read.

40

IN A GIANT WAREHOUSE by the airport, in an overindustrialized Chicago suburb called, with a certain amount of comic bravado, Elk Grove Village, Alberto Cepeda watched as a lifetime of accumulation was wheeled out in boxes and lots. Four estates, including the possessions of Dr. Marlena Falcone, would be auctioned to the public today.

Alberto had driven here from Indiana in a quiet rage, rain like bullets attacking his Honda on the Indiana Toll Road and the Tri-State. He couldn't even listen to public radio, which seemed to have been prattling on with the appalling news every hour for two days: Jonathan Prentiss had just won the Abel Prize. Square-jawed, shallow-brained, curly-maned Jonathan Prentiss of NYU, a game theorist and columnist for *The New York Times Magazine,* who had once appeared with his laptop in an Apple computer ad and who, like a carpenter fixing a sink with a hammer, approached every math problem with the same part of his ordinary brain, had just been given the math world's highest honor: a glass monolith and a million dollars, and a trip to Oslo besides.

A caustic mixture of envy, jealousy, outrage, and injustice burned on the back of Alberto's tongue.

The fact that Alberto had taught his classes dutifully but had not published anything in more than a decade that had even raised an eyebrow of respect from his peers only fueled his anger. He had wasted his life, and by rewarding a twit like Jonathan Prentiss, the gods of his profession were rubbing it in.

Alberto's contributions were apparently important enough for the most exclusive and important society of intellectuals in history, but no one would ever know.

Perhaps the insight he provided had even been worth killing Marlena for.

Cepeda parked and found his way inside the hangar-size building through an almost invisible glass door where an Eagles song played softly on a portable radio and a receptionist with a pointy white collar and black vest asked him to sign in and then handed him a numbered paddle. He followed a confusing series of yellow signs with the word AUCTION to a corner of the massive warehouse floor, sectioned off with curtains.

A handful of buyers from interior design firms slumped uncomfortably in padded folding chairs, prepared for the all-day tedium. A retired couple, probably auction regulars, probably pursuing the thrill of a bargain more than the items themselves, chatted in whispers. Surely the rainstorm combined with the massive blackout in nearby Chicago had tempered attendance.

He sat on the perimeter as a stranger's possessions were presented to almost complete indifference. He removed his phone, texted his wife, read part of a magazine he had folded lengthwise into his pocket. He wondered about his own accumulation of things, if they would matter so little to the people he would one day leave behind. His grandmother's sideboard, which he had personally shepherded from Puerto Rico to his dining room in Indiana. The humidor on his desk, a gift from a Dominican poet he had escorted about campus during a literary festival ten years ago. His books. *God, my books,* he thought. Would nobody care for them, read them, treasure them when he was gone?

Jonathan Prentiss would never suffer this angst. His family would fight over his things, especially that goddamned Abel Prize and his goddamned million dollars.

A young woman arrived. She was about the age of his graduate students and soaked from the rain. She wore a yellow slicker with matching boots and had a big canvas bag over her shoulder that looked mostly empty. He watched her for a moment, saw her snap her head to attention when the auctioneer announced a break before the presentation of the Falcone estate. The woman made a short phone call, and when she hung up, Alberto approached.

"Did you know Dr. Falcone?" he asked.

She said she had. She was much younger than Marlena, small and shy.

Her name was Laura and she said Marlena had been a colleague of her father, but she had known her since she was a child and in recent years, since Laura had moved out on her own to an apartment in the city, they had become close. Alberto could tell that the murder had affected her profoundly. He wondered briefly and gratuitously if they had been lovers but then decided no. She was just a woman living alone, wondering when the wheel of random city violence would stop and find her as it had found her friend.

"I was her professor, once, years ago," Alberto explained. "I couldn't make the wake. I thought maybe this would be a substitute."

Laura shook her head. "The wake was private. I wasn't even allowed to go."

"What do you mean?"

Laura hesitated. "Marlena lived her life in boxes. Boxes inside boxes. The funeral was only for the . . . the people in the innermost box."

Riddles, Alberto thought. *Who talks in riddles except* Batman *villains and people who think they know something they shouldn't say?*

"May I?"

He sat and they spoke in whispers within the cavernous space. Laura explained that Marlena's family had disowned her years ago when she came out as a lesbian. She told him that after the wake her brothers had claimed the body coldly and without a ceremony of their own and were now auctioning off all Marlena's possessions, scattering her life like ashes to the highest bidders.

"Her family, her brothers, they weren't at the wake, either?"

Laura shook her head.

"They weren't *in that box*."

"No," she said.

Alberto sensed the meaningful silence and he leapt into it, regretting that he had almost as soon as he did. "How did she get in? The smallest box, I mean."

Laura examined his face, as if wondering where these questions were leading her. "They *adopted* her. She had something they could use, so they adopted her. And then—" She leaned away. "Who are you?"

"I told you who I am."

"What do you think you know?"

Alberto swallowed the next words and analyzed the situation, coming to a conclusion with Euclidean certainty. Laura had already volunteered that she was not in the "innermost box." Laura was not a member of the

Thousand, but she was close to Marlena, close to the box. She knew something.

"The Thousand." He whispered as low as he could while still being heard. "She was mathematici, yeah? That's the box. The mathematici. The Thousand."

She picked up her bag. "I need to go. This was stupid."

"Please don't."

Laura sidled down the row of chairs and stepped quickly toward the rear opening in the curtain. A bald man in a dark suit appeared twenty feet ahead of her and Laura stopped abruptly. Alberto watched as she covered her face with the canvas bag, waited for the man to take his own seat, and then ducked out behind him, unnoticed.

Alberto slumped a bit in his own chair before remembering that the bald man, whoever he was, must not have any idea of his identity. Alberto Cepeda was no threat. He was a nonperson. For once in his life, it felt like an advantage.

He followed Laura's steps through the curtain, but she was already out of sight, the clicks of her sprinting high heels just barely reverberating from somewhere behind pallets and stacks of unmarked boxes.

Damn.

Behind the stage, the lots were still open for inspection, and Alberto peered at each one: furniture, dresses, photo albums, books, shoe boxes of pictures and miscellaneous papers, a large wooden harp with the label *Lyon & Healy, Chicago.* Alberto didn't find what he was looking for. Of course, he hadn't really expected to.

In his fantasy, he would uncover a mother lode of Pythagorean secrets, truths passed in whispers from generation to generation. There was one in particular he hoped most of all to read—the missing piece of a true story he had told his students many times.

In his classes, Alberto described how a long-ago ship had arrived from Samos and sat at anchor for three rainy days and how the hundreds gathered on the hard sand soon became thousands as word spread that this single-masted vessel ferried a god. Some said it was Apollo himself come to address the people of Croton, who had prospered for two centuries under his protection. Others insisted he was a *son* of Apollo, his birth to a mortal fulfilling a prophecy by the oracle at Delphi. Still others claimed he was a spirit recently arrived from his home inside the sun or the moon.

By the time the skies cleared and he disembarked, the Crotonians knew him as Pythagoras. With help, Pythagoras mounted a short wall that protected the city from the tides. If he knew about the rumors of his divine lineage, he did nothing to dispel them. When he spoke, he pinched his white beard, as if the wavy hairs were conduits for rushing waters of great wisdom. He asked that no one repeat what he was about to say, and forbade anyone who was capable of doing so from writing down his words.

Mostly, they obeyed.

Pythagoras taught and campaigned and preached for perhaps half the day. Exactly what he said is unknown, although he likely spoke of the immortal soul and the family of man and the relationship between Earth and heaven, between the visible and the invisible. About the mathematical order—the language of music and numbers—upon which all creation was based.

When he was done, a thousand men and women abandoned their former and comfortable lives to follow him.

As the years passed, their numbers would grow even larger. They would be cited as a community, a school, a cult. Those closest to Pythagoras were known as "disciples." They would dominate the society and politics of Croton for decades, until they were exiled from the city in a bloody purge. Pythagoras himself might have perished when his enemies set fire to a home where he was visiting, but his followers, scattered throughout the Mediterranean, would influence Western philosophy, science, mathematics, and religion for all time.

Over the centuries and millennia, they would become known as "The Thousand."

More than anything, more than divine equations and solutions to the universe's darkest mathematical mysteries, Alberto longed to know exactly what Pythagoras said that first day. What brilliant and inspiring words could move so many to surrender their lives, their families, their fortunes to a complete stranger? What words of inspiration could still bind their descendants to him? *That* was real power.

An announcement was made and then halted after a few words. Alberto returned to his seat. The bald man was whispering to the auctioneer, who nodded, and as the bald man disappeared behind the curtain, the auctioneer declared there would be no presentation of the Falcone estate. An offer had been made and accepted for all lots. The next estate would be presented in half an hour.

Cepeda found his way to the end of the row and up toward the microphone. As the auctioneer walked away, he whispered loudly, "How much?"

The auctioneer turned. "Excuse me?"

"How much did they pay? For the whole estate, how much?"

The auctioneer squinted. "Are you making a counteroffer?"

Back through the chairs and through the white curtains. The bald man was with the cashier. Alberto wanted to look over his shoulder, see what name was printed on the check, what name the bald man signed, but of course the names and organizations would be many times removed and laundered from the Thousand. Boxes inside boxes.

Alberto walked quickly back the way he'd come, following the trail of yellow signs. He slowed by the receptionist's desk and asked if he had dropped his pen there on his way in, a black pen, a nice pen, a *Waterman* he'd hate to lose, and as she glanced under papers, he focused on the sign-in sheet and saw the name just below his own and then declared that he had found his pen, thank you, and went out the glass door and stepped quickly to his car.

He started his Honda and turned toward the Tri-State Tollway, repeating the name Laura Russo so he wouldn't forget, as he was too afraid to write it down.

41

MONDAY, AUGUST 2

SHE WAS HOLDING the phone—his phone—monkeying with it. She had it turned on.

How did she get my phone?

Wayne shook himself awake. The passenger door was open and he quickly slapped the phone out of Cynthia's hands, knocking it to the ground, picking it up again, dropping it, finally turning it off.

"Oh, sorry," she said, startled.

Wayne tried to smile. The much-needed sleep had made his head heavy, but the pain was better all over. "No, I'm sorry. Woke up and forgot where I was for a second."

"I opened the door and then I saw it lying on the ground. I wasn't sure if it fell out of the car or if somebody else had lost it. I was trying to see who it belonged to."

"It's mine," Wayne said.

"I didn't know you had a phone."

"Pretty much useless in the desert."

"Now that we're back in civilization, why don't you call your friends?"

Damn. "I did. Last night. A buddy is going to pick me up in Lincoln. Sorry I freaked out. I'm just trying to save the battery."

Cynthia dropped him the same look Nada did when she was skeptical, which was often. "Huh. Where in Lincoln is your friend picking you up?"

Wayne wondered if she'd poked around on the phone, if she'd checked to see if he had made any calls. *How long has she had it on?* "I said I'd call when we got closer."

"Huh."

Wayne helped Will break down the tent while Cynthia set up breakfast on the wobbly picnic table. Will had walked to the campground's general store and picked up coffee and some doughnuts and a *USA Today*. As they ate, Will grabbed the sports section, handed Cynthia the business and entertainment sections, and offered Wayne the main section. "Anything in there about Palo Verde?" Will asked.

"Doubt it," Wayne said. The lead story on page one was about a massive blackout covering almost a quarter of Chicago. Cooling centers had been established across the city. Commonwealth Edison was asking people to conserve but was confident it could restore power quickly and subsequently meet the people's increasing power demands. A spokesman asked for patience. The mayor was urging everyone to check on elderly relatives and neighbors, mindful of a heat wave disaster some years ago that had left hundreds dead. The most urgent need was fresh water. Trucks and trainloads of bottled water were being diverted from all over the country to Chicago.

Wayne followed the story as it jumped inside and his hands froze as he had one of those alarming sensations you get when you see a familiar thing in an unfamiliar place—that paralyzing combination of recognition and confusion.

What the hell is my picture doing in the newspaper?

On page four, adjacent to a story about the murders of Las Vegas ADA Beatrice Beaujon and her husband, was Wayne's employee photo from the Colossus, the same photo that had been on the front of the badge he had tossed in the Tornillo brush. He knew from the mirror in the Subaru that he didn't look much like it anymore. But he looked similar enough. Some things, second-degree burns and a beard won't cover up.

The story said police were following several avenues with regard to motive, including the possibility that an individual named Wayne Jennings, an associate director of security at the Colossus Casino, had been an obsessed former lover of one of Beatrice Beaujon's friends. Another murder in the city might be related, they said. Jennings was missing after having been seen fleeing the latest crime scene. Calls to Jennings's mother in Sparks, Nevada, the story said, had gone unanswered.

Canada Gold was not mentioned by name.

Wayne felt the sweat building at his hairline despite the morning chill. His mother had become one of those parents, the parents of infamous criminals. *Jeffrey Dahmer had a mother, right? And Ted Bundy and those Columbine kids.*

Oh shit. Mom, I'm so sorry.

When he was nine or ten, one of the neighbors called his mother and accused Wayne of breaking her garage window while playing street hockey. Wayne was guilty, the perpetrator of an errant slapshot that rocketed high and to the right, but he denied it. His mother didn't believe in his innocence, but she defended him at the cost of a mostly cordial relationship with the woman. She defended his lie, and that was the last time he ever lied to her. He wanted to call her now to explain, his silence being something of a lie itself, but whatever brief conversation he could risk would only confuse her. He'd call her when it was over. He'd say it then.

"Can I see that front section when you're done?" Will asked.

"Yeah," Wayne said. His mouth was dry again. "Is there a bathroom near here? I mean besides the Porta-Potty I used last night."

"The store's got a bathroom if you want to clean up," Will said.

Wayne drained his cup of coffee and shoved the rest of a doughnut in his mouth and tucked the paper under his arm. How many people on the campground had read this newspaper? How many of those people would recognize him?

He walked around the bend, down the road, and into the store, which was nearly empty. He smiled at the woman behind the counter, who watched him with suspicion, or maybe even disdain for his shabby appearance, but then ignored him. In the bathroom, he rubbed cold water on his face and arms, then watched the gray mixture disappear down the drain. After just a few days, his beard was thick enough that it disguised his features pretty well. It would be difficult for a stranger to connect him with the photo that appeared in the paper. He assumed it had been on television, too. The problem was his shirt and hat, both advertising the Colossus. He removed the cap. His hair underneath was an unfamiliar matted nest. He looked even more disheveled, and even less like himself. Wayne stuffed the hat and the newspaper in the garbage.

Leaving the way he'd come, Wayne noticed that the woman behind the counter barely gave him a glance this time. As he walked toward the door, she ducked behind the counter and Wayne heard her rummaging in a box. He was tempted to lift a sweatshirt off the table, a XXXL with the campground logo, but he knew he wouldn't be able to explain to Cynthia and Will how he'd paid for it, and when he walked outside, he was glad he hadn't taken it. He wouldn't let them turn him into a thief just by accusing him of being something worse.

Back at the picnic table, Cynthia and Will were cleaning up. "Where's the paper?" Will asked.

"Oh shit," Wayne said. "I left it in the can. I can go back and get it."

"I don't want a paper that's been sitting in a public toilet, but thanks." Will smiled. "It's weird being unconnected. I haven't even checked my e-mail in a week." The tent was rolled up and packed away in a green canvas bag, which Wayne helped Will lift into the back of the car. "Cynthia said you had a nice phone. You get the Internet on that?"

"Yeah," Wayne said without thinking.

"Any chance I could look at it later? I got a phone, but it's not that fancy."

"I'm really trying to save the battery."

Will nodded. "Yeah, I understand." He looked a little peeved. Wayne knew he must be pushing limits with his freeloading.

"How about I drive awhile?" Wayne said.

Wayne took the wheel, pinning the needle right at the posted seventy-five miles per hour and keeping the radio on FM rock stations and away from AM news. He squinted into the sun and patiently let traffic pass him. Three times he spotted patrol cars, but they showed no interest in the Subaru.

About a half hour after they'd crossed the Nebraska border, they switched drivers again. "Do you mind if Will sits up front with me?" Cynthia asked. "I like him to keep me alert while I'm driving. No offense, but you're not much of a talker. I know you're still tired."

There wasn't much legroom, so Wayne tried to fold himself across the bench seat and finally maneuvered himself into a position that was not exactly comfortable, but far better than the desert floor. Will and Cynthia chatted about Labor Day plans. Wayne tuned them out. Cynthia started fidgeting with her own phone, which Wayne wished she wouldn't do. The last thing he needed was an accident right now. Accidents brought cops.

He thought about the dream he'd had. Nada playing roulette. *Red or black.* He didn't even feel he had as many choices as that right now. He was just pushing forward, trying to disappear long enough to get to Chicago.

He considered the evidence they might have against him. He had never met Bea Beaujon, but he'd been at the scene of Amoyo's murder and then fled before police arrived. He had been calling Amoyo's workplace and asking for him. On the hard drive of Wayne's computer, now certainly in the possession of Las Vegas police, was an amount of information about Canada Gold that, to a suspicious mind, might be described as—

"An obsessed former lover," the paper had called him. It wasn't completely untrue.

Oh shit.

He heard the siren and popped his head up, peering over the seat and the canvas bag holding the tent and out the hatchback's rear window. A Nebraska State Patrol car, either black or dark blue— *Shit, a Mustang, just like mine.*

"What did you do?" Wayne said with more than a little desperation.

They were crossing a bridge and Cynthia had slowed down but couldn't pull over.

"Yeah, Cynthia," Will said with an accusing hiss. "What did you do?"

Cynthia glanced in the rearview and gave her boyfriend a look that said, *later.*

"What did you do?" he asked again.

The cop was right behind them, Mars lights spinning, headlights blinking, one side and then the other. "Look," she said. "He's not who he says he is. His name is Wayne Jennings, not Daniel something. He's from Las Vegas, not Chicago."

"What?"

"I read a couple of his e-mails this morning," she said. "The cops are looking for him. He's in some kind of trouble. This whole problem you have back in Lincoln. We can turn him in and get you leverage with the county attorney. Being a good citizen counts; that's what the lawyer said."

"Are you crazy?" Will said.

"That's why I waited until we were in Nebraska before I turned him in."   •

"When did you call?"

"I texted."

"Goddammit."

"This will be good."

"He hardly did anything!"

"He lied to us, Will. He's not who he says he is. And we were hours and hours from Palo Verde. That story was bullshit. He's wanted, and for something *bad,* I bet."

"Goddammit!"

They were almost over the bridge. Now Wayne could see two patrol cars following just car lengths behind. He lifted the door handle to his right, but the door didn't budge.

"Child locks." Cynthia gave him a smug smile in the mirror.

Wayne wanted to tell them about the mistake they were making, that they had no idea what they were doing. Instead, he leaned forward, pushing his left arm between them, and gripped the key fob dangling from the ignition. Cynthia shrieked, slapping weakly at his hand. With his thumb, Wayne popped open the hatchback.

He climbed into the way back and pushed the tent over Cynthia's and Will's backpacks. Will was shouting for her to pull over as they got to the edge of the bridge. The cops were close enough that Wayne could see their faces. They burped their sirens. Cynthia slowed.

Wayne pushed open the rear hatch and slid onto the moving pavement, riding the tent like a sled, spitting gravel behind him. The first Mustang swerved onto the side of the road; the second slammed into the back of the first one with an abrupt crunch of metal and plastic and glass, some of which stung Wayne's forehead and cheek. In an instant, he was on his feet and running—lumbering, really—toward the median, which offered a line of old trees as cover. He must have surprised the cops, because he was already dodging honking cars on the westbound lanes before he could even hear them shouting after him.

In a few more seconds, he was into the woods on the other side of the highway, running, running, running. He heard the jingling of three pennies in his pocket—all the money he had left in the world.

42

THERE WAS SOMEONE DOWNSTAIRS.

Nada hadn't even digested everything she had learned from the mess of journals and documents she had organized into a neat circle around her, hadn't really recovered from the shock of it. She had sorted and read—and resorted and reread—until it became too dark to see, and then she slept as best she could, rolled up in a ball on the carpet. At first light she was back at it, desperately trying to complete the puzzle of surprises Marlena had left behind, but now she had a person to deal with, a person she could follow as he walked quietly across the first floor, gently setting each foot down before shifting his weight onto it. She assumed it was a man, estimating his size by the creak of the floorboards and assessing the baritone behind his heavy breaths.

It could have been just a Realtor, but then Realtors usually weren't so stealthy. She wondered if it could be the man from the coffee shop, still following her. Her first instinct was to hide in the secret room—the panic room or whatever it was—but then she'd be trapped there. Trapped was bad.

She grabbed her purse and stepped quietly across the carpet to the window. There was one more car on the street, but it looked empty. She lifted the sash and pulled out the screen and ducked onto the roof over the front porch. Scooting on her butt to the edge, she peered over and found a boxwood below. She maneuvered herself until she was over it and put both hands around the gutter, which pulled away from the house with a moan of stressed aluminum as she lowered herself to the ground.

Stumbling from the bush, scratches on her arms, Nada ran south through the wet heat, the answers to unasked questions now spawning new paths of inquiry, questions that multiplied and branched like a giant family tree, each question a sister or distant cousin to every other one.

She had been spooked by the intruder in Marlena's house, but she was more afraid of the image she'd created on Marlena's bedroom floor. A pair of tiles forming a partial but distinct picture. A picture intended, it seemed, specifically for her.

The eyes, the nose, the mouth. The ears. A glimpse of teeth bared.

She spotted a cab and waved for it and told the driver an address she had remembered but hadn't used in more than five years. She hadn't spoken it or written it on the front of a Christmas card or printed it on some emergency contact form.

The cab continued south.

"Are you to call on your mother?" Patrick had asked her.

A year or two after Solomon Gold's death, Nada's mother sold their Lincoln Park mansion and moved to a large apartment in the South Loop. As soon as she graduated from high school, Nada moved out and had never returned. Heading there now, she was breaking a promise she had once made to herself.

The cabbie was complaining about the outage and the gas he wasted driving to get gas, and the long lines at the pumps on the edge of the blackout zone. With the police force overtaxed, busy intersections had become lawless, honking fields of gridlock, especially the six-way crossings along the Lincoln and Milwaukee hypotenuses. On every block, slouching men and women remained tethered to stoops and porches, waiting to dash inside the minute the power returned.

South of Chicago Avenue, the lights were back on. At one time, Chicago Ave. separated the up-and-coming Near North neighborhood from the slums of Cabrini Green, and Nada wondered if the electric grid had been constructed specifically that way, like the Dan Ryan Expressway, to isolate rich from poor, white from black.

Of course, Cabrini had more Starbucks than tenements now. There were hardly any poor North Side neighborhoods anymore. Not really.

She was a trembling, exhausted, sweaty mess, but she couldn't go back to Jameson's yet, couldn't go back to her room, to her lovely "night and nothing else." There was too much she didn't understand. She trusted no one, including her mother. But her mother was at least family, which might be the kind of shelter she needed.

Jameson, whom she had trusted, seemed like all secrets and shadows to her now. She didn't feel anywhere near the truth. Nothing was green. Everything was all black.

At her mother's building, she announced herself to the doorman, who called up and let her pass, and she rode the elevator wearing needles of anxiety and dread. Nevertheless, she felt there might be resolution in her mother's apartment. Canada Gold was chasing answers, horrible as they might be.

On the twenty-second floor Elizabeth Gold, so surprised, opened the apartment door and tears exploded from her eyes as she reached out to embrace Nada. Icy air blasted from inside the apartment and Nada began to tremble, and her mother responded by holding her tighter. When she pulled away, Elizabeth sniffled and led Nada into her chilly home.

The apartment smelled like cigarettes and air freshener. It was all ivories and blues, more like a beach house than an apartment, Nada realized, and she remembered that if you pressed your temple to the living room window and looked northeast, you could see a sliver of calming lake between buildings. "I heard you were in town. I wondered if you would come to see me," Elizabeth said.

Not *hoped*. *Wondered*. "How did you hear I was in Chicago?"

"Gary Jameson called me."

The circle of conspiracy in her head was getting tighter. "You know Gary Jameson?" It was not an expression of surprise. It was more like a prosecutor's question, one to which she already knew the answer.

Elizabeth said, "He's donated money to your father's foundation. Gary called this morning to say you were sick. He thought I should know." It was undoubtedly the truth, but truth tangled in so many lies, Nada wasn't sure how she'd begin to unravel them.

Nada found a knit blanket on the back of the couch and wrapped herself in it. There were many photos in frames, most of them of Elizabeth. Others were of Nada's cousins. There were none of Nada as a child, perhaps because Nada had never sat still for a picture, but there *was* a photo of grown-up Nada sitting at the final table of a World Series of Poker side event. It had been clipped from a magazine and there were creases across it, as if a friend of the family had folded it before slipping it into an envelope and mailing it to her mother. There was also a photo of her father. The muscles of Nada's face formed an imperceptible cynical smile. Elizabeth would always keep up appearances. The cost of being the grieving widow was a few visible photos of the man she despised.

Her mother's eyes refocused and she must have just now noticed how dirty and tired Nada looked. "Honey. Do you need help? Do you need a bath?"

"I'm fine."

"Do you want to sit? Do you want something to eat?"

"I'll stand." She paused. "But I could eat."

Elizabeth led her from the living room into the kitchen, which was more up-to-date than her mother required. She was a competent, if unen-thusiastic, cook. "I'll make you a sandwich."

"Thanks."

A pause. "So why are you here?"

Nada didn't answer.

"I assume you didn't come just to be short with me. It's so embarrass-ing."

"I know a little something about being embarrassed by your family," Nada said.

Elizabeth Gold conceded with a nod. "So what do you want?"

Information. "It's not easy to come out and say."

"What isn't?"

Nada watched her mother pull sliced turkey, roast beef, cheese, mus-tard, onions, lettuce, and tomato from the refrigerator. Almost as if by muscle memory, she remembered exactly what her daughter liked, how she preferred her sandwich stacked. "Have you ever heard of Wes Wood-ward?"

"Wes Woodward stairs?"

"Yes."

"Expensive."

"I know. I'm talking about the man. Did you know him?"

With the ends of her lips turned down, she said, "They're just the name of a kind of staircase to me. Spirals. You see them in magazines. Why do you ask?"

The familiar background sounds here—the air conditioner, refrigera-tor, microwave, dehumidifier—formed a nostalgic major chord. "Because I'm stalling."

Her mother said, "What are you mixed up in, Canada? What are you even doing here? What are you doing for Gary Jameson?"

"He didn't tell you?"

"No. I asked. He wouldn't say."

"He didn't mention Burning Patrick?"

"What? Who?"

"Patrick Blackburn."

Her mother looked at the ceiling, gathering patience the way she had when Nada was a child. "Who's Patrick Blackburn?"

Nada caught something in her mother's face just as she asked the question. "Patrick is what I'm doing here, Mom."

"Riddles," her mother said with indifference, her eyes, between blinks, glancing up and to the left. "Another boy?" Her mother said it as if she thought there had been too many in Nada's life, although Elizabeth Gold hadn't the slightest idea what that number was. There were almost certainly more lovers in her mother's resentful imagination than there had been in Nada's bed.

Nada compressed the courage inside her the way you might press on a spring and then she let it out: "I know Dad had a spider."

"The sports car?"

"No," Nada said, suppressing an unwanted chuckle. She did the short-hand, tapping her collarbone. "A brain pacemaker. A neurostimulator. Like me. He got it six months before." Although she and her mother hadn't spoken in years, their special mother-daughter code didn't need to be reexplained. *Before* meant *before the murder of Erica Liu.* Before everything changed forever.

Elizabeth Gold expelled an angry breath. "Awful thing. How did you find out?"

"I'm more interested in why you didn't tell me."

Her mother began speaking quickly, as if relieved. "He got it for his back pain. Then he insisted that you should get one. I didn't want either of you to get the damn things, but you know once something got in your father's head—" She stopped to laugh at the unintended joke.

"He didn't get it for back pain, Mom. Or arthritis, which he didn't have."

"What are you talking about?"

"That was what Dr. Falcone's phony paperwork actually said. Arthritis. I saw it."

Nada watched her mother recalculate and her mask of a face changed dramatically. "Where did you see this? What do you think you know, Nada?"

"I know a lot. I just don't know how it adds up yet."

"Tell me." The eye twitch again.

"I don't know why Dad got the implant, but I know arthritis was just a smoke screen. And I know something happened to him after he got—"

"He went crazy, dear."

"No."

Elizabeth halted production of the sandwich and pressed both palms against the counter. "What do you call the affair with that . . . that *girl*?

What he did to her? And then what *he did to her?*" The last part was said in something like a controlled shriek, her voice increasing in urgency and disgust but not volume.

"I'm not talking about that. He thought the spider could help me. And it did."

"Everyone who got those things went crazy. Including your father. Including you. Listen to yourself."

"He saw something. He told Marlena he was like an 'engineer peering inside a massive machine.' That he could 'follow the wires, the gears, the oil, the pistons, each part linked to the next all the way'—and this is what he said—'from here to the One.' "

Elizabeth made an exaggerated show of disgust, rolling her eyes, waving her arms, leaning dramatically into the counter for support. "Your father and that crazy idea. *The Unity.* It wasn't a religion. I don't know what it was."

"Burning Patrick had a spider and he told me he could see almost the same thing."

"Who is this Burning Patrick again?"

Nada ignored the question, only partly because she thought her mother was playing dumb. "After Dad got his spider, he wanted Marlena to give one to me. The same one he had. She told him she couldn't. She said something about not having the 'votes.' "

Elizabeth stared at her blankly, betraying nothing, but not displaying confusion, either.

"What does acusmatici mean?" Nada asked.

"I haven't the slightest idea."

"They were holding it up somehow. The acusmatici. Are they some medical group? I don't know. But then Dad told them—I guess he must have been in jail at this point—Dad told them he wouldn't let them see something—these acusmatici—unless they allowed my surgery to go forward."

"Who told you this nonsense?"

"It was the requiem, right? Is that what these people wanted to see? He was going to trade the requiem for my surgery."

"Where are you getting these ideas?"

"From Marlena Falcone."

Elizabeth blinked. She was definitely confused by that. "The doctor who performed your operation."

"Yes."

"The doctor who was recently murdered."

"Yes."

"The doctor who was murdered with the same gun that killed your father."

Nada held her breath. "What?"

"You didn't know that? It's been in all the papers, although since this horrible blackout happened, they've hardly covered anything but ComEd."

"I didn't— Why wouldn't Jameson tell me that?"

"I don't know. But when exactly did you speak to her? When did she tell you all this craziness?"

"I didn't speak to her, Mom. I read her notes. Some e-mails. Medical records. Receipts. I pieced it together."

"Where did you see these papers?"

"At her house. This afternoon."

"Why were you at her house?"

"Burning Patrick sent me there."

Elizabeth drew in a long breath that added two inches at the top of her head and two inches at her shoulders. "I'm going to ask this again, but I'm not expecting an answer. *Who is Burning Patrick?*"

"He's an artist. After Dad's operation—and I guess mine—Marlena felt she'd discovered an effective treatment for ADHD. She faked a bunch of records, same as she faked mine and Dad's, claiming the devices were really for some nonexistent condition that had FDA approval. Burning Patrick got one. Wes Woodward got one. But they and some of the others went crazy. Woodward and another guy killed themselves. Marlena had to recall the device, and her medical license was revoked. She might have gone to jail, except none of the families of the victims wanted to press charges. None of them sued."

"I wanted her to take yours out, too."

"You weren't even there when they put it in."

"I wanted nothing to do with it. It was all your father's idea."

"He was in jail until two weeks before. You could have stopped it."

"If you think that, you don't remember your father very well." She trembled. "But you're right and I regret it. I never, never, never should have let him go through with it. I knew it was the wrong thing to do and I just sat on my hands."

"It wasn't the wrong thing to do, Mom. The spider saved my life."

"Stop calling it that. Ugh. It's awful enough." She rubbed her lip with her teeth. "I haven't seen you in years. Then you come in here and I'm so happy to see you and you only want to talk about this horrible nonsense."

Nada continued to reshuffle the pieces in her head, the way she had with Marlena's notes and Blackburn's tiles on Marlena's bedroom floor. "I find it hard to believe you don't know any of this, Mom. About Dad. About Marlena. About the requiem. About these people Marlena called acusmatici."

"Your father and I had different lives. Different interests."

Nada stepped toward her mother, ten feet and two stools and a kitchen counter between them. "Your initials were in Marlena's notes, too."

"I doubt that very much."

" 'EG,' several times."

"What did these notes say my initials did?"

"It's not clear. But EG knew Marlena better than you say you did."

"Is EG one of these ah-kooz-mah-tee-chee?" She drawled the word mockingly.

"I don't think so."

Elizabeth Gold's posture became dismissive, shoulders slumped, hands high in the air. "EG could stand for a lot of things."

"I'll agree with that," Nada said.

Elizabeth looked over at the big oven she rarely used. They stood there for a long time, not talking, the same way they hadn't talked for years, for Nada's whole life, the weight of two decades of spoken lies and unspoken truths pressing on them both.

The phone rang. Nada took a step toward her, blanket trailing on the carpet behind her like a cape. Elizabeth mumbled quietly into the receiver and hung up.

"Who was that?" Nada asked, more from paranoia than familiarity.

"Reggie Vallentine." She pushed the plate across the breakfast bar. "I left a message for him while you were on your way up because I was afraid you might be in trouble." She picked up the other triangle of the sandwich but didn't bring it to her mouth. "I just told him to come over here right away."

Nada accepted half a sandwich and walked to the window, blanket tight around her shoulders, and she pressed her head against the glass, searching for the narrow stroke of blue water in her mother's skyline view.

43

SHE APPEARED in the open doorway of his tiny office, prettier than she had looked at the auction, her black hair curling at the ends around her face, her blouse and skirt fashionable and dry. Alberto wondered how long she had been waiting down the hall for one of his students to leave.

"Oh. Hello." He stood. "Laura."

She said, "I came to tell you not to call me."

"I'm sorry. You didn't have to drive all this way to do that."

"I did." For a long moment, it seemed that was all the explanation she would give. "Every other way I could contact you would be"—she looked to be debating the most circumspect word in her head—"discoverable. Unless they follow me, which I don't believe they have any reason to do, speaking in person is mostly safe."

"Please. Sit."

"No. That's all I came to say."

"I don't believe that. Not with gas prices what they are."

She smiled. "My house is an oven. When I leave here, I'm going to my sister's place in Michigan until power in the city comes back."

"I thought they were close. Paper this morning had an interview with the CEO of ComEd."

She laughed. "The power's not coming on until they want it to."

" 'They'?" Cepeda said. "Commonwealth Edison?"

She laughed again.

He corrected himself. "The Thousand."

She said, "You shouldn't have signed in at that auction yesterday. Not with your real name."

"You did."

"They already know who I am," she said. "And I'm protected."

"By whom?"

She didn't respond, so he tried to guess. "Protected from the mathematici. Did they cause the blackout, too?"

Laura didn't answer, but she didn't leave.

"Why?"

"I don't know," she said. "That's the truth."

"How are you protected?"

"The important thing is, you're not. They've noticed you now."

He didn't like the sound of that. "Please. Tell me. Why are you really here?"

"Marlena liked you. She said you were her favorite teacher."

He nodded modestly.

"Can we go for a walk?"

"It's boiling outside."

"It's cold in here."

Walking to the elevator, they passed two dozen turquoise office doors, each identical to Alberto's except for the notices, editorials, and cartoons tacked to adjacent bulletin boards by the resident professors. They stepped over a cross-legged student, lost between headphone hemispheres, waiting for Dr. Walker's office hours to begin. The student acknowledged them with a surprised smile, then closed his eyes as they passed.

Outside, the tops of the elms wilted in the sun. There were few students on campus this time of year and they passed unnoticed across the manicured quad, away from the empty football stadium.

"Your father worked with Marlena. He's in the box—the boxes within boxes—a member of the Thousand," Alberto said finally, since she had said nothing. "But you're not."

He knew she wanted badly to tell him, that she was just filling herself with courage. "It is customary to pass the tradition down through families. But it is discretionary, as well. My father chose my brother but not me."

"Because you're a woman."

"Gender has nothing to do with it," she snapped, as if an insult to the organization that had rejected her was still an insult to her. "He passed me over because I believe in God."

"I don't understand."

"There is a division."

"Yes, I know. The mathematici and the acusmatici."

"You think you know," she said. "Actually, you probably know more than I do. The difference is, ninety-nine percent of what *you* know about them are lies. Lies they want you to believe."

They walked past the Doric columns of Sampson's administration building, off the path, over the stiff grass of the Chem Quad (called so because of the visual dominance of the ugly steel and stone chemistry building, rechristened last year for an aging colleague Cepeda disliked), and across a newly paved access road to St. Joseph's Lake. It wasn't much of a lake, really, home to a handful of small inedible fish and the faint but foul scent of decaying algae.

"What they know, their secret, it's not *complicated*," she said. "My brother once told me that everything that remains of the tradition, the basics anyway, could be explained in an afternoon to any person who'd taken college calculus. And I believe him. Not all of these people are geniuses."

"What does it matter if you believe in God?" Cepeda said. "Pythagoras believed in God."

"Some of the followers today believe the knowledge of Pythagoras was so far ahead of its time, it had to be divinely inspired. Others, while acknowledging the man's brilliance, do not."

"Nouns and adjectives," Cepeda said.

"What?"

"It's an old debate in my profession. Some mathematicians believe numbers are adjectives. That they were invented by man to describe the world. Others believe numbers are nouns. That they have been here as long as the universe, that they *are* the universe. That numbers weren't invented by man, but discovered."

"I can tell which one you are."

He nodded. "So you don't really know?"

"Don't know what?"

"What they know."

She shook her head. "I know *about* it. I know it's more like ratios than long equations, like secret recipes jealously guarded by chefs. I know the body of what they keep secret gets smaller all the time as science catches up to Pythagoras. I also know they all believe, mathematici and acusmatici alike, that when everyone knows what they know—and that day is inevitable—civilization will cease to exist."

"Why?"

"This is what my brother told me." Laura took a long breath. "He said, 'Imagine there is a button, a big red button, in the middle of a field or a jungle or a desert, and pushing that button will destroy the world and everything in it. The button is completely unprotected. There are no soldiers around it. No guards. No fences. No doors. No locks. Any person can walk right up to it and push this button whenever they like. Can there be any doubt that before long, someone will do just that, even though pressing that button will destroy him and every other life on the planet?' The tradition believes it is protecting mankind from itself."

Looking beyond the water, Cepeda could see a pair of old Gothic residence halls next to the ranch-style credit union, and not for the first time, he quietly cursed the lack of planning and logic and especially *symmetry* in campus architecture.

The face of a building—*or a man, for that matter,* Cepeda often thought—should articulate its purpose. For instance, El Morro Castle, the fortress that stood guard over his beloved San Juan, with its pointed snout and narrowed brow, must have seemed like a dragon's head to old-world invaders approaching from the sea. *Here be monsters, ye damn right.* The Brits took the fort once, but by land, without ever looking the great stone beast in the eyes. What El Morro's reptilian walls and fire-breathing cannons could not do, however, alien bacteria in the water could, and the English navy retreated weeks later with a brutal case of the shits.

"Man can be creative in his cruelty," Cepeda said out loud, almost to the water, "but nature has always fashioned the more efficient weapons."

She laughed. "You should be one of them."

Cepeda took a regretful breath. "There is a rumor that one of the secrets is a number that doesn't work. That if you had a circle the diameter of which equaled this number and you multiplied that number by pi, you would not get the circumference of the circle as you should. Allegedly, this number causes trouble in nature—hurricanes, tornadoes. It's said to have caused the *Challenger* disaster when the onboard computer stumbled randomly across it. It's also said that the Thousand know what it is."

"I don't know," she said.

Cepeda swallowed his disappointment. "I still don't understand. What does it matter that you believe in God?"

"The acusmatici and mathematici are almost evenly split at the moment. And while both groups believe that the end is near, that soon all their secrets will be known and that modern civilization faces an apocalypse of sorts, they disagree about what to do in the meantime. Acusmatici believe Pythagoras gave them the inspired word of God and it is their obligation to protect it, to prolong mortal life on this planet as long as possible. Mathematici believe that even if it puts their secrets at risk, they should use the remaining time to aggressively pursue a truth that eluded even Pythagoras."

"*Harmonia.*"

She nodded. "Some mathematici have no use for religion. Others are Catholics, Protestants, Jews, Muslims, Buddhists, and on and on. But my father thought my strong faith, my mother's faith, put me at risk of being recruited by the acusmatici. He feared they would get my vote. So he turned to my brother, whom he saw as being more loyal."

"So it wasn't religion so much as politics."

"I guess that's true." She smiled. "But there are many just like me. Orphans of the tradition. We keep the secret but don't enjoy the benefits."

"Why not go public?"

"Fear is a powerful motivator, right? Fear of them. Fear of spoiling my very comfortable life, which, I have to admit, is financed by my father. And fear that they're right. That it would lead to catastrophe. I've seen evidence of that. You have, too."

"The planes," Alberto said. "The blackout."

She looked away, toward the water.

"You're telling me a lot, though."

"Lots of people know about them, Professor. You know about them. Speculative books have been written. Novels even. The Internet is saturated with legends and theories. They don't care if people know *about* them. They have contact with outsiders at every level—science and politics and business. Their power comes from fear, and no one would fear them if they were completely unknown. But I need you to know that this is not an urban legend or a conspiracy theory. You need to understand that they are real. And they are very, very serious. And that you need to just let it drop."

Alberto pressed on. "I was one of those contacts. Marlena was working on something. I helped her for years. I answered her questions—"

"There might have been a dozen outsiders like you, each working unwittingly on a small part of some huge project. No one person would ever see the big picture."

"But that's the work I was doing? *Harmonia?* A theory of everything?"

"Might have been. Might have been a gadget to be manufactured in somebody's factory. A widget for Marlena to put inside somebody's head. A computer operating system to compete with Microsoft, or maybe a virus to take Microsoft down."

Alberto said, "I'm afraid the work I was doing was what got Marlena killed: Jesus Christ, I might have helped crash those planes, for all—"

Her tone sharpened. "Drop it right now."

"I don't know if I can."

"There was a man named Reuben Contreras," Laura said. "He lived in L.A. Like you, he got a glimpse of the tradition, got his fingers on just a tiny piece of it. And he wouldn't let go. Find out what happened to him, and then decide if it's worth it. But don't tell anyone you talked to me."

She refused an escort back to her car, and because he didn't feel like going to his office, Alberto took the long way, past the library, across the main quad. He turned and looked about, noting students, administrators, tourists, and alumni dispersed across the campus at some distance—random and uncorrelated plots on a grid—none, it seemed, paying particular attention to him.

44

SHE WAS SUSPICIOUS of him, guarded and cautious. Maybe that was just the way she looked at all people, or at least all lawyers. Still, Reggie thought there was something spooky about a girl with a half-robot brain, especially to a guy like him, someone who was keeping a secret she'd no doubt like to know.

"It's good to see you again, Canada," Reggie said.

She smiled, and it looked sad but sincere. Pretty. She was smaller but had many of her mother's best parts—around the chin and the cheeks and the straight white teeth. Her eyes were longer-lashed versions of her father's, round and penetrating and intense.

"You didn't have to call your lawyer, Mom," Canada said.

"Believe it or not, I'm worried about you," Elizabeth said.

A pile of dirty clothes in a Treasure Island grocery bag stood by the door. Canada looked scrubbed but uncombed, unmade, and so he assumed she must have showered here and pulled something clean from her childhood closet—a rock tour shirt and torn jeans with ballpoint tattoos above the knees, relics from long, torturous days at school. They still fit, but they looked to be from another time, like a costume at a theme party.

Reggie said, "Let's get to the reason I'm here, all right? The immediate concern is for Canada's safety. I've been in touch with the Las Vegas police and confirmed that I am representing Canada. They will want to talk to her, but that won't happen today. I'm not even sure what the logistics of that would be, whether it will take place here in Chicago or back—" Reggie stopped in mid-sentence because he could tell she wasn't listening. Canada had a distant look on her face, like someone rewinding through a video, looking for a particular scene.

Not until just then did Reggie realize that Canada hadn't read a newspaper in a week. He understood now why Elizabeth Gold had called him here in the first place. He turned to the mother. "Does she know?" he asked.

Elizabeth shook her head. Canada jerked her chin up, eyes alert now, lips tightening into a frown.

"Canada, have you been in touch with anyone from home?" Reggie asked.

Elizabeth said, "I hadn't heard from her in five years."

Reggie said, "From Las Vegas, I mean. That home."

Canada said no. "I was taking a break from that place."

"That's your problem," Elizabeth said. "You're always running away."

Reggie quieted her with a glare. "Canada, we've been looking for you. A lot of people have been looking for you."

"What do you mean?"

Reggie's father had always told him that if you do something you enjoy, you'll be successful. The truth is, if you become good at something *no one* enjoys—like delivering the worst kind of news—you'll become rich.

He said, "Beatrice Beaujon and David Amoyo are dead."

The look of comprehension came quickly. Her face melted into a horrible mask, mouth open in a trembling kidney shape, eyes flooded, nose wrinkled to a pug. Her mother reached out, but Nada pulled away.

Reggie hoped his intense discomfort couldn't have been read from the expression on his face. His had been the invisible hand that shaped the lives of these women, and although he had not brought them directly to this moment of grief, he had taken so many choices away from them, had driven them to estrangement and then back again, the daughter suddenly fearing for her life, the mother wanting to protect her but not at all sure how to do it.

Which was exactly why she had called him when Nada suddenly appeared—*To break the bad news.*

"How?" Canada asked.

Reggie paused to let her worst thoughts be confirmed. "Murdered. In their homes. Ms. Beaujon's husband was killed, as well."

A whimper and then a whisper. "Lori?"

"Who's Lori?"

She could barely form the words. "Bea's daughter."

Reggie nodded. "She wasn't home."

Canada took a long breath, assessing where the holes in her life would be now and mentally filling them. "Who?"

Reggie's tongue found the tops of his teeth, upper and lower. "Maybe you want to take a break before we go on with this."

Canada's head shook in a wide path, shoulder to shoulder. "Who killed them?"

Reggie reached into his briefcase and removed a creased and coffee-stained *Sun-Times*. "Police are looking at a casino employee named Wayne Kenneth Jennings."

Nada scanned the story and touched the photo with her finger and then sat upright. Something almost like a smile formed on her lips, as if this were the lie that exposed the mistake, as if she now knew everything they were telling her was untrue. "There's no way."

"Apparently, he's the main suspect at the moment, although the police never call them that anymore. They aren't ruling out potential involvement by others."

"It's not possible."

Reggie assessed her the way he would a witness. Eyes and lips—the parts closest to her brain—were all confidence. The farthest parts were less certain. Her hands fidgeted slightly. Her knees bounced twice. She believed what she said. But she wasn't sure.

Elizabeth said, "Good Lord, you won't even give your own mother the benefit of the doubt, but here you'll stand up for some stalker. A murderer."

Reggie quieted her with a hand. "How well do you know him?" Reggie asked.

"He's my friend."

"How good a friend?"

Her eyes turned to anger that quickly. "How much fucking detail do you want?" The transition reminded Reggie of Solomon and it chilled him.

"Did you know that he's missing?"

That surprised her.

"Did you know that the last time anyone saw him, he was fleeing the scene of Amoyo's murder just before the police arrived? Or that Amoyo's blood was found inside Jennings's abandoned car."

She didn't.

"Did you know he was spotted at Ms. Beaujon's funeral? Did he know her?"

Slowly: "I don't think so."

"Did you know that he broke into your apartment? That he has a professional reputation in Las Vegas for violence?"

No response.

"Did you know that on his computer at work police seized a sizable amount of material related to you?"

" 'Related'?"

"Photographs. Many of them apparently taken without your knowledge. Digital security footage taken of you in the casino. A map indicating which gambling tables, nightclubs, and even restrooms you favor within the hotel. Checks on your background, your credit history. Journal entries. Poems. Love letters to you. He even had a massive spreadsheet, apparently compiled from watching hundreds of hours of televised poker as well as surveillance video from the Colossus. It details your decisions in *tens of thousands* of hands. Poker, blackjack. Every raise, every bluff, every hit, every stand."

The head shaking slowed. "I know he likes me."

"He is *obsessed* with you, Canada," Reggie said. "After you left Las Vegas, he broke into your home. Murdered your best friend and your ex. He's looking for you, he's possibly very dangerous, and police don't have any idea where he is."

She thought about all this for a long moment and then started bobbing her body like she had something to add. "Okay, look, this is insane."

"Regardless—"

"Wayne is about as dangerous as a chocolate sundae. I need to think about this." Nada picked up the paper and examined the article.

Reggie said, "Canada, look. Just stay here until we learn more. I'll try to make some arrangements to keep you safe."

"Oh my God," Nada said, leaning over the paper again, the weight of it hitting her at once. "I missed the funeral." She put her hand over her mouth to cover the fear and remorse. That she had done something unforgivable.

They sat in silence and Reggie watched Canada cry for a long time. She refused any attempts at comfort, anything more to eat, just rocked on the couch, holding a pillow to her chest like a stuffed bear.

In a low voice, Reggie at last asked Elizabeth, "She can sleep here tonight, right?" Elizabeth nodded. "Canada, I can tell you're tired. But you're in a safe place and you and your mother can talk about all this tomorrow."

Canada looked at Reggie and then at her mother. The tears were still full in her swollen eyes. She stood finally and walked down the bedroom hall.

Elizabeth shook her head at Reggie. "Your bed's made," she called.

They heard a door open and shut.

"Is this the most dysfunctional family ever?" Elizabeth sighed.

Reggie smiled. "No, believe it or not." He told her everything was going to be all right.

"She's home, right?" Elizabeth said. "Not the way I imagined it, but she's home."

45

PERHAPS BECAUSE he had no idea where he was headed, the police never caught up to Wayne. Thick weaves of branches protected him from helicopters (he heard rotors) and his pursuers must not have had a budget for the kind of heat-seeking technology Peter had described.

He walked for several hours, sometimes losing the sound of the highway in the distance but always managing to find it again. He heard a train whistle far away. Peter once said something about hopping freight trains. He said it was extremely dangerous, but that didn't matter much to Wayne, who was desperate and also probably capable of taking out the average hobo. If he just wanted to get away to anywhere, it might be an option, but even if he found a freight train, he wouldn't know where it was going or when it had arrived. He couldn't risk hitchhiking, but he also couldn't think of any way to get to Chicago without taking the highway.

Eventually, he came to a dirt road, which he followed because it seemed to be modestly more promising than tramping through the woods. On top of his scabby crimson sunburn, he now had hundreds of bites from mosquitoes and flies. His eyes and lips swelled; his joints thickened. He didn't just feel exhausted; he felt old.

The dirt path led him to a paved access road, which he followed to a busy rest stop along I-80. He was on the westbound end, but the restaurant and shops were suspended over the highway, so travelers could enter and exit from either side. Wayne walked across the parking lot, swollen eyes bouncing in his head, this way and that. He didn't see any cops. He pushed inside.

The facility had a Wendy's and a Krispy Kreme and a little convenience store and an information kiosk where you could buy an electronic toll pass or a lottery ticket. Wayne was starting to entertain the idea of stealing a car. He didn't want to, didn't want to be pushed to that and wasn't even sure how he'd do it unless somebody had left a door unlocked and the keys inside. He didn't know what choice he had. Just being out in the open like this seemed like an unacceptable risk.

Wayne wondered at what point he would stop calculating risk altogether.

He saw them across the center food court. Two state troopers unwrapping foil from their cheese-melted Wendy's. On the table between them was a stack of flyers with what looked like a photograph and several bullet points. Wayne couldn't see it from where he stood, but he was willing to bet he'd recognize the photo.

He stepped quickly inside the men's room and turned to a urinal, face toward the wall, before anyone could get a decent look at him. He unzipped his pants and tried to take a leak. He looked up. Taped to the wall, exactly at eye height, was his Colossus staff photo. His full name, his height and weight, his age. "Assumed dangerous. Wanted for questioning in connection with murder." A toll-free tip line. No reward. Yet.

Wayne stood at the urinal, staring at his own hastily produced wanted poster for far too long. He flushed and zipped and washed and brought cupped handfuls of water to his mouth, all without raising his head. He stepped outside and quickly ducked behind a display of tourism brochures. The troopers were standing, getting ready to leave. They balled the ketchup-stained detritus of their meal and unconsciously brushed the backs of their fingers against the guns buttoned into their holsters. On the way to the door—the eastbound door, where Wayne needed to go—they stopped several people and showed them the flyer with Wayne's picture. Each traveler shook his head and walked on.

Wayne counted to one hundred and followed them out. No cops in sight. He peered into three or four locked cars before feeling exposed, then walked briskly to the adjacent lot, where about twenty semitrucks were parked. He hid himself on the hot pavement between trailers and tried to decide what to do. Turn himself in, perhaps. Maybe he could explain it. Maybe they'd believe him, even if he still had Amoyo's blood on his pants. Maybe they'd figure it out. Hoover might vouch for him. Maybe when they calculated the time of Amoyo's death they'd realize Wayne couldn't have killed him. He'd sure acted guilty to this point, though. And if someone was really trying to frame him, if someone had planted his knife, Wayne had no idea what other evidence they'd planted or how he would explain it away.

He looked up and to his left. That truck had a logo for some hauling company he'd never heard of. The truck to his right was wrapped with a colorful ad for bottled water, which reminded him how thirsty he was.

Wait. Water.

What had that newspaper said? Trucks and trainloads of bottled water were being diverted from all over the country to Chicago.

Wayne crawled under the water truck and came out on the other side. More bottled water. He ducked under that truck to the next one. More water.

These trucks could be headed toward Nada.

He walked to the back and pulled the lever. Padlocked. So was the next one and the next and the next. The fifth truck in line, however, had a lock that had been left undone.

It was better than no plan at all.

Wayne pulled the lever and started to lift the heavy door, when he was struck hard between the shoulder blades. He fell four feet and crumpled to the ground. His eyes were filled with red glare and every one of his recent wounds and bites and burns caught fire at once, and for a second he was almost glad to be caught.

"Motherfucker!" said a voice. "Motherfucking water is only a mother-fucking dollar! Just pay for it, you cheap shit, instead of stealing it out my truck!"

Wayne rolled onto his back and crossed his arms over his chest. The driver kicked him in the side. More pain, this time like needles all across his stomach. He tasted blood.

"Get up!"

Wayne tried, but he wasn't fast enough, and the trucker pulled him to his feet. Wayne's vision started to return. The man was probably in his late forties. He had a beard with some gray and unwashed hair under a union hat. He was strong but not that big, maybe two-thirds the size of Wayne.

"Holy shit," the man said, glancing at the logo on Wayne's shirt, and Wayne knew what he was thinking. He'd recognized Wayne. From the posters. From the newspaper. *Wayne Kenneth Jennings.*

Wayne felt like crying. He never used his middle name. His friends, good friends like Peter, wouldn't even know what it was. Now to the world he was a three-name killer, like John Wayne Gacy. They even had one name in common.

He had fractions of a second to decide what to do next. Or not even so much what to do, he realized quickly, as what to be. He could choose to be himself, the innocent man, the man who just wanted to explain. The man who, in spite of everything, still hadn't broken any laws, not even a misdemeanor, honest. The man who hadn't even stolen that sweatshirt in the store.

Or he could choose to be someone else. In those fractions of a second, he could become a person he had never met, the person they thought he was, the "dangerous" person described in that poster, instead of the innocent man pictured on it. He could choose to be that person. To act not as a desperate innocent would do, but as a desperate killer.

He pushed his fist into the driver's face, exploding it in a shrapnel of blood, broken capillaries and nose bone flattening against his knuckles. Wayne scooped up the heavy padlock the driver had used to strike him and let it hang menacingly from his right hand. He grabbed the driver by the collar, halting his slow stumble backward. Both the man's hands covered his bloodied face, trying to staunch the flow.

The driver was crying as Wayne told him what he would need to do to stay alive.

46

TUESDAY, AUGUST 3

NADA WOKE UP GROGGY, daylight punching between the blinds and dragging white daggers across the carpet. She didn't know what time she had gone to bed or how long she had been curled under the heavy sheet, eyes closed and dreamless. Eight hours? A whole day? Normally, her spider had kept time like a stopwatch, but the deep, opaque sleep had dulled her everywhere. She remembered her mother coming in with water and pills, and she'd taken them without asking what they were, taken them because she had wanted to escape the bad news, and now, as she remembered the evening in reverse, as she remembered herself crying, then denying, and then the words out of Reggie Vallentine's mouth, shocking her a second time, jolting her, wounding her, the denying and the crying started all over again.

She was anxious and angry. Angry at Wayne for what they said he'd done. Angry at Vallentine for telling her. Angry at her mother for *not* telling her. Actually, she could pick the things she was angry at her mother for. Some of them hadn't changed in ten years.

Sleep and presumably Valium had dulled the previous night's headache but not vanquished it, and she could feel the pain waking, too, now, sitting up and stretching behind her eyes. A light blanket over her shoulders immodestly covering her underwear and T-shirt, she walked out into the hall and called for her mother. No answer.

The puzzle was getting more complicated, not less, like a Rubik's Cube unwinding, every turn taking her farther away from the solution. And now the horrible news about Bea. David. Wayne, *Jesus.* None of it could be true, and yet there was the previous day's *Sun-Times,* still on the coffee table, proving it was.

And there was also the unknown man who had followed her into Marlena's house.

She found her purse, still on the floor next to the bag with her sweaty clothes from the day before. She felt for the two tiles inside and set them next to each other on the counter. A dog. A dog's snout. Blood on the teeth and on the gray hair around the mouth.

She wiped her eyes and turned away, toward the photo of her playing poker. She picked up the frame, flipped it over, tried to imagine her mother shopping at Target. Almost laughed at the thought.

The world was small and uncomplicated when she played poker, never bigger than the table, population never more than nine, each of the players alike except for the cards. There was only one puzzle to solve at a poker table—what was in the other guy's hand. Nada was so good at solving it that on a prop bet she once played a guy heads up at the Bellagio without looking at her own cards. Of the hands she didn't fold, she won seventeen out of twenty.

The world was even smaller when she played blackjack. Her and the cards and the dealer—not really a person, an automaton—and his cards. That was it. All the possibilities of existence limited by combinations of fifty-two. The choices narrowed to four: hit, stay, double, split.

Next, the photo of her father and her mother. Life was uncomplicated then, too. For Nada anyway. Living with her must have been hell. Part of her wanted to forgive her mother for being bad at a difficult job, but her father had managed it. Her father had loved her unconditionally. Had wanted to make her life better, more than she even knew until yesterday. He had given her the gift of her spider, and even if she couldn't see what he'd wanted her to see—it, everything, "the wires, the gears, the oil, the pistons, each part linked to the next all the way from here to the One"— it had saved her life nevertheless. She had been someone else before the operation, an impossible someone else, utterly lost and incapable of being found.

She touched the photo with a finger. Mo. That's what her mother used to call him. Sometimes Big Mo, after his beloved Mozart. And Loopa. He used to call her Loopa. She now realized she didn't know why. Or if she had once, before the spider, she didn't remember now. An itch in her head, the itch that was always making connections, was telling her it was important, though.

Wait. Not Loopa. *Lupa.*

She went to her mother's tiny laptop, anachronistically set on a Federal card table under the window. She found Google, typed the word, found a few references in a few languages, Czech, Indonesian, Finnish. *No, no, no.* Latin. Italian. That was more like her father.

Wolf.

Feminine for wolf.

She backed away from the computer, over to the tiles, and looked at them again.

Not a dog. A *wolf.*

Weird.

"Are you to call on your mother?" Patrick had said.

She retreated to the kitchen and poured a cup of lukewarm coffee and surveyed the apartment that had once been her home. It had always been like this, minimalist and immaculate. She would live here for a few weeks or months, padding around in her stocking feet so as not to scuff the slivers of hardwood that presented themselves between area rugs, then spend a few days on the street until her designer sneakers were covered in gas and tar and insects and gum.

That story seemed like it had been lived long ago and by somebody else. She thought about a recent scandal she'd heard of, a woman who'd written a memoir and manufactured details of a sordid childhood. When your own life seems like fiction, how easy it must be to think the details can be altered after the fact. How easy it is to believe lies are memories and memories are not truths.

Nada stepped from behind the kitchen counter and inspected the living room floor. The varnish was like new. Not a single mark.

No exclamation points like the one she remembered in her father's study. The scuff mark once made by her mother's shoe in anger.

She returned to the tiles and studied them again. Clearly a wolf now, menacing, fearsome. Nada's heart pounded against her ribs. She wondered what to make of the letters: *a s s/a s s.* Was it a joke? A simple vulgarity? Blackburn was not above that. Nada tried to make connections in her head between wolves and donkeys. She drifted back to the computer and searched for the phrase, the word *ass* twice in a row, but she didn't dare click through to any of the sites she discovered. The puzzle pieces turned in her head once again and she searched for the same letters, this time as one word—*assass.* Still nothing but vulgarity.

Assass. Lupa.

She clicked on Google's Italian language site and searched again.

The second result gave her a new word: *assassino.*

It wasn't two words. It was a fragment of one. Somewhere in Patrick's head, on a tile perhaps not yet painted, were three more letters, no doubt making the word a feminine match to *lupa.*

Assassina. Killer.

She placed her coffee on the table, holding it there while the thought congealed. So many leftover pieces of her life slowly turning and snapping together. She walked down the hall to her mother's bedroom, painted dark, with lots of long horizontals—the bed frame and the windows and two tones of blue paint on the wall. Inside the master closet, almost as big as the bedroom, she pulled out several tall wooden racks of shoes and scanned the pumps and clogs and flats and sandals for three minutes or more before she found the match to the black high-heeled pair in her head—the shoes her mother had always worn to the symphony. Nada remembered a picture of Elizabeth, head to toe, standing next to her father before the concert that preceded Erica's murder. It had been in *Chicago* magazine just prior to the trial.

Fathers are never who they seem to be. A mother with a secret is the scari-est thing of all.

Nada found a box and emptied it of red sneakers. Then she grabbed some tape from her mother's gift-wrapping station and carried the box back to the kitchen, where she printed a note in small, neat letters on her mother's monogrammed stationery.

Dear Mr. Vallentine,

As I remember, Erica Liu had an oval-shaped bruise on her neck where her attacker had crushed her windpipe. She'd also been gouged in the eye. Police never found the weapon. You made a big deal about that at trial.

  Compare the bruise in the evidence photos to the bottom of this shoe. It never occurred to them the weapon might be a woman's foot because it never occurred to them that the killer might be a woman.

Sincerely,
CCG

She taped the note inside the box and found the address of Reggie Vallentine's law firm on an envelope in her mother's file of bills. Then she walked downstairs to have the doorman call for a messenger, passing her mother with a bag of bagels coming from the other direction in the hall.

47

KLOSKA STUDIED the indentation she had left in his soft mattress. It was deep where her hips had been, where the weight of the two of them together had been centered, where the force of their coupling had made its most direct impression.

He couldn't stare at her yet—they hadn't been together long enough, hadn't made any commitment that made staring not weird. But he could stare at her absence, stare at the place where she had just been.

She returned from the bathroom and started a CD, some college orchestra playing Shubert's Unfinished Symphony—"I bought it just for you," she said, "because you're like that, a beautiful unfinished masterpiece"—and she lowered herself perfectly into the hollow she had left, like a child's puzzle piece into a frame.

"Did you see this?" He nodded at the television news, volume down.

"What?"

"Looks like a whole bunch of your old neighbors have moved into the park because their apartments are so hot. They're pitching tents. It's like a goddamn Yuppie refugee camp."

"They should call them 'Whole Foogees.'" She giggled. He rubbed her side absently and she reciprocated along his forearm. He smiled at the thought of her staying for the duration of the blackout. "Let me ask you something," he said after a minute.

"Yeah."

"What do you think of your boss?"

"You mean Reggie? Why?"

"Just curious."

"You probably know him better than I do."

"I don't think anyone knows him better than anyone else," Bobby said. "That's why he's a good lawyer."

She laughed. "That's probably true. Kind of sad, though."

"So what do you think?"

"I think I admire him. I don't know." She pulled the sheet up with unnecessary modesty. "He's nice. He's smart. Kind of aloof, but he puts up with my shit. I learn a lot."

Bobby blurted it out. "He's been hiding something."

"Like what?"

"I knew something wasn't right the night Gold was killed. Reggie seemed to be cooperating, but you could tell he was holding back."

"What do you mean?"

"I had forgotten, but it was in my old notes. He had a briefcase with him. He wouldn't let me look in it. We even talked about getting a judge to compel him, but the state's attorney put the kibosh on it."

"Duh. Lawyers don't let cops paw their files."

"I looked at the forensics report today. First time in ten years."

"I thought you were suspended."

"So I got time. First thing I notice, Solomon Gold had one of those things." He pointed to his chest. "Those pacemakers for your brain."

Della lifted her head upright. "Solomon Gold had a neurostimulator?"

"Right."

"You didn't catch that the first time around?"

Kloska raised his hands like a captured shithead. "It wasn't relevant to the fatal gunshot. It was just a general health notation the ME wrote down, like height and weight and condition of his bladder or whatever. Lots of people have those things. It didn't mean anything until now."

"It's another connection between him and Marlena Falcone."

"Not that we needed another one."

"Did Falcone do the procedure?"

Kloska frowned. "I'd know that if Dr. Dickwad at Executive Concierge would let me see her files. He's put a tourniquet on this way up at the state's attorney's office."

"Did you ask Elizabeth Gold?"

"Won't talk to me without her lawyer."

"Ask Reggie."

"He's a little pissed at me right now."

Della blew the stale air out of her lungs. "What did you do?"

Kloska waved. "It doesn't matter. I couldn't officially question Elizabeth Gold anyway while I'm suspended."

"What did Solomon have the device for? Was he sick?"

Kloska laughed. "The ME didn't say, and I doubt anyone could tell by looking at it. The neurothingy is buried along with Gold, so without an exhumation order I'm not going to get my hands on it. But weren't some of those devices bad? Weren't they making people go crazy? There were suicides, right?"

Della rolled onto her back, a sign of either waning interest or thoughtfulness. "Some. Only the ones for ADD, I think. I don't think they ever proved a connection or anything. I mean they still use them for all kinds of stuff."

"Maybe Solomon's *neurothingy* made him go psycho and that's why he killed Erica Liu."

"That's a stretch, babe."

Kloska pulled the sheet over his hip. "Here's something else. There was gunshot residue on Reggie's hands."

"Yeah, and on his clothes and in his hair and on the carpet."

Bobby pulled his head back by millimeters. "You really are a geek for this case."

She shook her head, bangs waving. "Taking a forensics class. Gunshot residue goes everywhere, on everything. Especially indoors and at close quarters. You'd need a specific concentration of it on his hands to prove he fired a gun. And even then it wouldn't prove it. It would *suggest* it. And the defense would suggest otherwise."

"Okay. It was more *concentrated* on his left hand than on his right."

She nodded. "Proves my point. Before he was shot, Reggie was right-handed, remember? 'If he used his right hand, then he can't be your man.'"

Kloska remembered. In one of the more amusing moments of the Gold trial, Reggie had argued that based on Erica's bruises, a person who was right-handed—as he demonstrated for the jury both he and his client were—could not have committed the murders. *If the defendant favors his right, the prosecution must be wrong. . . .*

"But he'd been wounded in the right shoulder. Maybe he couldn't aim the gun with that hand, so he picked it up with his left."

Della's voice was several decibels louder now and several octaves of incredulity higher. "Why would Reggie murder his own client?"

"As I was just saying—"

"You think Reggie is a member of the Thousand?"

"Or maybe he was hired by them."

Della was sitting up now, her breasts distractingly exposed. "He's an attorney, Bobby, not a hit man."

"All I want to know is what was in that briefcase that he didn't want me to see. It could have been the murder weapon, right? The gun that was used to kill Marlena."

Della wiped something from the corner of her eye. "Look, Reggie was probably on the floor and the killer leaned over him to shoot Gold at close range. Residue everywhere. Was he bagged at the scene?"

Bobby remembered how Reggie had crucified him on the stand over the sloppy tech work at Erica Liu's crime scene. Actually, Reggie had been polite about it. It was Brad Spelling who had nailed him to the boards after the verdict. "He was bleeding. We took him to the hospital and he was tested there."

"Residue decays quickly."

"Right. So there could have been even more."

"Okay. But if Reggie shot Solomon Gold, who shot Reggie? Was there significant residue on Solomon's hands? No, right? So we still have a third person in the room. And we know Michael Liu was there."

Bobby leaned back and closed his eyes. Frustration bubbled into heartburn and he let it subside. "Damn, Della. Sleeping with you is like dating a grand jury."

His cell phone vibrated on the bedside table. Indiana number. He ignored it, but it got him thinking. To Della, he said, "Do you think they could really pull something like this off?"

"Who pull what off?"

"The Thousand. Could something like that really exist? Could anybody really keep secrets like that, generation after generation? I mean, somebody always confesses eventually, right? Somebody always talks."

Della turned so her lips were just inches from his ear. "That's a myth, Bobby. Probably started because two out of three cops in this city are Catholic. You guys all think guilt is an unstoppable force that will just squeeze the truth out of people. You think you just have to wait long enough until somebody can't hold it in any longer. Reality is, everybody goes to the grave with a secret. It's easier than you think."

"There's a weird kind of honor in that, isn't there?" Bobby said. "Keeping each other's secrets. Being able to trust other people that much. That'd be nice."

She giggled again and it made him crazy. "Bobby Kloska, are you asking me to move in with you?"

He pinched her. "You won't tell Vallentine I went off the rails with this, will you?"

She beached her upper body on his chest and pressed the side of her head to his shoulder. "Attorney-boyfriend privilege," she said, which he laughed at, even as it reminded him that sex with Della, in that it required him to get up every day, if not out of bed, was the closest thing he had to a job.

48

THE TRUCK'S CAB was pin neat, almost luxurious, with leather seats and a satellite radio and a cozy sleeping area behind the seat. Paperback mysteries, some of them decades old, with lurid covers and forgotten authors, were bound together with long rubber bands. A small fridge was stocked with water and fruit. Photos of young twin girls, nieces of the driver, Wayne would find out, were clipped to the windshield.

Wayne had ripped the CB radio from the dash, and as the trucker pulled from the rest area back onto the interstate, Wayne climbed around the spacious cab, roomy even for his frame, feeling around in every compartment and cranny.

Under the seat, in a wooden box, he found a hunting knife, sharp on its hooked end, serrated on the side.

And a gun.

Here we go, he thought.

He held the pistol the way murderer Wayne would, carelessly, confidently. He tried to see if it was loaded, couldn't find the magazine release right away, then stopped looking because murderer Wayne would know where the fucking magazine release was. He at least found the safety and then scratched his head with the grip and had serious doubts he could pull this disguise off.

The trucker looked nervous, which was the only important thing for the time being; the whole point of pretending was to make this guy afraid. But not *too* afraid, not desperate like Wayne was. A desperate person might do something crazy, might call his bluff, might drive the damn semi right through the wall of a state police station. Wayne was ready to go that far—he had no choices now—but he needed to keep the driver on just this side of the edge for another eight hundred miles.

His name was Denny Waller and his face was pretty fucked-up. The bleeding had stopped, but his nose was crooked where it had broken and would have to be reset. He had a tissue, brown from dried blood, stuck up one nostril. His right eye was black and his whole face from the cheekbones up was a topographical map of busted capillaries. He'd taken about half a bottle of aspirin and some other pills Wayne didn't ask about. If he was still in pain, it didn't show.

"You still use a CB?" Wayne said after about an hour of silence, which seemed to be doing the trick, tensionwise, but was making Wayne tense, too, which he didn't need. He fingered the wires that used to connect the radio to the dash. "I would have thought cell phones had made these things obsolete."

Denny jumped a little when Wayne started talking, but he swallowed and nodded. "Cell phones ain't much good if I need local info. I'd have to know who was around. Have to know their number." His voice was anxious, clipped and nasal—there wasn't much air getting through that nose. "And sometimes you just want somebody to talk to, right?"

"Yeah," Wayne said. "But now you got me to talk to."

"Yeah," Denny said with a nervous wobble. He nodded at his radio on the floor. "It's even better these days, they say, because you don't have the . . . the *douchebags* sitting at home with the CB on. That's what the old-timers say. Course, a lot of them used to get laid like that."

"Really?" Wayne said.

"Yeah, that's what they say. Back in the seventies, you know. Lonely trucker hag sitting at home alone with her CB."

"Do you really believe that 'Dear Penthouse' bullshit?" Wayne said.

"Nah," Denny said, and they laughed and for the first time Denny loosened his hands on the wheel.

Wayne asked, "You got enough gas to get to Chicago?"

"Yep." Wayne was surprised he was so honest. The easiest way to escape would be to say they needed to fill up.

"What kind of gas mileage does this thing get?" For some reason, Wayne felt the need to correct himself. "Rig. What kind of gas mileage does this rig get?"

"It doesn't get any gas mileage; it's diesel." Denny glanced quickly at Wayne to see if being corrected had pissed him off. It hadn't. "With the load I got, all that water in back?" Denny said. "About five, six miles to the gallon. But I got a pair of one-hundred-and-fifty-gallon tanks, so we can drive a long way. I don't usually like to go deep into the second tank, but you don't look like you want to stop."

Wayne laughed until he started coughing, and soon Denny was laughing, too. "No, I don't, Denny," Wayne said, and as a gesture of goodwill he put the gun on the floor between his feet and cleaned four days of dirt from his nails with the knife. Just a little bit scared, a little on edge, that's all he needed Denny to be.

It turned dark and Denny drove mostly in silence. Wayne wanted to sleep but knew he couldn't. Denny took more pills. They passed the Grand Island exit, and Wayne thought it could be a casino name, the Grand Island Resort, and a series of comforting images from home—his apartment, his office, laser tag with Peter, the In-and-Out Burger off Tropicana—started him drifting, head bobbing, but he shook himself awake and picked up the gun. He didn't think he could fall asleep with a gun in his hand.

"You married, Denny?" Wayne asked.

Denny considered it. "You could call it that. State of Illinois does."

"You live in Chicago?"

"Yeah."

"Your house have power?"

"Apparently. Don't call home often. Wife don't say much when I do."

"Sorry."

"You know them trucker hags I was talking about? Iris'd be one of those. She'd be on the CB right now, wavin' 'em on off the highway right into bed. She's had so many truckers on toppa her, she's like a goddamn weigh station."

Wayne wasn't sure it was a punch line, so he didn't laugh.

Across the miles into Iowa, Wayne heard the litany of wrongs done to Denny by his wife, Iris. She had cheated on him, abused him mentally and physically, borne children by other men, cuckolded him—he actually used the word *cuckolded*—stolen from him, made a fool of him, black-mailed him, spied on him, called the police on him, set his motorcycle on fire. Denny hadn't done anything to deserve this, and he admitted that he loved her once, and even started to cry again as he described their first dates together, back in high school—going to the movies, playing minia-ture golf, and necking down by the lake.

"I've been around some rough characters and I know a few who seem crazy enou—" He stopped. "I know a handful who probably *have what it takes* to do it. But it seems like every time you turn on the TV there's some stupid moron tried to hire somebody like that and the person they thought would do the job calls the police and wears a wire, and it just seems like a good way to get caught."

What the fuck? Wayne thought. "Denny, stop it," Wayne said.

"I've thought a lot about this," Denny said, and Wayne believed him. "I got about seven grand in a safe, unless she's been dippin' in it. Make it look like a robbery and get paid at the same time."

"Denny, get a divorce."

"The guy'd do his thing, cutting and shooting and whatnot. Then open the safe. There's almost seven grand cash in there from some off-the-book jobs I didn't want Uncle Sam to know about. He could take it and be on his merry getaway. I'd come home and report a robbery and I'll *boo hoo hoo*. No one's the wiser."

"Bad idea, Denny," Wayne said.

Mile markers rolled by far below the cab. Wayne didn't think he'd ever been this high above the road. It was almost like flying. He turned on the AM radio and tried to find some news. After about twenty minutes, he heard a story about the crisis in Chicago. Cooling centers had been set up across the city. Eight hospitals had closed, and the ones that were open were overcrowded and chaotic. A man had been shot in the ER of Stroger Hospital when he wouldn't give up his seat. There was pressure on the Commonwealth Edison CEO to resign. A spokeswoman asked for patience. The mayor was urging everyone to check on elderly relatives and neighbors. An expert came on and compared the disaster in Chicago to a hurricane hitting a coastal city. "We might see the death toll rising very suddenly, exponentially, if the power doesn't come back on soon," he said.

"You mind if I ask you?" Denny said.

"Ask me what?"

"Why you did it?"

"Why I did what?" Wayne wasn't even sure what they were saying about him on the news.

"You know." Denny had some balls to come out and ask a stranger to kill his wife, but he seemed afraid to be too forward with Wayne. "How you got here. You know, *wanted* and on the run and like that."

Wayne slid down in his seat so he could just see the crest of the road on the dim horizon.

"A girl," he said.

49

SOME 41,000 FEET over the American prairie, six men were seated around a table covered with heavy linen and set with oversize silver and fine china, all framing a dinner of lobster bisque and Kobe beef. An expensive Australian Shiraz blossomed in a large crystal decanter. An elegant bottle of thirty-year-old scotch, offered but as yet unopened, was held by a clip to the table, which was bolted to the floor, protecting the meal from turbulence.

The owner of the pencil-thin yellow plane was mostly silent for the trip, but his friend, whom the others called "Sheik" with a mixture of respect and playfulness, had been on the aircraft on many occasions and he passed the time dictating its specifications in Arabic. African waterfall bubinga wood appointments and gold-plated fixtures. A state-of-the-art cockpit with a dozen LCD touch screens tracking not just the plane's vital signs but the weather and air traffic and sports scores, as well. Rolls-Royce engines. Five redundant generators in the extremely unlikely event four of them broke down in flight ("There are some things even Stephen Rhodes doesn't gamble with," he said).

The Sheik had been doing a lot of dictating, in fact. He had dictated that this meeting be conducted on the plane, to shield it from possible eavesdropping. He had dictated that it was too risky for Rhodes, who hadn't been invited, to attend the gathering of mathematici in Chicago, that the mission could be accomplished alone by his emissary, a young man who had proven himself worthy and who had clearly earned the Sheik's respect. Rhodes was uncertain if he had yet earned that respect, as well.

The four individuals—three men and one woman—whom the Sheik had invited were familiar to Rhodes, but he had never been friendly with them. Until recently, they had been his rivals, adversaries among brothers. They were acusmatici. And although it was difficult for him even to think it, Rhodes presumed he must be acusmatici as well by now.

When they boarded the plane, the pilot, a man who, like most of Stephen's close assistants, served out of some combination of loyalty, fear, and greed, had gone over his usual preflight checklist, and when he got to the part where he asked everyone to shut off their cell phones and electronic devices, the acusmatici laughed heartily and nodded at one another and double-checked their phones and laptops and digital assistants and anything with a battery, really, because they were aware of recent history and they knew the ways of the mathematici well, although not as well as Rhodes did, and Rhodes responded that he didn't find any of it funny. They rolled their eyes, and that was about the time Rhodes stopped talking and the Sheik started dictating.

After a while, Rhodes retreated to the rear section of the plane, where the emissary sat straight upright in a leather captain's chair, alone with a book and a soft drink. He was a legacy, his father one of Stephen's longtime mathematici friends, which is how the emissary had come to work for Rhodes. He had a bit of a rebellious streak in him, however, and the Sheik and Rhodes had given him several tests of his allegiance and he had passed them with ease—*with disturbing ease,* Rhodes thought to himself, marveling at the extraordinary lengths to which a son will go just to piss off his father.

"We'll be landing soon at O'Hare."

The emissary nodded.

"The single most authoritative daytime sighting in history happened there. Do you know about it?" The emissary indicated that he did, but closed his book to listen nevertheless. "November seventh, 2006, at four-thirty p.m. More than a dozen people—ramp workers, maintenance crew, *pilots even*—all observed a metallic disk between two and eight meters wide hovering about fifteen hundred feet in the sky over gate C-seventeen at O'Hare Airport. After a few minutes, it accelerated straight upward, punching a distinct hole of blue sky into the low ceiling of clouds."

Rhodes continued, "A pilot allegedly opened the windscreen of his plane and took a digital photo, which has been suppressed by the airline. The FAA denied any knowledge of the event, until a Freedom of Information Act request by the *Chicago Tribune* proved that they had been informed months earlier. They knew and they lied about it.

"As frustrated as that makes me, because I want to know the truth, as you do, I understand why they did it. With power comes responsibility, and anything that can't be understood must be suppressed until people are ready. Most people aren't ready for the truth about what it was that hovered over gate C-seventeen at O'Hare."

The emissary indicated with a thoughtful nod that he understood the point of the story.

"Are you ready for this part?" Rhodes asked over the noise of the engines, which were louder at the back of the plane.

"Yes."

The plane banked and turned. Gazing through the haze, Rhodes could see across the lake to the spectacular Chicago skyline. But even in the daylight, the area to the north of downtown seemed dark and dead. "We'll land just long enough for you to deplane. A car will be waiting, of course, but the driver will have only minimal instructions and he won't budge from that itinerary, no matter what you say. Other than him, you'll be on your own."

"Understood."

"Everything else has been seen to—money, alibi, an irrefutable paper trail that shows you were nowhere near this place. Don't do anything to fuck that up."

"I won't."

"Give it all to me. License, debit cards, gym membership. Everything with your name on it."

The emissary did and Rhodes handed him cash in a thick roll. Then Rhodes reached into his bag and carefully pulled out the gun.

"Wear tape over your fingertips," Rhodes said. "Jennings's fingerprints are all over it. We've sprayed to preserve them, but your prints would add a contradicting detail, and gloves would be conspicuous in this heat. We want this to be cut-and-dried."

"How did you get him to touch it?"

Rhodes almost smiled at the story. "I told him it was used to kidnap Patty Hearst."

The emissary laughed.

"Do you have a good knife?"

The emissary nodded.

"This will be gruesome. Difficult."

"I practiced a little. On Amoyo. The lawyers, too."

The flaps of the plane adjusted with a whir and the sudden drop in altitude felt like someone plucking a string connecting Rhodes's heart to his testes. "Police thought it looked personal. Fit with their theory that Jennings did it. Impressed the Sheik."

"Unintended consequences and all that. But good. I want to do this well."

Rhodes smiled and stood, then walked reluctantly toward the front of the plane, toward the Sheik and the acusmatici, leaving Peter Trembley a few minutes with his own thoughts before they landed.

He hadn't mentioned that Peter would be leaving the plane in an old steamer trunk.

50

OUTSIDE JAMESON's dining room was a twisting piece of black metal that rose straight toward the fifteen-foot hallway ceiling and then curled forward like a man with old bones. In the walk between her room and here, down two stories of Woodward spiral and through the narrow hall-ways of the first floor, Nada could count more than two dozen paintings and sculptures, many of them as disturbing as this one. She had been inside many mansions, including her own childhood home, and stared at many a rich person's wall, and she knew wealthy people mostly liked sub-jects in art that celebrated their wealth—lush landscapes and portraits, fox hunts and horses, still lifes and jeweled eggs.

Jameson surrounded himself with art that seemed intent on undermining, even devouring the good life he had made. This was not the studied art of the aristocracy. Not the art of the status quo. Not the art of leisure. Jameson had embraced the art of revolution—of instinct, of reaction, of death.

Most days, she had eaten breakfast in the kitchen with Molly and Hugh, but this morning Myra had come to her door and insisted she eat in the big dining room. "I want to be sure you get out of this room," Myra told her. Pulling up to the table in a dress she didn't remember packing, the news of Bea's death—and David's, too—still had her feeling like her head and her arms were made of lead. Then there was the ongoing reevaluation of her mother. She was hungry but didn't feel like eating. She had lots of questions but didn't feel like talking.

"We're sorry about Canada's friends," Gary Jameson said, as if she weren't there.

"It's disturbing." Canada turned to the voice and was surprised to see Elizabeth Gold at the table. "I don't think she's safe."

Myra said, "This Jennings from the casino. Do they really think he did it?"

"It appears that way." *Dr. Russo. When did he sit down? How come she wasn't noticing people until they started to speak?* "That could mean a lot of things."

"The correct answer is usually the simplest," Jameson said. "It's certainly easy to see how someone could become infatuated with Ms. Gold. She has charisma. She could easily attract a stalker." It sounded sort of like a compliment. She tried to smile.

"Bullshit," her mother said. "Rhodes sent him. Rhodes and the Sheik. They hired him to kill her."

Steve Rhodes? Nada thought. She remembered the couple in the coffee shop.

"What about Rhodes? What do we do?"

"His plane landed an hour ago."

"Is he really coming? That takes balls he doesn't have."

"He didn't get off the plane."

"More like it. So who did?"

"Nothing but cargo."

"Are we on top of that?"

"We're trying."

"Shit."

"Who else is on the plane?"

"We can guess."

"The Sheik."

"If the Sheik is there, so are Svahn, Hage, Elkan."

"Crawford."

"An acusmatici who's who. St. John, too, probably."

Nada remembered a high school trip to the island of Saint John—six kids, with two parents chaperoning. One of her friends brought some weed late at night to the beach and another pointed out that Canada Gold would be a good name for a type of marijuana. Nada realized then that she couldn't smoke pot that night or any other if she didn't want that joke to follow her around the rest of her life. Drugs never really agreed with her spider anyway. Except vodka.

"I need the cell towers back on," Jameson said. "I want the calculations on paper only and double-checked before the wireless goes live."

"Why don't we turn the *lights* back on?" Her mother. "The event had its purpose. Nada has remained here at the house. We kept her from the hospitals. She's not going anywhere. And as far as diversion goes, look at the crowd out front. We're just calling attention to ourselves."

Jameson cleared something from his throat. "With regard to that, we have a problem. I was worried about the, um, *restlessness* in the park, as well. I ordered the power back on three hours ago."

"So what happened?"

"I don't know. Equipment trouble, I suppose. It's out of our hands now."

"I hate fucking ComEd."

An argument followed that didn't much interest Nada. She turned her attention to the art on the walls. Myra Jameson was framed by a large cartoony image of an angel in a pink robe holding a sign with some words on it, probably from the Bible, although Nada was no expert. Jameson had said he had purchased dozens of Finsters before he'd become obsessed with Burning Patrick. He also said Patrick would have to be as prolific as Finster if he was going to finish his mural.

"—none of the risks I take is unacceptable," she heard Jameson say when she started paying attention again. "Jesus, you sound like him. Like the Sheik."

Hugh arrived with a skillet, from which he spooned an omelette onto plates for Jameson and Myra and Russo and her mother. Then he returned to the kitchen for a fifth plate, a fried egg placed in a large piece of sourdough bread for Nada. He smiled. "Molly allowed your mother into her kitchen to make it. She doesn't do that every day."

"Rhodes and the Sheik are a devious combination. Poisonous."

"The Sheik's pissed about the airplanes. Matuszak and Butler were close to him."

"The Sheik believes Matuszak and Butler will be reincarnated, so what does he care?" Halfhearted laughter.

"So will Marlena. At least that's what the Sheik would say."

"He knows I don't believe that shit. Marlena wasn't finished in *this life*."

"And now they're coming for Canada? Rhodes and that horrible Sheik?" Her mother again. "They put this Jennings up to it. Sent him to kill her."

"He won't come anywhere near her. I promise."

"Same way you said you could turn the power back on whenever you wanted?"

Myra said, "We can't have people living in the park. Right outside our home!"

"We've prepared for this. It won't be long."

"What about Canada?" Elizabeth now. "How much will she remember?"

Jameson sighed. "We couldn't have known what she'd find at Marlena's. A panic room? Son of a bitch. Between our people and the police, that house had been swept a dozen times."

"I can't wait for that awful thing to be out of her head. It's been between us all these years. Keeping me from my daughter. A 'spider,' she calls it. Did you know that?"

"We'll do both things tonight. The surgeon is ready. The room is sanitary; it's controlled. The place will be locked down and everyone will be there, including Ng. We'll do Canada before the concert and we'll do Ng just after."

Her mother let out a long breath. "*The Viola in My Life Two,* is that right?"

"Yes, and some of Ng's original pieces. I think you'll be impressed."

"I'd better be," her mother said.

Cheerily, Jameson said, "It's exciting. This ensemble has never performed outside China. Some say the violinist, in particular, might be the best in the world."

"Who says?" Myra said it with the sloping tone of a straight line.

"Well. The *Chinese*." Everyone laughed, even Elizabeth.

The dining room was paneled in oak and lined with more Finsters and square abstract canvases, the effect of which, regardless of the perhaps revolutionary intentions of the artists, only made Nada feel underdressed even in this smart outfit she couldn't remember. The last thing she remembered clearly was walking down the street, trying to decide where to go, what to do. Whether there was anyone she could trust anymore. Bea was dead. Wayne was coming after her. Maybe to kill her. And then her mother, sitting right here at the table, her own mother, a murderer. Her father innocent all along. She was convinced of it now, although she couldn't really prove it, even if she wanted to. She'd left any evidence on Marlena's bedroom floor. All the people she trusted were dead. Except Patrick. She needed to go see Patrick. To find out what he knew about her mother. She'd been trying to remember where she had left her car, and that was when the pin had gone through her brain.

The sensation had been immediate and crippling, all down the right side of her body, different from the last time she'd collapsed, in Hugh and Molly's kitchen. This was worse. This was painful. There was something wrong, but she couldn't see. She couldn't feel. She didn't even know if she was standing or sitting or lying on the sidewalk. She had hardly any sensation at all, and then she had the sense that she was flying, or maybe being carried, and then somehow she'd ended up here.

"We should never have let her leave the house," her mother said.

"You know we couldn't make her a prisoner," Jameson said. "We had to give her the illusion that she was free to come and go. We watched her everywhere she went."

The pain in her head had subsided, but except for the sandwich at her mother's house, she hadn't eaten in a day. Nada tried to take a bite of bread and eggs, but they kept sliding off her fork before she could lift it to her mouth.

Nada tried to speak. "How come I don't get them? These visions. Wes Woodward had them. Patrick Blackburn has them. Dad had them. I have the same spider as they had. How come I don't *see it*? The *Everything*? How come I don't have an *art*?" Nada tried to frown. She had to admit she was jealous. Not of the going-batshit part, of course, but she had always hoped her spider served some purpose. That it compelled her to do something huge, something great. Something like Burning Patrick was doing. "Gary, he's for real. That's what I was trying to tell you. Patrick Blackburn is for real."

No one answered her.

Hugh arrived with a second egg for her. "From your mother's recipe," he said.

She had no more success eating this one.

Jameson finished his omelette and wiped his face. "Shall we get started?"

Elizabeth: "And now I'm not so sure."

Russo stood up. He pulled a syringe from underneath the table. "This will wake her up first." He walked to Nada's side and stuck the needle in her arm. She didn't pull away and it didn't hurt, although she felt heat radiating out from her elbow, crossing her body in a wave.

Nada woke up in her bed, in the room of light and nothing else. They were standing around her, Jameson and Myra and Russo and her mother. There was a clear plastic line from a bandage in her arm to a bag above her head. Russo was still holding the syringe with which he had injected a substance through the IV.

"What the hell?" She tried to sit up, but it felt like bags of cement had been piled on her chest. "Mom?" She had no idea how long she'd been asleep. An hour? A day? A week? The scene at the breakfast table had been a dream, but she wondered how much of the conversation might have been real.

"Hello. You collapsed again, dear," her mother said.

"It appears you've had the equivalent of a stroke, Canada."

"That horrible thing in your head." Her mother again. "It's damaged and your seizures have returned. It has to come out."

"Who found me? How did I get here?"

"I followed you from the apartment, of course. You seemed disoriented. You wouldn't answer when I called you. I watched you collapse from not ten yards away. Of course I called 911."

"Why aren't I at a hospital?"

"The hospitals that are still functioning are completely overflowing," her mother said. "Gary has generously volunteered to let the operation take place here."

"You said you called 911. If I had a stroke, they would have taken me to a hospital."

"The city is in a state of emergency," Jameson said. "Right now a hospital is a dangerous place for someone in your condition. Since you were incapacitated, your mother directed the paramedics to put you in the care of Dr. Russo."

Nada tried not to slur her words, but it was difficult. "They wouldn't do that. What the hell?"

Her mother: "You're not thinking clearly, dear."

"Wait. What operation? What are you going to do?"

"Your neurostimulator has to come out. The procedure is long overdue, actually. Marlena wanted to remove it years ago."

"Not a chance."

"We're protecting you, dear," she said. "We're not the ones who will hurt you."

Russo produced a small black plastic gizmo. A remote. She hadn't seen anything like it since she was a teenager and a nurse had shown one to her in the hospital.

Just before her father died.

Just after they put the spider inside her.

The phrase repeated itself in her head, as if parts of her brain were whispering to each other: *thespiderinsideherthespiderinsideher*.

"Don't touch me," Nada said.

"Canada," her mother said.

In a shriek this time: "Don't you fucking touch me!"

"Don't worry, dear," the nurse had said then. "It's not like the average Joe can just walk into RadioShack and buy one."

Russo checked the face of the remote. "We don't need to," he said, and then he pointed it at Nada's chest and squeezed it between his fingers.

The light slipped away, past her and behind her and gone. She felt her guts drop to her knees and her head braced against the spinning effects of sudden vertigo. She screamed as if in pain, but she didn't feel pain anymore, exactly.

Her mother, distant: "Do we have to do it this way?"

Russo: "We'll never get her all the way under unless we deactivate the device first. Don't worry. We're controlling the pain."

For Nada, it was as if she had been cleaved in two, as if she were falling away from herself. The other part of her, the part with her spider, was disappearing like a shiny satellite into the blackness—into the night and nothing else—becoming smaller and smaller, reaching out to her with the same desperate shrieking sadness with which she, in turn, called out to it.

51

TEN YEARS AGO, news cameras had tracked every step Reggie Vallentine took in this place. Kate had made certain, always alerting the media an hour before Reggie would arrive, posting bulletins with the model and color of the car he was driving and even which vehicle door he would exit. For almost a year, he had been the Elvis Presley of the county courthouse, the De Niro of what reporters covering the Gold trial had called "the Twenty-sixth and Cal red carpet." Every eye had been on him. Every microphone had been tilted his way.

This morning, he left the office without explanation and drove himself south and west along a trio of expressways—Congress to the Dan Ryan to the Stevenson—and quietly waited in line with all the other jurors, defendants, spectators, and lawyers. He passed through security with hardly anyone but the courthouse regulars taking notice. Back at the office, Kate no doubt wondered silently if he was headed for some hotel rendezvous.

Better she think me an adulterer than what I really am, he thought.

Like most of the courtrooms at Twenty-sixth and California, this one was a distant relation to the oak-paneled theater upstairs where Solomon Gold had been tried. The walls were crudely whitewashed, the confines cramped. The judge and jury and prosecutors and defense lawyers and defendants were all in such close quarters that one Cook County judge had famously decreed that anyone sitting in his courtroom had to apply deodorant before entering, and he kept a case of miniature travel roll-ons in the jury room just in case. *Today's hearing would benefit from such a mandate,* Reggie thought.

Derek Liu was seated on the other side of the partition, his head bowed until it almost touched the defendant's table. One of Reggie's associates sat next to him, hand on his back in empty reassurance. Prosecutors were relaxed and professional. This hearing would be short. The judge would decide on a bond and a date for the next court appearance and then this defendant would be escorted out and the next one escorted in.

Reggie nodded at the bailiff who opened the door to the fishbowl courtroom. A handful of reporters and gawkers, dispersed throughout the glass-walled gallery like flies trapped in a windowsill, gasped.

"*Jesusmary,*" the judge whispered.

Reggie handed a thin folder with an appearance form to the clerk, who stamped it. Reggie then took a step backward and came to a full stop before saying, "Your Honor, Derek Liu is my client and I request a moment to confer with him."

One of Bradley Spelling's prosecutors jumped like a cricket. He was watching a routine day at the courthouse topped off by drinks at the Brehon Pub spiral down the toilet. "Oh *bullshit,* Reggie. I'd like to see those invoices." There was muffled laughter from the gallery and the judge let the expletive slide. "We're all very honored that Reggie Vallentine has decided to join us on a routine hearing. But, Your Honor, the city is in crisis—a state of emergency even. Desperate people are living in their cars and in the parks. Neighborhoods are literally burning to the ground. This hearing has already been delayed. We have no time for Mr. Vallentine's drama."

The judge sighed. "No, Mr. Downs, we don't have time. None of us has the time." He turned to Reggie. "Counsel, this is just a bond hearing, not a trial." He took a drink of water and woke his laptop keyboard with a swipe of his finger. "But you may confer with your client. And we'll wait."

52

"LIKE AN INVADING FORCE of well-groomed zombies, they shuffled into the park, hundreds of them with pillows and blankets, bottled water and flashlights, battery radios and air mattresses, winding alarm clocks and golden retrievers. With high-rise water pumps no longer functioning, the inhabitants of expensive parkside apartments—now oven-hot and bone-dry—have retreated to the slightly less stifling outdoors. . . ."

Bobby was sitting at a police desk for the first time in a week, listening to a newscaster describe the scene in Lincoln Park on a small flat-screen TV mounted on the wall. Technically, he wasn't supposed to be there, but technically the city was in the middle of a full-blown crisis, and if anybody cared that Bobby was violating the terms of his suspension, nobody was saying. Hell, if a fourteen-year-old kid could get away with imperson- ating a cop like one had at the Grand Crossing District station a few years back, he figured a suspended cop could get away with impersonating an active one. Since he'd arrived, he hadn't even spotted anybody who out- ranked him. Bobby figured they were all downtown at some blackout task force meeting. Either that or they were hiding. Apparently, the shit was really starting to go down on the West Side, and Bobby had heard rumors about cops just walking off the job—panic attacks, that kind of thing— but he hadn't seen any signs of that here on the South Side. Everybody here looked determined. Maybe a little angry. Certainly hot.

But that was true of everybody in Chicago.

Bobby had just hung up the phone with Alberto Cepeda, who really did sound like he was having a panic attack. After explaining unnecessar- ily that he'd tried to call Cepeda back but that the cell towers in Chicago were overtaxed and he couldn't get a signal and he'd dropped in here at Area 1 to use the phone because the power was still out up at Belmont and Western, he let Cepeda try to tell his story in a long, hysterical exhale. The professor claimed to have proof that the Thousand had killed Mar- lena Falcone. Well, not proof, exactly, but he knew it was true. They'd killed another man, too, an ex-cop in L.A. The papers said it was a murder- suicide, that this cop, Contreras, after being kicked off the force, drove his wife and three kids down the coast in a minivan, parked at the beach, and shot them all before shooting himself, but it was really the Thousand who'd done it, and the Thousand who'd made it look like murder-suicide. They'd killed him and they'd killed his wife and kids and they'd killed all those people on the airplanes, and Cepeda was scared now, really scared, and Kloska should be scared, too, because this cop had been a cop exactly like him, a cop who'd picked up a case just like the Falcone murder and the evidence had led him to the Thousand, too close to their secrets, and so they'd killed him and they'd killed his family and who knows how many other people they'd killed.

Bobby told Cepeda to calm down, but Cepeda told him more, that he knew the name of one of these mathematici—his name was Russo and he was a doctor in Chicago. When Bobby stopped him and asked him to repeat the name, Cepeda said he'd been told to forget the whole thing but that he didn't know if he could because they had used him—"These ass- holes used me and tossed me aside while no-talent kiss-asses like Pren- tiss get feted in Oslo"—and he was scared it might be too late for him in any case, but he wanted to warn Kloska, because Cepeda had been right all along about the acusmatici and the mathematici, that they were killing each other, they'd killed Marlena, and they were killing innocent people, too, women and children. Then when Bobby asked him how he knew all this, Cepeda told him he shouldn't say, he couldn't say, and Bobby told him again to settle down and he asked him if he was going to do anything rash—because at this point, Bobby thought he might be a suicide case—but Cepeda said no, and Bobby told him he'd look into it, and Cepeda said *no,* he was just trying to convince Kloska it was true, that he should walk away so he didn't end up like Contreras, but Bobby told him a third time to calm down, and finally Bobby hung up.

Kloska rubbed his face. An expert on TV was explaining that the area that was now Lincoln Park had been used as a refugee camp after the Great Chicago Fire. A newspaper had been disemboweled and left in pieces across four different desks. The Cubs had moved the next day's game against the Pirates from Wrigley, which was right in the middle of the northern blackout zone, to Sox Park, which was dormant now with the White Sox out of town. *Baseball.* In the summer, he was normally obsessed with it. He hadn't watched a White Sox at bat or even glanced at a box score since Marlena Falcone had been murdered. Baseball seemed unimportant to him now, like the collection of foreign coins he'd had when he was nine years old. That cigar box of metal disks had been the most important thing in the world to him right up until the day that it wasn't, and then it just disappeared. He remembered the coppery smell on his hands after he played with them each day, stacking them and ordering them by size or color or value or geography. Maybe his mother still had them, or maybe they'd been thrown out or given away.

He found another part of the *Sun-Times* stuck to the bottom of a chair. He saw a picture inside of a husky dude with black hair next to an explanation why that ADA in Las Vegas, the friend of Canada Gold, hadn't called him back. *Damn,* he thought as he read the gruesome details. This Wayne Jennings, this person of interest, was nowhere to be found. He hoped that really was Canada Gold whom Della had seen the other night.

Then his mind started making connections, the kind of connections Alberto Cepeda might make. *You have Marlena dead, and you got this woman in Vegas. They both have Canada Gold in common. What if these Vegas killings were connected to Marlena Falcone's murder?* Just as quickly, he remembered what his first sergeant had told him twenty years ago. "Every coincidence has got an eyewitness," he'd said, "and that guy always sees a damn conspiracy." Bobby knew if you took two random murdered corpses in America, they were bound to have *something* in common—an acquaintance, a car dealer, a church, diabetes. Didn't mean it had anything to do with their deaths.

Area 1 was practically empty now except for one sergeant and a couple of exhausted patrol guys looking for a place to crash between double shifts. If the police were making routine arrests today, he didn't see any evidence of it. Bobby borrowed a computer and searched news stories for Reuben Contreras, and reading the articles, the story came back to him in pieces. He now remembered just a few months ago the bad jokes about an ex–L.A. cop with post-traumatic stress disorder taking his own life in a minivan after offing his family. "Hey, Kloska, you know what LAPD stands for? Left'em in a Previa dead."

He looked up the division where Contreras reported and after about twenty minutes of wheedling and inquiries over the phone, he found a sergeant who would talk to him.

"Christ, don't you cops in Chicago got enough to deal with right now?"

"We got everything completely under control," Bobby said.

"Wiseass. You really want to talk about Ben Contreras?"

"What can you tell me?"

"He was a psych case, what do you want? Killed his fuckin' wife and kids and did us the courtesy of offin' himself. The papers all want to blame the job, but the guy had an axle screw loose."

"Contreras ever talk about something called 'the Thousand'?"

"He was always talking, that guy. Nine-eleven was an inside job. Kennedy was killed by the North Vietnamese. If this Thousand thing was crazy shit, Ben used to talk about it. This department's got more black eyes than a muddy potato and the *Los Angeles Times* reamed us for a month because of that guy. Ben Contreras can go fuck himself in hell."

Nice.

Bobby turned toward the TV. The stations were pooling their helicopter feeds. One was following an unknown disturbance on the West Side. Blue-and-whites blocking off streets. Fire trucks angling for position. A glimpse of riot gear.

Cut to a shot over the Lincoln Park Zoo, where six animals had died this week, traveling north over the displaced Yuppies—the Whole Foogees, as Della had called them—and then over North Avenue, where dozens of people were agitating in the heat, spilling out into the road, fists pumping in the air. They were right at the gates of the old cardinal's mansion, practically the only building on the North Side that still had power. ". . . now the home of philanthropist Gary Jameson," a disembodied anchor's voice was saying.

"Gary Jameson?" Kloska said out loud, and he was pretty sure he knew where he had seen it before. Gary Jameson had been one of the vaguely familiar names on the partial list of people Cepeda suspected of being members of the Thousand. A list Bobby had hardly taken seriously when the professor had showed it to him.

Kloska watched a kid throw a rock at the house as another guy leapt up and down, hands over his head, egging the first dude on. No cops in sight. He scanned the screen, trying to figure out what had instigated all this anger. The helicopter rotated and then he saw it.

Rich bastard had turned on his lawn sprinklers.

53

"I figured you wouldn't leave my defense to some second stringer," Derek Liu said. They were in an unadorned conference room more often used by the kind of jurors who would take hours to deliver their guilty verdict just so they could prolong their service through lunch.

"Sorry I'm late."

Derek smiled. "I knew you'd come. You're scared."

"Right now I'm more interested in knowing your side of what happened."

"This cop wouldn't let up. I told him, 'Don't you have better stuff to do?' But he wouldn't let up and he kept saying I knew what my father must have done with that gun, but I wouldn't say nothin', and then he got in my face and I just gave him a little shove. Or maybe a big shove. I got a temper."

Reggie looked at the complaint. "Had you ever seen Officer Borkowski before?"

"We got a little history."

"What have you told them?"

"Nothing. Not a word, not a peep."

"I need the truth if I'm going to defend you."

"I told you if it came to it I could always trade my freedom for everything I know about that gun. It hasn't come to that yet. And now you're here."

"Okay." Reggie stretched his back, pulling his bent arms behind him like wings. "We'll get it dismissed."

"How?"

"I know the judge. I know the assistant state's attorney. I know this court. In a few minutes they'll be forced either to knock it down to a misdemeanor or let you go. Right now I suspect the court will be disinclined to put any more stress on the population of the county jail. If they believe you don't know where that gun is, they'll let you out on bond. I just need to convince them of that."

Derek Liu shifted his weight hard to the back of his chair. "Good. But you realize that if at any time I'm ever dissatisfied with my representation, I'm holding cards here. What I know . . ."

"You don't know anything," Reggie said.

"Really?" He snorted his contempt.   •

Reggie lifted his thick briefcase and set it on the table. With his left hand, he removed a brown envelope and then a black high-heeled shoe. One at a time he placed six grisly black-and-white evidence photos on the table, producing each with a snap, like cards in a magic trick. "Solomon Gold did not kill your sister."

The tendons in Derek Liu's neck tightened and his face stiffened into a mask, disguising the pain and shock and horror these photographs could still deliver. Reggie wondered if Derek Liu could hear ten years of false justification and self-delusion collapsing like an imploded building inside the attorney's mind. Reggie wondered if, through his grief, Derek Liu even noticed that these photos represented not only Solomon Gold's innocence but also Reggie Vallentine's guilt.

As the photos imparted the truth of one murder, Reggie recalled the true story of another.

A story he could never tell.

THE REST OF THE TRUTH

THE NIGHT Solomon Gold was murdered, he gave a loving glance at his violin, the Guarneri, before turning to face Reggie, his feet on springs.

"That whole 'Solomon Gold is also a victim here' crap. I was skeptical. I was *skeptical*. You hardly even discussed whether or not I was guilty."

Without looking up, Reggie said, "A defense attorney isn't supposed to care whether his client is guilty."

Gold rubbed his jaw and said something under a low chuckle.

"The *prosecutor* is the one who's supposed to care about guilt," Reggie said. "He has the power to bring charges. But you were a political opportunity for Brad Spelling. He didn't care whether you were guilty or innocent, only that you were convicted." Reggie raised his chin and tried to find Gold's eyes in the poor light. "That offended me." He had motivated himself throughout the trial with the thought that it was possible for both propositions to be true: that Solomon Gold was guilty *and* that the prosecution was unethically and politically motivated.

Gold said, "I wish I could have been in the ballroom with Spelling on election night. Toasting his misery with bad, oaky Chardonnay from a plastic cup."

Reggie was tired and he was angry and he was not very drunk, but the inside of his skull was numb enough that he shouldn't have driven. The effects of the whiskey had matured as the hours passed and the buzz slithered from his head, down his throat, slowing his heart. Reggie heard thoughts now that didn't seem to be in his own voice. *If a person hearing voices can have thoughts that are not his own, then what is the difference between your thoughts and someone else's? Aren't all thoughts by definition imaginary? Inside the human mind is there any difference between the real and the pretend?*

For the first time, Reggie noticed the binder on Gold's desk. Leather, four rings. Thick with paper pages in plastic sleeves. Reggie had seen a similar object in evidence, and several of the pictures of Erica Liu he had projected in front of the jury had come from a binder just like it. They had come from a collection of applications. Applications for the training orchestra. Applications from Erica Liu's class.

This binder represented a new class. Students from Juilliard, Yale, the Manhattan School of Music, the New England Conservatory, the Curtis Institute, Cal Arts, the Royal College of Music in London.

Some of the pages had narrow Post-it notes protruding like balconies from the stack. When he'd retrieved it from the prosecution, Erica's page had had a similar marker.

Gold said, "I know there are people who will come for the requiem. There are people who will come for me."

Reggie didn't understand.

"They will want the dirty original—*the perfect, dirty original*—in my own hand, with all my notes and corrections, my thoughts and inspirations," Gold said. *"If I protect the requiem, the requiem will protect me."*

Reggie tried to hand the manuscript back. "This is my last visit." He shifted his weight forward in the chair as a prelude to leaving. "Find another attorney, Solomon. I'll recommend one for your divorce."

Gold contemplated that. "Why would you think Elizabeth is leaving me?" He looked surprised, even hurt.

Reggie said, "I thought she already had."

"That woman loves me, Reg. When the requiem is performed for the first time, she will be where she always is, in the seventh row center, I promise. And afterward, Elizabeth and I will eat and drink and make love to celebrate."

"If you say so," Reggie said.

Gold said, "You should love me, too. You owe me everything, Reggie. Fame. Money. Every dollar you deposit, every column inch of fawning press you receive, every pretty girl who flirts with her eyes when she passes your table at Charlie Trotter's."

The idea made Reggie sick, but he knew it was true.

A dull thump from outside the office. An accidental noise that Reggie would have dismissed as an idiosyncrasy of an old, settling house. Gold knew the sounds of the place far better, and from the intense look on his face, the finger held up in a plea for silence, this one was clearly unfamiliar.

Reggie did not know then (and he could not explain ten years later) why it was that when threatened by the sound of an unknown intruder, his first instinct was to hide the requiem inside his briefcase.

"If I protect the requiem, it will protect me," Solomon had said.

Before he could react further, amid multiple concussions in his ears, Reggie felt an explosion in his right shoulder.

He collapsed from the chair onto the floor, more from shock than pain, his legs tucking themselves instinctively underneath his torso like a child in an earthquake diving under a desk. His left hand pressed the fabric of his jacket against the wound—two wounds, he would realize later, an entrance and an exit about three inches apart in the muscle of his arm.

He thought he had heard several shots, but as far as he could tell, he had been hit only once. Fearful of an expected, more deadly second volley, Reggie held his briefcase in front of his torso and turned his face slowly toward the door, toward his assailant.

Michael Liu's pupils were black bull's-eyes ringed in red from crying. His cheeks were bowed from lack of sleep, his nose raw from rubbing, and his clothes were stiff with old sweat. His black shoes were scuffed after weeks of not having the strength to lift them even half an inch off the pavement. He was holding a black gun, shakily, at arm's length. Mr. Liu looked unsurprised to see Reggie there. "You haven't returned my calls," he said.

Gold was on the floor, too, bleeding from his leg. He looked startled but not panicked. In fact, he seemed in Reggie's brief glance to look vindicated, almost as if he'd been expecting *something* to happen that night, if not this.

"You know he killed her," Mr. Liu said to Reggie. "You defended him anyway."

Lifting his bloodied left hand away from his body in submission, Reggie asked himself if he had suspected all along that Michael Liu was capable of a solution this drastic, and he realized the answer should have been yes. He had watched the man become smaller in the courtroom pews every day of the defense presentation and Reggie knew well that a proud man in a shrinking body is always wound too tight.

A thin extension of the man's accusing hand, the gun vibrated at Reggie as Michael Liu fidgeted with the grip. A heat rash erupted across visible patches of Mr. Liu's skin. "When I was a child, I asked my mother how God could allow all the evil in the world. Do you know what she told me?"

Reggie didn't answer, but he glanced briefly again at Solomon Gold, who was alert but ice still. The pain was tolerable if Reggie didn't move his arm, and his head was starting to clear, along with the ringing in his ears. Just as he would in a courtroom, he considered every possible action and outcome—freeze, lean forward, lean backward, a verbal challenge, an apology. Like Gold, he decided to remain still and, for now, silent.

Michael Liu continued to focus on Reggie, "She told me that God allows evil to exist so that good men may confront it." He jerked the pistol suddenly, as if it were a hammer meeting an imaginary nail. This time, Reggie jumped. "If he asked you today, Mr. Vallentine, would you be able to tell God that you have faced evil and won? Or would you be forced to admit instead that you have succumbed to it?"

Reggie tried to will saliva into his sticky, dry mouth. The tremors in Mr. Liu's hand almost reached the point of seizure. He was a desperate man, a man who had had the most cherished thing in his life ripped from him in an instant and then was forced to become a helpless observer while lawyers picked at his open wound for months afterward. Gold's acquittal had been a terminal diagnosis for Michael Liu. He would never heal, never move on, never stop grieving. The insane urge that lured him to this house, the voice that whispered in his ear to bring this gun and to point it at Reggie, who had been the public face of his anguish, would persist for the rest of his life. Reggie Vallentine would always prosper from having been Gold's lawyer and Michael Liu would always suffer from having been Erica's father. That was what Michael Liu must have been thinking when he shot Reggie first instead of Gold.

Or maybe he had just decided to kill Solomon last.

Reggie managed to prop himself up against a leg of the chair behind him. "You're right, Mr. Liu. Everything you say is exactly right. If you think that shooting me is going to bring you satisfaction, then you should do it. But fifteen minutes from now, would you rather be on your way home to your family or on your way to a long prison sentence for murder? What would Mrs. Liu want right now? Or your son, Derek? Would they really want to lose a husband and father in addition to a daughter and sister?"

Tears pooled in the wells of Michael Liu's eyes. Reggie knew how to keep score in a debate and he figured if he could just prolong this moment, this intense and horrible feeling of self-doubt, Michael Liu would put down the gun.

Reggie allowed himself another look at Gold. The composer's teeth were clenched and he was jerking his head at something just behind Reggie and to his left. The movement attracted Michael Liu and he turned the attention of the gun's barrel to Gold, who feigned an innocent look. Reggie took advantage, reaching back with his good arm and finding a small cabinet door above the molding, and then a knob and then, upon opening the door and feeling inside, a cold gun—thin at the end, round in the middle.

Reggie pulled his left hand back and looped his fingers inside the briefcase handle and with a roar of pain flung the bag in Michael Liu's direction.

Paper, dozens of pages, spilled free and floated in the air as the briefcase tumbled from his hand. Startled, Michael Liu didn't fire, but he watched the pieces of the requiem, Solomon Gold's masterpiece, flutter like giant snowflakes to the floor.

Under the cover of paper, Reggie was able to reach with his good arm and grab the gun inside Gold's cabinet, which he quickly pointed at Michael Liu.

"God, yes," Gold said, eyes recharged with adrenaline and hope. "Yes!"

Reggie didn't feel hate or anger, only certainty. Self-preservation. *Purpose.*

Mr. Liu wiggled the barrel of his gun roughly at Reggie's chest. Reggie pushed himself to his feet and then the tears were released in long streaks from Michael Liu's eyes, sobs convulsing his torso.

Cool and detached, Solomon said, "Vallentine could kill you right now, Liu, and never be prosecuted for it. You've invaded my home. You've already shot both of us. You clearly came to my house to *assassinate* me. Your death would be in our self-defense." Liu's gun was still pointed at Reggie's chest, but Michael Liu and Solomon Gold were staring into each other's eyes and the place where fear and hate met between them was almost visible, like heat on asphalt.

"Tell him, Reggie," Solomon said. "Tell him how we could kill him right now. Tell him how ironic it is that just a few weeks ago you were groveling for my life in front of a judge and jury and this sad little man was cheering on the executioner. And now it is Mr. Liu who has to beg *you* for his life. Even if you choose to put this gun down and grant him a reprieve, he will spend most of the rest of his pitiful life in the same prison cell where he once wrongfully willed me."

Still hobbled in a sitting position on the floor, Gold reached up to the corner of the desk and snatched a cordless phone with two fingers.

"MynameisSolomonGoldandthereisanintruderinmyhomepleasehurry-hehasagun." Gold gave the emergency dispatcher his address and hung up quickly. "I'll enjoy sitting in the victim's pew, cackling through your trial for attempted murder," he said to Liu. "I'll enjoy seeing you in leg irons. You'll have it much worse than I did, too. They treated me pretty well in there, but you are not an extraordinary man. You'll find no friends among inmates or guards. Perhaps if you had the courage to kill me, they would have some respect for you, but instead they will look at you and they will see a pathetic and cowardly old man. And every time I sit down to a meal of Kobe beef and foie gras and Cabernet, I will think of the white bread and bologna they are feeding you. Oh, I should write an opera about this, the irony is so fucking perfect."

Reggie studied Michael Liu's face for a sudden shift in despera-tion, some sign he had decided to go down shooting. Liu had not yet surrendered the gun, and Reggie wondered and worried if he could even hit the man from this distance—twenty feet or so—if he were forced to. Mr. Liu's sobs had turned convulsive. Their standoff was just an argument with guns, and once again Reggie felt like he should be winning. He could feel what Derek Liu was thinking—that he had slowly been driven to a rash act and would now pay for that rashness for the rest of his life.

He should have put the gun down by now, Reggie thought. *Why hasn't he put the gun down?*

And then Reggie knew.

He's going to shoot at least one of us. Gold or me. If I don't kill him first, he's going to kill one or both of us. Then maybe himself.

The headlines flashed across Reggie's mind. The headlines if Reggie Vallentine killed the father of his client's victim. No matter how justified, no matter that it would be a clear case of self-defense, it would only cement his bond with Solomon Gold. They would be a killing team. Butch and Sundance. Leopold and Loeb. The wealthy and unsympathetic killers of undeserving father-daughter victims.

Vallentine and Gold. History would put Reggie's name first. It sounded better.

Reggie Vallentine, who had become famous by taking on the impossible and winning, by thinking quickly on his feet, by making prudent decisions in a split second's time, figured out what he was supposed to do next.

With the gun in his left hand, he turned forty-five degrees and from just four feet away fired a fatal shot into the center of Solomon Gold's face that shook inside Reggie's ears like a cymbal crash.

The sound had caused Mr. Liu to recoil and now his gun was pointed away as Reggie turned the revolver again toward him. Liu was confused and frightened. Although he might have arrived here with the intent to murder a man, he had clearly not prepared himself for seeing a man murdered.

Reggie nodded at Gold's body, which had fallen on its back, away from Reggie, toward the desk. "Take Solomon's wallet," Reggie said. "And his watch. Hurry."

Michael Liu nodded slowly. It wasn't clear if he understood what Reggie had planned, only that he was compelled to submit. He felt in Gold's pants and removed his billfold, but he had difficulty with the latch on the watch. Searching pockets, he found Erica's necklace and he paused for a moment, sobbing, before stuffing it into his pocket. He turned to look into Gold's vacant face, as if some final words Reggie couldn't hear were escaping the composer's mouth.

A siren outside, still at a distance, around corners. Reggie spun Solomon Gold's revolver and, gripping the still-hot barrel through his coat sleeve, offered its handle to Michael Liu. "Get rid of it."

Michael Liu took the gun and traced a line with his eyes from it to Reggie's face and back again, perhaps imagining what it would be like to finish the job he had come to do. With both guns in his possession, and his enemy dead, he could delete Solomon Gold's representative, the public face of his enemy, with little resistance.

He said instead in a nervous rasp, "We will share a secret, Mr. Vallentine."

Reggie said, "Call it a retainer."

Michael Liu nodded and left at a run, hunchbacked over the watch and wallet and guns cradled inside his arms. Reggie, in great pain and bleeding but still alive, began contemplating the murder he had committed. He hadn't killed Solomon in self-defense, at least not the way the courts would see it, but he had killed in *self-preservation*.

He wondered now about the story he would tell. Perhaps there was a way to show the world the monster Solomon had been—if they could only hear the cruel words he had just spoken to Erica Liu's father. But he thought of Gold's innocent daughter. She had suffered so much and would suffer still. Perhaps standing by Gold's memory, maintaining his client's innocence, perpetuating the slightest bit of doubt, the smallest, last pebble of hope that her father *might not* have been a savage killer was a gift Reggie could give to young Canada Constanze Gold.

With one hand, Reggie swept up the scattered pages of the requiem and stuffed and locked them inside his briefcase. It will look like a robbery. They will think Solomon was killed for his manuscript. He listened for Michael Liu's steps out the door and down the stairs of Gold's home—now the widow Elizabeth's home (transferred without a protracted divorce, one more favor the overburdened legal system owed Reggie Vallentine). Just ahead of the sirens he heard the gate clang as Liu passed through it, out onto the empty sidewalk and into the shadows of Lincoln Park.

Where Solomon Gold had said the wolves would be.

55

A FEW HOURS in a police station had made Bobby feel like a real cop again, so he got in his truck and headed north on the LSD. The LaSalle exit was barricaded, so he drove on to Fullerton and from there maneuvered his way through a handful of improvised roadblocks—garbage cans and benches—erected by the Whole Foogees. He left the truck in the street and pushed through the park back toward North Avenue.

New refugees from the heat were fleeing the steaming high-rises along the lake and joining the camp every hour, couples mostly, but also singles in groups, friends treating the blackout like a holiday, as if they were renting a Wisconsin lake house instead of squatting on a piece of city parkland. As the crowd grew, it became inevitably unrulier—noisier, rowdier, unpleasant. Nevertheless, Bobby couldn't see a single cop in any direction. The air smelled mostly of sewage and a little of ash. The fires had started on the West Side and eventually causes would be determined. Blame would be assigned. Arrests would be made. But at the moment, the distant plumes of smoke above the trees to Bobby's right were only an unwanted answer to a question no one had the courage to ask. *How much worse can this get?*

Dogs, as irritable and hungry as their owners, barked and fought and snarled and howled. Some people were trying to camp on the beach, across a pedestrian bridge over Lake Shore Drive, as if that were more romantic than the crowded park. Without shade, Bobby knew, the sun there would be too hot during the day, the sand too gritty at night. The urban beach was a lovely place to spend a morning, its waters the only real refuge from the heat, but it was an inhospitable place to live. Beyond them, an armada of boats had dropped anchor offshore, a new settlement on the cool water.

Bobby estimated some three hundred refugees from nearby apartments were now settled uncomfortably into their Eddie Bauer tents, their Land's End air mattresses, their lean-tos improvised from custom-made curtains. The previous day, the city had delivered six portable toilets, which had been quickly overwhelmed with use. Another six arrived that morning, allegedly courtesy of Gary Jameson, who might or might not be in the Thousand but who was definitely the asshole with the generator in the big house at the edge of the park. Peering between tent flaps, he caught glimpses and snippets and smells of people making love, sleeping, smoking pot. Everyone was agitated and he could hear bits of conversation as he passed.

"Fucking ComEd. What's their problem?"

"That house pisses me off. They got the lights on during the day, for Christ sake."

"Some kind of fucking gesture. That's all I want. Common decency. A gesture."

Most North Siders of means were waiting out the crisis with friends and relatives or in suburban hotels. Bobby wondered about the Whole Foogees, the ones who had stayed behind. They believed the power might come back anytime, he guessed. They were young kids, mostly, who still saw adversity as adventure or an excuse to party, or both.

Bobby checked in at a small improvised first-aid tent—a white canopy, really. It was manned by volunteers from the neighborhood—a few nurses, a med student, a paramedic, a vet. There had already been one death, cause undetermined, but probably a heart attack, body moved to the beach, covered and quickly grieved over, waiting in the sun for the coroner, who hadn't yet arrived. The makeshift funeral had only briefly disrupted the all-day volleyball games just a few yards upwind, they told him.

Trash now completely obstructed the road that cut through the park, linking LaSalle Street to Lake Shore Drive. That meant freer access to the less spoiled southern end of the beach through a tunnel under the highway. In twenty-four hours, Bobby guessed, the sand there would be just as saturated with feces and glass and garbage.

The media must have been stretched thin, too, but unlike the cops, the newspeople had managed a full-time presence in the park, a far safer beat than the West Side, where, it seemed, the real action was. Television helicopters hovered overhead, the noise of their rotors constant as cicadas.

And where's the damn National Guard?

At North Avenue, the mini-riot was over, but there were still a few agitators who would periodically rush at the house, waving arms and screaming curses. Bobby noted a few shattered windows on parked cars, some burn marks in the pavement where firecrackers had smoldered, red spray paint on the mansion's locked gate.

Across the street from the house was a statue of a seated man, bald and bearded, wearing a suit, with one hand on a book, the other in his lap. The engraving called him Greene Vardiman Black. Bobby was a South Sider, but he'd been to this park dozens of times. He'd never paid any attention to this statue.

Of course, Chicago had statues erected to all kinds of pricks and douchebags.

He leaned against it just as his phone vibrated in his pocket, startling him.

"Yeah?"

"Where you at?" Traden. "I been calling you all morning."

"If you haven't noticed, cell reception has been inter-fucking-mittent," Bobby said, even as he heard dozens of discordant ring tones suddenly calling out from all over the encampment, accompanied by cheers. "I'm over by Lincoln Park, checking things out. Where you at?"

"Madison and Pulaski."

There was a lot of muffled noise on Traden's end. Bobby could hear sirens. "Say, you gotta put a call in, Jimmy. I haven't seen a patrol over here since I showed up. The park's turned into a goddamn refugee camp. They almost rushed that big house with the generator at North and State. You know, where the archbishop used to live."

"Not gonna happen," Traden said. "West Side's going to serious hell. Everybody's out in the street, gats going off. We got fires, looting. I don't know if there's a body count yet, but it's only a matter of time. And the force is already burning oil. The union's screaming at the chief about overtime. The park's all yours for the time being."

"Christ, Jimmy. I'm on forced vacation."

"Well, you're showing real initiative. You got your gun, right? Your citizen piece?"

"Christ," Bobby said again. "Hey, Jimmy."

"Yeah?"

"If your last name was Black, would you name your kid Greene?"

"What are you talking about?"

Bobby didn't know.

"Anyways, I got some Canada Gold news," Traden said.

"What?"

"Did you hear about that Vegas fugitive? The dude who killed the ADA we were looking for and then disappeared."

"Yeah, I saw that."

"Dude is apparently obsessed with Canada, and I hear the latest theory is she's come home to Chicago and he's lit out after her."

"Serious? Della thought she saw Canada the night the lights went out, but I told her she was losing it. Anybody seen the doer?"

"It's taking some time to piece it together from different jurisdictions. Wayne Jennings is his name. They found his car in Nevada, stolen by some joyriding kids. They nabbed a methhead in Arizona who had Jennings's wallet and a knife that looks like it might have been used to torture one of the Las Vegas victims. The state boys almost nabbed Jennings in Nebraska, except he went Boogie boarding right out the back of a moving station wagon and beat it into the woods."

"Holy shit."

"We're still getting the details, like I said. Looks like he's hitchhiking. He could be laying low, or he could get caught, or he could be here anytime."

"Great."

"Just thought as long as you were playing amateur detective, you could work on that case awhile."

"No thanks," Bobby said. "I'll hang out here for a bit, but tell them I'm not staying all day and night. My girlfriend and I have serious under-the-sweatshirt plans."

But before he finished saying all that, the cell lines went dead again. Frustrated cursing and groaning and screaming followed from all quarters of the park.

56

THEY WERE SOMEWHERE OVER OHIO, with another big lake to their left, when Rhodes heard the sound, and he almost didn't recognize it. He stood and glanced at the acusmatici, who appeared as confused as he was.

"Turn it off," he said calmly. "Find that phone and turn it off. I'm serious." They began searching their bags and their pockets, but not with the urgency Rhodes wanted, and this time he said, *"Goddammit, find that phone!"* as the Sheik watched him with curiosity evolving into concern; by then it wasn't one phone, but three, and then six, and then he heard a bong of a laptop turning itself on and the tweet of a digital reader, and the tinny chirping of a music player, and by this time there was no mistaking what this was, which was not just one cell phone left on vibrate out of carelessness, but an attack, an all-out attack, for which Rhodes knew there was little defense, and he said, *"The batteries! Take out the batteries!"* And now it was Rhodes who was doing the dictating as he and the Sheik both fumbled for their phones and then there was a pop and a scream and Rhodes saw the lone female acusmatici and her face was burned and her hand gnarled by acid from an exploded battery.

Rhodes wanted to explain what was happening, that the mathematici were using their phones as transmitters to interfere with everything electronic on the plane, including and especially the cockpit controls and communications, that they had found a cell phone that had never been turned off, just switched to vibrate or silent, and used that one to turn on the others, and Rhodes remembered now the day years ago when the possibility of such a thing had first been raised—"It would be like crashing a plane with a lowered tray table," somebody had said—and Rhodes had laughed with all the rest of them, and of course he didn't explain any of that now, but as the plane pitched violently to the right on its way into a roll, as he was hurled painfully against the bubinga wood of the bar, as he heard a champagne bottle smash amid the terrified screams of his colleagues, he wondered what would have happened if he hadn't laughed that day, if he'd taken more of a leadership role. If only he'd had his own vision of what the mathematici could be, he could have used the charisma and persuasive powers that had made him a success in the most charismatic town in America and maybe everything that happened afterward, Butler, Matuszak, all those innocent people on those planes and this one, his pilots—*Christ, I know their families*, he thought just before passing out—everything might have been different.

57

SHE HADN'T HAD a sleep like this in forever. A deep, penetrating, hallucinatory sleep. Not since the day they'd put the spider inside.

That really was forever ago. Canada Gold's whole life. The years before that were lived by someone else, that little girl's memories having been passed along to Nada like a shoe box of old photos.

Sleep had always come easy to her. Just a switch in her head, a twitch in one of her spider's legs. But sleep rarely transported her into complete unconsciousness. Her spider—a machine, after all—was always awake, even if the rest of her wasn't.

This sleep, with her spider turned off and with the needle feeding her arm, this was a deep and dreamful something else. She could get used to this.

Life without her spider.

Everything became white. Whiter than this room at its whitest. Or maybe *bright* was the better word. Light surrounded her. Enveloped her. Warmed her. But the light didn't seem infinite and terrifying. It was close. Personal. A womb of light.

Then she was high above the old Marshall Field warehouse, looking down from the foreman's office at the empty space. She was alone. Her tile was on the floor far below. She heard a metronome sound, like water dripping, but loud and reverberating. The office smelled like wet rug. Paint peeled from the moldings. The sliding window was open, creating a double pane of glass opaque with grime. She leaned out the opening.

Her tile had become two, hers and Marlena's together making the eyes and snout of a wolf.

She imagined a grid set over the concrete, and this second one had been placed three imaginary rows up and fifteen imaginary spaces across. It was too far away to make out anything but a sense of color. Green or blue.

But there weren't only two tiles. Not anymore. Now there were four. Next eight and then sixteen, each a mostly equidistant speck across the massive warehouse floor. In another instant there were hundreds and a moment later the hundreds had become thousands. They were multiplying, growing, and the great big picture was coming into focus, the entire magnificent mural of lava and waterfalls and dragons and birds, and soon the warehouse was too small to contain it and the tiles were crawling up the walls like ivy—*like insects*—crawling like spiders, but not like her friendly spider, for these were fearsome, biting, dirty things and they were fast, so fast, and when she spun around, they were coming into the office, under the door and over the windowsill, and she begged them to spare her, and now the dripping sound had become a long tone, a violin, and she leaned out the window and gazed again into the completed mural and saw how lovely and malicious it was, with planets and comets and cities of steel and all the living things, trees and lizards, tiny proteins and mitochondria, bears and wolves.

Wolves.

Then as a long slow note was played across a single string, the light was back, like a knife slicing between the hemispheres of her mind.

She was upright. *A wolf. She's a wolf!* She might or might not have said it out loud. The IV pulled painfully at the bandage and she arranged herself on top of pillows so she could look around. She was in her bed in Jameson's home, the room of light and nothing else, fully illuminated and scrubbed clean. Her comfortable queen-size bed had been replaced by the hospital kind, but even besides that it looked different, strange, and she knew right away that the difference was her. The difference was not what she saw but the way she saw it. There was no focal point, no order, no priority attached to any of the items in the room. The bed, the nightstand, the vase, the closet door, her shoes placed neatly beside the bed, the bag hanging from an IV pole, the white box of fireplace matches on the mantel, the blanket over her legs and feet, machines that blipped and blooped, medical machines on wheels arranged in a semicircle about her—they seemed all of similar importance, no one thing more prominent or precious than any other. The light was so bright, it seemed to make everything vibrate and hum and pitch and yaw. The brightness even had sound, a high, piercing frequency like a needle in her ear.

Canada realized now that her so-white room, the spare quarters she had fallen in love with when she arrived, had been an operating room all along.

She didn't know what day it was, but she rubbed her head and tried to remember what she did know. Right. Her best friend was dead. Her mother was a murderer. The good news was her father might not have been. Also, her last living friend was trying to kill her. She wondered if any of that was true, if all of it was true, if none of it was true. If all of that had been a dream or if this was. The uncertainty was crippling. She wondered about the others with the spider, the ones who had killed themselves. She wondered if this was the same break with reality they had experienced. She knew if it went on too much longer, the confusion and uncertainty and the ringing in her ears, she wouldn't feel any resistance at all to the allure of suicide.

The room did one full rotation and fell away. She was staring up now at the ceiling. Lying on something cold. The floor. She thought there had been a carpet here once, but now it was hard. Linoleum or tile. White like the rest. She turned her head and tried to find where the floor met the wall and couldn't. It was one continuous plane of white with no horizon.

Canada tried to swallow, but her dry mouth stopped her. She drifted from thought to thought, question to question, unsure if her thoughts were real, or if they were ideas like dreams, emerging from some mysterious unconscious self in her head.

WhatwilltheydotomewhatdoesmymotherhavetodowiththiswhoarethesepeopledidtheykillDadwhatisthishotliquidtheyarepumpingintomyveinwasallofitatrickisanyofitrealwhydidn'tIseeitwhydotheywanttocutmeopenandyankoutmyspider?

She tried to stand but felt a tugging under the skin of her forearm. She clumsily removed the bandage and yanked on the needle, which burned and tore on its way out. She rested the side of her head against the cool floor. From below came the sound of musicians setting up, plucking strings, chairs being dragged across the floor, coughing, laughter, fast conversation in short syllables she didn't understand, maybe Chinese.

She pulled up onto the side of the bed and gagged into the sheet. Mucus and bile formed a bubbly yellow mass against the white, but it was a shock of color introduced to the room, and it gave her a jolt that prompted more gagging. Acid burned in her throat.

She tried to stand up quickly and felt so light as she did it, so light that she could fly, and she gave into the sensation immediately, arms extended at her shoulders, the air lifting her up as easily as a dozen hands taking her away, and then her chin hit the cold floor, rattling the thoughts and teeth in her head hard against her skull.

58

THEY WERE PARKED behind a Jewel supermarket near an empty loading dock. The neighborhood was empty and silent. It looked like there had been power as they pulled off the highway, but there wasn't any juice here. Crouched in the sleeping compartment, under the dome light, Wayne traced routes with his finger in a thick blue atlas of detailed Chicago street maps. Denny was reconnecting his CB and Wayne was letting him. They were like that now.

"This is us." Wayne was working through the maps out loud. Denny was being awfully helpful, considering what Wayne had done to his face, and also considering that he still thought Wayne was a murderer.

"This is your guy's address," Denny said, glancing up only briefly from his repairs. "The city's on a grid, so it should be easy to find your way."

Wayne turned to the index and then flipped to a page showing a big park by the lake. Denny had maneuvered them as close to Jameson's house as he could, but many of the main streets were closed, some with roadblocks manned by cops. By Wayne's estimate, he was probably fifty blocks west and north.

As Denny tinkered under the dash, the CB came to life with sudden static and mumbles and Wayne jumped. He ripped a page out of the book, then another, then another and another—all the pages that connected this parking lot to Jameson's address. Denny started to object but didn't. "Why don't you just take it?" he said, but Wayne tossed the rest aside.

"Burn that," Wayne said, thinking like Peter now. "Get a new one. I'll burn these pages when I'm done. Nothing to link us, right? Keep your mouth shut."

"You know where I live," Denny said quietly, as if the implications of that were just occurring to him.

"Move out, Denny," he said. "Get a divorce."

Wayne tucked the gun in his rear waistband, saluted casually, and reached for the door handle. Denny started to say something, but the CB squawked under him as he did and Wayne only halfway heard what either was saying.

"Shush!" Wayne said, and Denny did, quickly.

Wayne shut his eyes and listened to the chatter on the CB.

"—ed back to Canada."

"Chicago is out of control. I'd take the Tri-State if I were you. Go around. Go around."

"It's like *Escape from New York* in there. You ever seen that movie? With what's his name, Kurt Russell? I was afraid to get out of the cab."

"What about the Edgewater neighborhood? Anybody got a feel for what's going on up there?"

"It's ugly everywhere. I saw this shot on the news of Lincoln Park. Ritziest neighborhood in the city and there're tents all over the place. Looks like something out of the Civil War."

Over the reports, Wayne said, "For a minute, I thought they were talking about someone I knew."

"Not likely," Denny said.

"Which way's east?"

Denny pointed. Wayne felt the urge to thank him, but he didn't. Murderer Wayne wouldn't have.

He hopped down from the cab and limped as best he could across the parking lot. After a hundred yards, he turned. The glow from the truck cab was the only illumination in any direction. He pictured Denny sitting behind the wheel, all that love and hate churning inside him.

Wayne pushed on through a working-class neighborhood of bungalows and ranches. Every window was open. Some people had moved into their cars, which were idling in driveways with the seats reclined and the air-conditioning cranked. He could see elongated shadows moving slowly inside the houses. The air was thick with the smell of smoke, but Wayne couldn't see any flames except for the occasional candle burning on a living room bookcase.

59

FROM THE THICK charcoal plume in the sky, it was clear the fires to the west were not under control, and from the AM radio, he knew the flames were advancing slowly east. Despite the lake on its edge, the city was short pressure for the hydrants, just as the park was short clean water for drinking.

With the help of some of the less agitated Whole Foogees, Bobby had moved some makeshift barriers and repositioned his car on North Avenue, directly between the park and the big house. From there, he could keep an eye on the unrulier elements from the relative safety of the driver's seat.

There was a constant volley of noise from the park, punctuated with angry spikes. As the day grew late, boredom and thirst were giving way to drunkenness and stupidity. In the sweltering lawlessness of the park, arguments turned too quickly into fights. Weapons were plentiful—a rock, a knife, a pillow, scissors, a flashlight, a rope. There would be no investigations, no questions, no autopsies. Bobby knew it was just percentages, a matter of time before there was a body count here, too.

Someone had toppled a barrier and parked a huge black pickup in a clearing of brown grass, where it now operated as a gas-powered generator, providing loud music and keg refrigeration and battery power for a medium-size television. For twenty dollars, anyone could enjoy fifteen minutes of air-conditioning, a service for which there was now a long and impatient line. The overstressed portable toilets still hadn't been emptied, and the stench radiated into an unpopulated fallout zone, which widened in radius every hour.

Very few of the Whole Foogees had been diligent about climbing the many flights of hot stairs to their steaming apartments for a change of clothes. Most everyone was wearing the same thing they'd had on when they had decided to retreat to the outdoors. The entire park was costumed in filthy outfits of despair.

A large gray cloud promising rain but never delivering paused overhead. *Just pour already.* Another rain would help push back the insurgent fires and help cool their roasting bodies and help heal the eczematous ground and help wash away the grime and shit.

Instead, the darkest clouds always passed silently overhead, sometimes exploding into a shower over Lake Michigan, the one place in the Midwest that didn't need relief.

Throughout the evening, a dozen or more cars had arrived, passing through the gate and disappearing into an obviously massive underground garage. Black sedans and SUVs and limousines, all of them with tinted windows and all of them, Kloska imagined, chauffeured. Not only had

Gary Jameson not gotten the message from the near riot in his front yard, it also looked like he was having a party.

Jesus, Bobby thought. *That's balls.*

A line of refugees three deep had lined up across the street, protesters booing each arrival. Bobby felt like booing himself. Instead, he identified himself as a cop again. This time, they hesitated, and he wished he had his star, but with some stern looks and clipped shouts, he was able to push them all back.

Something struck him as different and Bobby looked up in the sky. The news helicopters were gone, to the West Side probably. A firecracker made him jump. And then another sound he knew too well, like a firecracker but more menacing, followed by the *thumpthumpthump* of rocks meeting the side of his truck.

60

"OH JESUS," the voice said, and it wasn't a voice inside her head, it wasn't a dream voice, and it wasn't coming out of her own aching mouth. She was being rolled over, stiffly, like one of those convenience store hot dogs on steaming metal rods. A beam shot into her eyes, but the room was so bright anyway, she hardly flinched at it.

"Why are you awake? Did you hit your head?"

Canada wondered if a voice asking if she was awake was proof that she must be, or if it was a trick, a fancy twist employed by her dream self. She blinked at the dark figure between the beam of light in her eyes, one of those tiny flashlights, and the unsparing fluorescent illumination overhead. He was the doctor. She couldn't remember his name.

"If you have a concussion, that will complicate things."

That made her laugh, possibly out loud. Complicate things? Things, at the moment, were already hopelessly complicated, beyond any possibility of comprehension. She was like a mouse born into a house where the doors tasted like trees and the countertops felt like rocks and there seemed to be an infinite amount to discover, but for all the thinking and exploring and questioning the mouse might do, she could never hope to understand how that house was conceived, how it was built, or for what purpose. And she realized now that her whole life had been like that:

Everything she thought she understood was really something else, created for some other purpose. She had been that mouse and the universe was that house, able to be explored but never understood.

Now she was flying again, for real this time. No, she was being carried. She could feel the fabric of his shirt sleeve against her thighs under her short hemline—what dress was this?—and another hand around her shoulders and she could smell him, his sweat and cologne, her face pressed against his neck and she knew he was carrying her back to the bed, the hospital bed, and she remembered that they wanted to cut her open and take out her spider, but she'd never had a chance to explain to her mother that the spider was really her, and now that it was turned off, she knew it for sure, that this thing that was left behind when her spider was off was somebody else entirely, that just like the dream self who hides inside your head when you're awake but can tell you a story in your sleep that you don't know the ending to, the spider was her real self, her first self, *Nada,* and if they took it from her, they would be taking *her,* killing her, leaving a stranger in charge of her body, but there was no way for her to explain that, no combination of words that she could assemble in her mouth to say all that now, no way for her to be understood, and so she opened her eyes and followed the tendons in his neck up to the doctor's ear and she opened her mouth like she might whisper something to him.

Instead, she bit hard into the rubbery flesh, straight through the cartilage, until she tasted copper, and she clenched her teeth and gave her head a violent shake and then he dropped her and fell away howling, hands to the wound, while she still had a bloody crescent-shaped piece of him in her mouth, and before she spit it to the floor, the doctor's blood pooling in the well between teeth and lip, she sucked the severed lobe against her incisors, and it reminded her of the mouthpiece they used to give her during those prespider teenage seizures to stop her from swallowing her tongue.

61

A HUNDRED Whole Foogees were lined up along North Avenue, assaulting the Mercedes sedans and limousines with a shower of rocks and sticks. Bobby cut the ignition and climbed out of his truck and tried to shout them down, but they ignored him. When he grabbed a forearm in full windup, ready to hurl a baseball-size stone, the kid punched him in the stomach with his weak hand, hard enough to double Bobby over his knees. He coughed and straightened. Bobby felt for the place on his chest where his star should have been hanging. "I'm a cop!" The kid spit in his face and threw the rock anyway.

What am I going to do? Kloska thought. *Arrest him?*

Bobby sent the kid sprawling with one punch to the middle of his face. He howled, covering his nose with both hands as blood gushed between his fingers. "Pig!" the kid shouted. "Pig!" A few of the others stepped toward Bobby, and Kloska drew his weapon. They stopped in ready stance, eyeing him closely.

"I want everyone here to sit the fuck down," Bobby yelled, shaking the pain from his hand. A few did as he said, but others continued to hurl rocks and epithets just yards away. All the cars were inside the gate, and down in the garage, so the mob occupied the street and aimed projectiles at the house. The scene had quickly devolved past Bobby's ability to contain it.

Frustrated, and still angry from being sucker punched, he pointed his gun in the air and fired.

Big mistake, he thought as soon as he had done it.

Panic all around. Shrieking, running. Some were flat on the ground, covering their heads. Men and women held sticks like bats. Rocks were being thrown in every direction. One hit Kloska on the left cheekbone, stinging him, cutting him. His hands in front of his face, warding off stones and fistfuls of gravel like swarming bees, he dashed for his truck, which was already beset with rioters. Bobby yelled and waved his gun as he ran, and the panicking Yuppies opened a path for him.

He was steps away from the door when he heard his name: *"Bobby!"*

Jesus, Della.

He spun around, scanning faces. He saw her, buffeted by the crowd, its anger focused intensely on Jameson's house, which, as the sun drifted lower, seemed to glow even more brightly. A hundred people were now lined up, banging on the fence with metal tent poles, throwing rocks. Bobby fought his way toward Della, absorbing elbows and shoulders and a few more stones to the body. He grabbed her hand and the two of them ran in a crouch to the door of the truck, which Bobby unlocked with a button hanging from his key. He pushed Della inside, threw a would-be assailant to the pavement, and closed the door behind him, locking it tight.

"What are you doing here?" he asked her.

"Forget about me. What's going on?"

Outside, half a dozen twenty-something men were pounding on the body of the truck, rocking it and chanting, "Turn on the lights! Turn on the lights!"

"Things just sort of blew up," Bobby said. The windshield was smashed into a concave web of white lines.

"Can they tip this thing over?" Della asked with admirably less fear in her voice than Bobby thought was warranted. He pressed the barrel of his gun against the driver's window and snarled. The vandals dispersed, at least for the time being.

"What are you doing here?" he asked again, almost shouting over the din.

"Traden was trying to get your cell," she said. "You weren't answering the radio."

"I was busy."

"Wayne Jennings is here."

"What? Where?"

"Here in Chicago. Some trucker flagged down a cop. Said Jennings overpowered him at a truck stop and forced him to give him a ride."

"Some trucker?"

"He says Jennings has a gun and a knife."

The rioters were shuttling back to the park for more ammunition— bigger rocks, bigger sticks, tree branches. Bobby saw one kid wielding a stop sign, banging it on Jameson's gate. Unsober battle cries all around, long days of anger and frustration simmering in the dark, were now diverted at the house with lights on.

"We need to get out of here," Della said.

Bobby turned the key and the engine responded with a horrible dull clicking.

Shit!

"You didn't replace the battery, did you?" Della said.

"Shit!" Bobby could feel himself blaming his ex-wife. That was unfair, as she had warned him about the battery, but there was nothing fair about the present situation. He picked up his phone and tried to call Traden.

"What are we going to do?"

"You're going to get down as low as you can," Bobby said. A big rock banged hard into the driver's door. Della shrieked and squeezed herself into the foot well. Bobby scanned desperately from window to window. He couldn't see anything out of the windshield, but it provided them with a thin veneer of protection, at least for now.

At a distance, he heard an engine. He spun around in his seat, hoping it was a patrol car.

"Fuck me," he said. "Stay down!"

The pickup that had been parked in the middle of the camp was roaring across the lawn, tires grinding up yards of turf, headlights bouncing on the low, rolling berms of the park. It dropped off the curb with a screech of metal, then accelerated across the street, clipping Bobby's truck in the rear, throwing Bobby and Della against each other and spinning them a quarter turn.

Della screamed again and Bobby gripped his gun tightly. He could see the other driver, clearly drunk, kegs of beer and a generator still loaded into the box, airborne with every rough bounce. With a grin, he backed up, and Bobby prepared for another hit, but the driver redirected the front of his truck toward the mansion's gate and slammed down on the accelerator. The crowd roared approval, even halting their own mayhem to watch.

The gate stopped the truck with a horrible crunch, but as the Ford backed up, Bobby could see a significant bulge in the black iron bars. The truck slammed into it again. Again. Again. The Whole Foogees cheered each assault with increasing volume.

And then, with a long, low rev, a ramping of rpms, the totaled front end of the other pickup screeched and sprung forward and rammed a final time into the gate, tearing the upper right side of it from its hinge. An exuberant crowd rushed forward, dozens of them crawling over the smoking truck and crippled fence on all fours, like spiders, like insects, a metamorphosed army of giant ants.

62

THE WOMAN HAD BLOOD down her face in long lines—strands of blood, strings of it, tendrils of dark red, and she was crying as she passed Wayne on the sidewalk, not noticing him, not responding to his nonspecific offer of help. The sound of it was still distant, but Wayne could hear the chanting, screaming, yelling, smashing, honking—a *riot*—growing louder with each step, and he knew he was going to have to walk into it, pass through some hell to find Nada.

He had been walking east for hours, following the torn pages from Denny's map, past looters and loiterers, empty stores, desperate families waiting out the blackout on stoops, and a few cops, who paid no attention to them or to him. Block after block, he never heard a laugh, never saw a smile. A National Guard truck passed him, going in the other direction, toward the fires. A woman cheered. A man cursed.

Following the sounds of tumult, he finally reached Jameson's address, a big house at the end of a big park, engulfed in confusion and panic. Hundreds of people were swarming over a smashed black truck and onto the grounds of the estate. Another pickup was nearby, at an angle to the curb, its rear end dented to hell. Closer to the lake, a police car turned the corner, its Mars lights bathing the chaos in impotent strobes of blue. Nobody got out.

Touching the fabric of his khakis, Wayne put a hand on the small knife and gun in his pocket and advanced carefully into the riot. Rocks flew over his head, bouncing off bricks and gutters, and every time one struck a window of the big house, the crowd cheered. Wayne lifted himself onto the truck and pushed himself through the narrow opening where the gate had separated from the fence. People were running, dancing, spinning across the yard, most without purpose. Some had approached the sloping entrance to what looked like an underground garage, blocking the driveway, pounding on the metal door. A dozen people were cooling themselves in a large stone fountain.

In the midst of an angry rampage, they were the first smiling faces Wayne had seen since arriving in Chicago in Denny's truck.

Flashlight beams cut through the dusk above his head like machetes through thicket. More people were flooding onto the grounds, boosting one another over the intact sections of fence, hurdling and hurtling themselves onto the estate. Wayne was jostled. He put his hand inside his pocket, protecting the gun.

Then, a familiar face. A familiar form. A familiar posture. He was tall and wide and he was walking up to the house, to a door that had been torn from the frame. Wayne had already watched four or five people storm inside, but this guy was different.

He turned and looked in Wayne's direction. A surprised grin.

Wayne knew him.

Impossible.

What would he be doing here?

A body in full trot struck Wayne in the back, almost knocking him over. Wayne turned to the man, who was clearly drunk. He had something heavy and metal in his hand. Like a crowbar. Or a piece of the iron fence.

"What the hell, man?" He raised his weapon and struck. Wayne blocked it with his left arm, which swelled from the pain of the blow. With his right fist, he punched the guy in the chest, reeling him on his feet. Furious and numb, he attacked with the bar again, this time hitting Wayne hard in the head, knocking him down. He stood over Wayne and reared back for another blow.

Wayne reached into his pocket and pulled out the gun. He flipped the safety and fired it quickly and defensively, striking the guy in the thigh and dropping him to the grass like a collapsing marionette.

A woman screamed at the sound of the report. Wayne pushed himself to his feet, his arm throbbing, his head screaming, the infected wound in his side cutting deeper into his abdomen. He was only upright for a few seconds before a dizzying gray spiral filled his vision and he fell back to his knees and then forward on his face. His ears rang. The noise all around became faint.

Wayne remembered the figure at the door. And he knew who had killed Bea Beaujon and David Amoyo. Who had framed him. Who was here now for Nada.

But he couldn't imagine why.

Then he heard another gunshot, this one from high above, probably out a window. A shot fired from inside the house.

63

"Now!" Bobby yelled.

He pushed the door open with his shoulder and pulled Della out by the arm, his weapon covering her as they ran east down North Avenue, away from the house, toward a patrol car that had magically appeared off the frontage road along Lake Shore Drive. A white-haired cop jumped out the driver's side and pushed them into the backseat and then he slipped quickly back into the car and locked the door.

"Jesus, Detective, what happened here?" the uniform said. The man's face wasn't familiar, but Bobby thanked God the cop had recognized him.

"Good to see you, too." Kloska was staring at one of the still-intact windows of the Jameson estate, a semicircle of glass with a metal grille like the top half of an old clock, and framed by thick bloodred curtains. This was a creepy, beautiful old house for sure. Kloska wondered about the generations of priests, the years of faith and superstition, of good works and bad thoughts. Too bad there probably wasn't going to be much of anything left inside it.

"It's like New Orleans," said the white-haired cop Bobby didn't know.

"What?"

The cop spread his arms, indicating the scene taking place around them. "New Orleans. Katrina. All over again," he said. "Half the cops off the job. Assholes running around, smash and grab. Civilians with guns. People calling 911 and not getting any reply." He sniffed the air and waved his hand at the burning neighborhoods off to the west. "We got fires instead of floods. That's the only difference."

Bobby ignored him. "What's the plan?"

"Plan?" the cop scoffed. "There's another car on its way. And an ambulance."

"One car? We're not going to put this down with one more car."

"Who said anything about putting it down?" the cop said. "I got orders to stay out of it. Supposed to keep off the grounds until somebody higher up can contact the people inside. Apparently, some gold star is afraid Monday morning quarterbacks are gonna say the police made a bad situation worse." It sounded like an accusation aimed at Kloska.

"Of all the ass-fucking-backward—"

"This is exactly what I'm talking about," the cop said. "We're standing here picking our asses while lawlessness abounds. Just like Katrina."

Bobby glared at him. "What the hell are you talking about?"

"I'm just saying . . ."

Della calmed him with a hand on his back. "So we're just supposed to let this whole thing fizzle out?" Bobby asked.

"I guess," the cop said.

Bobby hunched down to get a better look at the house through the window. A door had been torn off its hinges and a couple of Whole Foogees were playing a game of chicken, running a few steps inside and then retreating at full speed, cackling the whole time. The gate had come mostly down now and looters were running back and forth from the property. Dozens of windows were smashed and the landscaping and fountains were in the process of being trashed. Many of the rioters, the ones who weren't drunk, probably, had disappeared into the dark of the surrounding neighborhood, or just returned to the tent city in the park, like it had never happened, like they'd never been part of it.

The cop said, "Even if we could round everybody up and arrest them, we got no way to transport them, no way to process them. I'm not sure where we'd even keep them at this point. The city's just failing right now. Falling apart. Until the power's back on and those fires are finally out, a few broken windows and stolen knickknacks at a rich guy's house, especially a rich dickwad who's been rubbing everyone's face in it with his air-conditioning and whatnot, that's an insurance matter."

Bobby leaned back in the seat and made an obscene gesture at the house. "I've been thinking over what we talked about," he said to Della as if the cop weren't sitting right there. "You think as a cop at least you're making some kind of difference. But we're just oiling the machine, aren't we? Whoever the shitheads are who killed Marlena Falcone, or the prick who lives inside this house, there won't ever be a difference made unless they let it, which they won't, because if this prick decided to change something, some bigger prick would just stop him. There is always a bigger prick, Della. Anytime we get close to making a difference, they take us off the job or they tell us to sit back and watch a fucking beautiful old house get torn apart. Because some prick'd rather gut it to the bricks than let us see what's in there. Fuck that. Fuck them."

He reached into his pocket and inserted a new magazine into his gun. Then he kissed her quickly, told the uniform to let him out of the car, and dashed across the street.

64

NOT FOR THE FIRST TIME since he had fled Las Vegas, a voice in Wayne's head told him to stay facedown in the dirt, to surrender to the pain and chaos, to let himself be trampled by the riot, to let the police handcuff him and push him into the back of a van somewhere, to stop running and fighting and turn his fate over to the universe and the courts. Let somebody else choose red or black for him. He was probably physically incapable of doing much for Nada anyway. He doubted he had the strength to find her, much less save her.

But then the image of his friend Peter Trembley stepping through that door, closer and nearer to Canada Gold, and now the gunfire from inside the house motivated him to his feet, to full adrenaline alertness. The fellow he had shot was alive—a relief—and Wayne hobbled toward the open door and then inside Gary Jameson's home.

A looter skipped out over the shouts and ran past, his pockets no doubt full of stolen treasures. Wayne heard screaming within and without, and crying and wailing and laughing, too. Stepping inside, he felt an air-conditioned breeze.

It felt so good, he didn't notice right away that the long foyer had been destroyed—furniture turned on its side, paintings ripped from the walls, canvases torn. Shattered glass crunched beneath his thick-soled shoes. A massive wooden door had been toppled, and now it leaned against the cracked plaster of the opposite wall.

Wayne walked down the hall in a crouch and turned the corner into another mess of a corridor. No one in sight. Most of the looters had already departed, it seemed, smashed and grabbed and fled from the bullets.

He slowly turned another corner into the kitchen. Boxes and canned food spilled from open cabinets. A man Wayne recognized from earlier, outside, was on the floor, whimpering in pain, bleeding from his leg. A small television, tuned to local news, showed the outside of the house from above, three police cars now and an ambulance and maybe fifty confused drunks, half of them on the estate and half of them on the street. The volume was down, but Wayne could hear the sounds of crisis through the walls—sirens and helicopter rotors and muffled shouting all around.

Here in the kitchen, a fat woman in white polyester and a tall old man in black pants, dress shirt, and tie were sobbing and embracing, her short arms not able to meet around his waist, his long arms draped like warm scarves down her back. They saw him and the woman gasped.

"Where is she?" he said.

The fat lady whimpered. The tall man hugged her tighter and looked at Wayne with calm, deliberate hate. "What are you people doing to this house?"

"Is Canada Gold here?" He was trying to sound menacing, like murderer Wayne, but he was grunting and wincing over the words, the pain being everywhere now, through his head, down to his side, and all the way up from the bleeding feet-shaped blisters at the end of his legs.

The old man didn't answer, but his eyes gave it away, a change of focus, a connection with something behind Wayne. With quickness that surprised even him, Wayne dove to the floor just as a bullet deflected off a stainless-steel appliance with a reverberating ping. A warning. The fat lady screamed and Wayne scrambled over to her on hands and knees as quickly as he could. He could feel the inflamed cut in his side splitting wide. Wayne held a painful breath and pulled himself up by the counter. By the time the shooter, who had fired from the hall, had entered the kitchen, gun pushed out in a two-handed grip, Wayne was crouching behind the old lady's girth, Denny the Trucker's gun at a halfhearted angle to her temple.

The shooter was wearing black jeans and a black T-shirt and he held a pistol, bigger and newer than Wayne's, expertly in both hands. "Police," he said. "My name's Detective Bob Kloska. Put the gun down."

Wayne gave the guy what he hoped was a menacing stare. He wasn't dressed like a cop, but he sounded like one. He held a gun with a lot more confidence than Wayne did.

"There's going to be twenty more of me here in a minute," the cop said.

"There better not be." Wayne didn't know how convincing it sounded.

The cop bit his lip and studied him a minute and then he turned his head with recognition. "You're the shithead from Nevada. Jennings."

Christ, Wayne thought. "I guess you know I'll do this, then," he said.

"Let's talk about this, Wayne," the cop said. "Where's Canada?"

Wayne fired into the ceiling and the gun wobbled and kicked in his hand with the shot. He looked not so much like murderer Wayne, he guessed, as a guy firing a gun outside a range for only the second time in his life. "Go!" he yelled anyway.

The cop looked at the old woman and then the old man, and with an unpleasant snarl, one more realistic and menacing than anything Wayne could manufacture, he backed slowly into the hall.

Wayne limped over and shut the door behind him and locked it with a cheap hook and eye, probably meant to keep important guests from wandering accidentally into the large but unglamorous kitchen. He did the same to the door on the other side of the room.

"What do you people want?" the old man demanded.

"I'm not people. I'm alone." He bent over the kid—*I'm sorry*—and promised he'd get him to an ambulance, even though he wasn't sure how.

"Fuck you," the looter said.

The old woman wouldn't stop sobbing.

The tall man asked, "What do you want?"

Wayne said, "I'm looking for Canada Gold." He counted his wounds with his hand, one at a time, and winced.

The old woman's wails turned to guilty shrieks and she buried her head into the old man's side. Wayne was just now figuring that they were husband and wife.

"He called you Jennings," the old man said. "You're here to kill Nada."

Nada. Only her friends called her that. Wayne said, "I'm here to save her," and realized how insane that sounded, how insane the truth had become, so crazy that he would never be able to convince anyone of it. Wayne wasn't prepared for it to come out so dramatically. It sounded false. Scripted. The truth was more complicated than that.

The truth was, he needed her to save him.

"Oh my God!" the cook said into a dish towel. "You're here to save her from us!"

The old man comforted her, told her that was nonsense. They did what they were told, he said. They were doing their job. They were doing it well.

"Goddammit!" the kid said. "I'm bleeding everywhere!"

On the little TV, the helicopter followed a looter running alongside Lake Shore Drive, a large painted canvas in his hands. The cook pulled down an unmarked ceramic canister from a cupboard and opened it, revealing a white powder inside. "I did what they told me. Oh the poor girl. She got so sick! The seizures!" The sobs came between each word now. "I should have to eat it myself!"

Wayne stepped over and put a little bit of the stuff on his pinkie finger and dabbed it to his tongue. It tasted chalky, but it stung his tongue a little, like bad garlic. "How much did you give her?"

"Enough to make her think she was sick." The old man thought about that and maybe he heard something sincere in Wayne's concern for Nada, or maybe the guilt he was feeling was interfering with his judgment. "Her room is upstairs. Third floor. Something was going to happen tonight."

"What was going to happen?" Wayne asked.

Instead of answering, the man said, "You'll be killed if you leave this kitchen." He was the butler, Wayne decided. "Open either door, you'll be shot. And the cops aren't your biggest worry."

Wayne could hear footsteps beyond the kitchen walls. He looked at the looter, whose life was probably on the minute hand now. "You need to get him out of here." He pointed to flashing lights on the little TV. "But I can't be here when you do it."

The man opened a cabinet above the counter, revealing a large cavity, a chute, maybe as wide as a dorm-room fridge. "Most of them are on the second floor. In the chapel, unless they've gone somewhere else to hide. There used to be a dumbwaiter here. If you could wedge yourself in the shaft, you might be able to climb past them. There's still a rope in there somewhere."

Wayne grabbed his bad knees. "I'm so tired," he said out loud, with nothing remaining of murderer Wayne in his voice.

The butler ignored him. "There could be a man on her door. Dr. Russo might be in with her. And I don't know where Jameson and the others are."

Wayne looked up the square opening. "I'll never fit."

"Stay here, then. See if I care."

Even as he folded himself into the shaft, the rip in his side stretching and bleeding and screaming, Wayne still suspected it was a trap, an ambush, that he would get stuck between floors or that the guards would be waiting to yank him through the sliding second-floor door. He had accepted it was probably a trap right up until the point, as Wayne strained to push his own moon weight even a few inches up the shaft, that the old man helped him cut the rope away from the pulley and said, "My name is Hugh. Tell her we're sorry." And he closed the door.

The pain was incredible, worse now than it ever had been, but proximity to her was an analgesic, and by the time he could hear the paramedics and the cop back in the kitchen shouting, "Where'd he go? Where'd he go?" Wayne had advanced far up into the darkness, not quite to the second-floor opening yet, but he figured he had to be close.

Wayne straightened his legs as much as he could, pressing his back against the plaster, and rested for a moment he couldn't afford. Only seconds maybe.

Then, with his nearly three hundred pounds suspended in a painful wedge between his giant feet and his big ass, Wayne gripped the thin cord, barely a thread cutting into his bleeding hands, a rope that for a century or more had lifted modest meals prepared by nuns to busy priests in their ascetic quarters, and wondered how long it could continue to lift *him.* How long before five days' worth of exhaustion and the infected wound in his side and the tremors in his head and arm and his bad knees and this old rope all conspired against him at once and he tumbled down with a crash and a bellow that would send the whole house running right to him, probably armed to the incisors.

The third floor might be twenty more feet up. Or fifty.

The hunting knife he had taken from Denny's truck was in his teeth. There was muffled commotion from all around—shouts and barked orders and a siren on the street outside. He could hear the kid in the kitchen moaning in pain, which at least meant he was still alive. He could hear the cook in the polyester whites sobbing with guilt. He heard a car alarm from somewhere distant.

He pulled on the fraying rope and hoisted himself another few inches, a few inches toward Nada, the wound in his side opening up in a scream, a monster making its presence known, pushing itself out with every step, every squeeze, every foothold, every pull.

Then he felt the gun slip from his pocket and he heard a terrible bang and an awful rattle as it struck the tin floor below.

65

SOMETHING CHANGES inside you when you bite another human's flesh, when you sink your teeth clean through and tear a part of someone away, when you split a person into two parts. She even knew the name for the catalyst of that change, could still find the word *adrenaline* somewhere in her head, which made her think that maybe she wasn't completely gone. But she quickly knew that wasn't true. Nada Gold had been turned off with her spider and she had left behind a brain full of truths and trivia and fuzzy memories, the same way Marlena had left some trace of herself in her notebooks and journals. Nada was as far gone as Marlena was, replaced by anger. Rage resided in Canada's head now; fury was calling the shots.

She reached up and grabbed the IV bag from its little metal coat stand, bit into that too until the stuff inside squirted out, tasting of medicine and formaldehyde and mint, and she stood over the doctor and squeezed the bag in front of his terrified face, half covered with his hands, but the liquid didn't seem to be stinging his wound like she wanted, so she spun around and saw a bottle of a familiar shape, wide at the top and bottom, skinny in the middle, and she unscrewed the top and poured it over the doctor's head, waterboarded him with its contents, as he gasped and screamed, and she remembered the name of this catalyst, too—*isopropyl alcohol.*

When the last of it had bubbled from the bottle, she dropped it in his lap and the anger searched the room for something else it could use to reduce this doctor the way he had reduced her, to whittle him away until there was nothing left but pain and fury.

She found it on the mantel.

She found matches, long fireplace matches in a box like a carton of cigarettes, and as she struck one and stood over him, the anger stared at the flame and it played back one of Canada's memories, of that summer before the spider, when her father was in jail and she and her mother were up at the Michigan lake house and Nada was hiding behind the garage with Solomon's cigarette lighter in her hand. It was broad and heavy, like her dad. Silver-topped, also like him. Nada brushed its wheel with her palm and the flame appeared.

She had wondered that day what life would be like if the jury convicted her father. The rest of her life would be a lot like the last year of it, since the day they took him away, and the last year of it had been terrible, between the horrible truth of her father's crime and the unrelenting scrutiny of the media. She and her mother had lived life not so much under a microscope as under a magnifying glass, with the media's heat directed into a laser that burned them relentlessly every day.

She flipped the lighter's lid closed with her thumb.

What would life be like alone with her mother? Weird. Impossible. Cold. The two of them would be like that clacking thing on her science teacher's desk with the five metal spheres on wires—"Newton's cradle," he called it. The balls on the ends were constantly going at one another, taking a hit and then hitting back, always in conflict, constantly in opposition, but never directly connecting with one another.

That was Canada and Elizabeth Gold all right. *Balls on the ends.*

She smirked and ignited the flame again. And, just as quickly, extinguished it.

She watched a bug, a beetle as big as her thumb, make its way under one neighbor's fence and march toward the property behind them. That neighbor had a pool and a dog that crapped freely in the yard. That's why the beetle was headed there, for supplies of feces and water.

Flame on.

An instant later, she could see thousands of them, thousands of bugs she hadn't even noticed before, ants mostly, and tiny flies and a handful of bees, a whole bug underworld, and they were all commuting behind her garage for some purpose, flying and crawling this way and that. Bugs were busy, industrious, purposeful.

Does that make bugs happy? Does that make bugs normal? Do bugs even notice when their father goes missing? Do bugs even have fathers?

Thousands of them. They had been there all her life and she'd hardly noticed. Hardly noticed them except one at a time, when an ant traversed her sandwich or a bee buzzed her ear. Certainly they had noticed her, a giant walking across the grass. They had known her, feared her presence, wondered about her nature without ever comprehending it, and, like her father's indifferent God, she had hardly given a thought to them.

She stomped her foot twice, warning them with a tremor. Canada Gold held her father's flaming lighter at arm's length in front of her face and dropped it into the long, dry grass.

Ten years later, standing over the doctor, she let the match burn out, and then she pulled him to his feet, the sedative wearing off now, her rage providing direction and adrenaline giving her strength. She opened the door and pushed the doctor down the empty hall, the box of matches against his back. His right hand was cupped over his half an ear and every few steps he would expel a noise like a whimper.

On the way out of the room, she grabbed the little black box he had used to turn off her spider.

A floor away, the house had erupted in a chaos of shouts and orders. Canada stopped to look out a half-circle window and saw a riot outside, and she wondered again if it were real. The gate of the house collapsed by a big truck, people running on and off the grounds, looters, vandals, mischief makers. The world had changed in the few hours she had been asleep. She approached the steps—Woodward's twister—and could hear voices from below. She silenced the doctor with a pinch and pulled him backward.

She marched him down a dead-end utility hallway. Instead of being oak-paneled, the doors here were whitewashed. The hardware was brass, but the maintenance fell below the standards of the rest of the house.

Even without her spider, she noticed spots of tarnish and traces of dried green polish left on the knobs. She glimpsed a utility room through an open door and pushed the doctor inside. The room was the size of a walk-in closet. There was only a folding chair, nothing else she could push up against the door besides empty white wicker baskets. A countertop held piles of folded sheets and towels and clothes, which had been carted up from the second-floor laundry and were waiting to be put away. Mops and brooms and two vacuum cleaners were lined up against the back wall. On a higher shelf were bottles of window washer and bowl cleaner and miscellaneous household chemicals. Everything smelled of soap and softener. There was no lock on the door, not even a cheap push button on the knob. No doubt, in answer to a long-ago question from her contractor, Myra Jameson had replied, "When would anyone need to lock the utility room?"

She motioned for the doctor to sit with his back to it. He didn't try to run.

"I need to tell you some things. Please," the doctor said. His voice was raised to a desperate pitch, although, she noticed, her mind no longer correlated the syllables with notes. He winced at a horrible metal-on-metal crunch from downstairs.

She didn't care. Burrowing through a pile of clean laundry, she found a pair of Myra Jameson's black stretch pants. Canada only now looked down at what she had been wearing. A thin hospital gown, tied in back, her own underwear underneath, thank God. She pulled the leggings on under her gown and then, discarding a few of Myra's blouses with a grimace, found one of her own T-shirts, gift-bag swag from a long-ago poker tournament with a Horseshoe Casino logo on the front. It was big and worn soft and she liked to sleep in it.

"Turn around," she ordered. He did.

Voices outside. Close. In the main hall. She quieted the physician with a hand and went to the door, leaning over him. She could feel the doctor's eyes peering up at her and she kneed him not so gently in the chin and cinched the billow of her T-shirt at her waist.

"Goddammit. I was right. We should have done this at a hospital." It was her mother. Unmistakably Elizabeth. Even the anger recognized the resemblance. Two pairs of footsteps rushed down the hall toward Woodward's spiral and she didn't hear the reply, if there was one.

Canada knocked her forehead hard against the upright washer, as if she could restart her spider with a tap.

"Your mother loves you very much," the doctor said.

That caused her to laugh, although the staccato noise she expelled didn't sound much like one.

"She never wanted you to have it. The implant. There was too much risk. And she had other plans for you. Large plans, Canada. But your father insisted. And with that thing in your head, your mother couldn't go forward. She couldn't trust you when you were part machine. Not after what it did to your father."

She shook the matches at him.

"She wanted you to join us, Canada. To join the tradition."

She couldn't imagine what that meant, but the term was familiar to her from Marlena's journals. That and another one. *"Harmonia,"* she managed to say, almost in answer to herself.

The doctor nodded. "Marlena tried to contact you. You were supposed to think it was all part of the product recall, just ten years overdue. No one would suspect anything, not even you. You'd think you were sick. That the seizures had returned. Then after it had been removed and placed inside another who could use it to its greatest potential, your mother would ask you to join her, join us, in the tradition. But there are people, people among us, who want you dead. They want to destroy your device. They think killing you would please their God."

"Shut up." She scratched her temple with a corner of the matchbox. She didn't want to get to the next part. That the people who wanted to kill her included Wayne Jennings.

The doctor said, "The mathematici believe you could be trusted to join us. Unfortunately, acusmatici seem to have brought Steve Rhodes to their way of thinking. But we're talking about a world, believe it or not, in which your mother is more powerful than Steve Rhodes. She can protect you, Canada. I doubt anyone else can."

He said, "She's had people following you since you got here. Keeping an eye out for your safety. This Jennings fellow who killed your friends in Las Vegas, he's likely working for Rhodes. For the acusmatici. If he kills you and gets away, they'll set him up with a new identity somewhere. If he gets caught, they'll cut him loose and no one will believe that he's sane. Anything he says about Steve Rhodes or the tradition or anything else will be written off as a delusion. The police will say he was just a stalker. It's so easy to turn the truth into a lie and the lie into a truth."

Canada couldn't make sense of any of it. Everything coming from his mouth was just raw, meaningless data.

"Rhodes betrayed us. He was supposed to be watching you for us. For your mother. After Marlena died, we suspected he might have turned, and your mother sent Jameson to save you. To bring you here for the procedure."

Jesus Christ. She rubbed her sweaty forehead into her arm, her mind spinning. The truth of it was finally hitting her. Nada had told Bea that English Judson had been in her apartment. But it had been Wayne all along. *Vallentine was right about Wayne.*

She counted the friends she had left, friends as good as the rapist's friends.

"After you left your mother's apartment, you had another attack. We plucked you off the street and brought you back here. To help you. Protect you. We're not the bad guys, Canada."

Sadly, that might even be true, Canada thought.

She pushed the remote at him, shaking it at his face in lieu of instructions.

The doctor shifted, like he had been sitting on his wallet. "You don't want that."

Words were coming to her slowly, but not quite the right ones. She tried to explain that some other self had taken over since the spider had been turned off—some angry, uncontrollable self—and she wanted the spider back on and the real her to come forward, to take charge, but it all came out of her mouth this way: "Kill this bitch."

"It's going to hurt."

"It hurts." *Now,* she meant. *It hurts now.*

"Canada, let us help you. You think the neurostimulator helped you see the truth, but it only showed you a high-definition illusion. We can show you reality, which only a very few people in history have ever been witness to. We can complete your father's dream. But we need to free you from that device in your head. We need to give it to somebody who can put it to good use. He's from China. A composer like your dad. He's had ADHD his entire life, like your dad. Like you. Marlena identified him as a candidate. He's going to use it the way Solomon did, to peer into corners of the universe that none of us has ever seen, and he'll produce a glorious work of art, and we will show you how to appreciate it, and your new life will make your old life seem like a foolish waste. We will take care of Steve Rhodes and this Wayne Jennings and this mess outside, and your new life, reunited with your mother, can start right now if you just trust us. If you just trust me."

She thought, *Nada isn't here right now, which is too bad for you. You might have been able to reason with her.* But she doubted it.

She didn't say that or anything else. Instead, she shook the remote at him with one hand and with the other she flipped the top off a gallon bottle of bleach and took one step toward the bloody cartilage dangling from the side of his head.

66

ACHING, cramping, having made the long, painful climb to the top of the dumbwaiter shaft, Wayne followed Hugh's directions down the third-floor hallway. It smelled of alcohol and must. He looked up and down the empty hall and then a door started to open next to him. He panicked and pulled the knob and held it shut.

A long pause and then a loud "What the hell?" A man's voice.

Wayne put his hand on the knob and lowered his voice into a half-understandable mumble. "She in there?"

Another pause and then a slow and skeptical, "No. Who is this?"

Holding the door shut tight with his left hand, he fished in his pockets with his right and found the three pennies Ginny had returned to him in the desert, the change James and Hale and the Rain Man didn't want. On the other side, someone pulled hard on the door, and Wayne squeezed the knob tight to make sure it wouldn't turn. With the thick fingers of his right hand, he arranged the three pennies into a stack and pressed them at lock height between door and frame. Now the knob couldn't be turned from the inside.

"Hey! Who are you? Get me the hell out of here!"

Wayne didn't reply, but he sidestepped the door and tapped the point of the knife on his chin. Even now, under extraordinary circumstances, he was feeling jealousy and confusion—all the emotions that always accompanied the thought of Nada Gold.

"Where's the girl?" Wayne said, muffling his voice against his shirt.

The man on the other side of the door paused. "Who is that?"

Wayne said nothing.

After a few frustrated beats, the voice said, "Come on! Get me the hell out!"

Footsteps around the corner.

Wayne took two long, quick, quiet steps to a door he hoped was unlocked and opened it to a room he prayed was empty. It was dark. A closet. He shut himself inside.

He could hear someone pulling and pushing on the knob to Nada's room, trying to shake the pennies loose. The first voice, unmuffled: "Son of a bitch! Who did that?"

"The place is crawling with that filth from the park!" said another voice. Female.

The first guy now: "I don't know where your daughter went. Or Russo." They were inches away, walking right past the closet door. Wayne could see shadows on the carpet.

"Goddammit. I was right. We should have done this at a hospital. Or the clinic. This whole plan was screwed from the beginning."

"Calm down. We'll find her."

"Downstairs. She must be running."

"We'll have to search every—"

They were gone. Wayne opened the door a crack, saw the hallway was empty. He ran up the carpet runner and collected the pennies from the open doorway. Then he crawled back to his closet, shut the door, and, just as he heard more footsteps, put the penny lock on the inside, so no one could open the door from the hall.

He sat on the floor, knife in his hands, breaths in and out like a bellows.

67

A CORKSCREW in the middle of her head was drilling through her brain, pushing, grinding hard against the top of her skull.

The instant the doctor pressed the last digit of code into his remote, the nanosecond after two tiny pieces of metal kissed inside his little black box, she felt the pain advance along the wiry paths of her spider's legs and Nada shrieked and held her ears and collapsed at the knees. She felt her face twist into a horrible mask, heard the matches hit the ground beside her. No doubt they could hear her screaming downstairs.

Now this was what it was like to want to die.

The doctor stood up, staring at her. His face looked half worried for her, but his body was turning away, hand on the door. She growled at him between screams.

"I'm sorry," he stopped to say.

It felt like she was being tasered from the inside, like the robot part, the half of her she was trying to save, was trying to kill off the flesh part. And now her brain was pushing on the backs of her eyeballs, pushing her eyes, those eyes that always saw everything, right out of their sockets, and she fought back, shutting her lids tight.

She couldn't lie here forever waiting for the pain to subside. The doctor would bring them right to her—Jameson and her mother and the rest of them, whoever they were. They were all trying to kill her.

Nada forced herself to her feet and pried her eyelids apart. Her vision was blurry, but she could see up close. She climbed up on a folding chair and pawed through a cabinet of cleaning supplies. She found furniture polish and a bottle of disinfectant, other household cleaners. She squinted at the labels, looking for familiar-sounding chemical endings from high school science class, which started coming back to her in perfectly organized sets.

Footsteps in the hall just outside. She grabbed the gallon bottle of concentrated bleach and crouched on the floor, still blinking at the agony behind her eyes.

The door opened. Not the doctor. Someone bigger than he was.

Someone with a gun.

She swung the arm with the bottle once, twice, three times. Chemicals splashed toward the door in waves. The big man, almost as big as Wayne but not Wayne, screamed a profanity as he covered his face and ducked. She heard a smack against the Pergo floor and she dove toward it, feeling with her hand until she came up again with the gun.

"Fuck!" said the man.

She rubbed her eyes with the inside of her elbow—her hands reeked of chemicals—and she tried to point the weapon with authority while her vision slowly cleared. *The gun smells of powder,* she thought between the screams in her head. The man was dressed in a black T-shirt and blue jeans. Boots. He had a knife in his hand.

"Who are you?"

"A friend," he said.

Nada's life was coming back to her in chunks and pieces as her spider was rebooting. "You look familiar."

The big man listened at the door and then said softly, anxiously, "I work at the casino. With Wayne."

She leveled the revolver more seriously. The gun seemed familiar, too, which was crazy. She began to wonder if any of this was real. If she was still in the hospital bed. Still under sedation. If they were doing the operation right now, if this sudden feeling of clarity was just the result of the doctor poking around in her head, if everything she was feeling and seeing and hearing was just one of those *high-definition illusions.*

The big man shook his palms at her. He still held the knife in one hand. "Wait, wait. There are a lot of people trying to hurt you."

"No shit."

"The people in this house."

"I know about them."

"Your mother."

"I know about her, too."

"Wayne."

"Steve Rhodes sent him to kill me."

"Mr. Rhodes has been trying to protect you. He knows about these people who want to hurt you. He wants to stop them."

Knowing who was lying and who was telling the truth seemed impossible without her spider at full strength. "Why would he want to do that?"

"He feels responsible. He's trying to do the right thing."

Nada squeezed the grip of the gun. It felt so right in her hand. None of this made sense. "I can't think," she said.

"You don't need to think. But we need to run," the big man said. "Hand me the gun and follow me out of here. I know how to get us out."

"Peter," she said. "That's your name. Peter."

"Just give me the gun and we can get out. It's a mess down there. Rioters are running all through the downstairs. We'll slip out in the commotion."

"I'm not giving you the gun."

"They've been putting poison in your food, Canada. You've been having seizures, right? They've been making you sick so they'll have an excuse to slice you open."

The doctor had almost admitted as much. She tried to remember, tried to think if that were possible. *Poison in my food?*

"You'll never get down three floors by yourself," Peter said. "Jameson was expecting thirty guests tonight. Most of them arrived before the riot. Every single one of them wants to slice you with a scalpel."

"How did you know where to find me?"

"Mr. Rhodes brought me here. He's been involved with these people, with your mother, too, but he wants to do the right thing. He's betraying his own people to save you. I can explain it all later, or Mr. Rhodes can explain if you like, but we need to leave right now." He put out his hand for the gun. She drew it back.

"I can protect you, keep you safe, but I need you to trust me," Peter said. "It's fucking *Lord of the Flies* out there. There's no law. No cops. It's every man for himself."

"Yeah," Nada said, holding the revolver with both hands. "That's true in here, too."

Commotion all around them now. Shouts from the floor below, from the yard outside. Nearer, she heard men barking. Boot steps. They were close.

"We can't just walk out there," Peter said, blinking and gasping between words. "Even if they're checking every room, they've got to be almost on top of us by now. They'll see us if we go out. And Wayne's out there somewhere, too. I guess you know about him. He's gone crazy. God knows what he wants to do to you."

She ignored the last bit. "Do you have a phone? We can call the police."

Peter scoffed. "You aren't listening. There are no cops. It's jungle law now. Riots and fires. Even if cells were working, you couldn't get through to 911 in a million tries."

Nada climbed back onto the folding chair and looked again at the labels on the bottles she had set aside. She limped down and pulled some sheets and socks and other whites from a basket. She uncapped each bottle and soaked the linens. Loose from their bottles, the chemicals burned her nose. Glancing around, she scooped up the fireplace matches.

"Let's go." She noticed the doctor had left the remote on the counter by the door, the keys to her spider. She picked it up and tried to examine the inside of her head for signs of herself. Clearly, she wasn't whole yet, still confused, still uncertain, but she could feel parts of her returning, the anger receding. Nada set the remote on the counter and smashed it with the grip of the gun and then swept it to the ground, crushing the circuits with the heel of her bare foot. She retrieved all the pieces and shoved them between folds of the soaking-wet sheets.

Peter pinched his nose. "What's that stink?"

Nada said, "Alcohol, varnish, paint thinner."

They walked out into the service hall, Peter in front with the knife, Nada pointing the gun at his back under the pile of laundry, which reeked of gasoline. When they approached the corner, Peter pointed down the hall and to the left, toward her room, and he motioned for her to hold back. She peeked around the wall just as two men in suits were disappearing into a bedroom, only steps away.

Peter nodded and Nada rushed into the wide hall. She raised the sheet up over her head and snapped it like she was making a bed. Socks and other laundry now soaked in household petroleums and phenols dispersed every which way. Nada pointed in the other direction, toward the Woodward stairs, and then pulled out a match and struck it against the side of the long box.

The sheet lit up like flash paper, igniting the thick red drapes on the north windows with a *whoosh* and trapping the two men inside the bedroom and a third, from his shouts at least, on the other side of a hot wall of fire and smoke.

Within seconds, the expensive wallpaper began to peel and melt and burn. Oil paintings in gold frames lit up like castle torches. The carpet runner underneath, fringed with some unknown flammable dye, caught like a fuse and two narrow columns of flame chased them down the hallway, toward the Woodward stairs, like runway lights.

68

WAYNE HEARD A SOUND almost like a race car speeding down the hall outside. He felt the heat and smelled the smoke as it rolled under the door. He groped around in the dark for a thick bath towel, which he placed over the crack.

This was bad.

In a panic, he tried to find the back wall of the closet. He fantasized it might be made out of particle board or paper or some other material he could rip apart with his bare hands or cut through with his knife. Plaster. If there was time, maybe he could dig through it, but there would be another wall on the other side and the shelves were deep and the spaces between them small. He would die trying to escape that way.

His clock was down to seconds. He couldn't see anything, but the air in this closet was half smoke now and the door, pressed against his back, was uncomfortably hot, burning him through his shirt.

Wayne had one knee on a wooden shelf that wobbled under his weight. He put his hand underneath and it lifted, as if on a hinge. He pushed the towels that were sitting on it to the floor and lifted the shelf as high as it would go, maybe ten inches, and he felt below it with his arm. He couldn't touch the bottom. A laundry hamper maybe?

Or if he was very lucky, a laundry *chute*.

He tried to get his legs inside, but the shelf would only lift so far, and the space between the shelf and the closet was only so wide and his body just wouldn't fold that way. He stuck his head in and by throwing his shoulders, one and then the other, he was able to force himself into it, almost with the same determination with which the smoke was forcing itself around the frame of the door.

The only way in was headfirst.

His hands explored the space—still no bottom. Knife in one hand, he braced his arms against the sides and tried to drop his hips through the opening. A week ago, before those days and nights practically starving on the road, Wayne Jennings never would have fit.

The rest of him followed in jerks and stops, as if the house were eating him. Finally his feet cleared the top of the bin and he let himself go, wherever this went, into the dark belly of the old house.

69

Kloska didn't know how he was supposed to tell the good guys from the bad guys. He wasn't sure there were any good guys. Hell, without his star, he wasn't sure which kind of guy *he* was.

After Jennings had forced him from the kitchen, he waited outside, trying to interpret the muffled conversation on the other side of the heavy door. After a few minutes, it opened.

"Where did he go?" Kloska asked the butler.

"Up," the butler said without explaining.

Bobby checked the wounded kid. He would probably live, but Kloska had no idea when the paramedics were coming or how many others might be hurt. "Did Jennings do this?" he asked.

The cook shook her head.

"Who did it?"

"Another big guy," the butler said. "But not him."

Now Kloska was on a giant spiral staircase, working his way toward the third floor. One step following another, not sure if he was chasing one killer or two or ten or if Canada Gold was even in the house.

He stepped off onto the second floor, down a wide hall, following the sounds of voices behind one of the doors. He opened it carefully, his gun drawn, finger just off the trigger.

It was a chapel, no doubt a holdover from the days when priests lived here. Instead of an altar, there was a small stage with music stands and chairs. A dozen nervous people dressed for the opera in black ties and long gowns. Seven were Chinese, three men and four women, most of them holding instruments—a violin, a viola, a flute, a cello. They didn't look like they spoke English.

The Chinese were the only ones in this house who seemed frightened of his gun.

"Is everybody okay in here?"

Nods, murmurs. They didn't seem happy to see him, which made him a little annoyed to be rescuing them. "It's not safe here," Bobby said.

"You want us to go outside? It's craziness out there."

Bobby said, "Somewhere in this house is a man wanted for murdering at least three people, and I can't look for him if I'm worried about you people. There's an officer outside and more on the way. You are safer out there than you are in here."

They stared at him, not moving. Someone mumbled a translation to the oldest Chinese man. The defiant way he looked at Bobby reminded Kloska of Solomon Gold, which was enough for Bobby not to like him.

"What is it going to take to get you people to move your asses?"

The answer came in an explosion from upstairs—a sucking of air, a wave of heat, and the painful, pungent odor of chemicals and smoke.

70

SMOKE CURLED, descending slowly behind them, a member of their improbable party. Each step down on the Woodward twister was a leap of faith to the next invisible plank of wood. They heard voices below, lots of them, and footsteps becoming faint.

"They could run up these stairs right into us and we'd never see them," Nada said.

"People run *away* from fire, not toward it," Peter said. "We're going to run away, too, right behind everyone else, and we're going to get lost in that mess outside."

She could feel her spider again, the two halves of her cleaving together. The pain was gone, but she still had double vision caused by the reactivation of the device or maybe by the smoke, and she kept blinking it away as they moved slowly down, down, around toward the short bridge to the second floor.

Maybe Peter really was here to help her.

Farther below, she saw the body of the doctor, arms and legs at unlikely angles, the right side of his face browned with old blood, his shirt soaked with stuff that was newer, wetter, more crimson. It looked like he'd been shot.

Russo, Nada remembered now. *His name is Russo.*

And just as she thought it, the billowing smoke cleared, like clouds halfway down a mountain. Materializing on the first floor were two of Jameson's dressed-up guests and a third man with a gun. He had cop hair and cop shoulders and he wore his T-shirt tight like a cop.

But this was no time to trust anyone.

Nada leapt to the second-floor bridge and dashed down the hall. The cop shouted after her and she heard Peter running behind her.

The second-floor hallway was long on this side and formed a rectangular circuit around the floor. In the center of the rectangle was the chapel and on the outside of it were alcoves with windows and guest bedrooms and the gallery of Burning Patrick's art that looked like her father's den, plus adjoining offices for Jameson and for Myra.

If that cop was coming up the stairs, he'd be there before they could make the end of the hall.

Nada pushed on the chapel door and slipped inside. Peter followed. She turned and pointed the gun, still keeping him at bay.

"This is a bad idea," he said, his hands exposed to her, the knife slowly twirling in his right hand. He asked again for the gun.

"Hide," she said.

The ensemble had set up on a small stage for that evening's performance, and Peter dashed around the back of it and crawled underneath a heavy black tarp that had been left there. Nada stepped to the wall, parts of which were ringed with thick blue drapes. She slipped her entire body inside just one of the fabric's folds.

She glanced toward the ceiling, which she couldn't see in the dark. She'd started a fire. Russo was probably dead, either from the fall or from being shot. She sniffed at the end of the revolver's barrel, freshly fired, and wondered what it meant if Peter had killed the doctor. Possibly that her enemies were also his enemies, and that Rhodes had instructed him to save her at any cost.

Crap. She was only about thirty feet closer to getting out of this place. And with no idea what to do next.

She felt the drape move. Nada tensed, fingering the trigger, waiting for somebody's paw to feel through the curtains and land blindly on her. When it didn't, she knew something wasn't right. She extended her hand, careful not to disturb the fabric, in case someone was watching it from the other side.

Her hand touched flesh. And when it did, she heard a gasp.

Nada had her fingers around an arm. A biceps. A very small one. Like a child's.

She moved slowly toward it, pulling the person toward her at the same time.

The gasp had turned to a sob.

Nada moved her face toward the sound slowly, slowly, until, just inches away, she saw the face of a young woman. Younger than Nada by a few years.

A young Chinese woman holding a violin to her chest. Not just any violin, either. Even in the nearly absent light, she knew its luscious patina and its sensuous shape and the grain of the maple wood and the tint of the stain.

Dad's Guarneri.

For a moment, Nada, still not quite whole, wondered if she could be facing the ghost of Erica Liu.

"What are you doing here?" Nada whispered, but the girl didn't speak English, and it was obvious besides. She was one of the musicians sched-uled to perform tonight. She was petrified. Paralyzed. Too scared to flee the house with the others. The entire second floor must have been evac-uated, but she had remained.

Instead of running, she had decided to hide.

The reverberating click of a door shutting in the chapel. Nada put a hand over the Chinese girl's mouth. *They* were here, whoever they were, and whoever they were, they probably meant to do Canada Gold one kind of harm or another. She had to start making quick and difficult decisions. Her only chance was to surprise and shoot. She wasn't a killer, didn't want to be a killer.

They, whoever they were, kept refusing to give her any choices.

Nada put a finger to her lips and raised the gun, which drew another frightened short breath from the violinist. Then Nada jumped out from the curtain, revolver out in front of her, finger half squeezed.

71

THE WORD FELT LAME as it slipped from his mouth and he also knew he looked like hell, and then it really hit him, the guns and the knives and the murdered bodies and the threats and the possibility of going to prison for a very long time. There she was, the woman he loved, wide eyes wild, perfect jaw tensed, aiming a gun at him like a pro.

"Hi," Wayne said.

But the thing that happened next was a surprise. He hadn't really expected her to be glad to see him. He hadn't expected Nada to throw her arms around him and to touch his wounds softly, to caress his tired shoulders and legs. He hadn't expected her to cry with delight at the sight of him. He had daydreamed all those possibilities in the long days before, but he hadn't really expected any of them.

He had never contemplated that she might shoot him.

There was an explosion and burning inside his triceps and his left arm flung itself behind him and the rest of his big body turned toward it, and all the pain up and down his weary body just shuddered from the intensity of it, every nerve ending he had just afire now, and as he howled in pain and called her name—"Nada!"—there was another assault, a fist hard into his cheek, spinning him back the other way, and he saw it was Peter—"Peter, no!"—and he saw Peter had a knife.

Wayne's own knife had gone flying with the impact of the bullet, and with the back of his head pressed against the floor he felt survival panic, wondering how he could defend himself without a weapon, and all this pain and hardly any strength left.

His body had to find it somewhere.

Bridging himself with his feet and shoulders, he kicked his right leg over and managed to swing all his weight into an excruciating reversal. Lifting himself over Peter, he punched him twice with his right fist, neither time hard but once square in the nose. And while Peter was stunned, he pushed up onto his nearly crippled feet with a groan and hobbled back toward the door, praying the woman he loved, the woman he had come to save, the woman he needed to save him, wouldn't shoot him in the back.

72

THE VIOLINIST CRADLED the Guarneri as gently as a baby Jesus. Nada held her other hand as they followed Peter back toward the magnificent staircase at the end of the hall. The house appeared empty now. It was hard enough to think with the pain in her head and the spider shrieking in her ears, but she started to process all that was happening. Minutes earlier she had shot Wayne in the arm. Jesus. And he was only one of who knew how many people in this house who apparently wanted her dead, or worse. Peter said she'd been *poisoned*. She remembered now, the meals always arriving on separate plates. There had never been any sharing in the Jameson house. Nothing family-style. Even in the kitchen, Nada's food always came from a separate pot. Hugh always complained of his arteries. His stratospheric cholesterol. Molly ate after everyone had been fed.

How had she not noticed? *Molly and Hugh.*

They had manufactured her illness. Made up an excuse to remove her perfectly functioning spider.

They were on the stairs, Peter barely on the third step, knife held in an almost comically ready position, Nada and the whimpering violinist trailing behind. Shouts and screams from inside the house and out. She could barely feel the heat from the upstairs fire here, but she could smell it for sure, hear it crackling above, and wisps of smoke had kept pace with them down the stairs, providing something of a cover and also something of an obstruction. It was hard to see. It was hard to be seen.

Eight more steps, almost to the bottom. Nada could make out the shadow of Russo's broken body still on the floor where it had landed.

Another person dead because of her, and she didn't even know if the counter on that statistic had stopped.

Then a voice: "Everybody hold it."

He was either a cop or a goon hired by Jameson and her mother. Nada hadn't yet decided which. He looked familiar. He was just to the side of a hallway door, gun covering the three of them. Peter lifted his hands in the air, but he didn't put down his knife. Nada noticed he had odd little pieces of tape around his fingertips. Bandages, maybe.

The cop said he was a cop. He ordered them to put their weapons on the ground and for the three of them to descend slowly. They had to get out of the house quickly, he said. Nada wasn't sure how to do something quickly but slowly.

"Don't move, Peter," Nada said. Then to the cop, "Let me see your badge."

The cop cleared his throat but didn't produce one. "I'm Detective Kloska." He gestured with his gun at Peter.

"You're the cop who arrested my father." He didn't answer. "That's a big fucking coincidence, Detective Kloska. Where's your badge?" No answer. "Are you working for them? For my mom? Nobody's doing anything until I figure this out."

"Are you kidding me?" Kloska said.

The heat from the fire upstairs singed the back of her neck now. "If I follow you outside, I'm either dead or they're taking my spider, and there's practically no difference." She looked down at Russo's body.

"I'm not working for anybody, Canada," Kloska said. "You're going to put down that gun and we are getting the hell out of here. This house is about to become a brick skeleton."

"We need a minute, we'll take a minute," Nada said.

She was forcing the pieces together in her head, but they just wouldn't fit. The idea that this was a dream still appealed to her, although she dreaded waking up to find it was already done, the spider torn from her head.

"Here's what we're going to do," Nada said, but before she could finish the thought, which was only half formed in her mind anyway, there was a low whistling sound and a growl of pain and panic and a large black blur collapsed her field of vision, and for a moment she thought she was having another seizure, but it was Wayne, giant Wayne, who had leapt or maybe fallen from the stairs or maybe the bridge just above them and landed hard on the steps between her and Peter. Peter turned with a determined scowl, not as surprised as Nada thought he ought to be, and lunged with his knife. Wayne kicked the hand away, sending the knife flying, and leaned forward to counter with an attack of his own, but Kloska was on them quickly, separating them, pushing Peter away, forcing Wayne against the steps with his knee, Wayne roaring at the pain. Kloska was in good shape for his age and she could see he was a strong man under his shirt, but she also knew how tired and beaten up Wayne must have been that he allowed himself to be subdued so easily. Kloska put a flex-cuff in his teeth and, with his knee at the base of Wayne's spine, yanked Wayne's left arm behind his back, no doubt setting it on fire where Nada had shot him, and Nada watched his face contort in pain and thought he might be about to pass out.

She wanted to say something to him, but she thought about Bea and said nothing.

The violinist sobbed and Nada pulled her closer, and the violin dropped momentarily at the Chinese girl's side. Wayne blinked away at the pain, looking Nada in the eyes for the briefest of seconds, a passing, honest, meaningful look, and then he swung his right arm hard behind him, catching Kloska in the jaw, sending him backward. Freed from the cop, Wayne reached up with his right hand, his left arm still mostly immobilized from Nada's bullet and Kloska's manhandling, grasping for anything, and his fingers found the violin. The Guarneri.

He ripped it easily from the musician's grip and smashed it against the iron railing. It splintered—*exploded*—in his hand, and, horrified as she was, Nada couldn't help notice that even in its last violent moments, as solid black metal smashed through old spruce and maple, it made a beautiful sound.

The violinist shrieked in horror. Wayne spun from the step, falling over the crouching cop, landing on Peter. Wayne stabbed the air with the violin's scroll and end piece, whipping the four strings once around Peter's neck, finding the other ends of them with his half-paralyzed left hand and pulling them all tight against Peter's throat. He got a better purchase on the strings with his teeth and lifted Peter, the strings cutting hard into Peter's neck as he gurgled and flailed, and then Wayne pulled Peter's body over the top of him and the pair of them tumbled to the bottom of the stairs. The cop clenched his teeth and poked his own gun in frustration at the two hulking bodies struggling, rolling, fighting until gravity stopped them on the first floor.

With Peter on top of him, Wayne pulled his right hand and twisted his jaw, tightening the noose of wire around Peter's neck. Peter's face was purple, and thin horizontal lines of blood appeared across his neck around the violin's strings. But Wayne didn't have the strength—or maybe the will, Nada realized—to finish it, not with only one good arm, and Peter rolled off him, gasping for air, and then he shook his head and retrieved his knife and looked about to pivot his body and plunge the blade directly into Wayne's chest.

"Stop it!" Nada and Kloska yelled.

Peter looked up at the barrels pointed toward him and then collapsed, wounded, thin cuts and burns etched all around his neck. His lungs bellowed for oxygen, which was diminishing in the smoky air, and Wayne and Peter were both lying on their backs, bruised and swollen, limbs at all angles, blood oozing from multiple wounds, most of them Wayne's. Russo's corpse was only a few feet away, already looking days dead.

"*Jesus Christ!*" Nada and Kloska said, again at the same time, guns at the ready, but unsure where they should be pointing.

"Peter killed Bea. And Amoyo." Wayne struggled to get the words out. The strings had bitten into the flesh around his mouth, causing a grotesque and bloody extension of his lips on either side. He had lost one prominent tooth and the ones that remained were painted red. "He was going to kill you."

"No," Peter said, and he coughed and a small amount of vomit surfaced on his lip, which he wiped against his shoulder. "If I was trying to kill you, why didn't I already?"

"You are all coming with me right now," Kloska said, but Wayne and Peter didn't look like they could walk and Nada wasn't yet interested in what the detective had to say.

"The only thing I can figure . . ." Wayne took a breath. "He didn't kill you because you have a gun." Another breath. "Figure it out, Nada. You always make the right play."

But she couldn't figure it out. She didn't know. There was a crash from above, another critical part of the building's upper support being consumed by the fire, inching closer to collapse. Kloska was right—they had to get out—but she was terrified of what would be waiting for her if she did. There were still too many people who wanted to take from her what she was unwilling to give.

"Wayne," she said. "How did you find us?"

"Jameson used a credit card at the Coloss—"

"No, I mean in the chapel. How did you find us in the chapel?"

Wayne winced a few times, searching for both the words and the strength. Kloska shouted over them, "People, we are walking out of here *right now*," and he tried to take a step toward Wayne, but Nada warned him off with the revolver.

"Shut up," Nada said.

Peter said, "There are debit-card receipts and eyewitnesses that prove I was hundreds of miles away when the Beaujons were killed and that I was at work when David Amoyo was murdered."

"How do you even know that?" Wayne said.

"Because I know where I was."

"Because Rhodes manufactured your alibi."

"Bullshit."

"Shut up," Nada said.

Peter didn't. "Half a dozen people saw Wayne flee the scene of Amoyo's murder. His fingerprints were all over the room. All over the body. They have DNA. His footprints in blood. Amoyo's blood all over his car."

Nada looked at Wayne.

"I don't think I can prove I didn't do it," Wayne said.

Nada said again to Wayne, "How did you find us in the chapel?"

Wayne reached slowly into his pocket and barely held up his phone.

"How are you even getting a cell signal in the blackout?"

Wayne said, "It's GPS. Satellite. It's homing in on a chip from the Colossus that you must still have in your pocket."

Nada shook her head. "I don't have any chips on me. I don't have any *pockets*. These aren't even my pants."

Wayne closed his eyes. "I don't know."

Nada stared at Kloska for a long moment, as if the answer were on his face. Her look, intense as it was, must have paralyzed the detective for a moment. Nada pointed the gun at Peter. "Pull your pockets out."

Peter said, "What? No."

Nada pointed the gun at Kloska. "You. Pull his pockets out."

"What the fuck?" Kloska said, but he stepped over and kicked Peter's knife away and dug around as Peter struggled against him, and he came out with a large wad of bills and change and keys, which clattered to the floor. And a single green casino chip with the silhouette of the Colossus of Rhodes.

"That's gotta be . . . one of yours," Wayne said to Nada.

Peter said, "It's mine. It's mine. I work there. I gamble there, too."

Wayne waved his phone limply. "It's hers. This says."

"Maybe your batteries are low," Peter said bitterly. "Take it up with Hassan."

Kloska examined it, then held it up for Nada, who was not at all convinced that a casino chip in Peter Trembley's pants was incriminating evidence, and who thought the more troubling revelation was that Wayne had some sort of homing device in his pocket that could track her halfway across the country. "Hugh and Molly say they're sorry," Wayne said, possibly delirious.

Nada said, "Let me see it," and Kloska flipped it carelessly to her, mumbling something about "goddamn fingerprints," but his attention and his gun focused on the wounded men.

Nada studied the disk, turning it slowly, studying the edges, wondering about its provenance, finding at last an imperfection with her finger, an almost invisible scratch across one face of it, a scratch that ran right through the crotch of the silhouette of the Colossus of Rhodes, and as if everything snapped back into sharp focus at exactly that moment, she remembered how she'd amused herself by looking at the scar on this chip and thinking how pleasant it would be to witness the forced castration of the rapist Phillip Truman right before she'd wrapped it up with Kerry Meadows's phone number and tossed it across the room.

To Bea Beaujon.

For the first time in her life, Nada felt the wolf inside her, the wolf she had always feared, the wolf her father had warned her about—*I just couldn't stop the wolf.*

The wolf she once thought she'd inherited from him.

She had been mistaken.

Nada pointed the barrel down and away, firing in the same motion, startling Wayne and the violinist and Kloska, too, with the sound of the blast, but not Peter, who took the bullet silently in the cheek from just a few feet away. A small amount of blood squirted out the hole in front; a small amount of bone followed the slug out of the soft part of the neck in back as blood and spinal fluid oozed onto the floor.

After three long beats, the violinist screamed. Wayne let out a staccato breath and without opening his eyes mouthed, *Thank you.*

"Jesus," said the cop, but he didn't move as two figures appeared in the doorway behind him.

"Hi, Mom." Nada bounced the sight of her gun from head to head. She stepped slowly backward and upward into the haze of smoke. The violinist repeated every step beside her. "Hi, Gary." She tried to load her voice with as much sarcasm and loathing as she could manage.

Jameson watched the smoke drop behind them. Alarms beeped from every room, every hallway, every floor. "You're burning down my house," Jameson said.

Nada said, "Let's call us square."

Jameson looked directly into her eyes and then into Wayne's and the violinist's, as well. He glanced at the bodies on the ground without changing expression. "There are more important things than my house." He stared again at Nada, which meant he was also staring directly into the barrel of her gun.

Another crash from above and behind her, the fire consuming another room. Kloska took a step toward Nada, restraints in one hand.

Nada turned to her mother. "Looks like I'm going to need a favor, Mom."

Elizabeth looked at Peter Trembley's body. "Detective, my daughter clearly killed this man in self-defense. You can take Jennings, and my daughter will give you a statement in the morning."

"Not that simple, Mom," Nada said. She pointed the revolver up, and then she turned the barrel around, pointing it at her own chest, thumbs on the trigger.

"This is where it is," she said. "There's a little nub there, you know, like those tabs at the top of little plastic soldiers. I can take me and my spider out with the same shot. Just like the guy who made these stairs. That makes nobody happy, except maybe me, am I right?"

Jameson lifted his arms and stepped back. Wayne barely moved, but she watched him mouth, *God, Nada, no,* and she could almost hear the sweet anguish in his voice.

Calmly, Gary Jameson said, "What do we do now?"

Nada, who couldn't possibly have steadied herself on her own feet, put an arm around the violinist, who stiffened to support her. "Call an ambulance. Call the fire department. Mom, get me your lawyer."

Kloska said, "What the fuck do you all think is going on here? I just witnessed a goddamn murder."

No one else seemed to be paying attention to the detective, so Nada continued to ignore him. "And when you call him," she said, "tell him I've figured out who killed Dad."

73

REGGIE'S CAB couldn't get any closer than LaSalle and Division before it was stopped by police barricades and standing traffic. He walked through the hot night, following sirens and smoke. As dark as the street was without lights, the air felt even blacker in his lungs, and by Clark and Schiller he could see the tops of the flames, and by Dearborn he could even hear them, hissing and popping, licking and puckering. On State Street, he realized the extent of the devastation, all the second- and third-floor windows golden with fire, spewing smoke. A Chicago landmark, one of the first magnificent downtown homes built after the Great Fire of 1871, was eating itself from the inside out.

Reggie was halted for five minutes or more by a fire department barrier, until he found Della Dickey pacing on the other side. "What are you doing here?"

"Bobby's inside the house." Her voice was full of worry.

"Was there really a riot?"

She said, "I've seen them pull three bodies out so far, and I don't think they're done. What are you doing here?"

Reggie's phone rang in his coat pocket, surprising him. "Can't tell you." Into his phone: "Yes?"

"Where are you?" Elizabeth Gold.

"I'm as close as they'll let me."

"Inside the gate?"

"No."

"I'll send somebody to bring you back to the coach house."

"Is Canada all right?"

"Yes. She says she knows who killed Solomon."

Reggie hung up.

She says she knows who killed Solomon. Jesus.

"Is Bobby okay?" Della asked.

Reggie said he didn't know. "How come you get to stand on that side of the sawhorses?" he asked.

Without embarrassment, she said, "You mean whom did I have to sleep with?"

That stung a bit, although Reggie wasn't sure why.

"Reggie . . ."

"Yeah."

"Are you going in there?"

"In where?"

"You're meeting with them."

"Meeting with who?"

She studied him until her head was nodding slowly. "You really don't know."

"What are you talking about, Della?"

"Take me with you."

"What? No."

"I can help you."

"How can you help me?"

She said, "I know what they want."

Reggie exhaled through his nose. "Della, I'm here to meet a client, and from the sound of it, she's in a world of trouble. But *I* don't even know what she wants."

Della put a hand on his arm, perhaps to hold him there while she thought about it. "The most famous lawyer in Chicago is summoned to Gary Jameson's house in the middle of a riot. A fire. A civil emergency. City-wide chaos. The cops don't even know what's going on. They've been told to sit tight from somewhere so far up the chain, you can't see it from here." She apparently didn't find what she was looking for in his stoic expression, so she continued. "Whatever trouble your client is in, the people in there have the ability and the juice to make it go away. You just have to give them what they want. The problem is, they won't ask for it because they don't know you have it."

"Who are you talking about?"

"The Thousand," she whispered.

"The Thousand?"

"You really don't understand what you're walking into, do you?"

"And you do?"

"Yes."

"How? How do you know what they want?"

He could see her building the wall of courage inside, brick by brick. She drew a deep breath. "Because I want it, too. Because this might be as close to them as I'll ever get. It's the only reason I was ever interested in the Gold case. It's the reason I came to work for you. But I didn't figure out that you had it until just the other day. Not until Bobby told me you wouldn't let him look in your briefcase. That's not a detail that was in the news. Not in the police report. Not in your book."

Briefcase? What's she talking about? "Della, you should go home." He scanned the yard for Kloska.

The next thing they heard sounded like an animal. A giant bear maybe. A bear thirty stories tall awakening from a long sleep and stretching his jaw as far as it would go and letting out a loud, tired, groaning yawn.

One by one, the restaurants and houses and apartments along Lincoln Park West lit up, like a Christmas tree on its side. The streetlights were next, flickering at first before producing their full white blooms, and then the high-rises along Lake Shore Drive, and then a cheer, a sustained cheer from all around, and the last of the rioters ran away from the ruins of the smoldering house and toward their own homes.

Della pulled on his tie. "They want what's in your safe, Reg."

He became like stone. He leveled a long stare, which she accepted with hardly a blink.

She knows. Della Dickey knew about the requiem. And perhaps she guessed that he had killed Solomon Gold.

He understood now that when he got to the coach house he would discover what the Thousand really was.

He also knew that Della Dickey was going with him.

74

IT WAS THE DAMNEDEST negotiation he'd ever been part of, so full of conflicts and ethical breeches and outright illegality that it would mean disbarment and jail if anyone outside this room knew. But this was the damnedest bit of trouble a client had ever been in, and Reggie was up to his neck in it, too.

Della Dickey sat at his side in a hot second-floor coach house guest room. Across the estate, maybe forty yards away, the great main house, ignored by cops and firefighters under orders and busier elsewhere, had burned to the bricks. Gary Jameson, wrapped in a blanket, sat in a chair opposite. Canada Gold sat three seats and a world away from her mother. Bobby Kloska had been ordered back onto the street by a gold star who rarely showed up at crime scenes. There wasn't anyone in this small circle who didn't have secrets, awful secrets, and they were there to trade them, with Reggie trying to get as many of their secrets in exchange for so few of his.

When he had arrived, up the old and dark painted wooden steps, Elizabeth said Canada wanted a word with him in private. Elizabeth looked worried. Reggie said what he always said—"Everything's going to be all right." He had never been less sure of it.

In a small square room, once the barren bedroom of an old nun, Wayne Jennings lay semiconscious on a musty cot. Canada Gold nodded at a revolver lying on a blue blanket. The gun was at once familiar, and a weight formed in his stomach, a cancer round as a pearl. "Peter Trembley brought it to kill me with," she said. "I killed him with it instead." Reggie didn't reply. "I figure it's the gun that killed Dr. Falcone, which means it's the gun that killed Dad."

Reggie nodded and waited for her to continue. It took a long time.

She showed him the letters on the grip of the gun. *EKG.* "My mother's gun. Dad gave it to her as a present. He loved guns. He thought it made them rebels, what with the gun ban in the city and all. Why are you covering for her?" she asked.

It took him longer than it usually did to process. *She thinks Elizabeth killed Solomon.* Reggie wasn't expecting her to be so right about everything else and so wrong about that.

Canada said, "Are you sleeping with my mother? Have you been having an affair with her all this time?"

"Your mother is my client." He hoped that would serve as a denial of the accusation and also an explanation for why he wouldn't comment further. An old lawyer's crutch, but a sturdy one.

"A friend told me the truth, that my mother is a killer. I figure Marlena must have told this friend of mine," she said. "Steve Rhodes had the gun. I figure Mom gave it to him. It would fit right in with his creepy collections. Rhodes tricked Wayne into touching it. Guess they figured at least one of his fingerprints might still be on it after Peter shot me and left it behind at the scene."

Reggie almost corrected her. He almost told her that he knew how Steve Rhodes had purchased that gun and from whom. But her misconstruction of the facts wasn't so bad for him, and as an attorney secretly representing himself, he saw no reason to correct the record.

"I'm going to keep her secret," she said. "But first you're going to get me everything I want." What she wanted was for the Thousand to leave her alone. Forever. She wanted Wayne Jennings off the hook. For everything. She wanted Reggie to tell her mother that she would have nothing more to do with Elizabeth.

In the end, Reggie gave up nothing and everything. He got to keep his own secret, leave his life mostly the way it was, yet he had to surrender the key that could bring it all tumbling down.

Reggie introduced Della Dickey, who explained that she had found an item among her father's effects when he had died seven years ago. Her father had passed before he could hand down his legacy to her, his only child, as he'd always intended. When Della spoke the man's name, Reggie understood from the recognition on their faces that her father's legacy was the same one that Gary Jameson and the others would quietly pass down to their own children. And when she told them what she had supposedly found among her father's things, Reggie could tell from their shock that they would give her, and him, everything asked for in return.

But Reggie could tell by the long, silent stare he received from Elizabeth Gold that Solomon's widow wasn't buying any of it.

The rest was details: what could be done, what couldn't be done; what was within their power, what wasn't.

The last list, Reggie marveled, was shockingly short.

75

THE FOLLOWING SPRING

It felt something like a Vegas casino in scale, with ceilings high enough that you'd never notice them and air cold enough to pinch you awake and waitresses revealing enough to make you stare and slots paying just enough to keep you in your seat after twenty or more dry pulls.

The headliner in the theater had been a has-been before Wayne and Nada were even born, however. And the steaks were tough and the pasta overcooked and the drinks were poured of cheap stuff and everyone on staff would have been on probation for some combination of incompetence or indifference if they'd been working at the Colossus.

Wayne let it all slide because he loved being her whale.

The doctors at Executive Concierge had secretly stitched up Wayne's side and his arm and they'd offered him, and Nada, too, some minor plastic surgery. Nada declined but dyed her hair—red to black. Wayne had his crooked nose straightened and shortened, had a bit lifted from under his chin. He thought it was a handsome face now. He also colored his hair and kept the beard, and disguised his old thick body with the modestly trimmer one he had found on his hungry journey to Chicago. Nada received payment for her summer of work, a quarter of a million dollars in a Cayman account, and her mother signed the papers, giving her full access to the trust fund, and they had assurances from her and Gary Jameson that the Thousand would leave Nada and Wayne alone.

With respect to the Federal Bureau of Investigation, which was still engaged in a manhunt for the fugitive killer Wayne Kenneth Jennings, Wayne and Nada were on their own.

One day soon, when everything had quieted down, Wayne would risk a phone call to his mother, or his brother, just to say he hadn't done it.

There were new driver's licenses and birth certificates and Social Security cards and passports, even credit histories. Wayne's papers gave his name as Cameron and Nada's was listed as Gwen, after one of Peter Parker's girlfriends in her old Spider-Man comic books. It was only a few days before they were using those names without giggling, settling into their new skins and shedding the old ones as unsentimentally as they might trade in a car. They did that, too—her yellow Miata for an invisible silver Accord.

What had been exchanged for all of this, Wayne wasn't sure. Nada said it was something that had belonged to her father, something she believed her mother must have known about, must have kept hidden all these years. It was also the final bit of proof, in Nada's mind, that her mother had killed her father as well as Erica. For that reason, she was disappearing once more, and this time Elizabeth Gold would never be able to find her.

They drove east from the suburban hotel where they had been hiding and healing, up through Michigan and then Ontario to test their new passports, and then to the Finger Lakes and the Adirondacks and up the New England coast, stopping at every blackjack table along the way. They never went back to the same casino twice, and always paid cash, and they always kept track of their winnings and always quit before their pile grew so big that some pit boss would throw them a tax form.

Invisible.

They played the count much the way Nada had with David, probably better, as Wayne knew everything a casino—especially one with limited resources—would be watching for in a counter. They were never greedy. Under hats and behind sunglasses, she was never recognized, or if she was, no one ever approached. They always had fun. Wayne did anyway. He thought Nada seemed to.

The papers along the way—*Buffalo News, Oneonta Daily Star, Albany Times Union, Hartford Courant*—printed good news and bad, most of which they ignored. Wayne showed her a short paragraph with a Las Vegas dateline reporting that Phillip Truman had been sentenced to fifteen years. Peter Trembley hadn't killed Bea before she had had the case locked up good.

Nada asked Wayne about the photos and video the police found on his computer, about the credit reports and other personal information. What could he say?

"I didn't keep any crazy record of the hands you played," he said, copping lamely to all the rest. "Someone else put it there."

"Who?"

"I don't know. Peter. Rhodes, maybe. To frame me after Peter killed you."

"Rhodes was watching my play? Why? To catch me cheating? If he wanted to know, I'd have *told him* I was cheating." She laughed, or maybe *cackled,* cackled to say that Rhodes's idea of cheating and hers were very different.

"Maybe he was collecting your hands the way Jameson collected tiles. Maybe cheating is your art." Wayne intended it to be funny.

Every so often, Nada would make a phone call and a week later a package would arrive at some post office up ahead, always with the same return address: 3414 North Ravenswood, Chicago. She would pick it up with Wayne in the car and then open it in the passenger seat and, after a long examination, put the contents in a large container in the trunk with the rest of Patrick Blackburn's tiles. He was making them for her now, it seemed, so that one day she could see what he once saw. And her father. And Wes Woodward, too. She and Wayne joked about buying a hitch and a trailer for the tiles, when it got to that point.

They traveled as friends and occasionally, at her invitation, maybe once a week, as lovers. They never discussed it. During long silent stretches, though, she held his hand in the car. And sometimes in a casino, especially when they were winning, she would touch him casually and secretly on the shoulder or the face or even brush a lone finger hip-to-hip across the back of his pants, signifying nothing, just to let him know she was there.

He asked himself, sleeping alone, if this would be enough for him the rest of his life, wanted, on the run, never in contact with his disgraced family, never leaving a mark or a trail, ever so rarely sleeping with the only friend he might ever have, certain that she would never love him exactly the way he loved her.

In the morning, he would always answer yes, and every morning he expected her to be gone.

76

IT WAS A MASSIVE and ancient castle of a church, forgotten on a remote and overgrown Austrian mountainside. The only road to it had been covered many times over with fallen trees and vines and dead rodents and dust. Thirty vehicles of different makes and colors—Land Rovers and Humvees, mostly—traversed the rough terrain all the way from Vienna, leaving from seven different hotels at more than ten-minute intervals. A *convoy*, after all, would attract attention, which the mathematici never did, according to their unwritten, unspoken motto, in Latin for some reason instead of Greek.

Imperium Sine Fama. Power Without Fame.

Thirty-nine sworn members of the tradition had made the trip along with one they called "the initiate." Or even sometimes "the novitiate."

Over 120 musicians and choir singers, none of them German-speaking, had been brought to the site in blindfolds. They rehearsed for three days under a famed Chinese conductor, learning this single variation on a work that was untitled on their sheet music but which each of them already knew well. At night, they slept in a large complex of luxury safari tents that had been arranged in a nearby clearing. Only in brief hushes did any of them speak about their strange circumstances and most of the time they acted as if this were the most ordinary of command performances. Each had been sworn to secrecy by a confidentiality agreement that stipulated a penalty none could ever afford, as well as, many felt, an unspoken threat. The name of the organization that had hired them was never revealed. They had been promised that when they returned to their homes after the performance, fifty thousand euros would be placed, via wire transfer, into each of their accounts.

But when they saw the music they knew. Few of them saw the entire piece—each musician glimpsed only his own part. Still, they knew what it must be and they were awed.

The night of the performance, they dressed formally in their tents and took the stage. The audience of twenty-seven men and thirteen women sat politely in tuxedos and evening gowns. Each wore the mask of an animal to hide his or her identity from the musicians onstage. There were pigs and birds and dogs and cats and foxes and horses and even dragons.

All wore black except for one woman, seated in the center of the first row, dressed in brilliant white cotton, somehow undusted by the remoteness of the landscape outside and the years of neglect within. Her mask was a sheep. A lamb, more precisely. In whispers within the small cliques of musicians thrust together by common language, all agreed she must be the guest of honor.

There were no introductions, no speeches, no toasts. The masked men and women greeted the orchestra's arrival with enthusiastic applause. During the performance, they wept. Many of the musicians did, too, and in the newly elongated Dies Irae, some ten minutes into the piece, one large section of the choir erupted in a contagion of tears and the appreciative audience responded with a gasp.

•

The woman in white, who could not help being both thrilled and disturbed at the resemblance of her simple dress to a wedding gown, did not know if the mathematici had really caused three planes to crash, or the blackout in Chicago, or if their rivals and brothers, the acusmatici, had killed Marlena Falcone. This was business that had been settled and dismissed long before this night of her induction, but she was also not discouraged from suspecting it. She had been fascinated by the Thousand when they were only a rumor to her, when she first discovered evidence—

later confirmed—that her father had been one of them, and now that they were real, sitting all around her, feting her, paying tribute to her, now that she was about to join them, they terrified her.

She realized only now that members of the Thousand were not joined by knowledge so much as by fear.

There was so much Della wanted to share with Reggie, but so much she couldn't. "They're going to make us all wear animal masks" was all she told him about the ceremony, and it was more than she should have. "The masks are supposed to reflect our essence. An animal we were in a past life. It's totally weird."

••

The orchestra began the Benedictus, the longest sequence in the Gold Completion, and in the seventh row was another woman who now understood that, contrary to the lies sworn by Della Dickey to gain acceptance here, Reggie Vallentine had murdered her husband and stolen the requiem. She had said nothing because she had her own secret—a secret, thanks to her daughter, Vallentine no doubt now suspected, as well.

She would need to be careful and creative when she eventually moved against the lawyer, an act that would be both preemptive strike and revenge.

Like Della, she was also a legacy, also a daughter of one of the mathematici, a great-great-granddaughter, and more, a member of this organization since the year she graduated from Vassar, a woman who, since a night of perfectly rational violence ten years ago, owed a long debt to the power and cleverness and resources of the Thousand for not just her position but her freedom. That night, she had watched from her car as her husband and Erica Liu rendezvoused inside her husband's big Cadillac SUV. They were in plain sight, in a metered space on Division, but also invisible behind the opaque windows of the truck. It was less comfortable but far more discreet than a hotel. And it was also very dirty, which was part of the allure for the thing that her husband had become. She knew how expert Solomon was at making those rear seats go away, and there was no doubt plenty of room, even for his large frame to be enjoined with a doll-like, dirty cello-playing slut in their filthy, adulterous sex. But Elizabeth was not bothered by her husband's incursion between the whore's legs so much as she was by his indiscretions into her ears. He was telling her too much. Hinting at the grand visions he was allowed with that damn robot chip in his head, the chip Elizabeth never wanted him to have, and now he wanted her daughter to have one, too, and soon Canada would turn against her, as well, the family turned against itself. She couldn't let that happen. She was a mother. She would keep the family together.

At any cost.

When she noted the slight, almost imperceptible side-to-side sway of the parked vehicle, she left her own car and walked quietly up beside her husband's truck and with her own duplicate fob and key she beep-beeped the driver's door open and slid into the seat. The screams from the whore, the shouts of *"Lupa! No! Lupa!"* could no doubt be heard outside, but it was late and the street was empty. As one of the mathematici, she had used the power of numbers, the tension between order and chaos, to eliminate untold numbers of people anonymously and from a distance. The whore needed to be done up close. The acusmatici way. In front of her husband, who needed to be taught a lesson.

Ten years later, sitting in this beautiful, neglected church, she grieved for him and for the estrangement of her daughter—another fact for which the lawyer would have to pay—and listened to the performance with a widow's pride, tears welling behind the tiny holes for eyes cut into her wolflike mask.

• • •

In a tree near the church ruins, the ex-detective perched with a camera and a long lens, snapping photos as they arrived, preparing himself for more when they departed. He hadn't anticipated the masks, which would obscure their identities. But the photos might go partway toward redeeming him.

In Chicago, he was now known as an incompetent cop who had let the murdering Solomon Gold off the hook with sloppy policework. They called him a drunk, a philanderer, a sex addict even, a serial harasser. A conspiracy theorist. An obsessed ex-lover. A stalker. A liar. The evidence was allegedly on his computer at his desk at Area 3. It was also in his delusional statements about an ancient society of number worshippers, about Solomon Gold's daughter, Canada (who, Bobby alleged, had killed a man), and about the wanted murderer Wayne Jennings, whom Kloska had claimed to have placed in custody, however briefly. They said he had no evidence for any of this and that reliable and credible witnesses, including some of the city's most respected citizens, even contradicted him directly. A mathematics professor in Indiana, whom Kloska had said could back up some of his most outrageous assertions, declined to comment as he mourned the sudden and tragic deaths of his wife and daughter in a car accident.

Kloska had tracked his ex-lover across an ocean and two continents, something he doubted even two of the traitor detectives in Area 3, and none of the goddamn backstabbing sergeants, lieutenants, captains, commanders, and certainly not the fucking deputy chief, who had sold him out before the first scandalous *Sun-Times* article hit the sidewalk tin cans, could do. Della no longer spoke to him, even had a restraining order, one with fantastic and outrageous assertions that any asshole with a blog could gape at on the Internet. Fuck them. While they found other targets, he would continue to follow Della, taking pictures from afar until something irrefutable and remarkable happened, as he was certain it would, an irrefutable, remarkable something he could capture with his camera, incontrovertible and incorruptible evidence of his sanity.

• • • •

In a rented car down the road, just beyond the lightly guarded perimeter of the church, a man, once a twin, said a short prayer of apology and lifted the Merkel shotgun from the passenger seat and set it across his lap. He glanced at the folded paper the lawyer had provided to see if any unused wisdom remained scribbled there and then ripped it into tiny pieces and fed them to the wind.

He had been given a date, and an approximate location. He had traded his new television to a neighborhood acquaintance, a gangster rumored to be a member of the 14K Triad, for a contact in Linz from whom a foreigner could buy a gun. He'd exchanged everything else he owned to pay for this trip.

After identifying a few members of the orchestra before they had been trucked into the forest, bribing them, imbibing with them, it had been relatively simple to follow them here, even for a conspicuous man, a young Asian man, because he was looking for the Thousand and it was not looking for him.

The last thing he had to know, the most important thing, had been whispered by the lawyer in their final phone conversation. It was not written anywhere. The lawyer's motives for telling him this went unsaid, but he could guess.

"She'll be wearing the mask of a wolf."

He left the car on the side of an unpaved road, keys on the seat, and walked into the woods. When it was over, he expected to be dead as well, but this weird cult of wealth would no doubt clean up his mess. He guessed the bodies would disappear, his rental car returned. Back home, she would be missed more than he would be, and even if his absence was noted, the tenuous, long-ago connection between these missing persons might be a curiosity, but nothing more. That was all right. This was justice, not a publicity stunt. What he was about to do wouldn't change anything. He was fine with this.

When he was close enough, he could hear music between the trees, beautiful music like his sister used to make, and he couldn't help feel a sick thrill that he was stalking this woman the same way she must have stalked his twin, her husband's lover. He would wait until they were leaving, until they were mingling exuberantly outside, the beautiful requiem mass sustained in the mountain air, and after he located her wolf mask, locked in on it like a missile, he would make his surprise suicide assault. Another concert, another murder.

There was symmetry to that.

Acknowledgments

I shouldn't have to say that I have taken liberties in writing *The Thousand*. Nevertheless, the many fictional threads of this novel are interwoven with fact. Pythagoras was a far more interesting and important fellow than most history classes acknowledge. Much about him is a mystery, but there are some excellent books for anyone interested in discovering what we actually understand about the Pythagorean cult, the first among them, in my opinion, being Kitty Ferguson's terrific *The Music of Pythagoras: How an Ancient Brotherhood Cracked the Code of the Universe and Lit the Path from Antiquity to Outer Space*. Those looking for a more succinct overview might check out *Divine Harmony* by John Strohmeier and Peter Westbrook. And if you really want to go hardcore into the Pythagorean influence on the history of music, read *The Harmony of the Spheres* edited by Joscelyn Godwin.

The translation of the fragment from *Life of Pythagoras* by Nichomachus of Gerasa is from *Die Fragmente der Griechischen Historiker* by Felix Jacoby.

Thanks to my early readers, including Dr. Jon Svahn, Kevin Fry, John Warner, Michele Seiler, and Peter Bormes. Thanks to Joe Dickey, as well as to Thomas and Janine Pendergast, who donated generously at charity auctions and endowed this novel with its best two character names. Thanks to the Ninth Avenue Men's Club and everyone at theoutfitcollective.com. Thanks to Pete Henrici and Chris Manolis (better known in my house as "Mr. Chris") for help with Latin and Greek. Thanks every day to Max and Vaughn.

Thanks to Simon Lipskar, Katie Zanecchia, and Josh Getzler at Writers House, as well as Kassie Evashevski, Josh Getzler, and Nikki Furrer. Thanks to everyone at Knopf, especially Jordan Pavlin, Leslie Levine, Maria Massey, and Erinn Hartman. Thanks to Jim Coudal and everyone at Coudal Partners.

And special thanks to Leticia Mata, and to Elizabeth, Melissa, and Sean Pierson, who do the really important work while I make stuff up and write it down.

A NOTE ABOUT THE AUTHOR

Kevin Guilfoile has written for *McSweeney's, Salon, The Morning News,* and *The New Republic.* His first novel, *Cast of Shadows,* has been translated into more than fifteen languages. He lives in Chicago with his wife and children.

A NOTE ON THE TYPE

This book was set in Fairfield, the first typeface from the hand of the dis-
tinguished American artist and engraver Rudolph Ruzicka (1883–1978).

Composed by Creative Graphics, Allentown, Pennsylvania
Printed and bound by Berryville Graphics, Berryville, Virginia
Book design by Robert C. Olsson